Praise for *New York Times* bestselling author Maisey Yates

"Yates' new Gold Valley series begins with a sassy, romantic and sexy story about two characters whose chemistry is off the charts."
—*RT Book Reviews* on *Smooth-Talking Cowboy*
(Top Pick)

"Fans of Robyn Carr and RaeAnne Thayne will enjoy [Yates's] small-town romance."
—*Booklist* on *Part Time Cowboy*

"Passionate, energetic and jam-packed with personality."
—USATODAY.com's *Happy Ever After* blog on *Part Time Cowboy*

"[A] story with emotional depth, intense heartache and love that is hard fought for and eventually won.... This is a book readers will be telling their friends about."
—*RT Book Reviews* on *Brokedown Cowboy*

"Yates's thrilling seventh Copper Ridge contemporary proves that friendship can evolve into scintillating romance.... This is a surefire winner not to be missed."
—*Publishers Weekly* on *Slow Burn Cowboy*
(starred review)

"This fast-paced, sensual novel will leave readers believing in the healing power of love."
—*Publishers Weekly* on *Down Home Cowboy*

**Welcome to Gold Valley, Oregon,
where the cowboys are tough to tame, until they
meet the women who can lasso their hearts:**

Cowboy Christmas Blues (ebook novella)
Smooth-Talking Cowboy
Mail Order Cowboy (ebook novella)
Untamed Cowboy

**In Copper Ridge, Oregon, lasting love
with a cowboy is only a happily-ever-after away.
Don't miss any of Maisey Yates's
Copper Ridge tales, available now!**

From HQN Books

Shoulda Been a Cowboy (prequel novella)
Part Time Cowboy
Brokedown Cowboy
Bad News Cowboy
A Copper Ridge Christmas (ebook novella)
The Cowboy Way
Hometown Heartbreaker (ebook novella)
One Night Charmer
Tough Luck Hero
Last Chance Rebel
Slow Burn Cowboy
Down Home Cowboy
Wild Ride Cowboy
Christmastime Cowboy

From Harlequin Desire

Take Me, Cowboy
Hold Me, Cowboy
Seduce Me, Cowboy
Claim Me, Cowboy

Look for more Gold Valley books coming soon!

For more books by Maisey Yates,
visit www.maiseyyates.com.

MAISEY YATES

Untamed Cowboy

HQN™

Recycling programs
for this product may
not exist in your area.

ISBN-13: 978-1-335-90070-8

Untamed Cowboy

Copyright © 2018 by Maisey Yates

The publisher acknowledges the copyright holder of the
additional work:

Mail Order Cowboy
Copyright © 2018 Maisey Yates

CONTENTS

Dear Reader,

I'm so happy to welcome you back to the town of Gold Valley for another story about hot cowboys and true love.

It's true that the best-laid plans often go awry. But that doesn't stop us from trying to make them anyway.

That's exactly what Bennett Dodge, the hero in *Untamed Cowboy*, is doing. But his relationship with the woman he thought would be perfect for him has dissolved, and now she's fallen in love with someone else. And to top it all off, when he gets home one night, he finds a fifteen-year-old surprise waiting on his front porch.

About the only thing in his life that has remained the same is his friendship with Kaylee Capshaw. But with one kiss, that's about to change, too.

I loved writing Bennett and Kaylee's relationship. They were first introduced in *Christmastime Cowboy*, a book that's part of the Copper Ridge series, and I knew immediately that I was going to have to write their story. And even though Bennett was with another woman then, I knew that ultimately Kaylee was the right one for him.

Bennett just has to realize that the plans he had for his life weren't the best thing for him. And what he really needed was right within reach all along.

Happy reading!

Maisey

Untamed Cowboy

Haven, this book is for you. In the past nine years you've gotten a lot of them, but that's how it should be. You're the one who taught me that friendship is the perfect foundation for true love.

CHAPTER ONE

KAYLEE CAPSHAW NEEDED a new life. Which was why she was steadfastly avoiding the sound of her phone vibrating in her purse while the man across from her at the beautifully appointed dinner table continued to talk, oblivious to the internal war raging inside of her.

Do not look at your phone.

The stern internal admonishment didn't help. Everything in her was still seized up with adrenaline and anxiety over the fact that she had texts she wasn't looking at.

Not because of her job. Any and all veterinary emergencies were being covered by her new assistant at the clinic, Laura, so that she could have this date with Michael, the perfectly nice man she was now blanking while she warred within herself to *not look down at her phone*.

No. It wasn't work texts she was itching to look at.

But what if it was Bennett?

Laura knew that she wasn't supposed to interrupt Kaylee tonight, because Kaylee was on a date, but she had conveniently not told Bennett. Because she didn't want to talk to Bennett about her dating anyone.

Mostly because she didn't want to hear if Bennett was dating anyone. If the woman lasted, Kaylee would inevitably know all about her. So there was no reason—in her mind—to rush into all of that.

She wasn't going to look at her phone.

"Going over the statistical data for the last quarter was really very interesting. It's fascinating how the holidays inform consumers."

Kaylee blinked. "What?"

"Sorry. I'm probably boring you. The corporate side of retail at Christmas is probably only interesting to people who work in the industry."

"Not at all," she said. Except, she wasn't interested. But she was trying to be. "How exactly did you get involved in this job living here?"

"Well, I can do most of it online. Otherwise, I travel to Portland, which is where the corporate office is." Michael worked for a world-famous brand of sports gear, and he did something with the sales. Or data.

Her immediate attraction to him had been his dachshund, Clarence, who she had seen for a tooth abscess a couple of weeks earlier. Then, on a follow-up visit, he had asked if Kaylee would like to go out, and she had honestly not been able to think of one good reason she shouldn't. Except for Bennett Dodge. Her best friend since junior high, and the obsessive focus of her hormones since she'd discovered what men and women did together in the dark.

Which meant she absolutely needed to go out with Michael.

Bennett couldn't be the excuse. Not anymore.

She had fallen into a terrible rut over the last couple of years while she and Bennett had gotten their clinic up and running. Work and her social life revolved around him. Social gatherings were all linked to him and to his family.

She'd lived in Gold Valley since junior high, and the friendships she'd made here had mostly faded since then. She'd made friends when she'd gone to school for veterinary medicine, but she and Bennett had gone together, and those friends were mostly mutual friends.

If they ever came to town to visit, it included Bennett. If she took a trip to visit them, it often included Bennett.

The man was up in absolutely everything and the effects of it had been magnified recently as her world had narrowed thanks to their mutually demanding work schedule.

That amount of intense, focused time with him never failed to put her in a somewhat pathetic emotional space.

Hence the very necessary date.

Then, her phone started vibrating because it was ringing, and she couldn't ignore that. "I'm sorry," she said. "Excuse me."

It was Bennett. Her heart slammed into her throat. She should not answer it. She really shouldn't. She thought that even while she was pressing the green accept button.

"What's up?" she asked.

"Calving drama. I have a breech one. I need some help."

Bennett sounded clipped and stressed. And he didn't stress easily. He delivered countless calves over the course of the season, but a breech birth was never good. If the rancher didn't call him in time, there was rarely anything that could be done.

And if Bennett needed some assistance then the situation was probably extreme.

"Where are you?" she asked, darting a quick look over to Michael and feeling like a terrible human for being marginally relieved by this interruption.

"Out of town at Dave Miller's place. Follow the driveway out back behind the house."

"See you soon." She hung up the phone and looked down at her half-finished dinner. "I am so sorry," she said, forcing herself to look at Michael's face. "There's a veterinary emergency. I have to go."

She stood up, collecting her purse and her jacket. "I really am sorry. I tried to cover everything. But my partner... It's a barnyard thing. He needs help."

Michael looked... Well, he looked understanding. And Kaylee almost wished that he wouldn't. That he would be mad, so she would have an excuse to storm off and never have dinner with him again. That he would be unreasonable in some fashion so that she could call the date experiment a loss and go back to making no attempts at a romantic life whatsoever.

But he didn't. "Of course," he said. "You can't let something happen to an animal just because you're on a dinner date."

"I really can't," she said. "I'm sorry."

She reached into her purse and pulled out a twenty-dollar bill. She put it on the table and offered an apologetic smile before turning and leaving. Before he didn't accept her contribution to the dinner.

She was not going to make him pay for the entire meal on top of everything.

"Have a good evening," the hostess said as Kaylee walked toward the front door of the restaurant. "Please dine with us again soon."

Kaylee muttered something and headed outside, stumbling a little bit when her kitten heel caught in a crack in the sidewalk. That was the highest heel she ever wore, since she was nearly six feet tall in flats, and towering over one's date was not the best first impression.

But she was used to cowgirl boots, and not these spindly, fiddly things that hung up on every imperfection. They were impractical. And how any woman walked around in stilettos was beyond her.

The breeze kicked up, reminding her that March could not be counted on for warm spring weather, as the wind stung her bare legs. The cost of wearing a dress. Which also had her feeling pretty stupid right about now.

She always felt weird in dresses, owing that to her stick figure and excessive height. She'd had to be tough from an early age. With parents who ultimately ended up ignoring her existence, she'd had to be self-sufficient.

It had suited her to be a tomboy because spending time outdoors, running around barefoot and climbing trees, far away from the fight scenes her parents continually staged in their house, was better than sitting at home.

Better to pretend she didn't like lace and frills, since her bedroom consisted of a twin mattress on the floor and a threadbare afghan.

She'd had a friend when she was little, way before they'd moved to Gold Valley, who'd had the prettiest princess room on earth. Lace bedding, a canopy. Pink walls with flower stencils. She'd been so envious of it. She'd felt nearly sick with it.

But she'd just said she hated girly things. And never invited that friend over ever.

And hey, she'd been built for it. Broad shoulders and stuff.

Sadly, she *wasn't* built for pretty dresses.

But she needed strength more anyway.

She was thankful she had driven her own truck, which was parked not far down the street against the curb. First date rule for her. Drive your own vehicle. In case you had to make a hasty getaway.

And apparently she had needed to make a hasty getaway, just not because Michael was a weirdo or anything.

No, he had been distressingly nice.

She mused on that as she got into the driver's seat and started up the engine. She pulled away from the curb and headed out of town. Yes, he had been perfectly nice. Really, there had been nothing wrong with him. And she was a professional at finding things wrong with the men she went on dates with. A professional at finding excuses for why a second date couldn't possibly happen.

She was ashamed to realize now that she was hoping he would consider this an excuse not to make a second date with her.

That she had taken a phone call in the middle of dinner, and then had run off.

A lot of people had trouble dating. But often it was for deep reasons they had trouble identifying.

Kaylee knew exactly why she had trouble dating.

She was in love with her best friend. Bennett Dodge. And he was *not* in love with her.

She gritted her teeth.

She wasn't in love with Bennett. No. She wouldn't allow that. She had lustful feelings for Bennett, and she cared deeply about him. But she wasn't in love with him. She refused to let it be that. Not anymore.

That thought carried her over the gravel drive that led to the ranch, back behind the house, just as Bennett had instructed. The doors to the barn were flung open, the lights on inside, and she recognized Bennett's truck parked right outside.

She killed the engine and got out, moving into the barn as quickly as possible.

"What's going on?" she asked.

Dave Miller was standing there, his arms crossed over his chest, standing back against the wall. Bennett had his hand on the cow's back. He turned to look at her, the overhead light in the barn seeming to shine a halo around his cowboy hat. That chiseled face that she knew so well but never failed to make her stomach go tight. He stroked the cow, his large capable hands drawing her attention, as well as the muscles in his forearm. He was wearing a tight T-shirt that showed off the play of those muscles to perfection, his large biceps, and the scars on his skin from various on-the-job injuries, and he had a stethoscope draped over his shoulders. Something about that combination—rough-and-ready cowboy meshed with concerned veterinarian—was her very particular catnip.

"I need to get the calf out as quickly as possible, and I need to do it at the right moment. Too quickly and we're likely to crush baby's ribs." She had a feeling he said that part for the benefit of the nervous-looking rancher standing off to the side.

Dave Miller was relatively new to town, moving up from California a couple of years ago with fantasies of rural living. A small ranch for his and his wife's retirement had grown to a medium-sized one over the past year or so. And while the older man had a reputation for taking great care of his animals, he wasn't experienced at this.

"Where do you want me?" she asked, moving over to where Bennett was standing.

"I'm going to need you to suction the hell out of this thing as soon as I get her out." He appraised her. "Where were you?"

"It doesn't matter."

"You're wearing a dress."

She shrugged. "I wasn't at home."

He frowned. "Were you out?"

This was not the time for Bennett to go overly concerned big brother on her. It wasn't charming on a normal day, but it was even less charming when she'd just abandoned her date to help deliver a calf. "If I wasn't at home I was out. Better put your hand up the cow, Bennett," she said, feeling testy.

Bennett did just that, checking to see that the cow was dilated enough for him to extract the calf. Delivering a breech animal like this was tricky business. They were going to have to pull the baby out, likely with the aid of a chain or a winch, but not *too* soon, which would injure the mother. And not too quickly, which would injure them both.

But if they went too slow, the baby cow would end up completely cut off from its oxygen supply. If that happened it was likely to never recover.

"Ready," he said. "I need chains."

She spotted the chains lying on the ground, picked them up and handed them over. He grunted and pulled, producing the first hint of the calf's hooves. Then he lashed the chain around them. He began to pull, his muscles straining against the fabric of his black T-shirt, flexing as he tugged hard.

She had been a vet long enough that she was inured to things like this, from a gross-out perspective. But still, checking a guy out in the midst of all of this was probably a little imbalanced. Of course, that was the nature of how things were with Bennett.

They'd met when she'd moved to Gold Valley at thirteen—all long limbs, anger and adolescent awkwardness. And somehow, they'd fit. He'd lost his mother when he was young, and his family was limping along.

Her own home life was hard, and she'd been desperate for escape from her parents' neglect and drunken rages at each other.

She never had him over. She didn't want to be at her house. She never wanted him, or any other friend, to see the way her family lived.

To see her sad mattress on the floor and her peeling nightstand.

Instead, they'd spent time at the Dodge ranch. His family had become hers, in many ways. They weren't perfect, but there was more love in their broken pieces than Kaylee's home had ever had.

He taught her to ride horses, let her play with the barn cats and the dogs that lived on the ranch. Together, the two of them saved a baby squirrel that had fallen out of his nest, nursing him back to health slowly in a little shoebox.

Kaylee had blossomed because of Bennett. Had discovered her love of animals. And had discovered she had the power to fix some of the broken things in the world.

The two of them had decided to become veterinarians together after they'd successfully saved the squirrel. And Bennett had never wavered.

He was a constant. A sure and steady port in the storm of life.

And when her feelings for him had started to shift and turn into more, she'd done her best to push them down because he was her whole world, and she didn't want to risk that by introducing anything as volatile as romance.

She'd seen how that went. Her parents' marriage was a reminder of just how badly all that could sour. It wasn't enough to make her swear off men, but it was enough to make her want to keep her relationship with Bennett as it was.

But that didn't stop the attraction.

If it were as simple as deciding not to want him, she would have done it a long time ago. And if it were as simple as being with another man, that would have worked back in high school when she had committed to finding herself a prom date and losing her virginity so she could get over Bennett Dodge already.

It had not worked. And the sex had been disappointing.

So here she was, fixating on his muscles while he helped an animal give birth.

Maybe there wasn't a direct line between those two things, but sometimes it felt like it. If all other men could just…not be so disappointing in comparison to Bennett Dodge, things would be much easier.

She looked away from him, making herself useful. Gathering syringes, and anything she would need to clear the calf of mucus that might be blocking its airway. Bennett hadn't said anything, likely for Dave's benefit, but she had a feeling he was worried about the health of the heifer. That was why he needed her to see to the calf as quickly as possible, because he was afraid he would be giving treatment to its mother.

She spread a blanket out that was balled up and stuffed in the corner—unnecessary, but it was something to do. Bennett strained and gave one final pull and brought the calf down as gently as possible onto the barn floor.

"There he is," Bennett said, breathing heavily. "There he is."

His voice was filled with that rush of adrenaline that always came when they worked jobs like this.

She and Bennett ran the practice together, but she

typically held down the fort at the clinic and saw smaller domestic animals like birds, dogs, cats and the occasional ferret.

Bennett did large animals, cows, horses, goats and sometimes llamas. They had a mobile unit for things like this.

But when push came to shove, they helped each other out.

And when push came to pulling a calf out of its mother they definitely helped.

Bennett took care of the cord and then turned his focus back to the mother.

Kaylee moved to the calf, who was glassy-eyed, and not looking very good. But she knew from her limited experience with this kind of delivery that just because they came out like this didn't mean they wouldn't pull through.

She checked his airway, brushing away any remaining mucus that was in the way. She put her hand back over his midsection and tried to get a feel on his heartbeat. "Bennett," she said, "stethoscope?"

"Here," he said, taking it from around his neck and flinging it her direction. She caught it and slipped the ear tips in, pressing the diaphragm against the calf, trying to get a sense of what was happening in there.

His heartbeat sounded strong, which gave her hope.

His breathing was still weak. She looked around at the various tools, trying to see something she might be able to use. "Dave," she said to the man standing back against the wall. "I need a straw."

"A straw?"

"Yes. I've never tried this before, but I hear it works." She had read that sticking a straw up a calf's nose irritated the system enough that it jolted them into breathing. And she hoped that was the case.

Dave returned quickly with the item that she had requested, and Kaylee moved the straw into position. Not gently, since that would defeat the purpose.

You had to love animals to be in her line of work. And unfortunately, loving them sometimes meant hurting them.

The calf startled, then heaved, its chest rising and falling deeply, before it started to breathe quickly.

Kaylee pulled the straw out and lifted her hands. "Thank God."

Bennett turned around, shifting his focus to the calf for the first time and away from the mother. "Breathing?"

"Breathing."

He nodded, wiping his forearm over his forehead. "Good." His chest pitched upward sharply. "I think Mom is going to be okay too."

They stood watching for a moment as the calf stood up on shaky limbs, taking its first few tentative steps. It was all a good sign, but they had both seen enough to know that there was no such thing as out of the woods.

"Give me a call," Bennett said to Dave. "If you need anything, anytime of night, give me a call."

"I will. I'm going to set up in here tonight."

"Good. If he makes it through the night… Well, the odds will be pretty good from here."

Dave shook his head. "I didn't know how stressful all this was."

"I know people don't understand," Bennett said. "How you can care so much about animals you raised for food. But I know. They're your livelihood, and your whole life on top of it."

Dave nodded. "They are."

He shook Bennett's hand, then turned and shook Kaylee's too. As his hand close over hers she realized what a mess she was. She looked down and saw that her skin was streaked with the aftereffects of touching the recently birthed cow. A fine accessory to go with her flirty date dress.

They collected their gear, and Kaylee followed Bennett outside.

They both looked...well, a little bit ragged.

"You're wearing a dress," he said again.

Yes, she supposed that bore paying attention to, considering her typical uniform was plaid button-up shirts and worn jeans. If she was feeling really fancy maybe a belt with some rhinestones on it.

"I was on a date, Bennett," she said, articulating the *T*s a bit more sharply than necessary.

"Were you?" he asked, crossing his arms over his broad chest and leaning against the truck.

She pushed her now-completely-tangled red hair off her face. "I was."

"Anyone I know?" he asked, his tone overly casual.

He was asking so he could cast aspersions. It was what he did. And it rankled. He was never going to be her boyfriend. And yet he took great delight in judging every single one she'd ever had and finding them unworthy.

"Depends," she said, keeping her tone sweet. "Do you know Clarence the dachshund?"

He arched a brow. "I do not."

"Well, I had a date with Clarence's owner. And since you don't know Clarence that doesn't mean anything to you."

"I didn't think we dated the owners of patients," he said, frowning.

"Well, that's much easier for you, Bennett. If I eliminated every man in town with a pet then I would never be able to date." She pretty much didn't. And actually, tonight was the first time she'd been on a date in over a year.

Bennett let out a very masculine-sounding sigh, and she ignored the slight shock wave it sent through her. "Do you want to come over and have a beer?"

She really, really needed to say no. She was supposed to be on a date with another man, she was definitely not supposed to end the night platonically hanging out at Bennett's house again. It was her default. She did it too often.

She had done it all throughout his dating Olivia Logan, feeling so pointlessly jealous of everything the cute, petite woman was. Certainly everything that Kaylee wasn't. Refined. Fine-boned. Short. Definitely able to wear giant heels around any man without towering over them. Not that she would tower over Bennett in heels.

At six-four he was definitely tall enough to stand next to her in most shoes. Which had made his association with Olivia even more irritating, since the woman was barely five foot three. That was how that always worked. Tall men with tiny women. Irritating for women like her.

But he and Olivia had broken up a few months ago when Bennett had failed to propose quickly enough for Olivia's liking, and then, much to everyone's shock, Olivia had gone and fallen in love with Luke Hollister, who was her polar opposite.

She was from the town's most prominent family. She was prim. Luke was…not.

She hadn't really been able to gauge how Bennett

felt about it, and selfishly, she hadn't really wanted to either. She was just relieved. Relieved he hadn't married her, because even though she didn't harbor hopes of marrying him herself, if Bennett did get married, things would change.

She didn't want that.

"I…"

Bennett's phone rang, and he fished it out of his pocket and answered it. "Hello?" He frowned.

Kaylee took a moment to take stock of her appearance. Her dress was rumpled now, and she was…well, she was a mess. And Bennett still wanted to have a beer with her. Well, because she was like a guy to him, really.

He would invite a guy over to have a beer even if he was dirty.

"Really?" Bennett sounded suddenly irritated. Or maybe, irritated wasn't quite right. Intense. "Really," he repeated. "We'll talk about it later. I'm out dealing with a calf."

He hung up the phone, and looked at Kaylee. "That was Wyatt." Wyatt Dodge was Bennett's oldest brother, and the boss at Get Out of Dodge Dude Ranch.

"Really?" She unconsciously parroted Bennett. "What did he say?"

"Luke called him. Apparently, he and Olivia are having a baby."

CHAPTER TWO

BENNETT COULDN'T BEGIN to untangle the whole mess of feelings rioting around inside him like coiled-up snakes. He wasn't in love with Olivia. He never had been. But she had been his girlfriend for a year, and he had been planning on marrying her. They'd had an arrangement that had suited them both.

It hadn't been a love match in a conventional sense. Her father had asked for him to take care of her after a health scare, and Bennett had thought...

He'd thought she was damned near perfect. He didn't want a passionate love affair, he wanted stability. Wanted the kind of life he could plan. Put in careful order. And Olivia had seemed to want that too.

But right toward the end, he'd been putting off proposing. He'd known what she wanted and he just...

There was part of him that worried she wanted more than he was giving. At first he'd thought she wasn't any more in love with him than he was with her. Hell, they'd never gone past second base, at her insistence. And she'd never seemed tempted to go further. He'd respected it, respected her. Hadn't touched anyone else the whole time they were together, because he was a man of his word.

Then, she had broken up with him over the fact he was dragging his feet, and she had gone and slept with Luke Hollister. Who Bennett would have said was about the worst bet in the entire world. If asked, Luke would probably have agreed he was a bad bet too.

But apparently, not when it came to Olivia. Because that bastard had proposed to her in record time. And apparently had gotten right on starting a family with her too.

It was what Olivia wanted. He knew. Well, not to be pregnant out of wedlock. That would bother her. He had a feeling the wedding was about to get moved way the hell up.

But a family. That was what Olivia wanted. Domestic bliss and all that.

"Are you all right?"

Kaylee was looking at him with wide amber-colored eyes.

At the moment she made a pretty comical sight. Wearing a dress a hell of a lot fancier than he was used to seeing on her, the delicate floral material swirling around her long, pale legs.

And her arms were streaked with afterbirth.

Her red hair was disheveled, a smudge of something across her cheek. But she was also wearing makeup.

Frankly, the dress and the makeup were a lot more out of place than the afterbirth.

Kaylee wasn't a girly girl. She never had been. Kaylee had run with the boys from junior high on. She had been one of his best friends ever since then. The kind of friend that he called if he needed someone to help at two in the morning. The kind of friend who would leave a date—apparently—to come and help him birth a calf.

The kind of friend who knew everything about him.

Almost everything.

"I'm fine," he said, lying.

But he couldn't exactly articulate all the things this

was bringing up. Because it wasn't just Olivia. There was something else churning deep beneath the surface and he didn't want to get into that. He knew what it was. Whenever pain pushed up against that locked door down in his soul, he knew what that pain was. *Loss.*

All that loss in his life.

And mistakes. Regrets. A time in his life when he hadn't planned a damn thing, when he had lacked for control and decency, and had paid the consequences of that behavior. Consequences no one, not his family or Kaylee, knew about.

He was different now.

But that didn't erase the past.

"Do you still want that beer?"

"Maybe let's take a rain check," he said. "You're covered in…"

Kaylee looked down her arms and grimaced. "I can shower at your place." The suggestion was casual, and there was no reason it wouldn't be. He and Kaylee had known each other forever. Had showered in each other's homes more than once.

For some strange reason, probably because it was late, he was tired, and feeling like his world had been thrown slightly off its axis, he had a momentary blip in his brain, just one bright pop of an image. Pale skin and water sluicing over slight curves.

He blinked heavily in the darkness. He did not think about Kaylee like that. Ever.

She wasn't a woman. She was his friend. His business partner.

And he had more control than that.

"Yeah, I think… I think I might go over to Wyatt's."

Kaylee was clearly somewhat irritated by the fact he was rescinding his invite, but she would deal. They had spent so much time in each other's company over the years that it was inevitable they sometimes irritated each other.

Anyway, Kaylee was great if you wanted to talk. That was one of the perks of having a woman for a friend, even one who wasn't especially...stereotypical. She got into deeper topics and longer conversations than his brothers did. Than any of his guy friends.

He wasn't sure he wanted to talk now. He wanted to drink. And Kaylee would want to know what he was feeling about Olivia. She liked to pick that particular scab. He wasn't sure why. But it was something that she hadn't been able to let go since he and Olivia had broken up.

He shouldn't care at all about this news. Olivia deserved a man who loved her. She deserved to be in love. That kind of thing wasn't in the cards for Bennett. It wasn't what he wanted. He wanted a well-ordered life. He wanted one without complications, without big highs and lows. Because God knew he'd had enough.

The whole situation was tangled up, but his heart wasn't broken. And Luke Hollister was like a brother to him. Even given the circumstances. The man was always going to be part of the Dodge family. So having to deal with Olivia was unavoidable.

"Okay," Kaylee said, taking a step away from him. "We'll talk tomorrow I guess."

"Thank you," he said, meaning now and for the birth. "If you hadn't been here... The baby probably wouldn't have made it. I would've lost one of them."

"Hey," Kaylee said. "What's a date compared to the life of a baby cow? And that's not sarcasm. I can go out with Michael again anytime. He was very understanding."

"Michael, huh?"

He didn't know Michael, and he hadn't been able to place him when Kaylee had started talking about Clarence the dog either. He didn't know why he couldn't picture the guy. Gold Valley was small enough that he felt like he should know men about their age that Kaylee might date, particularly ones that owned pets and sometimes came into the clinic.

But no, he was drawing a blank.

"You want to go drink," Kaylee said, waving a hand. "Interrogate me some other time."

"Good night," he said, getting into the truck that served as a mobile veterinary unit. He might go ahead and crash at Get Out of Dodge tonight, he mused as he pulled onto the highway, putting Kaylee and her date out of his mind.

He could get hammered and sleep in one of the cabins that were currently unoccupied on the dude ranch. They were gearing up for their grand reopening, but it hadn't happened yet.

Wyatt was working tirelessly—and working the rest of them to the bone when they were doing their real jobs—getting it ready.

Although, his brother Grant officially didn't have a real job anymore. His real job was the ranch. Jamie, the only girl, and youngest in the family was in the same boat as Grant and Wyatt. Bennett was the only one that hadn't thrown himself wallet and soul into the place.

But it wasn't as simple as that for him. Veterinary medicine was his passion. He hadn't gone to school for all those years so that he could quit when his brother decided on a whim to stop flinging himself around on the back of angry bulls and focus on the homestead for the first time in fifteen years.

For as long as Bennett could remember, he'd liked to fix things. That need had only grown stronger after the death of his mother.

And stronger still later on.

He could have been a doctor, but he truly hadn't been able to face the idea of working on people and losing them. He lost enough people in his life. But having such a comprehensive veterinary practice in Logan County kept himself and Kaylee fully occupied. Being able to go into business with his best friend was a privilege.

The two of them had talked about doing that from the time they were kids. Usually when you made a pact with dirt and spit and a handshake underneath an oak tree when you were thirteen years old you didn't keep it.

But he and Kaylee Capshaw had.

She was the truest and most constant person in his world. His friend, his partner. Always. From the moment he'd met her when they'd been in seventh grade. She was new to school, and looked lost, but defiant right along with it. And he couldn't help but be intrigued by the redhead with a thousand freckles who didn't talk to anyone for the first half of the day.

Something in her reminded him of his own losses. The way it felt to feel like you were walking through a room of people all alone.

So at lunch he'd sat down and introduced himself.

She hadn't been friendly at all. Not until he'd asked if she liked horses, and if she'd like to come over to his ranch sometime and see them.

That had made her smile. And something about her smile had felt so damned good. He'd wanted to keep on making her smile.

She hadn't been smiling when she'd left the ranch just now.

He pushed away the guilt at not having her come over as he turned into the driveway that led up to his brother's ranch. Well, the family ranch, really. Bennett was part owner in the place, even if he wasn't working on it full-time. He had thrown a good lot of his money into it, but then, that was another thing about him staying in veterinary medicine. He made enough money to help Wyatt with this crazy scheme. Bennett was mostly a financial backer when it came right down to it.

Although, Wyatt had made a decent amount of money on the rodeo circuit. Bennett had no idea how much, because Wyatt preferred to be a mystery.

He shook his head and parked his truck, getting out and slamming the door.

He walked up the familiar steps, steps he had walked on thousands of times, and up to the door. He just opened it up and walked in, because he wasn't going to knock on the door of his childhood home. He might not live there anymore, but it still felt like home in many ways.

"Hey," he called out.

"Drinking in the kitchen," shouted Wyatt.

Bennett moved through the entryway and into the kitchen, where his brother Wyatt, his other brother Grant, and their sister, Jamie, were all sitting around the high counter on barstools, clutching various alcohols of choice.

"That's nice." Bennett said, "are you all having a drink for me?"

"Wash your hands," Jamie said, wrinkling her nose, her brown hair pulled back in a loose braid that had likely started the day tight, but had ended askew, a testament to the activities of the day. Knowing his sister those activities had been riding horses like hellhounds were biting at her heels.

Jamie didn't know caution, not on the back of a horse.

"All right," he said, looking down and seeing that while he had been wearing gloves for a good portion of the procedure he had not escaped unscathed.

He started to scrub up in the sink, very aware of the fact that all of his siblings were watching him. "Did any of you have a comment to make?" He gestured broadly.

"Olivia is pregnant." Jamie leaned forward, resting her chin on the lip of her beer bottle. "How do you *feel* about that?"

"I didn't know Jamie was going to be here," he said to Wyatt.

"Where else would she be? Anyway, you didn't ask."

"I just came over for a drink," he said pointedly, "not a talk. If I had wanted to talk, I would have had Kaylee come over."

"You should have had Kaylee come over here," Jamie said.

Jamie wasn't a whole lot more of a girl's girl than Kaylee was, and the two of them got along pretty well now that Jamie wasn't a kid. Though, at twenty-three she still seemed a lot like a kid to Bennett.

"She was tired. She had to leave a date to come help me deliver a calf. It was breech."

"Did you save it?" Grant asked.

"Yeah," he responded. "Hopefully it makes it through the night. But at this point I don't see why it wouldn't. Everything was good when we left."

"She left a date to come and help you deliver a calf," Wyatt said, his eyebrows raised.

"It was a life-and-death situation," Bennett said. "It's more important than dinner."

"Sure," Wyatt said, "but couldn't you have called someone else?"

"No," Bennett said. "She's the only person I can count on in a situation like that. And anyway, I didn't know she was on a date." Though, he probably still would have called her. Kaylee was always there when he needed her.

It wasn't like he'd needed help choosing a tie. He was trying to save a life.

"Careful," Wyatt said, "or she likely won't be at some point. Not if you keep taking advantage of her."

"I don't take advantage of her. First of all, we run our business together. So, she benefits from the extra time I put in and in the middle of the night. Second of all, she's my friend. And I would do the same for her, and she knows it."

"Still," Jamie said, her tone sly, "you have a history of losing women now, Bennett."

For one blinding second Bennett wished that he were still fifteen. Because if he were, he would have yanked on Jamie's braid until she apologized for that.

"I do not have a history of that," he said. "One girlfriend broke up with me."

"And now she's having Luke's baby," Grant pointed out. "Which I feel like is why you're here, even though you don't want to talk about it."

"I don't want to talk about it," Bennett returned.

"That's fine," Wyatt said. "We do have more important things to discuss than your lack of a love life."

Of course, Bennett hadn't had a love life when he was with Olivia, not that his family knew that. Olivia had said she wanted to wait until they were engaged to have sex, and he had honored that. It just wasn't the kind of thing that you discussed with your older brothers.

Well, it wasn't the kind of thing you discussed with anyone, first of all, because he wouldn't go talking about Olivia's business like that. But second of all, because he had no desire to get harassed. Not that Grant was in any position to harass anyone on that subject.

Since the death of Grant's wife eight years ago, Grant's love life had been in the deep freeze. Grant hadn't even gotten close to having another woman in his bed, let alone in his life. At least, that was the impression that Grant gave to his family.

They tried to get him to go out when they could, hoping to do something to heal that hollowed-out look in his eyes. But nothing ever did.

Though, that likely explained why his siblings enjoyed giving Bennett such a hard time about the situation with Olivia. It wasn't fatal. Not even close. It was just one of those things.

"Much more interesting," Wyatt supplied, "is the fact that we got our first few bookings online today."

"That is great," Jamie said, almost shimmering with glee.

His younger sister wanted this business to take off almost more than anyone. Because the opportunity to ride horses for a living didn't present itself often, and this was her chance to do exactly what she loved to do. He respected that. Understood it. Because this might not be his dream, but he certainly wanted his family to work it all out. And anyway, he had his work dream. So he wanted them to have theirs too.

"We're set to open with a big barbecue by June. Kind of a grand opening with tours and all of that, and then afterward, it looks like we're already halfway full."

"Fantastic," Jamie said.

Grant nodded. Grant didn't do much in the way of enthusiasm.

"You seem thrilled," Wyatt said, directing that comment at Bennett.

"I am," Bennett said. "But my primary focus is still my veterinary practice. You know I support this, but I have other things on my plate."

"I never said you didn't," Wyatt said. "But you do have a stake in Get Out of Dodge. I figure you don't want to lose all your money."

"I'm fine," Bennett said.

"Right. So you're fine if I take a stack of your cash and light it on fire? And you're fine with Olivia being pregnant?"

He really wasn't fine with any of that. But since Wyatt wasn't going to burn a stack of his cash, and Olivia was going to remain pregnant regardless of his feelings on the matter, he didn't see the point in rising to Wyatt's bait.

"Doesn't worry me," he said, grabbing a beer out of the fridge. He had every intention of drinking more heavily here. But he didn't want to expose the fact that he was bothered by all of this. He really should have stayed with Kaylee, who would have imagined that he was heartbroken or wounded in some way. He wondered if that was what his brother thought too. That Olivia had broken his heart. She hadn't. It was dredging up a past he didn't like to think of.

He wondered if it would be like this if he ever had his own children.

That was a strange thought. Because of course he had been planning on having children with Olivia. But it had seemed an easy thing. Part of that normal life he was planning for.

He hadn't anticipated that it would make him think of his first girlfriend and the baby that they had lost all that time ago. The baby that nobody knew about.

Nobody but Cole Logan—Olivia's father and Quinn Dodge's best friend. He'd been like an uncle to Bennett, and far enough removed from the situation for Bennett to feel like he could go to him for help without being terrified of being seen as a disappointment.

Not even Kaylee knew.

There was no point talking about something that had never become anyone else's problem. He had intended on bringing the issue forward with his family when it had become something they couldn't deny. But he'd been sixteen, and he'd been an idiot. He'd been caught up in feelings, and he sure as hell hadn't been thinking.

The acrid, burning shame of failure still sat in his gut all these years later. For that loss of control.

He had never acted like that ever again.

He had gotten caught up in passion, and he hadn't taken care of Marnie. Hadn't protected either of them.

And after all the emotional turmoil of going over what they were going to do, of deciding that he was going to put all of his dreams, his life on hold, so that he could do the right thing and marry her and make a home with her, she had lost the baby. Then she had broken up with him and left town, unable to handle the pain of what had happened.

He hadn't heard much about her since. She didn't stay in touch with her parents. He'd heard once through the grapevine she'd been arrested.

She hadn't been that person before. Not when they'd been together.

He blamed himself, in part. For the fact that what

had happened seemed to have damaged her in ways she couldn't come back from.

So of course when Olivia said she didn't want to have sex until they were engaged he had honored that easily. He would never, ever pressure a woman into doing something she didn't want to.

And he would never act out of control again in his life. The consequence for that kind of thing were too grave.

But nobody knew about that. They would all think he was acting weird because his ex was pregnant. They had no idea he'd nearly been a father once. And that this made him think of the baby he would have had fifteen years ago. That it made him wonder about what that might have been like. What that life might have been.

It hadn't even been a life he had wanted. It had just been the life he was coping with.

But it was hovering there now. And he couldn't even explain it to anyone.

"Well, maybe at the barbecue I can set up a free vet check booth," he said drily.

"Yeah, not sure we want you doing any of that near the food."

"Like having hayrides near a barbecue is any less problematic? I don't think it is."

Jamie sniffed. "Horses are not dirty."

"Just because you love horses more than you love most people doesn't mean other people love them near their burgers."

"Well, then, they're not people I want to know anyway," his sister said.

Sometimes Bennett wondered if Jamie had suffered the most from losing their mother at a young age. Jamie had been a newborn when their mom had died, and their dad had done his best with her—with all of them—but he'd had four kids, a working ranch and a shedload of grief to contend with.

Ultimately Jamie had been left to go a little bit wild, running around outside and doing her best to keep up with her brothers from the time she was barely knee-high to a grasshopper. But then, Jamie was happy. Normal shouldn't matter.

But it did to him. That was the problem.

It clearly did, because his entire set of goals had centered around having some version of a normal life. The house, the job, the wife, the kids.

And it had all crumbled down around him and he didn't know how he felt about it.

But then, when push came to shove he hadn't proposed to Olivia.

Now that her pregnancy news was rolling over him slowly, and he was dealing with various ghosts from the past, he wondered if that was why.

If, in the end, his past was part of what had held him back. The fact that he had known marrying Olivia and making a family with her was going to dredge up things he didn't want to think about.

But when it came to Jamie, he only cared about her happiness. And that much was easy. When it came to himself, it was a lot different.

Sometimes he wondered if he deserved to be happy.

Whatever, he had to quit sitting here feeling sorry for himself. He needed to go home. Now that he had given up on the idea of getting blind stinking drunk, he needed to get his ass in bed so that when tomorrow morning's wake-up call came it didn't feel like such an assault.

"Well," he said, "thanks for the… This little version

of support that you all are able to give." He tilted his half-consumed beer bottle upward. "I think I'm going to call it a night."

"You're not too drunk to drive," Grant said, his tone dry, "are you?"

"I don't know how you're ever not too drunk to drive," Bennett returned.

"I might not be," Grant said. "But, seeing as I live here, it doesn't really matter."

A couple of years ago Grant had sold his house in town and moved back onto the ranch. There were so many outbuildings and dwellings on the property that it was easy for them to all cohabit there and not see each other.

Bennett preferred to have his own space.

"Fair enough. Now you can just stagger across the property."

At least Grant wasn't drinking alone. He wasn't going to say that, but he was grateful for that. They all worried about Grant. They had thought that in a year, two years, five years, he would have done something in the way of recovering from Lindsay's death. But Lindsay had been his high school sweetheart, his first and only love, and the fact that he had married her even knowing their marriage wouldn't be a long one, knowing that eventually her terminal illness would take her, had made them a kind of tragic love story for the ages in Gold Valley.

And unfortunately, Grant, it turned out, excelled at existing in tragedy.

"I'm sure I'll see y'all tomorrow," he said. "If you end up needing any help on anything specific let me know."

He stood up and went back outside, feeling a little

bit like an unsettled boomerang not sure what target he was hoping to return to.

His hand itched, and he wanted to reach for his phone to call Kaylee.

But it was late now, and she had probably gone to sleep.

He had already interrupted her date, he didn't need to wake her up too.

Part of him wondered if she had called her date back, if they were resuming activities now. At her home. In her bed.

He gritted his teeth. What the hell was wrong with him? He didn't think about Kaylee and sex. He didn't think about Kaylee *showering*. Didn't imagine pale skin and her curves. Never.

He blamed this whole thing on Olivia because he didn't think of Olivia as being the mother of someone else's children either.

She was supposed to be the mother of his.

And whether or not he had a broken heart, he felt…

Well, thwarted plans were never fun.

Having built an entire life in his head that was now permanently crumbled around him was not fun.

He had encouraged Luke to go after Olivia, when the man had shown up at the ranch looking brokenhearted and generally hangdog. Because Bennett hadn't felt that broken when Olivia had left him. And he knew that Olivia deserved a man who *did*. When push came to shove, he felt like he had done the right thing.

But he kind of wished that he hadn't now. And in this moment, by himself, he was going to go ahead and feel petty.

Yeah, and he was going to take that home by himself. All of his anger, all of his unsettled feelings. All of the weird thoughts he had about his best friend tonight.

Tomorrow would be a new day. And he would start making a new plan. There wasn't another option.

CHAPTER THREE

BEFORE TEN O'CLOCK Kaylee had already dealt with a parakeet that had a fever, a ferret with a bad skin condition and an old dog that had gotten into some foxtails.

Business was never slow at Valley Veterinary, which was a good thing in many ways.

But at the moment Kaylee would kill for another cup of coffee and a moment to sit down.

And that was when Bennett walked in, looking like her salvation with his strong hands wrapped around two cups of coffee from Sugar Cup.

"Thank God you're here," she said, stretching her arm out.

"That's quite the greeting."

"I didn't mean you. I meant coffee. Hand it over, Dodge. I'm dying."

"Well, we can't have that, Kay." He thrust the cup into her hand, and she took it greedily, taking a cautious sip. It was scalding hot. Just the way she liked it.

She looked up at the clock, and then looked at the schedule sitting on the desk. Unless there was another emergency, she was clear for the day.

"Have you been out to check on the calf?"

"Yep," he said, "first thing I did this morning. Everything looks good. But it's just the start of busy season for me."

"Right," Kaylee responded. "It's the most wonderful time of the year. The time of year where you spend half your time shoulder deep in cows."

He chuckled and lifted his coffee cup to his lips. "It's a living."

"Indeed. Not jealous of you, just FYI. I prefer the small and fuzzy to the large and smelly."

Usually, she didn't have to assist with many births. Occasionally there were some breed-specific issues, and she would have to do something like give a bulldog a C-section, but that wasn't very common around here.

"Did you end up finishing your date last night?" Bennett asked.

It was a weird question, and there was something weighted in his voice.

"Did I end up…finishing my date?" She blinked. "I didn't go back to the restaurant at 9:30, if that's what you're asking. My steak would've been cold."

"That's not what I'm asking."

Heat flew into her cheeks, her heart slamming against her breastbone. "Bennett, are you asking if I brought the man home?"

His expression was overly bland. Overly casual. "Just out of curiosity."

"I have *never* asked you such question in my life," she pointed out.

"Well, no. And you probably never would."

Because the idea of Bennett with another woman burned her with jealousy, and she would have maybe had a blackout and stabbed him with the nearest medical instrument, but she wasn't going to say that.

Bennett was *not* asking out of the burning jealousy of his heart. Not even a little.

In fact, that Bennett was asking at all proved how

much the thought of her being with someone else didn't matter to him.

She blamed Olivia Logan for all of this. Yes, him being with her had hurt. Knowing that he was probably going to marry her had hurt. But she had also seen...the end.

If Bennett were married then there really wouldn't be a *them*. Not like part of her stupid heart had hoped there would be since junior high. If he married another woman then it really wasn't going to happen between them. So yes, it had been indescribably painful to know that was finally coming.

But it had been a relief in some strange ways. A relief because it would finally kill her hope dead.

And then the golden couple of Gold Valley had broken up.

Bennett being single forced her to ponder all the what-ifs again.

Which was why she had gone out on that date.

She hadn't been on a date in forever—it had been even longer since she had been with anyone, and she had just been...tired of that. Tired of the fact that her emotions, her body, seemed to be completely held hostage by a man who didn't want them.

"Normally I wouldn't," he said, "but the whole thing with Olivia has me thinking."

Everything inside Kaylee drew in tight, the breath in her lungs, her stomach, even her pulse seemed to narrow down to the tip of the pen, stabbing at her with each beat.

She swallowed hard. "You mean, you're looking for someone else to marry?"

She had survived the selection process of Olivia.

Had survived that relationship and near-marriage. She wasn't sure if she was going to survive it again.

The corner of Bennett's mouth tipped upward, the expression on his face turning wicked, which was not an expression normally present on Bennett's face. "Or maybe I just need to hook up."

Their eyes clashed and held over the tops of their coffee cups, and something seemed to spark the air, to catch and hold. They both took a sip of their coffee, as if to prolong the moment or let it settle, she wasn't sure. But it was something. Something to do. But she didn't look away from him. She felt like she couldn't. Like there was a magnet holding her gaze to his, and she couldn't fight it. Didn't want to.

The door to the clinic opened, and they both looked over quickly. A rush of breath left Kaylee's body, a strange dizziness washing over her as the tension broke.

It was Beatrix Leighton. Her sister-in-law Sabrina Parker ran the tasting room for Grassroots Winery in the neighboring town of Copper Ridge, and Bea lived on the winery property, which was owned by her other sister-in-law, Lindy. Both Sabrina and Lindy were polished and immaculate. Beatrix was…not.

She had a tangle of carrot-colored curls that always seemed to move independently of the rest of her, her cheeks often pink from the sun, her nose peeling because she had spent too much time outdoors. Kaylee had the vague idea that Beatrix was in her early twenties, but her slightly feral nature made it difficult to say.

In Beatrix's arms was a box. And in that box was what looked to be a mass of blankets.

"Can I help you?" Laura the receptionist asked Beatrix, who looked from her to Kaylee and then to Bennett.

"I found him this morning on the side of the road," she said, her eyes looking incredibly round and dewy.

"Found what?" Kaylee asked.

"Him," Beatrix said, setting the box on the counter and revealing the contents.

A tiny baby raccoon nestled down beneath the pale blue blanket, his little claws wrapped tightly around the woolen fabric like it was his safety.

"His mother was dead," Beatrix said. "And another baby. Hit by a car. But he was all right. I thought I saw movement, so I pulled the car over and got out. I think he might be injured, so I thought I should bring him to you."

Beatrix had dropped by the clinic often over the past few years for just this very thing. She was a chronic rescuer of wild animals. And Kaylee could never bring herself to charge for the service of helping the younger woman rescue them. Anyway, usually Beatrix ended up doing most of the work, as long as Kaylee could provide an antibiotic or set a broken limb.

She shot Laura a glance. "Your schedule is clear right now."

Kaylee looked at the mournful little creature, and then back at Beatrix. "Let's get a look at him."

Bennett was watching the entire thing with a kind of bemused expression on his face. Bennett was a veterinarian who cared deeply about saving animals. But Bennett was also a rancher from a long line of ranching stock, and when it came to offering medical aid to varmints, his opinion on the subject was more neutral than that it was a necessity.

Kaylee had spent a lot of her life feeling helpless. Useless. She hadn't had resources to control or help anyone or anything when she'd been growing up. And now that she could? She could no more turn down the raccoon than she could Beatrix.

"Let's take him into an exam room," she said, picking up the box and leading the way back to one of the enclosed patient rooms.

Beatrix followed, and Bennett followed slowly behind her.

Now his presence was just starting to irritate her. That weird moment from earlier was making a mess of her insides, combined with the fact that she had it in her head now that Bennett wanted to...*hook up*. With some woman. Any woman but her, clearly. That always seemed to be the case.

What's the alternative? He hooks up with you and then what? He's going to marry you? What will happen to your friendship?

All those typical questions came tumbling down on her head. The questions that she always asked herself when she got into a Bennett loop.

But she didn't just have a wayward heart and an overly excitable body. She had a brain.

And her brain knew a few things about Bennett Dodge. The first being that if he wanted her at all, he would have made a move. He was decisive. Honest. Not the type to sit and stew about hidden feelings.

The second being that she didn't really know how to have a long-term relationship. Her attempts so far had been unsuccessful.

A recipe for disaster.

And anyway, they had made the decision years ago to go into business together, which further complicated... everything.

Bennett was deeply ingrained in her life. Her friend, her business partner and a staple in the community.

They were tangled around each other. And untangling even one portion of it had the potential to unravel her entire life.

A good thing to remember whenever she got a little bit too wistful about him.

She had made her choices a long time ago.

What she needed was a man to tangle all up in her personal life.

What she needed was to call Michael because he had left that door open, and she needed to walk through it.

Kaylee got some gloves and carefully ensconced the tiny raccoon in a blanket before lifting it up and examining it. He was in fact a he, as Beatrix had stated upon first entry. Kaylee looked up from the raccoon and at Bennett, who was leaning against the door frame with his arms crossed, his muscles shifting interestingly, displayed nicely by the tight black T-shirt he was wearing. His typical uniform, and one that was really getting to her today.

"If you have commentary on my treatment of a baby raccoon, Bennett, I will thank you to take it in the other room," she said pointedly.

Beatrix turned to look at him. "You don't think we should treat the baby raccoon?" Her tone was almost comically accusatory.

Bennett looked somewhat thunderstruck by that. It was the complete lack of guile in Beatrix's question, the absolute shock that he might not think a raccoon was worthy of saving.

He looked between Beatrix and Kaylee.

"Treat the baby raccoon if you need to," he said, putting his hands up.

"The baby raccoon *needs* to be treated," Beatrix pointed out.

"Yeah, Bennett," Kaylee said. "The baby raccoon needs it."

Bennett suppressed what looked to be an eye roll, but continued to stand there and watch as Kaylee conducted an examination on the tiny creature.

"He looks like he's in decent health," Kaylee said. "All things considered. Though, I'm sure he's a little bit shocky. Was he behaving like he was injured when you took him home?"

Beatrix shook her head. "I haven't taken him home yet. I just pulled him off the road. I keep a blanket and a box in my truck just in case."

Of course she did.

"Well, I think he can probably go to your house. If you're up to round-the-clock feedings. I would assume that you could treat a small raccoon like a runt puppy. A little bit of evaporated milk and an eyedropper might help him pull through."

"That's reassuring," Beatrix said.

"Do you want me to give him some vaccinations?"

"Can you?"

"I don't see why not," Kaylee said, working her way through her supply. "I'll just make sure he gets his rabies shot, and then I'll send you on your way. Hopefully he makes it through."

"Well, if he does, then I'll have a rabies-free raccoon as a pet," Beatrix pointed out. "Lindy may not appreciate a raccoon living at the winery."

Kaylee suppressed a smile. "That is between you and your sister-in-law. I'm just going to treat the raccoon."

Kaylee took care of the vaccination under the watchful eye of Beatrix and the overly amused Bennett. Then she bundled up the tiny animal and put him back in his box and handed the box back to its owner.

"Good luck, Beatrix," she said.

"That was nice of you," Bennett said once Beatrix had left.

"It wasn't nice of me," Kaylee said. "It's my job."

"No, your job is to work on people's pets for profit. You don't have to patch up every sickly critter that Beatrix Leighton brings in on a whim."

"Why not? It's a small thing. But it's something."

"I suppose so."

"I'm very giving," she said. "The kind of woman who leaves her date to help a baby calf."

He chuckled. "Yes, you are. And I do owe you a massive thank-you for that."

"You're soft too, Bennett Dodge. Maybe not for raccoons. But for other creatures."

"Yeah," he said, "I'm less soft toward animals that are going to make themselves nuisances because Beatrix ends up turning them loose once they grow up, and they view people as their natural source of food. If I have to pry that raccoon repeatedly out of my garbage cans I'm going to be irritated."

"Don't worry about it," Kaylee said. "First of all, Beatrix is probably going to keep it. Second of all, it will wreak havoc at the winery, not your place."

"Well, Wyatt will be happy about that."

"Why would Wyatt care?"

"He has some kind of uneasy alliance with Lindy. Funneling business between the places."

"Uneasy?"

"They do not like each other. But then, Wyatt used to be buddies with Lindy's ex-husband. He did PR on the rodeo circuit back when Wyatt was still riding. So they used to be friends, and I think Lindy wants to castrate him."

"I can see where that would cause a rift."

"Yep."

"Wyatt wants to drive business to Get Out of Dodge so badly that he's willing to work with a woman who hates him?"

Bennett chuckled. "My brother used to ride bulls for a living. Drooling, angry, two-ton monsters that wanted to rip his guts out. I think one ragey blonde who wants to gut him doesn't scare him much."

"Well, that must be fun to be around."

"Fortunately," Bennett said, "I have my own business to keep me busy. And I'm about to go out on a call, so I will see you later."

"See you later."

When Bennett walked out of the clinic, her stomach bottomed out, the aftershock of everything that had happened in the past hour moving over her in a wave.

Why was it like this? All the time.

Why were there these moments? Thunder and lightning without the rain. A storm brewing that never seemed to break open. Tension. So much tension and nothing to ease it.

Maybe the tension was only on her side. Because it wasn't coming from him. And it all felt so big and real and raw to her, and he didn't seem to feel a thing.

The door opened again and she had to suppress a sigh, until she looked up and saw that it was Michael, holding Clarence in his arms.

"Is Clarence all right?" she asked.

"He is," Michael said, a smile spreading over his handsome face. "But I'm here to see you."

Utter resoluteness washed over Kaylee. She was going to take this opportunity. She wasn't going to let herself back out.

"I'm glad you did," she said, forcing herself to smile. Hoping that it looked like a smile, and not a tragic grimace.

"Good," he responded. "I'd like to try dinner again."

"Me too," she said quickly. "And this time I'll make sure that I'm not inadvertently on call."

"I like that you work," Michael said. "I feel like a lot of people are so insecure with first date stuff they act out of character. But I think that was really you. And I liked it."

"Well," she said, smiling. "Good."

She really needed to get a new life. Really, really. Not the whole thing. Because there were parts of it that she loved. But she needed something to fill that void her body, mind and heart kept insisting Bennett could fill. He wasn't ever going to. That couldn't have been made more apparent by their conversation this morning. He didn't feel anything asking about whether or not she had slept with Michael. He saw nothing strange in telling her offhandedly that he needed to find a woman to hook up with.

She was in the friend zone, and she should be fine with that. She was the one who'd put herself there, after all. She'd decided forever ago that she wasn't going to act on her feelings, so she needed to own that choice. Not in that intermittent, half-assed way that she had for more years than she wanted to count. But in a real way. A solid way.

And the only way she was going to do that was to actually try to have a relationship with a guy instead of simply sabotaging every opportunity that came her way.

"Dinner would be perfect," she said.

And she felt like if she said it enough times to herself over the next few days it might just become true.

THE LAST THING Bennett expected when he pulled into his driveway that evening was to see a police car parked out in front of his ranch house.

His dogs—traitorous, useless beasts—were lying on the porch, long noses resting on their front paws, their floppy ears draped down in total relaxation. The old horses—retired rodeo animals, former pets that had outlived their usefulness—and his solitary llama were all looking equally unconcerned out in the field.

But Bennett didn't feel as calm as any of the animals.

He was a rule follower, so there was no way that he had done anything wrong. Forgot to pay a parking ticket? No. Definitely not.

He had been so distracted by the sight of the cruiser that it had taken him a moment to realize that there was another car parked alongside it. An SUV with yellow plates and a gray-green color that those official-looking vehicles seemed to favor.

He frowned and got out of the car, and by the time he did the police officer was already rising up to meet him.

"Are you Bennett Dodge?"

"I suppose that all depends on whether or not I'm getting served."

"Not getting served," the officer said.

"Okay."

If somebody were dead he would have been called already. If somebody had died Wyatt would be here. Unless it was Wyatt who was dead. But then Grant would be here. Or Jamie. And if something had happened to Jamie… Well, Grant and Wyatt would both be here.

In a fraction of a second his brain concocted a thousand different events that might have happened to wipe out every last one of his siblings.

Or maybe it was his dad. Who was currently in New

Mexico with his new wife, Freda. Maybe something happened to one of them. An accident with that damned motor home of theirs.

"Just tell me nobody's dead," Bennett said.

The officer looked shocked for a moment. "Oh, no one's dead," he said. "But we're here to talk to you about a matter of custody."

"Custody?"

The only thing he could think that might mean was they needed to take him into custody, but he hadn't done anything. He was sure he hadn't. But of course, he found himself cataloging his every action from the past week. Whether or not somebody had seen him get in the car after his half a beer last night.

But that was ridiculous. Mostly.

"You look confused," the police officer said.

"I am," Bennett responded.

"It's about your son, Mr. Dodge."

Bennett frowned, no immediate emotional reaction bubbling up to the surface. Mostly because the guy was just plain wrong. He had to be.

"I don't have a son," Bennett said.

"The paperwork I have says you do. You're welcome to contest that. But what I have is a kid that's going to end up in a group home if he can't stay with his father."

As if on cue the door to that SUV opened and a woman in a severe-looking outfit got out, followed by a teenage boy. Fifteen years old or so, Bennett figured.

Brown hair, tall, lanky. And he looked up at Bennett with simmering fury in brown eyes that matched Bennett's perfectly.

"Hi, Dad," he said. "I guess it's been a while."

CHAPTER FOUR

"Your mother is Marnie Claire?"

Bennett was sitting at the kitchen table across from the boy and the social worker. The police officer was outside. Apparently, he had been required to act as an escort because the social worker wasn't confident in her ability to keep the boy from running off. The boy. Dallas.

Dallas Dodge.

That was his name. His legal name. Though, Bennett had had no idea of his existence. In fact, Bennett had been told that the pregnancy had ended in a miscarriage. He had lived with it like a weight ever since. Everything he had heard about Marnie, what had happened to her, the kind of life she had fallen into. He had blamed himself. She had been so distraught when she had broken up with him. When she had left and he had been convinced that any dire straits she was in was partly his fault. But if any of this was true, if this was his son… Then she had lied to him. She had lied to him almost sixteen years ago.

And he was a father.

To a teenager.

Dammit to hell.

"That's right," the social worker, who was named Grace, answered the question for Dallas.

"How old are you?" Bennett said, addressing the

kid straight on. Talking around him was insulting, and even if he did seem like he was a little punk, Bennett wasn't going to treat him like he was invisible. He knew what that was like.

When his mother had died that was what everyone did. They talked over his head like he was stupid, like he couldn't possibly understand what was happening. Addressing all manner of sympathy to his father, to his older brothers, and treating Bennett like he had no idea what was happening in his own life. "Fifteen," the kid said.

"There isn't a foster family that has been able to cope with him. And he's extremely lucky that the owner of the last store he robbed didn't press charges."

"It wasn't robbery," Dallas said. "You make it sound like I had a gun."

"That's *armed* robbery," Bennett supplied.

"Well," Dallas continued. "It wasn't as badass as that. It was shoplifting. Shoplifting would be a pretty pussy thing to go to jail for."

"But it is something you could have gone to jail for," the social worker said, clearly well versed in Dallas's brand of attitude, and pretty damned fed up with it too.

Which was fair enough, he supposed.

"What happened to your mom?" Bennett asked.

"I don't know." Dallas shrugged. "She used to come around sometimes, but I haven't seen her in a few years."

"His mother lost custody a few years ago," Grace explained.

Bennett rounded on her. "If this is my kid then why didn't anyone contact me then?"

"Because we didn't know," she said. "There is no father listed on Dallas's birth certificate. We didn't know where the last name Dodge came from."

"How did you find it now?"

"It was in something of my mother's," Dallas said. "Something that I kept."

"He showed it to me when I told him about the group home," the social worker said.

Bennett just sat there, shock making him numb. And it was probably a damn good thing.

But on some level, this angry, feral-looking kid wanted to be with him. Or at least, he wanted to be with him more than he wanted to be in a group home. But...it was clear he didn't want to be here that much. And... Bennett couldn't close the gap that he felt. With the facts in his brain, the words that had been planted there and the feelings in his heart.

This was his son. In all likelihood it was.

Not only did he look quite a bit like a combination of the Dodge brothers, the timing matched up. For Marnie's pregnancy. The one that she had said she lost.

That had been a lie. Clearly.

"You didn't know you had a son," Grace said.

"No," Bennett responded. "I didn't know. Do you honestly think that if I knew there was a kid out there that was mine, that had gotten taken from his mother and put in foster care... Do you honestly think I would've left him there?"

"I've seen everything," she said, her eyes exceedingly weary. "There is nothing in the whole world that would surprise me at this point. Nothing at all. Actually, what surprises me most of all is finding you here in a house with a career and a semblance of a normal life. Unless you have drug paraphernalia hidden underneath that very nice-looking sectional in the living room, it seems like you might actually be the best thing that could have happened to Dallas."

"He's sitting right there," Bennett said. "Maybe we should talk right to him, instead of just about him."

"Oh, it doesn't bother me," Dallas said, smart-ass grin tipping his lips up. "What's the point, anyway? You don't want me to stay here. I didn't have any idea my dad was living in such a fucking fancy place."

"It's not that fancy." The word *dad* was echoing in Bennett's head, and it was making him feel a little bit dizzy.

"Fancier than where I've been, believe me."

"You've been with some nice families," Grace said.

"Yeah," Dallas snorted. "Too nice for me."

"So let me get this straight," Bennett said, resolutely keeping his focus on Dallas, almost unable to keep his eyes off him. This kid that looked like a mirror image of him nearly sixteen years ago. This kid who was a year younger than Bennett had been when he'd gotten his girlfriend pregnant and had thought he had to face up to becoming a father.

It hadn't happened. Then.

But it had all come home to roost in a really strange way.

"You've been in trouble with the law."

"Just a little." Dallas smirked.

"Yes," Grace confirmed.

"What else? Why won't they keep you in the houses?"

"I run away. I cuss a lot. I was with a church family a few months ago and I taught one of the little kids the *F* word."

"That was a dick move," Bennett pointed out.

Dallas grinned. "Yeah."

"What else?"

Dallas shrugged. "Nothing really. I mean, they want to control me, or turn me into what they think a good kid is, so that they can prove that they made an impact, or whatever bullshit reason they have for taking in foster kids in the first place. I had a mom. I don't need another one. And as for the fathers… They all sucked. I haven't seen any evidence that dads don't."

"Mine doesn't," Bennett said, his voice rough.

"Well, so far mine kinda does."

Bennett couldn't argue with that.

"Did you ever hurt anyone?" he asked.

"Yeah," Dallas said, looking down.

Bennett's stomach tightened. "What happened?"

"Just a fistfight. One of the older kids was saying shit to one of the girls. I didn't like it."

Instantly, that tightening healed. Because if Dallas had that much of a barometer inside of him for what was right, for what needed to be defended…he wasn't all that bad of a kid.

And then Bennett realized it didn't really matter if he was. If Dallas was the one who had been punched because he had said something objectionable to a girl, Bennett would still have to take him on. If this was his son, then it didn't matter if he was the worst little troll on the face of the planet, Bennett had to take care of him.

They were all sitting around this table like there was a choice. But there wasn't a choice. No way in hell. There was no real choice here.

"What's the procedure for this?" Bennett asked.

"We can do a paternity test," Grace said.

"And that…does what? Makes it all official in the court?"

"Yes," she said. "Then there will be a family court date to grant you official custody. It's not an adoption if you're his biological father."

"Then we'll do all that."

"I have paperwork ready for you to be granted temporary custody in the meantime," Grace said. "He doesn't have anywhere else to go."

"He has this place. It's fine."

Nothing was fine. Bennett had a feeling that he was existing in some strange plane where nothing seemed real as a precaution against the reality of it all. A reality that was a bit too harsh, a bit too sharp for him to cope with just yet.

"I don't…" Bennett looked around his house, which was spotless because he had a cleaner that came in once a week and took care of everything. Spotless because he didn't spend all that much time at home. "I don't have anything for a kid."

"I have a bag," Dallas said.

Again, Bennett couldn't quite tell if Dallas was being dragged here on sufferance, or if he wanted to be here. He was wondering those things because wondering was a lot easier than feeling at the moment.

"Okay," Bennett responded.

"I'll go get it." The boy stood up.

Grace eyed him speculatively. Dallas put his hands up in a defensive gesture. "That cop is still outside. It's not like I'm going to run for it. Anyway, I don't exactly have the equipment to go live in the mountains. You drove me out to the middle of nowhere. Where am I going to go?"

He walked out of the room, and Bennett winced when the front door slammed.

"You didn't know?" The woman leveled her dark eyes on him.

"I had no clue," he said, keeping his words as firm as he could. "My girlfriend told me she lost the baby."

Grace looked suddenly sympathetic. "Oh."

"I believed her. She left. Said she couldn't stand to be around me after all that. That was the last I heard of her. We were dumb kids."

Grace raised her eyebrows. "You must have been. I was surprised by how young you were."

Bennett had aged about ten years in the last forty minutes, so that statement seemed especially funny right at the moment. But he couldn't laugh.

"What happened to him?" Bennett asked, his voice rough. "What happened to her?"

Grace sighed, long and slow. "I haven't been working with Dallas that long. But from what I understand his mother had drug issues. He was neglected and eventually had to be removed from her custody. He went back and forth for a while, but as he said...not recently. He's been moving between foster homes for couple of years now."

"And no one keeps him?"

"He's difficult," Grace said, folding her hands together. "I'm not going to lie to you about that."

A difficult kid who'd had more than a difficult life, and there had been no reason for that. No reason at all. Bennett had been here the whole time. And if he'd known...

"It's okay if he's difficult," Bennett said, firming up his jaw. "He's my difficult."

She nodded slowly, and something that looked like it might at least be a neighbor of respect flashed in her eyes. "I suppose he is."

Dallas came back into the room then, dragging a black garbage bag behind him. "Quick packing," he said, indicating what passed as his luggage.

For a moment, Bennett felt like he was staring into a black hole of rage. Despair. Denial.

And yet here was this kid who looked almost just like him. This kid standing there clutching a garbage bag.

Bennett had experienced loss in his life. He hadn't grown up with a mother. But he'd had stability. He'd had a father and a home. He'd never wanted for anything, and he had certainly never had to put all of his worldly possessions into a single bag and get carted to a place he'd never been before. Over and over again.

This was his son, and he would do the tests, or whatever they wanted him to do, but he didn't think there was a scenario in which it would turn out that Dallas didn't belong to him. In which it would turn out that this kid, this kid that had been abandoned and shuffled around, wasn't *his*.

But right then, with that reality crashing it, it hit him that Dallas was also a stranger. A stranger that was going to live in his house.

Bennett could not have picked a more surreal moment off a list. He couldn't imagine anything more bizarre than staring down a stranger that you were blood-related to. A stranger who was your child.

Bennett didn't *feel* like a father. He was thirty-two years old. He didn't feel old enough to have a fifteen-year-old son. That was for damn sure.

But he didn't feel *nothing*. There was something inside of him that burned for this angry boy standing in front of him. Guilt, mostly. Guilt that Dallas had gone through all of that when Bennett had been going on with his life, making something of himself. When he had been living in this big, comfortable house all this time. With a housecleaner, no less, and this kid had been bouncing back and forth between homes.

"I have a bit of a drive to get back to Portland," Grace said. "So, this is where I leave you. But of course you can have my number. And we will be checking in."

"So you can just…leave him with me?" Panic made his throat tight, made it hard for him to breathe. He'd stuck his hand up inside animals and faced down wounded, enraged creatures that were bent on killing him before they let him help them. His brother might have ridden bulls for a living, but Bennett had vaccinated them. None of that came close to the kind of fear he felt here.

"You are his father," she said. "His father with no criminal record or any reason that he shouldn't have him. That's simple enough."

Simple and complicated in ways that Bennett couldn't work out even within himself.

Grace paused and put her hand on Dallas's shoulder. "You can use my number too. I hope you know that. Goodbye, Dallas. I'll be checking in with you."

Then she left. Left him standing there with this kid who was a stranger. Who was his son.

The clock on the wall ticked, marking the torturous seconds where he couldn't think of a thing to say. Where he couldn't even move.

"I have a guest room," Bennett said slowly.

"Right," Dallas said. "Are you sure you don't want me to sleep in a barn?"

"No."

"You don't have a wife or anything?" the kid asked.

"No," Bennett said.

"Girlfriend?"

"Do you?" Bennett asked.

Dallas shrugged. "Hard to hang on to one when you're moving all the time."

"Sure."

More seconds ticked off.

"I bet if you touch any of the girls here their dads run you off the property with a shotgun, right?" he asked.

"I don't know about them, but I might chase you with a shotgun."

Dallas snorted. "That's funny. Especially because I know my mom is from here, and I know that you knocked her up."

"I did," Dallas said. "She told me she had a miscarriage."

Dallas looked shocked at that, and Bennett wondered if he should have said that. But honestly, there was no point letting the kid cast him as any more of a bad guy than he already had. Marnie wasn't here. Marnie was off mired in drug addiction somewhere. And any sympathy that he had felt for her situation was rapidly disintegrating. He would have helped her. He would have stayed with her. She didn't need to run away. He had no clue why in hell she had done that. No clue what had possessed her. If she hadn't wanted the baby, he would have taken the baby. He would never understand this.

"She didn't tell me that," Dallas said.

"I don't know what she told you. But I'll tell you, honestly, I found out she was pregnant, I was going to propose to her. She told me she had a miscarriage, and then she told me she was leaving town. She broke up with me. We were young and we were stupid."

"I'm younger than you were," Dallas pointed out.

"Yes. And you're young and stupid. Because when you're fifteen you're stupid. And when you're sixteen you're not much better. We were stupid. But I didn't know... I didn't know. You don't have to believe me right now. I don't know that I can really believe any of this. I feel like I'm going to blink and you're going to disappear. I'm going to wake up and it's gonna be some kind of weird dream. But as long as you're standing there... I didn't know about you. I'm going to be honest with you. That's what I'm going to do." Bennett made a decision then, and he decided to go with it. "Whatever else, I'm going to tell you the truth. I'm going to be really bad at this. I don't have any experience with kids."

"Not really a kid," Dallas said, shrugging.

"You're not," Bennett said, his heart clenching tight. Because the boy in front of him was really more of a young man, and the first fifteen years of his life were lost to Bennett. There was nothing he could do about it. That hurt like a son of gun.

"But you are," he continued. "And you need somebody. I'm going to be that person. And I'm going to be honest with you. Even if it's hard. So, that's my first bit of honesty."

"That doesn't mean I believe you," Dallas said. "Just because you told me to."

"That's fine. It's going to take a while for you to believe that, I know." He swallowed hard, and the sound of his heartbeat blended into more seconds ticking by.

"Do you have an Xbox or anything?" Dallas asked, breaking the silence.

"No," Bennett responded.

"Really? What the hell do you do?"

"I have animals," Bennett responded. "They're time-consuming."

Dallas frowned. "What the hell do you do for work?"

"I'm a veterinarian," Bennett responded. "Big animals. Cows. Horses. Llamas."

"Llamas?"

"Llamas get sick too."

"What do you do around here for fun? Did you... go cow tipping?"

Bennett crossed his arms and looked at Dallas. "Well, I got my girlfriend pregnant when we were sixteen, so I think that answers your question about what we do for fun around here."

Dallas blinked, and then huffed a reluctant laugh. "Great. But you just told me to stay away from the girls."

"I didn't say I recommended that kind of behavior," Bennett said. "I mean, I got my girlfriend pregnant. And now I'm standing here with you."

"Condoms, dude."

Bennett shook his head. "Okay. Too much honesty. Way too much honesty. I'll get you an Xbox."

Bennett was a terrible parent already. He was making deals and bargains and buying Xboxes. And he hadn't even told his brothers yet. Or his sister. Or Kaylee.

Dammit. *Kaylee.*

She was going to be so mad at him.

"Where's that bedroom at?" Dallas asked, looking around.

For just a moment a crack in the kid's bravado seemed to break. Right around the moment when Bennett felt his own beginning to crumble.

"I'll show you." He walked him down the hall and opened the door to a room that was fully furnished, and definitely not the kind of thing a teenage boy would find interesting at all. Because it was done up for guests he had never had. Hypothetical ones that he thought someday when he and Olivia had married they might have.

There was a plaid bedspread and a full-size bed with headboard. Art with Oregon landscapes framed on the walls.

Dallas looked around and dropped his trash bag next to his feet. "It works." He turned to Bennett. "Don't worry. I probably won't kill you in your sleep."

Bennett lifted a brow. "Probably?"

"I've lived with a lot of families. I only did that once."

Bennett had to laugh at that, a forced, short chuckle, because of course the thought had crossed his mind. And of course this kid was calling it out. Because he was just that kind of kid. Hard and direct and more than willing to put himself at odds with Bennett in the interest of not showing any vulnerability.

But it was there.

The very fact that the kid was standing here, and not running off in the woods was evidence of that.

"Can I take a shower?"

"Yeah," Bennett said. "Bathroom is across the hall."

"Cool."

He stood there for a moment, and then looked over at Bennett. "Is there any point in me unpacking this?" He gestured down to the plastic bag.

"Yeah," Bennett said. "Unpack it. Throw it away."

He'd get him a new bag. But not now. Not when it would just look like he was giving him nicer luggage for a nomadic existence. No. He'd make sure he didn't need a bag for a good while.

"I'm just checking. Because if you really didn't know about me, and you're really as surprised as you say you are, I figure it's going to take a little while for reality to set in. And when it does, you probably won't want me here."

"I'm going to have you here," Bennett said.

That was the truth. He was giving him the truth. Want was... He didn't even know what that word meant right now.

But he had been prepared sixteen years ago to upend his life to raise a child. To put everything aside for the baby he had made with Marnie, accident or not. That it was all happening sixteen years later didn't matter.

The kid was still his responsibility. And Bennett was still going to lay it all down for him.

Because outside of what he felt, Bennett knew what was right. And even if he couldn't feel it all, he could still do what needed to be done.

"You're staying," Bennett said decisively, resolutely. "Unpack the damn bag."

CHAPTER FIVE

KAYLEE WAS IN her pajamas when her phone rang. She'd just come inside after riding her horse, Flicka, around the trail behind her house and getting her put away, and was currently sprawled on the couch with her cat, Albus, lying across her chest.

Her heart kicked a little bit when she looked at the screen and saw that it was Bennett.

"Are you having more cow drama?" she asked. "Because I'm getting ready for bed."

"No, not exactly."

"What's going on?"

He sounded…he sounded weird. Not like himself. Bennett was cool and in control, always. He was the kind of guy you wanted to have around in a crisis, and he professionally handled animal crises on an almost daily basis. He was not the kind of guy who ever sounded… Well, whatever it was he sounded now. She couldn't quite put her finger on it. Only that it wasn't him.

"It's hard to explain. Can you come over?"

Thoughts chased each other around her head like rabid foxes. He was ill. He had some kind of terrible disease. He was quitting the business and leaving her.

"I'll be right over."

She hung up and started hunting for something to wear. She put on a pair of ripped jeans and a gray

T-shirt that had a logo for the veterinary clinic on it. By the time she had gone to her truck, she had thought of at least three new scenarios, each one more upsetting than the last, for why Bennett had sounded so grave.

Olivia wanted him back. Olivia, who was pregnant with another man's baby, wanted him back because Luke had abandoned her. Yes, that was it. Luke had abandoned her, and she was asking Bennett to raise another man's child.

Bennett was a good man. He was a good and faithful man, and he was going to do it.

She was going to tell him *not to do it*.

Kaylee was completely worked up in a lather by the time she was halfway to Bennett's place. Ready to fight him over his chivalrous nature. He was *not* marrying a woman and raising another man's child as his own. He wasn't doing it.

She couldn't imagine anything more terrible.

At least when they had been together at first she had thought Olivia was exactly the kind of woman he should be with. And yes, that had burned. Because Olivia was so different from everything that Kaylee was. And having to acknowledge that Olivia was going to fill a place in his life that he clearly didn't think Kaylee could fill was painful. Painful all the way through her bones in a way that forced her to clench her teeth to make them stop aching.

But nonetheless, it had been bearable. Bearable because she had thought that Olivia would make him happy.

But *this* wouldn't make him happy. *This* was outrageous.

She pulled her truck up to the front of his house and turned the engine off quickly, hopping down out of the cabin and slamming the door, only to stop once she'd climbed the front steps.

She was just about to raise her hand to knock when the door opened, and she was met by a shell-shocked-looking Bennett.

"It's Olivia, isn't it?"

It occurred to her just then that Olivia might have lost the baby. That she wanted to marry him now that she wasn't tied to Luke. That would be a lot harder to talk him out of. Especially if Olivia was upset and Bennett wanted to fix it.

"Don't do it," she repeated. "Don't take her back."

"What?"

She blinked.

Right. He hadn't actually said anything about Olivia. He hadn't said anything about anything. It was just that all of those scenarios had seemed so possible, and she had latched on to that one so tightly, and turned it over about fifty different times on the drive over.

"Never mind. What's happening?"

He stepped outside, closing the door softly behind him. "I don't know how to explain this to you," he said, his words rough.

"What?" He looked… He didn't look good at all. His eyes looked like they'd been punched, dark shadows spreading beneath them. "Bennett, you are freaking me out."

He shook his head and walked down the front steps past her, his boots making a hollow sound on the wood, then crunching on the gravel.

He sighed slowly, heavily, looking upward. She followed his gaze, staring at the inky sky, with the stars bursting through like a candle in punched tin.

"You're the first person I called," he said, sounding as if the realization of that was dawning over him slowly. "I'm going to have to talk to Wyatt. And Grant. Jamie. My dad. I'm going to have to explain some things to a lot of people."

"What? Do you have some kind of terrible disease? Do you have gambling debt? Have you lost the ranch?" She frowned. "Did you lose *our* business?"

He shook his head. "No. Kaylee… You remember Marnie Claire?"

"Yes," Kaylee said, and an instant spike of loathing burst hot and insistent through her chest. Yes, she knew Marnie Claire. Bennett's first girlfriend. Kaylee hadn't liked her, not at all. Not because there was anything wrong with her specifically, but because Bennett had been so obsessed with her. She'd seen less of him over the months he'd dated Marnie than she ever had since they'd become friends.

He'd told Kaylee before they'd had sex for the first time, a shy grin on his face as he'd confessed it was going to happen that night. And Kaylee had wanted to die. It was the moment that had forced her to realize that she was…jealous. That she wished it were her.

She'd decided very quickly after, sometime during his very messy breakup with Marnie, in fact, that she didn't want that. She didn't want to be his girlfriend for a little while. She wanted to be his friend forever. To become veterinarians like they'd promised each other, and work together.

To be something more, better, than a husband and wife. Her parents' marriage hadn't made the institution seem all that aspirational.

"There's something you don't know," he said.

"What?" He sounded so very, very grave. Grave enough she was starting to wonder if she was going to have to prove that she was a friend who'd help hide the body.

He lowered his head. "When we were sixteen Marnie got pregnant."

Kaylee felt like the ground tilted underneath her feet. *"What?"*

"Marnie was pregnant in high school."

"Whose baby was it?" The words felt numb and ridiculous. But they fell out of her mouth naturally. Because if it were Bennett's… It couldn't have been.

"Mine."

She was…stunned. She couldn't even process it. Because there had never been a baby. So how could Marnie have been pregnant?

"Marnie left. She moved away," Kaylee said.

"Yes," he said slowly. "After she lost the baby."

Kaylee's breath rushed from her body, like it was trying to flee the scene of this very difficult conversation. "Bennett, how did you never tell me any of this?"

"I didn't tell anyone," he said. He closed his eyes. "I told one person. I told Cole Logan."

"Olivia's dad. He's the one that knew." There were implications to that, and she knew it. But she couldn't sort them out, not right then.

"I was scared," Bennett said. "I was stupid and I didn't want my dad to know that I made such a big mistake. I didn't want him to be disappointed in me. At that point Wyatt was gone, off riding in the rodeo. Grant was getting married, and Dad really wished he wouldn't. He was still coping with Jamie being a little kid, being a single dad. I wanted him to be proud of me. I wanted to be something easy for him. Not something hard. So I talked to Cole."

"And not me?" she asked.

How weird that a secret kept from that many years ago could hurt. But they'd talked about everything back then. He'd told her when he'd gotten a note from a girl in math class asking him if he liked her, and to check Yes or No. She'd told him about the time she'd taken a cigarette some older kids had offered her, and she'd hated it.

She hadn't talked about her family, but that was different. The day-to-day things. School, friends, growing up. Hopes, dreams, fears. First kisses and first times. They'd shared that stuff. The parts of her life she cared about, she'd shared with him.

She'd thought he'd shared it all with her.

"I was scared, Kay. Scared of what you'd think of me. I went to Cole because he was the closest thing to an uncle I had. And I was terrified of telling my dad."

"But wait, why…" It was like the other shoe had dropped straight out of that starry sky and crash-landed between them. "What's happening now?"

"She *didn't* lose the baby," Bennett said, his voice raw. "She didn't lose the baby. She lied to me."

"Why?" She blinked. "How do you know that?"

"Because the baby is a damned fifteen-year-old boy and he is in my guest room."

Kaylee exhaled. "Dammit to hell."

"That's what I said. Well, that's what I thought."

"How do you know he's yours?"

"He looks just like me. He's the right age. She would have had to go and get pregnant again pretty damn quick for all to match up like this. And with someone who resembled me."

"Possible," Kaylee said, "I mean, if she had a type."

"She lied to me," Bennett said. "She lied to me, and she lost custody of our son at some point because of drug addiction."

"Bennett... I don't even know..."

"Me either. You were the first person that I called. Kaylee, I need you."

And there he was, standing out under a romantic, expansive Oregon sky, professing to need her, his dark eyes illuminated by the moon, the sincerity in them deep enough to steal her breath. He needed her. But not for what she had always hoped he might. He *needed* her because his life was falling apart. He needed her because everything was falling apart and he knew that she would help pick up the pieces, no matter how big or heavy they were. Because it was what she did. It was what they did.

He had called her. He *needed* her.

And yes, she'd just been in the process of trying to fix her narrowed, Bennett-focused world, but she didn't know how she could turn away from him now. How she could possibly spend less time with him when this was happening.

Dates with nice men who had nicer dogs were important. She needed to go on them because she needed to figure out a way to find some healthier balance inside of herself.

But not now.

Her best friend had just found out that he was a father. A father to a fifteen-year-old, and that child was sitting in his house.

The very fact was like a slap.

Bennett had just found out he was a *father*.

He was her friend. She needed to get over herself for just a few minutes and deal with the reality of that.

"Where is he now?" she asked, feeling numb.

"He's in his room. Asleep I think. Or maybe plotting my death, I don't know. It's tough to say."

"Are you okay?" It was a stupid question. *She* wasn't okay, how could he be okay?

"I'm not okay," he said, shaking his head. "I don't know what to do. I feel like I would be hard-pressed to find a paternal bone in my body if you handed off a baby to me. Much less handing me a fifteen-year-old and telling me he's my kid." He let out a long, heavy breath. "I don't know what to feel. I don't know what I'm supposed to do. I don't know what to do with the kid. Much less a kid that's half a man and all trouble. I don't know... I don't know what to do."

"You don't have to know right this second," she said.

She knew he felt like he did. Like he needed to regroup and come up with a plan of attack in five minutes flat without taking more than a second to panic.

It hit her then that his version of that had been calling her.

That she was the one person he'd been able to call when he'd been mired in the feeling of not knowing what the hell was happening in his life.

That mattered to her. That she could be that person for him.

That she was important.

"I kind of do," he said. "He's in there. And I have to...parent."

What would Bennett's son look like? Her heart stuck then, a dull ache spreading out through her throat. She would know the answer to that question soon.

But Bennett had said that the kid was asleep. Still, suddenly, she was overwhelmed by curiosity. Kind of a morbid curiosity because the idea of seeing a child that Bennett had made with somebody else walking around felt like it would be painful in many ways. But also... amazing in others.

Her throat tightened, emotion expanding in her chest. "I doubt he expects you to just…magically be perfect. He doesn't know how to be your son any more than you know how to be his father. You're going to have to… feel it out together."

"I told him he was staying," Bennett said. "He's staying. I don't know much of anything except that. I know that I want to…fix things somehow. But I don't know how. I've never felt more like I needed to do something and less certain of what that something was ever in my whole life."

She had no idea what to say to that. "Well, I don't know what the hell to do with a kid either. But I know that we can figure this out together. I'll help you with your family. I'll help you with him." She didn't know the kid's name. He hadn't said. "What's his name?"

"Dallas," Bennett said.

The name was very not Bennett. Not traditional enough. And Bennett had never been to Texas so there was no personal connection to it at all. "I guess it's too late to change it now."

He laughed. "Just a little bit."

Kaylee wanted to be what he needed. But she didn't know how to be. So she would just be there with him. That she could do. "Can I…can I come in for a little while?"

"For a little while." Bennett turned away from her and she went after him, following him toward the house on unsteady legs, her heart throbbing at the base of her neck.

Bennett pushed the door open and she followed him in, looking around the clean, well-organized home, which didn't look at all as if it had been disturbed today, much less like it had taken on a new occupant. Everything was in order, everything in its place, just as Bennett always kept it. Bennett liked to be in control of his world, and she'd always understood the compulsion. Her own home life had been chaotic, and her method of coping had been to close the door on it and pretend it wasn't happening. Bennett had lost his mother when he was a little boy, and she imagined his carefully ordered life was designed to give him control after feeling so powerless then.

They'd both gotten into veterinary medicine because they wanted to fix. To heal. To help. A small bit of control in a world that offered very little, in reality.

A teenager showing up and moving in was…anything but controlled and orderly.

"I'll take a drink."

"Well, I want about ten. Can you drink when there's a minor in the house?" he asked.

"Pretty sure you can. If not, my parents would have lost custody of me at some point." She hadn't meant to make that comment. She purposefully avoided mentions of her parents. Bennett had asked a few times why she didn't go visit them at holidays, after they'd moved out of town. She'd always been vague. That they drank too much. That they just didn't get along.

He'd pushed a few times, but she'd always shut down the conversation, and he'd backed off.

"Bring on the alcohol, then," Bennett said, jerking the fridge open and getting a bottle. He handed one to Kaylee, then took one for himself. Then he frowned. "I'm probably going to have to hide this," he said.

"You think?"

"Trust me," Bennett said, "he seems like the type to steal beer out of the fridge."

"Oh, really?"

"He's here because he's been in trouble with the law. Because nobody can handle him. I think underage drinking is probably in his repertoire."

"So is eavesdropping," came a rather sullen-sounding voice from the hallway.

Kaylee looked up, and her heart choked before tumbling down into her stomach. He looked just like Bennett. His build was more slight, his hair a bit lighter, but he had the same eyes. And, having known Bennett since he was about that age, it was just like looking at him. Like a carbon copy. She didn't see any of Marnie in him, and she really didn't want to, so that felt like a strange and selfish blessing. But he was Bennett's son. She would be more shocked to find out he wasn't. If she had passed him on the street she would have thought the same thing.

"Dallas," Bennett said, keeping his tone even. "This is my friend, Kaylee."

"Friend?" He looked her up and down. "Just so you know, I'm not in the market for a new mommy."

Kaylee felt the sting of those words like the crack of an open palm across her face. "Well, no danger of that," she said, her tone stiff. "I'm just his friend."

"She friend-zoned you?" the kid asked, directing the question at Bennett.

Kaylee wanted to laugh at the absurdity of it. Of course, in spite of her feelings, she kind of had. The only scenario where she could imagine her and Bennett becoming more than friends involved him confessing undying love for her and a desire to get married immediately. The alternative was way too risky.

Well, the real gut punch was that even that insane fantasy felt too risky.

"She's someone you'll see around," Bennett said,

choosing to ignore the dig. "Kaylee and I run a veterinary practice together."

"Okay," Dallas said, feigning disinterest.

"Nice to meet you too," Kaylee said.

"Did he really not know about me?" Dallas asked, leveling that angry brown stare at her.

"Well, I didn't know about you until five minutes ago," Kaylee said. "And he told me he didn't either. I've known him for a long time. He's a terrible liar. On that you can trust me. He's actually kind of a goody-goody. If he tells you something, I would be inclined to believe it."

"Well, you're his friend, so you're biased."

"It's true," Kaylee said, nodding. "But if I thought he was being a dumbass I wouldn't protect him. Count on that. That's real friends. Weak-ass friends just tell you what you want to hear. Real friends call you out when you need it. I'm a real friend."

There was something about the vulnerability that flashed through Dallas's eyes just then that hit Kaylee in a place she would rather not acknowledge. She didn't want to relate to this kid, but suddenly she did. Yeah, she had both parents at home, but she knew all about uncertainty. She knew all about what it was like to spend your life walking on eggshells and hoping that you didn't land on someone's bad side.

She knew what it was like to live on a system of earning affection. Earning your place. Earning the right to get through the day without getting slapped upside the head.

Not even Bennett knew that about her. But she wondered in that moment if his son might have guessed just by looking at her. Like she had found common ground with him the moment their eyes had met. And suddenly, all that hurt she had felt a moment before over Marnie seemed ridiculous. The kid wasn't a hypothetical anymore. He was real, and he was standing right in front of her.

A teenager who needed assurance. Who needed to know that he deserved to feel safe. That he deserved to have someone take care of him.

"He's a good guy," she said, tilting her head toward Bennett. "You can trust him."

"Well, this random woman that I don't know says I can trust you," Dallas said, his eyes going flat as he looked up at Bennett.

But Kaylee didn't care. Because he needed to hear it. She didn't know anything about kids. But she knew about the kid she had been. She knew what she would have wanted to hear. Even if she wouldn't have been able to believe it or receive it. But it would have sat there. If just one person would have told her that she deserved some kind of stability, it could have helped. Bennett had shown her that. As a friend, he had been constant and steady. And even though she had talked about the tumultuous nature of her home life, he had somehow seemed to know exactly what she needed.

He had given her focus. He had made her feel like she deserved to go for her dream of being a veterinarian. He and his father, Quinn, had helped her figure out how to get scholarship so that she could go to school.

Yes, having someone be interested, having someone be adamant that you could do something, that you could have something, mattered.

"If it's all the same to you," Dallas said, "I think I'll head to bed."

"I thought you already had," Bennett said.

"Which is why you were talking about me."

"Yeah," Bennett said. "I'm going to talk about you sometimes."

"Is this more of that honesty that you promised me?"

"Yes," Bennett said. "I plan on being relentless with that until you start believing me when I tell you things."

"Good luck. I have about fifteen years of people proving they're useless liars. I would say that in about fifteen more you could maybe undo that. But I doubt we'll be speaking by then."

"If we aren't," Bennett said, "then it won't be because of me. It won't be because I stop talking. Guarantee it."

Dallas reeled back, a deep crease between his brows. "Why?"

"Because you're my son. And that's how that works."

The fire and intensity in Bennett's eyes caught Kaylee by the heart and held her fast. She was useless and hopeless. Hopeless for him, and this only introduced a new way for her to be that.

Bennett was gorgeous to her, always. That was part of the problem. Maybe, if she had some kind of quiet, sweet love for him based only on *feelings* she could have redirected it. But it was more than that. It was a violent, intense visceral attraction that was physical on a deep and very sexual level.

So sexual it was impossible to pretend it was anything else. Feelings she might have been able to squish into another box. That deep, intense ache between her thighs was very difficult to pass off as anything but sexual attraction.

She'd tried.

And she would have never guessed that watching the man deal with fatherhood would have ratcheted that up a notch. She would have said that nothing could. But Lord Almighty, this did. Bennett full of righteous fury staring down his son. Fury at the world for what it had put him through. Uncompromising with a kind of deep intensity, a commitment that no one had ever offered to Kaylee.

It was more than her poor ovaries could bear.

Every little biological *thing* inside of her was screaming about the suitability of Bennett as a partner. A protector of offspring.

It was ingrained on a hormonal level. She was powerless against it.

That still didn't make it less disconcerting.

Somewhere in the back of her brain she felt a little itch.

Michael.

Michael was the itch. She had a date with him next week. She had a date with him next week and she was standing here getting hot and bothered over Bennett.

But then, that was kind of the normal state of things. Exacerbated in the moment, but relatively normal nonetheless.

And again, she was mired in her own stuff and she felt like a tool.

Dallas shrugged, as if he was fully unaffected by the proclamation that Bennett had just made. But Kaylee knew otherwise. She just did. Because whether it hit him today or in five years, he was going to realize eventually what Bennett was saying to him. What Bennett was offering.

It would matter then. When he needed it to matter, it would. Someday when a little bit of that anger had subsided, or when he was feeling particularly angry and his body needed a break from it.

She was certain because sometimes having the friend that she'd had in Bennett, having the support she'd had in his family, had been the only thing keeping her grounded, rooted to the possibilities of the future, rather than those old, ugly feelings of inadequacy. Of not deserving.

And that—she knew—was what all that bluff and bluster was.

Feeling undeserving. Unwanted.

"I'm really scoring points all over the place," Bennett said, when the bedroom door slammed shut.

"You are, actually," Kaylee said softly. "You just might be saving them up for later. Want to go back outside?"

"Yes," Bennett said.

They wandered out to the front porch, and Bennett leaned over the railing, lifting the beer bottle to his lips. "He's real," Bennett said. "You saw that too."

"Yeah," she said. "Sorry I can't tell you it's some kind of hallucination."

"I was actually almost afraid it might be," Bennett said, his voice rough. "That I was going to take you in there and he was going to be gone."

She didn't say anything. She had the feeling that he didn't want her to.

"I didn't want him to be," Bennett said. "As little sense as that makes… Now that he's here…"

"It makes as much sense as any of this does," Kaylee said. "If you felt like you wanted him gone in the next five minutes, that would be okay too, because nothing about this is normal. There's not exactly a guidebook for what to do when the son you didn't know you had shows up out of nowhere."

"I guess not," he said.

"I just can't believe it," Kaylee said, shaking her head. "I mean, now that I've seen him I can. He looks just like you, Bennett. And I mean in an uncanny way. It's like looking at you when we were in high school."

"He doesn't look that much like me," Bennett said, kicking against the edge of the porch rail with the toe of his cowboy boot.

"He does," Kaylee said. "And it's everything. The way that he stands, the set of his shoulders. He's just… you through and through, and he'd never even met you before today." She sighed. "He's not as happy as you were."

"Of course not," Bennett said. "Because he's had an awful life, and I'm partly to blame for that."

"You couldn't force her to tell you. She lied to you, and you had no reason to think that she would do that."

"My whole…everything since then…this is why I plan like I do. Why I make sure I have everything mapped out in my head, because I know what happens when you don't do that. When you just…think of the moment and not the future."

"I thought… I thought it was because of your mom." She reached out and touched his arm.

"Partly," he said. "You know things were hard after she died. We missed her, and Dad didn't do a great job organizing. Not that I blame him. I had to keep my part of the world organized or it would all fall apart."

Her heart twisted. "I know. I get that."

"I know you do," he said. "And then Marnie got pregnant. I knew that I had let us both down. I just wanted… I didn't ever want anything like that again. I was young, and sex was new, and I didn't think. I didn't think, and I put her through loss and pain. I blamed myself for everything that went wrong in her life. And maybe I still own part of that blame. Because I was dumb. Because I didn't keep control. I thought of my own physical pleasure over anything else."

Kaylee didn't like the way this conversation was going. Didn't like the way it made her feel like there was heat crackling beneath her skin. Didn't like how off-kilter she felt. Didn't like imagining Bennett, her steady, staid Bennett, losing control with a woman.

It made her feel hot all over, imagining Bennett making love with intensity.

Hell, she was about to have a hot flash.

"I've never felt anything like that," she said, the words sticking in her throat on the way out.

Bennett whipped his head sharply to the side, his beer bottle frozen midway between the porch rail and his lips. "You... Never..."

"I've never felt out of control. In that...situation. That's all I'm saying."

Something caught between them in that moment, and it was electric, intense enough that it was undeniable. It rolled over her like a wave, an ultrasonic wave, sharp and shocky and quite unlike anything she had ever felt coming from him before. Yes, there had been some small moments. Little pops of awareness, of both of them suddenly remembering that they were male and female, and not simply two genderless people sharing a friendship.

But not like this. Nothing like this.

"Well," he said, clearing his throat.

"Nothing good comes of it, apparently," she said, her throat feeling scratchy.

"No," Bennett said. "And I've made sure it never happened to me again."

"Does that mean..." She shouldn't be continuing this

conversation. She really shouldn't. "You didn't feel that way about Olivia?"

"I never slept with Olivia," he said, his tone rough.

Kaylee felt like she'd been slapped. This was a lot of weird revelations for one night. "You never…you never slept with her?"

"No," Bennett responded. "I never did. She wanted to wait until we were engaged. And we never got engaged."

"I thought that you…" She had spent so much time imagining dark-haired, petite Olivia wrapped around Bennett, had made herself sick thinking about it. And he hadn't done it. "She's so…beautiful," she finished lamely.

Olivia was everything Kaylee wasn't. Petite. Feminine.

"She was *safe*," Bennett said. He took another drink of beer. "I wanted safe. I wanted something that I could plan. I wanted to be able to plan my life. And she seemed like a pretty great thing to plan it around. She felt the same way about me. It was never… We were never in love, we were just hoping to make a good life together. And then I lost her, and now I have a kid. So I give up. I give up on sensible. I give up on control." He shook his head and took another drink.

She had a feeling he did not give up on control at all. That he was going to try to corral and take the reins of this situation, whatever he said now.

"I see," she said, looking up, her eyes clashing with his.

She hadn't imagined it. Hadn't for one moment fabricated that spark between them. It was there. It was there now.

And then he looked down at her lips.

She felt the impact of that shoot down between her thighs. Good Lord Almighty. Bennett Dodge was looking at her mouth.

Bennett Dodge was having a breakdown. And if he did something with her now, it was only going to be for that reason.

That snapped her back to reality. She took a swig of beer, needing for her lips to be busy so that they didn't decide to occupy their time with him.

"I should go," she said.

"Do you have to?"

"Yes," she said, not quite sure if they were talking over the top of the same subtext. She knew what she felt. She knew what she read here, but apparently she didn't know much of anything. Bennett hadn't slept with Olivia. He thought she was safe.

It was a totally different relationship to the one she had thought she had been witnessing. The one where he called her princess. Where he treated her like this beautiful, delicate and fragile thing that Kaylee was so certain she could never be.

This wonderful, deserving little creature that Kaylee knew she wasn't.

But his relationship with Olivia hadn't been passionate or physical. All that time she'd tortured herself over it and he'd never been with Olivia. She would never have guessed that.

So maybe Bennett was looking at her mouth because he wanted to kiss her, or maybe he was trying to figure out how much beer she was going to drink, or he was just spacing out because everything was weird.

Whatever, she wasn't in the space to try to figure it out and she needed to stop trying before she did something really foolish.

"I'm going to have to go over to the ranch and talk to my brothers tomorrow. Will you go with me?"

"Of course I will."

No matter what was wacky and off tonight, she was going to be there for him. There was no question about that. That was the kind of friendship they had. That kind of unconditional support that he had been the first person to show her.

"Thank you," he said. She shrugged and set the beer on the porch rail, turning to walk down the steps. And then, Bennett spoke again, his voice heavy. "Kaylee... I really need our friendship right now."

Those words were so weighted down that she knew in that instance he had felt the same thing she had.

That just made her mad. She had spent all this time subsuming her feelings, and there was one moment of mutual electricity and he was making veiled proclamations.

She'd been guarding their friendship for years. She didn't need him to go talking about the importance of it. She damn well knew.

"Good," she said, not offering him any indication that she had any clue what he meant. "I'm glad that I can be your friend. Very glad."

And with that, she turned and stomped her way back to the truck, not quite sure what the hell it said about reality that the earlier scenario where Olivia was pregnant with Luke's baby and wanted Bennett back was somehow less complicated than the one she found herself in now.

CHAPTER SIX

EARLY THE NEXT morning Bennett found himself em-
broiled in indecision.

His son—that was still the weirdest thought it was
possible to have—was still asleep, and Bennett had to
get to work in the next hour.

He went out and slowly, methodically began to feed
the animals. Pepper and Cheddar, his Australian shep-
herds yipping excitedly at his heels as he navigated the
morning chores with all the conviction of a robot per-
forming work on an assembly line.

He didn't know if he could leave Dallas alone. He
thought of the business card that the social worker had
left for him. Should he call her about that?

Logically he knew that a fifteen-year-old could handle himself for a few hours, but Dallas had only just
shown up and Bennett didn't know if it meant the kid
would run away if he was left unattended. Of course,
it wasn't like he could prevent him from leaving if he
wanted to, short of tying him up and locking him in a
bedroom, and that was probably frowned on.

He didn't feel comfortable about leaving him, though.
Whatever was technically acceptable and wasn't, he
knew he didn't feel right about it.

He had to talk to his family tonight. He had decided
that he wouldn't do it until then. Until they had all got-

ten through the workday and could see each other face-to-face.

But until then, he had patients to see.

Dallas could hang out at the clinic, or he could ride in Bennett's truck all day. That would work well enough.

Bennett couldn't think of what they would talk about if they ended up trapped in a vehicle together for the entirety of the day.

He supposed that was a stupid, selfish thing to concern himself with.

But he was concerned.

He walked back into the house just as the clock rolled over to six, and he knew that he was going to be tempting a lot of rage waking a teenage boy out of a dead sleep but he had to do something.

He knocked on the bedroom door and got no answer. He knocked again, this time more heavily, and nothing.

What if the kid had run off in the middle of the night? He should have like…slept in front of the door. But then, he could have climbed out the window.

Dammit.

He opened up the door, and his heart slammed hard against his breastbone when he saw the boy lying on his stomach, his face smashed against the pillow, a little bit of drool coming out the corner of his mouth. His arm was draped over the side of the mattress, his hand bent at the wrist, his knuckles pressing against the floor. He was so profoundly out that he looked entirely limp.

A flood of emotions butted up against some dam inside of Bennett he hadn't known had existed. And he felt it crack.

Dallas made a croaking sound and sniffed. And the dam inside Bennett burst completely.

It was like being caught between two points in time.

He could imagine then, what it might have been like to walk into a nursery when Dallas was a baby, to see him asleep like this in a crib.

But he hadn't. He had never gotten to see him then.

Were there pictures? Was there a video of him taking a first step? How old had he been?

Had his first word been *dada*, like so many other babies, but with no dad around to feel like his baby was talking to him?

He had missed that. All of that. And he hadn't even had a choice. He pressed a hand against his chest and staggered backward, suddenly so overwhelmed with the enormity of the situation that he couldn't breathe.

This boy was fifteen. He took up the length of this entire bed. There had been a point when he had been no larger than a loaf of bread, and dammit, Bennett had had the right to know him then. To *hold* him then. But he hadn't. And Dallas had spent all these long years with no one. Being bounced around, no safe place.

But he had slept easily here last night. He had slept deeply.

Whatever happened today, Bennett was going to take some solace in that.

And he was not leaving the kid here by himself.

"Wake up," Bennett said. "Dallas, wake up."

"What?" Dallas jerked up, rolling over onto his back and blinking hard. "It's still fucking dark out," he moaned.

"Yeah," Bennett said. "But it won't be for long. And I have to go to work."

"So?"

"I'm not leaving you here."

"I'm not a baby," Dallas muttered.

Bennett was well aware of that. It had all been driven home just a second ago.

"Yes. I know. But you are my kid. If you weren't a kid, they would have turned you loose. But you are. That means I'm the adult. And I make the rules. I'm your dad." He felt a strange, out-of-body sensation when those words fell from his mouth. "And I think that it would be best if today you weren't here by yourself all day."

"Afraid I'm going to steal the silver or whatever rich thing people get wound up about?"

BeΔnnett crossed his arms. "Do I look like I have silver?"

Dallas lay back down, his eyes on the ceiling. "I don't know what the fuck you have."

"Well, I don't fucking have silver."

He turned his head slightly to look at Bennett. "You shouldn't use that kind of language in front of me. I'm impressionable."

"Somehow, I don't think you are." Bennett made a jerking motion toward the door with his head. "You've got ten minutes. Then be out in the kitchen. I'll get you something to eat."

"What do you have to eat?"

"You know what? Nothing good. I'll take you to Sugar Cup if you can be ready in five minutes."

Dallas squinted. "What's that?"

"Coffee shop. Bakery. Food."

That seemed to get the kid's attention. Bennett gave him some privacy, and went out and paced the length of the kitchen while he waited. Dallas appeared not four minutes later, clearly motivated by offers of baked goods.

"They better have doughnuts," he muttered.

"They do," Bennett responded.

Dallas pulled on a hoodie and zipped it up, throwing the hood over his head and shoving his hands down his pockets. "I never get up this early."

"I always get up this early," Bennett said.

Dallas's lip curled. "Why?"

"I have animals to take care of."

Bennett pushed the door open. Dallas looked at it for a moment, then at Bennett, then walked out ahead of him.

"What animals do you have?"

"Well, there's the dogs. I know that you saw them. Pepper, she's the old lady. And Cheddar, the puppy."

"Those are stupid names."

"They're great names. For great dogs. Anyway, you'll get used to it. So we've got the dogs and then there's the goats, which are kind of rescue animals. All my ranch animals are. Kind of a hazard of being in this business. When there is an animal that someone can't take care of, I end up with it a lot of the time. Goats that people were finished with after their property was cleared. Three horses, retired from the rodeo. And a llama."

"Do they have names?" He was trying not to sound interested, Bennett could tell.

Bennett led the way across the gravel drive over to his mobile veterinary truck and unlocked it. "You would just think they're stupid," he said.

"Yeah, maybe I would. But it seems better than saying *hey, Llama*."

Bennett shrugged. "Get in the truck."

Dallas complied. Once they were on the road, Bennett started talking again. "Blanche, Sophia, Rose and Dorothy are the goats."

"That's weird."

"They're named after *The Golden Girls*."

"I don't know what that is."

Bennett shook his head. "This is what's wrong with kids today." In fairness, Kaylee had named the goats. Kaylee was the only reason he'd ever watched that show.

"I don't even know what to say to that."

Luckily, he didn't have to say anything, because that was right about when they got to Sugar Cup.

"The llama is Candace," Bennett said. "I didn't name her."

He killed the engine and the two of them got out of the truck.

"Okay. At least you didn't name her. And the horses?"

"Shadrach, Meshach and Lucy. She's the only girl."

"Well, at least now I know all their names. But I'm probably not going to remember them. And I'm probably not going to do anything with them."

"Pepper and Cheddar will force interaction, so good luck with that."

He and Dallas walked down the sidewalk together, along the quaint little storefronts in the redbrick buildings that lined Gold Valley's Main Street. None of the shops were open yet—it was too early. Only the coffeehouses and the Mustard Seed diner were open this early. Though, it occurred to him just then that people were going to take one look at Dallas and know they were family of some kind. It was undeniable, Kaylee was right about that. The way that Dallas walked reminded Bennett of Grant and Wyatt, which probably meant that really, he walked like Bennett. It was just that Bennett had never observed himself walking down the street.

It made his heart squeeze tight. Made his whole body feel a little bit numb.

"Right here," he said as they turned a corner. He pushed the door to the coffee shop open and held it, letting Dallas walk on through.

Sugar Cup was busy, even at this early hour, with tables filled with older people reading the paper and drinking their morning coffee, and the line full of people on their way to work. Ranchers, teachers and guys who worked in the mill out of town.

Teachers. The school year was about over, but eventually, Bennett was going to have to figure out school. In fact, Dallas might need some kind of summer school.

"How are you doing in school?" Bennett asked.

Dallas choked out a laugh. "Um. Not great."

"Why?"

"Could be the moving around. And also the hating it."

"Is it hard for you?" Bennett pressed.

Dallas shrugged. "It's boring. Anyway, there's no point to it. It's not like I'm going to college."

Bennett frowned. "Why wouldn't you?"

"Because I don't have any money, dumbass," Dallas muttered.

"I do," Bennett pointed out.

"That doesn't have anything to do with me. I'm not smart enough to get a scholarship. I'm not like a piano prodigy or really good at football or anything like that. So, I would have to get perfect grades, and I already don't do that. So yeah. What's the point of school?"

"I wouldn't… I wouldn't *make* you go to college. But know that you could."

Bennett had money, his family had it. And he was more than able to take out loans if necessary.

Dallas looked stricken by the information, and not really pleased or excited, or anything that could be construed as positive. "You don't mean that," he said.

"I do," Bennett said, the two of them moving up in the line. "I told you, I'm your dad. That means that you're my responsibility."

"And I told you we're not going to be speaking in a couple of years. You know how I know that? Because nobody that was in my life a couple of years ago still talks to me. Except for Grace, and that's because it's her job. It's because she's assigned to me and she has to. But believe me, the minute she doesn't have to deal with me anymore? She won't. I'm not telling you a sad story, I'm not fishing for sympathy. That's just the way it is."

"Not anymore," Bennett said. "We don't have to talk about this now. But eventually we're going to have to figure out how to get you caught up in school. Because you're going to have options. I know you're not used to that. But I'm going to make sure you have them."

Dallas didn't say anything after that. He occupied himself by studying the case full of pastries, and Bennett did the same. At this point in the day eating healthy seemed overrated. He needed something that paired nicely with the emotional turmoil that came with discovering you had a secret son.

He had no idea what the hell that was, but he imagined it contained a lot of butter.

"Good morning." Kelly, the usual morning shift worker at Sugar Cup, who never gave any indication that she felt like the morning was good at all, addressed Bennett and Dallas. "What can I get for you?"

"Coffee for me," Bennett said. "And a cinnamon roll."

He turned to Dallas and waited. "You're just going to buy me something?" he asked.

"Yes," Bennett said.

"A mocha. And a chocolate doughnut."

"Okay." Kelly gave them the total, and Bennett handed her his card.

They walked over to the part of the counter where the drinks came out, waited for a few moments and then were presented with their pastries and drinks.

While they waited in line he shot a text to Kaylee to check if she was in the clinic today and if she'd mind if Dallas hung out in the break room, in case he didn't want to drive around with Bennett all day while he saw to his appointments.

She shot back an affirmative text. "Let's sit for a minute," Bennett said, gesturing to the tables. They took their breakfast over to a table by the wall. "I have a couple of scheduled appointments today. I have to go out to some of the ranches and vaccinate some baby animals. Horses, mostly. But if you want to you can hang out at the clinic."

"What clinic?" Dallas asked around a mouthful of doughnut.

"Valley Veterinary. That's the name of the practice I run with Kaylee, the woman you met last night."

"Yeah, I remember the one other person besides you I was introduced to yesterday."

Bennett pressed on as if Dallas hadn't spoken. "I do a lot of work outside of town. My truck has all my equipment, so it's easy to travel around. If you want the chance to see some of the area, we can do that. Otherwise, there's a break room at the clinic. If you want to hang out there Kaylee will be around if you have an emergency."

"An emergency? Like blood or fire?"

"Is that…a serious concern?"

Dallas shrugged, which was clearly a favored gesture of his. "Maybe. I'm a problem after all."

"The kind that sets things on fire?" he asked. "No judgment, but I feel like I should know that."

"I haven't set anything on fire."

"Okay. Good."

"All right."

"All right to which?" Bennett leaned back in his chair.

"I guess I'll go sit in the break room. Not really interested in driving around. We just drove all the way here yesterday from Portland."

"Right." Bennett couldn't decide if he was relieved or disappointed that his kid was opting to not spend the day with him. But they'd only been together for about a half hour this morning and Bennett already felt...taxed. Full of emotion he didn't know how to sort through and weighted down by the idea he had to be something he didn't know how to be for this kid. "Okay. And then after that we're going to go over to my brother's place. Well, it's actually my brother's and my other brother's and my sister's place."

Dallas looked stunned by that. "You have all that family?"

"Yeah," Bennett said. "And they don't know about you either. Since I didn't know about you. But they're your uncles. And your aunt. I'm going to have to call your grandfather."

His dad was going to have something to say about being a grandfather.

"I have...a grandfather?"

"Yeah, and he's married. Not to my mom. My mom is dead. But he remarried a great lady a couple of years ago. They're down in New Mexico with her family right now. But you'll meet her. Then, for holidays and things like that. He'll probably want to make a trip up to meet you."

Dallas looked surprised by that. "They would?"

"Of course. You're family."

"That's never mattered before. My mom never talked to her family. I don't even know where they are. I just know they aren't here anymore. She told me that much."

"That's true. Her parents moved away after she left. She left home when she was sixteen."

Dallas nodded. "I know that much. She didn't want to be trapped in a small town anymore. She said she hated it here." He took another bite of doughnut. "She wanted to go somewhere more exciting."

"I didn't know she hated it here," Bennett said.

"That's what she told me. But I don't know how much of anything she said is true. And it's not because I trust you," he clarified quickly. "It's just because she's a liar. She always has been. At least, as far back as I can remember. Because that's how addicts are. She's not the only addict I know. Every guy she ever dated was one. They're all liars."

A sobering thought occurred to him then. "Are you... Do you have any problems with that? I mean, addiction stuff."

"Hell, no," Dallas said, taking another bite of doughnut. "I mean, I drink. Not all the time. But I have. I've had some weed. But I'm not messing with meth and shit. I get why it's tempting. Because it makes you forget. But then you forget everything. Including where the hell you left your kid. I just don't want that. I don't want to forget who I am. I mean, who I am isn't anything all that impressive. And it's not like I have much of anything. But I'm not going to be a meth zombie."

Bennett swallowed hard. "She wasn't always like that."

"Yeah. She wasn't like that until me, I guess."

"I don't know," Bennett said. "I figured that I screwed up her life."

"Yeah, she thought you did too. I mean, you definitely got your share of the blame. But I was part of it. When she would get mad and scream and stuff, she blamed both of us."

"I'm sorry," Bennett said. "I'm sorry she treated you like that. And I have to believe that in the beginning that isn't what she wanted. For some reason, she didn't want to be here with me. Probably because I wanted to marry her. And if she really did hate it here, if she really did want to get out, she probably figured she was going to have to do it without me. She probably thought that her only hope of escaping this life, and being a rancher's wife, or at least having to share custody with me, was to leave without telling me. Making me think that she lost the baby. I have to believe that she did it for what she thought was a better life. It's just that she probably got into the other things that come with finding freedom. And she was too young to have that kind of responsibility."

"Yeah, maybe." Dallas shifted in his seat, looking a little uncomfortable. "Either way, I've seen too much of it to want it," Dallas said. "There's not much mystery in drug use. She would have given it to me if I wanted it. I didn't want to let her poison me. Didn't want to let her make me as bad she was."

Those words burned. They hurt, all the way down. The stuff that kid had been through wasn't fair. It was all new to Bennett, and he was having trouble processing it. But it was Dallas's life. And he spoke about it in a matter-of-fact way. Way too matter-of-fact for someone his age. The effects of meth shouldn't be something a fifteen-year-old was so familiar with.

"I'm glad I don't have to worry about you and drugs anyway," Bennett said, his voice sounding like gravel.

"Would you really worry?"

The question was presented as something of a challenge.

"Yes," Bennett said. "I'm not taking responsibility for you because I don't care. I do care. If I didn't, why the hell would it matter to me where you were?"

"I can't answer that question. I don't know what it's like to have a parent care what I do."

"You will," Bennett said, the words a promise that came from deep inside of him. He wouldn't be perfect. He was going to make so many mistakes he felt stupid in advance. But he could be there. "You will."

WHEN BENNETT SHOWED up with Dallas in tow, the kid went straight into the break room and shut the door.

"Thank you," Bennett said.

Kaylee cast a worried look at Bennett. "Does he have a phone or anything?"

"Yes," Bennett said.

At least he'd have something to stay entertained on.

"I don't know what to do with a teenager all day."

She sounded petulant, but it was true. She had agreed to let him hang out, but now that he was here she felt a sense of responsibility she wasn't sure she could live up to. And if she did something stupid with Bennett's son and he...ran off or something she'd never forgive herself.

Bennett shrugged. "Put him to work. Give him cages to clean out or something."

"I only have two animals in kennels right now."

"Maybe Beatrix will bring you a box of orphaned weasels."

Kaylee snorted. "There are no weasels around here."

"I feel like that wouldn't stop Beatrix from finding some."

"He's going to be bored," Kaylee said, ignoring the weasel absurdity.

Bennett shrugged. "He might be. But he's the one who said he wanted to hang out here. You don't have to do anything with him. I'm going to come by lunchtime with something for him to eat. Don't worry about that. I'll check in."

He looked stressed, and she wanted to reach up and smooth the lines by his eyes. Wanted to do something to erase the concern on his handsome face. It made her palms feel sweaty. Made her stomach feel like it was tied up in knots.

Her date could not come soon enough.

She was at that critical point in her Bennett cycle. And yes, sadly, she had a very definitive cycle.

Things would begin to build up. Her attraction would begin to become unmanageable. Her feelings so sharp and intense she couldn't handle them. And she already knew why she couldn't act on those feelings. She'd made her decisions. So when she reached that point, she knew it was time to find a guy to date. And so she would.

Depending on how long they dated, it could lead to a real relationship. Which meant that there was someone else to focus some of those feelings on. A man that she could go to bed with at night and be physically close to.

But as she had made the silly mistake of admitting to Bennett last night, they were not men who necessarily lit her body on fire. Still, putting effort into a physical relationship with another man did something to help take the edge off the Bennett situation. It gave her a relief from that hyperfocus she began to feel. From that intense edginess she experienced whenever he was around.

But then, invariably, the newness of the relationship would begin to wear off. The general disappointment of the sex would begin to overshadow the fact that there was sex at all, and the buildup to her Bennett feelings would start again.

Then something would happen. Bennett would brush his fingers against hers, lean in especially close to brush a piece of dirt from her cheek, and her body would nearly combust.

That's when it would all tumble down on her. That feeling of how pointless and ridiculous it was to sleep with a man who made her feel less with his entire body than Bennett Dodge made her feel with the smallest brush of a fingertip against her face.

She'd have to end the relationship at that point. And the cycle would begin anew.

She had been…somewhat frozen in the terrible part of the cycle for the last year and a half. Because there hadn't been anyone the whole time that Bennett was with Olivia. And at the same time work at the clinic had gotten more intense, which meant they were together more, and her social life—never all that booming outside the Dodge family—had shrunk down.

Rather than going out on fifty-mile endurance rides with Jamie like she often enjoyed doing on weekends, she'd been melting into her couch, keeping her rides on Flicka short and in general reducing her activities to work and an occasional night out drinking with Bennett and his family or Bennett by himself.

And all during that time she had done nothing but fixate. Nothing but marinate. Trying to force herself to accept that he was going to marry this other woman. Trying to figure out how her life would reshape when that happened.

And then the breakup happened, and it had hit her that she needed to do something to get herself out of the loop.

So here she was, trying to deal. Trying to get that separation that she so desperately needed. To get another man in her life so she could focus on him.

She really needed it to work. She needed Michael to be more than a nice guy. Maybe he would finally be a guy who managed to give her an actual orgasm during sex.

Heat swept over her body, and she did her very best not to think about that too much. Because then it forced her to think about the only ways she'd ever been able to have an orgasm. By herself. With her mind inevitably wandering to places it shouldn't. To fantasies it shouldn't.

She needed to get a grip. Preferably on Michael.

And she could give Bennett emotional support in the meantime. Could help him out with Dallas.

There was no other option. She had to do that.

Because she was a true friend. Not helping him out because of her regrettable between-the-thighs feelings would only prove that she wasn't actually a very good friend. And she wasn't going to do that.

"Fine. I'll see you at lunch."

"Okay."

He seemed relieved to be getting a break, and she really couldn't blame him. She sighed heavily and looked around the empty office.

Technically, they weren't open yet. Though, if somebody came to the door she would obviously let them in.

But she liked to use the early morning hours to catch up on paperwork and get everything in order for the day.

She sighed heavily, and then charged toward the break room before she could think it through. He'd said she could leave Dallas alone, but she wasn't going to do that.

She was going to give this kid a task. He was not sitting back there on his phone the whole day. Why she felt that way, she really didn't know. But it definitely had something to do with that strange sense of connection she had felt toward him when they had first met.

"Good morning," she said, smiling a little bit when she was treated to a surprised expression from him.

"Why does everyone keep saying that?" Dallas asked.

"Because it's morning."

"Too early to be good," he pointed out.

"And yet, here you are. Awake. And Bennett…" She redirected. "Your dad…" Bennett as a dad. Good grief. "Is that weird?"

Dallas straightened slightly, pressing his hand flat on the wooden table. "Yes. It's weird."

"Bennett," she said, resolute. "I'll call him Bennett then. Because it's weird for me too. Anyway, he said that you were going to hang out here today."

"Because he thinks I need a babysitter," Dallas said. "Which is ridiculous. I've spent days by myself. I think I actually spent a week alone in my house when I was about seven."

He said the words flippantly, speaking of his neglect as if it were something as routine as going back-to-school shopping. But Kaylee wasn't fooled. Mostly because she knew how deeply that sort of thing touched you. Knew how it felt when your parents barely bothered to look your direction.

"But you're not alone now," Kaylee said.

"But it wouldn't matter if I was."

"I think it would," she said. "And not just because you don't have the resources to take care of yourself. But because we are made to need people."

"I've never had the time to sit around whining about whether or not I needed someone to survive."

She looked down, picking at her fingernails. "Whether or not you believe it, I actually understand a little bit. I never got taken from my parents and I was never in foster care, but I understand. Once I moved here, though, I had school. Friends. Bennett is one of them. We've been friends for years. His family…your family, they're good people. They supported me. Invited me to backyard barbecues on the Fourth of July, made me feel like I was part of something. And that was when I really understood what was missing from my life growing up. My parents drink. And they fight. And in general don't have a lot of time for me."

Her mother had told her once, in a drunken rage, that Kaylee was a Band-Aid that hadn't fixed a damn thing. That they'd had a baby to try to fix everything. To make life better. But she'd only made things harder. Worse.

She looked down. "I had to get up and get myself ready for school." This was one of those things she never talked about. One of those struggles she liked to leave behind the closed front door of her family home, every morning when she left for school. "Nobody was going to do it for me. If I relied on my mother or father to wake me up I would never have made it on time. I used to walk. I'd leave forty-five minutes early so that I could walk to school and get there on time. Anyway. I have a feeling that's something you understand. Having to depend on yourself. But let me tell you, things got better when I let other people be there for me."

"I'm not letting anyone do anything. I'm a minor. Which means adults interfere when the law says they have to, and for most of my life I've been on my own. Age has never meant a damn thing as far as my mom is concerned. Like I said, she just left me alone sometimes. I had to learn to take care of myself. To survive. And then, because some government agency suddenly notices, I have to go from house to house, listening to new bullshit rules everywhere I go. I had stuff worked out. Now, I had to leave Portland to come live here because this is where my sperm donor is?"

"That's what I'm saying. You're going to have to let people be there for you. Because you have a routine. Because you do know how to survive. You're going to have to figure out what else there is. Past survival. That I know something about."

"What about…" Dallas seemed to struggle for a moment. "Bennett. His family is good?"

"They are. They're the best. Bennett's mother died before I ever met him, but she sounds like she was wonderful. And his dad… Quinn. Quinn is your grandpa. He's the best man I've ever known. He's strong, and he raised four kids on his own. Not only that, he supported kids that weren't his responsibility at all. You'll meet Luke Hollister too. He came to work at the ranch when he was a teenager, and Quinn made him part of the family. Just like he did me. Included me in everything. Bennett's friendship has been a huge part of my life, and Quinn's support is probably the reason that I ended up trying for scholarships and going to college. Believe me. All this stuff that you think you don't need, that you've convinced yourself you don't need... Maybe you don't need it. But it could give you a whole different life than you ever thought you could have."

Dallas's expression was carefully blank. "So, did you just come in here to lecture me on how everything is going to be rainbows and puppy dogs from now on?"

"No. I came in to tell you that you're going to be cleaning some puppy dog cages, though," Kaylee said, making that decision on the fly. "I don't have very many dogs in residence at the moment, but they're going to need their cages cleaned, and Rufus the mutt is probably going to need to be walked. He's going to be able to go home later today—he just had a minor surgery, so he's moving a little bit slow, but some exercise would do him good."

"I don't like animals," Dallas said.

"Why?"

"They're pointless."

"That's the most ridiculous thing I've ever heard. Animals are important. Even if you don't like them as pets, don't tell me you've never eaten a steak. In which case, you definitely appreciate animals in one way at least."

"I don't understand pets," he said.

"There's nothing to understand. They keep you company. They love you. You love them."

"I still don't get it."

"Well, you can ponder the merit of dogs while you clean cages."

"And if I don't?"

Kaylee shrugged. "I can't make you. I mean, I can turn the Wi-Fi off, but I can't make you. And I'm not going to. But here's the thing. I asked you to, Dallas. I think that should mean something. Because someday you might ask me for something, and you're going to want me to do it, and I will. That's community. That's friendship. That's depending on people."

"You're really not my... Bennett's girlfriend?"

"Really not," she said, ignoring the slight tug at the center of her chest. "So, I have no special influence over him. I'm never going to be your stepmother. I'm really just someone who wants to get to know you. And wants to help you figure life out. And someone who doesn't want to clean up dog poop this morning."

Dallas stood up, the expression on his face strange. As if he couldn't really understand why he was doing it. "Okay. Show me where the stupid dogs are."

"I don't have any stupid dogs," she said, schooling her expression into one of total seriousness.

"Really?"

"They're good dogs, Dallas."

He let out an exasperated sigh. "Do you want me to clean up the dog poop or not?"

"I definitely do. Follow me."

As they walked out of the break room, Kaylee smiled to herself. Maybe she was a secret teenager whisperer, or something. She didn't have any experience with kids, so she hadn't really expected to find a connection with him.

But she was glad to know that she had.

Dallas mattered to Bennett. And that meant he mattered to her too.

She would do anything for Bennett.

She tried to ignore that thought as it tumbled around inside of her brain, repeating itself throughout the day.

It would be better if she wouldn't do anything for Bennett. She just needed to break the cycle.

Too bad there was a wrench thrown into her gears.

She looked over at Dallas, who was doing his best to wrangle Rufus. Yes. There was most definitely a wrench. But it remained to be seen what effect that was going to have.

CHAPTER SEVEN

BENNETT HADN'T REALLY known how he was supposed
to break the news to his family gently. So, he decided
that he would do his best to make it quick, and to make
it so he had to tell the story only once. That meant asking everybody to come for dinner at Wyatt's house on
the Get Out of Dodge property. He knew that making
a cryptic command like that would cause everybody to
be a little bit concerned. And he didn't want to say anything leading like *I have an important announcement*
either. Because then they might think he was sick, or
moving to a commune or something.

Probably, they all just thought he wanted to get together to continue to process the reality of Olivia having another man's baby.

He shook his head and laughed for no reason at all really because what the hell was funny? He kind of longed
for the days when that seemed like the most shocking
bit of information he could possibly get in a year.

He hadn't really thought of Olivia at all since Dallas had showed up.

He swung into the Valley Veterinary parking lot,
gripping the steering wheel tightly. He was picking Dallas up and then Kaylee was going to follow them over to
the ranch. He had checked in on them at lunch, and everything seemed fine. Dallas had been—surprisingly—

helping Kaylee wrangle some of the animals that had come in, and he didn't seem overly put upon by it either.

Kaylee, for her part, didn't seem especially put upon either. He could tell that this morning she had been a little bit irritated with him over leaving Dallas at the clinic. But it had seemed like the best option. Forcing the kid to ride around in a truck with him all day wouldn't have worked. Though, he had expected Dallas to hole up in the break room. He certainly hadn't expected him to engage in the goings-on of the practice.

He took a deep breath and killed the engine on the truck, getting out and heading into the little yellow cinder block building that he and Kaylee had painted themselves when they had first started out.

He pushed the door open and found Dallas sitting at the front desk, looking at the computer.

"Hi," Bennett said.

"Hi," Dallas returned.

"Did you have a good day?"

"Everyone is obsessed with me saying today is *good*."

"The alternative is that it's bad," Bennett said.

"No. It's not. It was just a day." He let out a slow breath. "I…did stuff with animals. It was weird."

"But not boring?"

"It wasn't Xbox," Dallas said, crossing his arms and leaning back in the swivel chair. The serious expression on his face was so familiar it was surreal. That same, stubborn Dodge expression he had seen on any of his brothers countless times. Or in the mirror.

"Well, nothing is," Bennett said. "Except Xbox. Obviously."

"True."

Kaylee came out from one of the exam rooms, her

red hair pulled back into a ponytail, her brow crinkled. She looked between them. "Everything okay?"

"It's fine," Bennett said, finding it strange the way that Kaylee positioned herself between himself and Dallas.

But then, he had left Dallas with her all day, and she hadn't ignored him. Which kind of surprised Bennett in some ways. He didn't imagine Kaylee as being particularly maternal. Not that she wasn't. Not that she didn't like kids, it was just that she didn't seem to ever go out of her way to spend time with them. She never talked about longing for a husband or children or anything like that.

And yet, she seemed to have taken the reins of this situation capably.

Guilt crept up the back of his neck. He shouldn't have left him with her today. He should have taken Dallas with him no matter what the kid said he wanted.

"He was great," she said, smiling at Dallas. "I probably wasn't supposed to tell you that. I mean, he was a total monster. Rebellious. Uncontrollable."

Dallas rolled his eyes. "I'm pretty sure I have dog shit on my pants. There's no protecting my street cred at this point."

"Sorry," she said, not sounding sorry at all.

"Time for the big family dinner," Bennett said.

"I've never been to a family dinner in my life. They sound horrible," Dallas said, still sitting resolutely in the chair.

"I don't know how it will be," Bennett said honestly.

"Can't we just, like…call?" Dallas asked. "Hey, surprise. I exist."

"You have to meet them all eventually. Might as well rip the Band-Aid off."

Dallas lost control of his face for just a moment. He looked vulnerable. Uncertain. And that made Bennett feel bad. Like there was something he should be doing differently. Except he didn't think there was a way to navigate this that wouldn't make people feel uncomfortable or emotional. His brothers and sister were going to have a reaction to this. He was going to have to get the news to his father over the phone, and he was going to have a reaction to it. He couldn't protect himself or Dallas from that fact.

"It's going to be fine," Kaylee said, reaching out and squeezing Dallas on the shoulder. "Tonight, I have a feeling it's going to be a little bit overwhelming. But they need you. I mean, that's what it's going to feel like to them. They're going to be happy. And you need to let them have that."

"Right," Dallas said. "I'm going to go to the bathroom."

He got up and walked toward the single-use bathroom at the back of the clinic, leaving Bennett and Kaylee alone.

"He doesn't have to be strong for my family," Bennett said. "That's a lot of pressure to put on a kid."

Kaylee shrugged. "I spent the day with him. He's not comfortable needing anyone. I have a feeling the only way he's going to get through this is to think that they might need him. I'm just trying to help."

"Yeah, but I'm his dad," Bennett said.

"And you left him with me today," Kaylee said, crossing her arms. "Plus, I relate to the kid, Bennett."

He looked at his friend, at her eyes sparkling with conviction. Kaylee wasn't an emotional person. She was coolheaded and steady. The one you wanted on your side in any situation. But she didn't look cool and steady now. She looked…she looked like fire. And it made him wonder if she would be that hot if he were to touch her.

"Why?" he asked.

"My parents are drunks," she said baldly, shifting position. "I know I make jokes and stuff, and I know you know I'm not close to them. But it's more than that. I just… I don't like talking about it."

"You won't talk about," he said. "Not beyond small comments here and there. I've asked you and…"

"Why do you think I never had you over? It's not just because my house is small or I was embarrassed. It's because it was a mess, and my mother was probably passed out somewhere. I didn't want you to know. I wanted to leave my house for the day, close the front door and go out into a world that wasn't about that. I don't want to think about it now, or talk about it. We built a better life and I want to live it, not think about a past I didn't choose and never wanted to be part of."

"Kaylee," he said. "If it hurts you then I care about it. I want to know about it."

She gritted her teeth, her eyes glittering with that stubborn fire that was essentially Kaylee. When that woman dug in, there was no getting her to move. "It's not important. You know who I am. The details of my home life don't change that. We've been best friends since we were thirteen. The life I had at Get Out of Dodge…that's what I chose to let shape me. Your family was real to me, they mattered. Your dad. The ranch, the animals, you."

He imagined Kaylee at Dallas's age, all elbows and knees and boldness. He hadn't known that her home life was quite so bad. He'd have thought something like that would make a person shrink, and Kaylee was anything but small.

But he could see it in Dallas. That hot, burning anger that flared up sometimes in his dark eyes. The stubborn set to his chin. And the occasional surprising and wicked sense of humor. It was strange to see a reflection of her in his son. But he did.

"I relate to Dallas," she said. "He's been through a hell of a time. He was neglected. Left at home sometimes from when he was seven years old, Bennett. It's going to take him a long time to admit that he might need somebody. To admit that he deserves love. I'm just trying to put it in a way that it would have made sense to me when I was his age. So that he can... I don't know. Accept your family now instead of spending years being too afraid to let them close."

His heart turned over in his chest, and he wanted to...do something. Reach out to Kaylee. Touch her. Offer comfort. She had never said that she was neglected. She had never seemed like she was.

Kaylee had always been a practical, self-contained force of nature. He knew her parents weren't involved. She didn't see them all that often, and she seemed okay with it. But people were varying degrees of close with their families.

And now he was justifying. Justifying how he hadn't realized that she wasn't simply distant from her parents. That it was more.

"Kaylee, we need to talk about this."

"No, we don't. You have enough going on without worrying about me and ancient history. It's stuff I've sorted out, Bennett. But like I was telling your son today, I wouldn't be where I am today if I hadn't learned that sometimes needing people, letting people be in your life, is important. Is necessary. You mean the world to me. You always have. You showed me that people were good. You taught me to ride horses and run barefoot in fields and…and that depending on someone doesn't always end in disappointment. But it takes a lot of years to undo the kind of hurt that I went through. I assume it will be the same for him."

She looked uncertain then. Vulnerable and young. Which Kaylee never did. She'd never admitted she didn't have a single thing handled as long as he'd known her. He was always proud of her, his brash, pretty friend who attacked the world like it was a bull coming at her horns first. She went straight for those horns, grabbed them, took control. Always. It was who she was. Right then she looked uncertain.

He wanted to shoulder it for her. Wanted to fix it. If he'd had any idea that she'd been in need back when they were kids he would have…he would have done anything to give her what she needed.

She didn't like that, his Kaylee. Didn't like asking for anyone's help. Didn't like leaning on anyone. He wished she could have confided in him. He wished she'd let him take care of her. Even just for a moment.

Without thinking, he reached out and brushed his fingertips along the edge of her jaw. She drew in a sharp breath, looking up at him, her blue eyes going wide. It was like last night. When everything had gone sideways for a minute when he had touched her. When they had talked about the fact that no man had ever made her lose control. When he had been forced to imagine what it might look like if she did lose control.

He had shoved all that down deep, buried it underneath the uncertainty and the general enormity of having to cope with having a son. Because dealing with this strange, electric sensation he felt in these quiet moments with her was the only thing that came close to being as unsettling as what was happening with Dallas.

"Ready to go?"

They turned and saw Dallas standing there, eyeing them with a speculative expression on his face.

He was a teenager. He was not supposed to be perceptive. But Bennett had a feeling that the kid was being far too perceptive at this moment about what had just crossed through Bennett's mind.

"Ready," Bennett said.

"Hey." Kaylee touched his arm. "Why don't I ride with you? We can all squeeze in."

For some reason, he was more than ready to take her up on that. He shouldn't. He should let there be some distance. He shouldn't lean on her quite so hard.

But she had just spent the entire day with Dallas, and having her on the ride over to the ranch was a comforting thought.

They all piled into his truck, with Kaylee sitting in the middle and Dallas by the door. Kaylee's thigh brushed up against his, and he did his best not to hyperfocus on it.

He and Kaylee had squeezed into vehicles like this countless times over the years. One denim-clad leg brushing against *his* denim-clad leg should not register on his radar.

But it was more than moving the needle right about now.

It was just because he was thrown off. He had been for days. Which was why he was experiencing these strange electrical currents when she was around.

But right now, he had two choices. To focus on the fact that he was driving over to his family ranch to announce to his brothers and sister that he had a son. Or he could focus on the fact that each bump in the road that brought Kaylee's body into contact with his sent an electrical spark right down through him.

He opted to focus on her.

But by the time they got to the ranch his teeth were set on edge.

"It's going to be fine," he said, mostly to himself.

"It's going to be weird," Dallas said.

"Well, I didn't say it *wouldn't* be *weird*. I said it would be *fine*."

Kaylee shook her head, the motion kicking up that scent that was uniquely hers. Soap and skin, no-nonsense. Clean, even after a day spent handling animals. It was strange to him, that the scent of her skin was so familiar, when it wasn't as if he had ever been pressed up against that skin. But it was. He knew her. His Kaylee. Better than almost any other person in the world. And he was damned grateful to have her with him right about now.

"Should I hide in the bushes or something?" Dallas asked. "Then I can jump out and surprise everybody."

Kaylee laughed. Bennett could barely manage to force a smile.

"We're trying not to give anyone a heart attack. My brother is pushing forty. We have to be careful."

Dallas shrugged. "I'm just trying to spice things up. You know, keep the whole secret family member thing interesting. We've got a good thing going here. I would hate for it to get too expected."

"Believe me," Bennett said. "Nothing about you is expected."

The group of them walked up the steps to the front of the house, Bennett feeling increasingly tense with each step.

He looked over at Kaylee, who looked resolute. He wanted to touch her. He wasn't sure why. Except that focusing on her on the drive over had been helpful, and maybe that was why his hands itched now to touch the soft skin on her face. He had done it earlier. A comforting gesture, when he had been thinking about her and all of the neglect that she had been through.

He had wanted to comfort her then, but now he kind of wanted her to touch him to offer him something.

He shook that off.

He and Kaylee didn't touch unnecessarily. They were *friends*. And it had never mattered that she was a woman and he was a man. Their friendship was deeper than that. He wasn't going to go reducing her now. Wasn't going to try to seek physical comfort in her softness just because she was a woman.

She was better than that. More than that.

She was the kind of friend that picked you up off the side of the road at two in the morning if your truck got a flat at the wrong place and time. The kind of friend who came right over when you found out you had a secret son.

The best kind of friend. The most important kind.

She'd been there for him when his grief had hit him hard at high school graduation, when he'd looked around and seen mothers watching their children, and he'd become so acutely aware his had missed so much.

They'd sneaked beer out of his dad's fridge and run barefoot through the field behind the house. Lying under the stars and getting buzzed and talking about what college would be like. A celebration that they'd both been accepted into the same program, and a memorial for his loss, all in one.

She made him pumpkin pies every year at college on

his birthday because they were his favorite, and were impossible to find in the store in February. In return he drove to the bakery outside town and got her favorite— filled, salted caramel cupcakes—for hers.

They'd watched each other grow up. The only other people in his life who knew him half as well was his family. And in many ways, she knew him better.

She was the kind of friend who'd lasted. This was real stuff. Hard stuff. The kind of stuff that didn't even seem possible to have happen in real life. Off-the-wall, crazy ridiculousness. She was here for it.

He took a deep breath, and opened the door, nearly colliding with Luke Hollister when he did.

"Oh," Luke said. "I was just heading out."

Considering that Luke was Bennett's ex-girlfriend's new fiancé, he wasn't exactly the person that Bennett wanted to see right now. Only because he couldn't possibly deal with one more layer of complication. It had nothing to do with Olivia or lingering feelings for her. It was just that…

He saw the exact moment that Luke's eyes collided with the young man standing next to Bennett.

"Who is…"

"Luke," came a voice from behind him.

It was Olivia.

She ran into Luke's broad back and then froze, her eyes connecting with his. Then, she looked at Dallas.

"Hi, Bennett," she said very carefully. Very, very carefully.

He had seen Olivia plenty since they had broken up. There had been a space of time when she had actively tried to make him jealous by throwing Luke in his face. But it was his understanding that at the time their rela-

tionship hadn't been real. But that through attempting
to make him jealous, it had become real.

He had interacted with them both since then, though,
not since the pregnancy revelation. There weren't hard
feelings. Just weird ones.

"We were just leaving," Olivia supplied.

"And we're just getting here," Kaylee said, looking
a little bit combative.

Kaylee was more protective of him than she needed
to be. He was a grown-ass man, and he could more than
handle running into an ex.

"This is Dallas," he said, not seeing any point in
delaying introducing the kid. It would seem weird if
he didn't.

"Nice to meet you," said Olivia. "I'm Olivia. This is
Luke."

And none of them told any of the others how they
were all connected. All things considered, it was probably for the best.

But then, Wyatt showed up.

"There's kind of a bottleneck at the door," Bennett
said drily.

"Apparently," Wyatt said. "Who is this?"

"Dallas," Bennett said.

"I'm your long-lost nephew," Dallas said, completely
unhelpful and at completely the wrong time.

Damned kid.

"What?" Wyatt looked like he could easily be pushed
over with a feather. Luke was frozen, his eyes fixed on
the situation, and Olivia's eyes were darting back and
forth, clear confusion written on her delicate face.

"I'm assuming you're the family that I'm supposed
to meet?"

"We're not family," Luke said, jerking his thumb between Olivia and himself. "Not officially."

"My bad," Dallas said. "But nice to meet you anyway."

"Long-lost nephew?" Wyatt asked, clearly trying to do the math here.

"Yes," Bennett said, his tone grave. "It's kind of a long story, and I only wanted to tell it once tonight, but it looks like it's not going to go that way. This is my son."

The eruption of profanity around him would have been funny if it weren't so tense. Dallas seemed to find it hilarious. He was obviously enjoying the fact that none of the adults around him seemed to have any clue what to make of the situation.

"Come in," Wyatt said, ushering everybody back into the house, including Luke and Olivia.

"Where are Grant and Jamie?" Bennett asked.

"On their way," he said.

"Well, maybe we should wait for the full explanation until they're here."

"How detailed is the explanation going to be?" Dallas asked. "Because if we're going to go over my conception I would like to skip that. I want to be able to eat dinner tonight."

"He's funny," Bennett said. "He doesn't get that from me."

"I'm not surprised by that revelation," Dallas said.

"I didn't know about him," Bennett said, turning his focus to his brother.

"How is that possible?" Luke asked. "I was a pretty big manwhore." He looked over at Olivia. "Sorry, honey, but you know it was true. And even I don't have random kids."

"That you know of," Kaylee said, her tone weighted.

Luke looked uncomfortable at that pointed statement.

"I mean…" Olivia looked at Luke pointedly. "You *did* get me pregnant when you didn't mean to."

Luke shot Bennett a glance. "I already know," Bennett offered.

"Oh. Okay then."

"It got overshadowed by this whole situation. But congratulations."

Luke appraised him, and then appraised Dallas a little bit more slowly. "Yeah, well. Congratulations to you too."

"Who is… I mean…"

Just then, the door opened, and Grant and Jamie came in. Grant took off his cowboy hat, looking around the room. "What is happening?"

"You wouldn't believe it," Wyatt said. "Have a seat."

"What?" Jamie asked.

"Just sit down," Wyatt said. "Bennett is telling us a story."

Jamie looked over at Dallas. "You look just like my brothers," she said. "Oh, shit. Does Dad have a secret kid?"

"That would have been easier to believe," Wyatt said. "Apparently, Bennett has a secret kid."

Jamie let out a string of truly inventive swears. "Bennett?" She looked scandalized and disgusted. It probably wounded her mortally to ever have to believe he'd had sex. But that was the least of his worries at the moment.

"This is so much more fun than I thought it would be," Dallas said. "But then, I imagined there would be a lot more hugging and crying, and I don't like any of that. I like the swearing a lot more."

"I'm sorry," Jamie said. "I didn't mean to swear because you exist."

Dallas laughed. "Are you…"

"I'm Bennett's sister. So I guess I'm your aunt."

Jamie was only nine years older than Dallas, so that had to hit her a little bit funny. Dallas too, if his expression was anything to go off.

"I always imagined that aunts had lipstick on their teeth and cat-eye glasses."

"Well, you're out of luck," Jamie said. "Because I don't have glasses and I sure as hell don't have a tube of lipstick."

"I'm starting to see a family resemblance between all of us," Dallas said. "The language we use."

Bennett shook his head. "Let's start over. I have a son. I just found out last night."

"And who's the mother?"

"Marnie. My girlfriend from high school."

"Yeah," Wyatt said. "I remember her."

Grant wasn't saying much, but then Bennett had had a feeling that this would hit Grant in an especially strange way. Grant was the one who should have a son. Who should have a family. Grant had been married. Married at eighteen, widowed by twenty-six. None of his life had gone the way that it was supposed to. And here it was Bennett who ended up with a kid. When it was Grant who had been ready for that kind of thing. Who had wanted it. But it was something that he and Lindsay had never been able to accomplish. Not with her health. Even adoption had been out of the question, though he knew that Grant had looked into it several times in the hopes of making Lindsay's dreams of being a mother come true before she passed.

And much like Olivia's pregnancy had brought up the memories of Marnie's pregnancy and the loss of it for Bennett, he knew that it was bringing up stuff for his older brother.

"Where have you been living?" Jamie asked, directing the question at Dallas.

"Portland, mostly. I've been in foster care for the past few years."

"What happened to Marnie?" Wyatt asked.

"My mom is a druggie," Dallas said succinctly.

"I knew that Marnie was pregnant," Bennett said. "But she told me that she lost the baby, and I didn't have any reason to suspect otherwise. But now the state put all the pieces together and figured out that I was Dallas's father. I can get tests done..."

"What's the point?" Jamie asked. "He looks just like you."

"And it isn't like the timing is off," Grant said, the first he'd spoken beyond the casual swear word since coming in. "Plus, you were with her."

"I know," Bennett said. "I don't doubt it. Not at all. At first, I felt like I might need to confirm some things, but honestly, since I've had time to absorb it a little bit... I feel like there isn't much question about any of this."

Grant cast a worried glance in Dallas's direction. "Sorry," he said. "It must not be any fun to have people talk about you like you're not there. I know how that feels."

"You people are always trying to relate to me. That, I find weird." Dallas stood up then. "I was promised dinner. That was the trade-off for the awkward family part."

Wyatt stood up. "Yeah. There's food in the kitchen."

"He doesn't cook," Jamie said quickly. "He gets big batches of food from the Mustard Seed diner in town.

He uses it to feed all the ranch hands, and then he feeds the rest of us with it too."

They all started to filter toward the kitchen, and Kaylee touched his arm. He paused, hanging back for a moment.

"It's going to be okay," she said.

"I thought you were supposed to tell me the truth. Isn't that friendship?"

"I am telling you the truth."

"You can't know how this is going to go. Not really."

Kaylee frowned. "I can. I mean, I'm not saying that it isn't going to be hard. I'm just saying…your family is a great family. And I know that things aren't working out exactly the way that you imagined. I know that you expected to be engaged to Olivia by now. And that you expected to have your first child with her. And that you most definitely didn't expect to end up single with a fifteen-year-old."

Bennett looked toward the kitchen, where said fifteen-year-old and the aforementioned ex-girlfriend had just disappeared to. "Olivia really doesn't have anything to do with what I'm feeling. I mean…I wasn't happy that the relationship ended. Mostly because we'd made plans and…having a plan is important to me. But that's the real problem. I'm not sure I have any idea what the hell is going to happen next. In fact, I'm pretty sure I don't. And that's about my least favorite situation to find myself in."

Kaylee pressed her fingertips to his shoulder, dragged them down to his elbow. It was a completely platonic thing to do. But for some reason the touch lingered long after she pulled her hand back to her side.

"But it's going to be okay," she reiterated. "Whatever

happens. They're going to be here for you. I'm going to be here for you."

She lifted her hand again, and then, Bennett heard someone behind him clear his throat. He turned, and saw Wyatt standing there. "Everything's fine," Wyatt said. "I just wanted to ask you a quick question while we weren't in front of an audience."

"Kaylee isn't an audience," Bennett said, taking a step back from her.

"Right." Wyatt looked between them. "Does the kid need work?"

"What?" Of all the things that his brother could have asked him right then, that wasn't what Bennett was expecting. But then, Wyatt was a man of action more than he was a man of words. And finding something concrete that he could offer was his way of acknowledging the situation in many ways, Bennett was sure.

"I have work on the ranch. I can pay him. It will give him something to do. Something to occupy himself. Actually, it occurred to me when Luke started asking Dallas what he does with his time. And he said he had no idea what to do around here. Well, remember Luke moved here when he was sixteen and got a job on the ranch. He credits it with keeping him out of trouble."

"Luke knocked up my girlfriend. So, whether or not he's stayed out of trouble is actually up for debate."

"She was your ex-girlfriend," Wyatt clarified. "Be fair."

"I put him to work today at the veterinary clinic," Kaylee said. "He was really good with the dogs. He says he doesn't like animals, but I can tell that isn't true."

"I have to figure out the school situation," Bennett said. "School is out in what…three weeks? There's not very much point in him starting now. But I'm going to have to figure out a way to get him up to speed to start school in September. Otherwise…I think working here would be good."

Money would give him an incentive to show up, and it would also give Bennett some assurance that during the day the kid was taken care of. Plus, Bennett was involved in Get Out of Dodge himself, spending a lot of his days off doing work on the ranch, so it would all work out nicely, really.

"Perfect," Wyatt said. "I'll offer it to him." Then, Wyatt shook his head, rubbing his hand over his forehead. "Damn. If I had a kid randomly show up out of the blue I would be losing it."

"You think I'm not?"

"You're doing it pretty quietly."

"No point freaking out."

"It's just… You seem like the kind of guy to wear two condoms at the same time to make sure nothing happens." Bennett shot a look over at Kaylee, whose face had turned a particular shade of scarlet. "Sorry," Wyatt continued. "But you do."

"How do you think I became that guy?" Bennett asked. "Also, that doesn't help, in fact, it can make it worse, because the latex rubs against it… Never mind."

"I'm going to go get some dinner," Kaylee said. "You can keep having this discussion without me."

Wyatt's gaze followed Kaylee as she walked from the room. "Sorry," he said.

"Whatever. She's fine."

"She didn't look fine."

"It's been a weird couple of days."

"Seriously. How are you?" Bennett knew that Wyatt did sincerity only if he absolutely had to. Which meant that the situation must be really messed up.

"I don't know how to answer that. I could say that

I'm fine, but it's not really true. I'm handling it. Because what else can I do? He's mine. He's my responsibility."

"I just can't imagine." Wyatt shook his head.

"Neither can I. But I'm living it. So, there it is."

"Have you called Dad yet?"

"No. That's going to be…a conversation."

"I have to tell you, I did not think you would be the one to have a skeleton in your closet quite like this."

"Neither did I. I thought…I made a mistake. And, it seemed like it was one that resolved itself, even though the resolution was pretty traumatic at the time."

"Did you ever tell Dad that your girlfriend was pregnant?"

"No." Bennett scrubbed his face. "You had moved out. Grant was getting married, and I know that Dad was worried about all of that. Knowing that Grant was marrying a woman who was going to die. Dad having gone through that himself. He didn't want that for Grant. Especially knowing that any other outcome was unlikely. I figured I'd have to tell him eventually. I figured I would have to tell everybody."

"Well, you were right about that. It just happened fifteen years later than you imagined."

Bennett tried to laugh. "Right."

"Come on," Wyatt said. "Let's go have dinner. We're Dodges. We've been through enough to handle this too. We lost enough together. It's about time we got something instead."

Bennett couldn't help but admire his brother's perspective on that. And so, on a heavy sigh, he followed him into the kitchen, and got ready to have dinner as a family.

KAYLEE WAS MOSTLY silent through dinner. She watched Jamie attempt to engage Dallas in discussion. Watched

Grant sink deeper into a bottle of beer. Bennett was on edge, obviously, waiting for someone to cause offense or take offense. Or maybe just waiting for the roof to collapse.

At this point, she didn't really blame him.

Wyatt, for his part, was trying to direct things. Because that was what he did. Bennett controlled his own life. He was steady, and responsible, while Wyatt was the wild card out of the brothers. Brash and bold, the oldest Dodge had never done anything according to convention.

But at Get Out of Dodge, he was definitely in charge. It was his place. He was the one with the vision for it. And she could see all of that reflected in the way that he kept things moving at dinner.

He was magnetic. A champion bull rider who had not only completed a record number of rides, but who had easily scored endorsement deals with his good looks. Wyatt was a force to be reckoned with. Always had been.

He was sexy as hell too. There wasn't a single Dodge brother who wasn't. But he had never appealed to Kaylee in the same way that Bennett did. Wyatt was much more rugged, scars on his face and body, and he possessed kind of an aggressive swagger and bravado that came with men like him. Cowboys who risked life and limb every day for a belt buckle and some money.

Bennett was rugged, but it was in a more low-key way. He had the kind of looks that almost would have been too pretty if it weren't for his height, muscular build and the scars on his hands betraying the fact that he never shied away from manual labor.

Grant was handsome too, in that steady sort of way.

Square jaw, brown eyes and a mouth that rarely smiled. The strong silent type was an understatement.

But it was Bennett, always had been, who had affected her physically. And she had gone and touched him twice in the space of the past hour. The whole drive over to the ranch had been fraught for her. Her thigh kept brushing up against his, and it…it affected her. She couldn't pretend it didn't.

Then in the living room…

She turned her focus back to the present.

"We are going to have a cleanup day over the weekend. I've enlisted the girls from Grassroots Winery to come over and share a meal with us, and then we're going to go over the logistics of this partnership. After that, it's going to be time to really whip the property into shape."

"Women," Jamie said crisply. "You will find that all of the females that work at Grassroots are women, Wyatt."

"My mistake," he said. "Though, if we're going to be pedantic, a few women and a harpy."

Grant chuckled. "Say that to her face sometime," he said, meaning Lindy, the owner of the winery.

"No thanks," Wyatt said. "I like my face as it is."

"Hmm." Jamie made a speculative sound. "Really? You do?"

"You're awfully punchy tonight for someone whose paychecks I sign," he said to his little sister.

She shrugged. "You need it. You need someone to keep you on your toes."

"No. What I need is a dictatorship that goes unchallenged."

"Sadly," Grant said, "for you, this is a partnership."

"We all own a piece of this ranch," Bennett said, for Dallas's benefit.

"Yes," Wyatt agreed. "And it's a pain in my ass sometimes."

"Except that we all help you," Grant supplied.

"Help is subjective."

"Speaking of help," Bennett said, looking at Wyatt meaningfully.

"Right," Wyatt said, taking the cue. "I'd like to hire you to work at the ranch, Dallas. I'm going to pay you."

Dallas looked surprised. "What?"

"Do you want a job?"

"Doing what?"

"Whatever the hell I ask you to do. Like I said, we are going to have a big cleanup day over the weekend. I'd like to start you then. Because we'll have all hands on deck I can train you to do a few things. But I need a basic ranch hand. I have horses and other animals to take care of. Luke here just started his own ranch, so I don't have as much help as I used to."

That drew Kaylee's attention back to Luke and Olivia. It was strange how being near them wasn't really all that strange. She was used to being near Olivia and feeling a constant burning sensation. All that jealousy. But there was nothing to be jealous of now. She was with Luke. They were happy, clearly, in a way that Olivia had never been when she'd been with Bennett. She'd always seemed a little stressed and overly serious with Bennett. With Luke, she smiled. And he smiled back. They were *in love*. That was the difference. And if she felt any kind of jealousy it was…different.

Well, she had that dinner date with Michael coming up. Maybe she could fall in love with him.

The idea of that felt strange. Wrong.

Her place felt secure here at this table. With this family. Making a new one wasn't even something she was sure she wanted.

But maybe that was the problem. Maybe the problem was that Bennett's family had always been her surrogate family. And part of her feelings for him were wrapped up in that.

That was pathetic. She didn't want to be pathetic.

Anyway, it didn't matter how she felt. The Dodges felt like family sometimes, but it didn't make her family. Sometimes watching them interact with each other made her feel like a kid with her nose pressed against the window of a toy store. All that wonder and glory and none of it for her.

Pathetic.

"That sounds...not terrible," Dallas returned.

"We have to work schooling out," Bennett said.

"The year is almost over."

"I know," Bennett said. "But we're going to do everything we can to get you caught up so that you can move on to your sophomore year. Is that the grade you should be in?"

Dallas laughed. "Yeah."

"Well, we're going to do that. If there has to be some summer school, then there has to be summer school."

"I'm not failing or anything. I should just be able to do the last few weeks at home."

"Okay. Well, you made it sound like you were failing."

Everyone at the table was watching the exchange with rapt interest. And Kaylee couldn't deny that she found it pretty interesting herself. To watch Bennett assume this position. The way that he was dealing with Dallas was... Well, it wasn't doing anything to calm her feelings down.

She had always thought he was the best man in the entire world. And this was only confirming it. If only he could be decent and have feet of clay. But no.

"Not failing."

"Well, I'll call the school and see what we need to do."

The meal moved on, Wyatt gleefully listing the various tasks that Dallas would probably be made to do. She could see that at a certain point Dallas was a little bit overwhelmed. Not because his uncle was promising to make him dig holes for a fence, but because he had an uncle at all. He got quiet, no longer making mouthy asides to fill the silences.

"I'm getting tired," she said softly.

"Oh, right," Bennett said. "We rode together."

Whether or not he realized that she was making the excuse for Dallas, she had a feeling that he was grateful for it.

"We have to go," Bennett said, standing. "We all rode over together."

"I have an early appointment," she lied. "But thanks for dinner, Wyatt."

"Yeah," Wyatt said. "Thanks for...well, coming."

She felt like he was actually thanking her for being here at all. For being there for Bennett.

Dallas's shoulders sagged with relief once they told everyone goodbye and were outside on their way to the pickup truck.

"Are you okay?" she asked underneath the sound of their feet crunching on the gravel.

"Me?" Dallas asked.

"Yes," she confirmed.

"Fine. Tired."

Bennett didn't say anything, he just got into the truck and started the engine. She and Dallas followed suit.

She had forgotten that she would end up sitting next to Bennett again. That her leg would be smashed up against his. The heat of his body seeping into hers. Suddenly, she was exhausted. It was all just...a lot. And she knew that Dallas wasn't her responsibility, but it still felt weighty. Like something she was carrying, an extra burden, on behalf of her friend.

Bennett's house was between Get Out of Dodge and the clinic. After making sure he was completely all right, Bennett dropped Dallas off at the house, telling him he wouldn't be long, before heading back onto the highway to take Kaylee to her car.

"So I guess he has a job now," Bennett said.

"Yeah," Kaylee said, scooting all the way to the door, as far away from Bennett as she possibly could. Her leg still burned.

"I'm glad. I'm glad that he has something to keep him busy."

"And something to give the two of you some distance?"

"It's definitely a uniquely exhausting situation. And he's not a toddler or anything. He doesn't need constant care. But I feel like...I don't know him. He's a stranger. But I care about him. What's going to happen to him. If he's happy. And I don't know how to gauge any of that. I don't know how to control it. I hate not being in control, Kaylee. I really do."

"Well, if it's at all comforting, I don't think you've ever been in control. I just think sometimes it's easier to pretend that you are."

"That's not particularly comforting."

"Sorry. But it's the truth."

"Can he come by the clinic again tomorrow?"

"Sure. He was fine today."

"Are you going to come over for cleanup day?"

Spending the day watching Bennett do manual labor sounded like a recipe in sweet sexual torture. She wasn't sure she was up for it. But she didn't feel like she could leave him alone either. Not that he would be alone.

"Sure. Oh. Is that Saturday?"

"Yes."

"I have a dinner date. So, I'm going to have to leave early to shower all the…you know."

"Right. With the dachshund guy."

"Michael," she said.

"Right. Not like I really have to remember his name."

Kaylee frowned into the darkness of the truck. "I'm sorry, what?"

"It's not like I have to remember the guy's name, Kay. Let's be honest. Your boyfriends don't last very long."

"What the hell, Bennett?" she asked, rage breaking out over her skin like hives. She could feel it. Just beneath the surface of her skin. Itchy. Hot.

"How long has your longest relationship lasted, Kaylee?"

"I don't know. But that's completely…asinine. I know the names of all of your girlfriends."

That just made her sound sad.

"Sorry. I didn't know that would be an offensive observation. I'm just saying, it's not like you're going to go on more than a couple of dates with him."

"I dated Kyle for three months."

Surely he wasn't her longest relationship. *Ryan.* She snapped her finger in triumph. "I dated Ryan for six months."

"When? Five years ago?"

Probably.

"Just stop," she said. "Stop while you're only a couple steps behind and you have a hope in hell of catching up at some point."

"Sorry," he said.

She stewed. The only sound the tires on the rough road. She looked out the window, the darkness concealing any view she might have been able to use to distract herself with. She looked up, the dark, ragged silhouettes of the trees and inky blur bordering the clear night sky.

She took a deep breath. "I can't believe that you think it's not worth remembering the name of my date." Apparently, she couldn't let it go. Even if he did drop the subject.

"I'm just saying that unless he puts a ring on your finger or something, it's very likely I'm not going to need to know his name."

"I was right in the middle of all of your Olivia drama."

"I was with her for a year. Plus, she was somebody that you knew before I started dating her."

"No. That's not it. I care more about what happens in your life than you care about what happens in mine."

"The hell *I don't care*."

"Sure. You just let me never tell you about my home life."

"Come on, Kaylee. Because I didn't drag the story out of you by force? You never talked about it, I had no reason to assume that what you'd told me wasn't the whole truth of it."

She was being petulant. She was being driven into petulance by the fact that he didn't care she was going on a date. That was the real issue. She knew the name of every woman he had ever gone out with because those women had each hooked a manicured nail into one of her insecurities. Olivia was so petite, and Kaylee, with her Amazonian stature, couldn't compete. Then there had been Brandy. Who had looked exactly like her name suggested. Big breasts. Small waist. The kind of butt you had to do squats to get, because nobody got it on accident.

Yes. There had been many, and they had all been different than her in some way. He had never gone out with a lean, athletic-looking redhead who was pushing six feet.

She had made a choice. A choice to keep her friendship with Bennett as it was, but it didn't stop her from resenting every woman who was brave enough to take what she didn't feel like she could.

She remembered all the women because it *bothered* her. And he couldn't remember the men, because they didn't matter to him.

That hurt. No matter how much she wished it didn't, no matter that it didn't make sense because she'd decided their friendship should never change.

The certain knowledge that no part of him harbored secret fantasies about her...

It sucked, basically.

About a second before she crawled out of her skin, and then maybe crawled out of the moving vehicle, they arrived at the clinic. As soon he put the truck in Park she basically scrambled out of the passenger seat.

She heard the driver-side door slam a second after she slammed her own door. She ignored it.

"Kaylee," he said. "I'm sorry."

She stopped, closing her eyes. "Don't, Bennett. I'm just tired."

And there she was, pushing it all off like it was nothing. It wasn't fair to get angry at him about her parents.

To get angry about this. When push came to shove, when rubber met the very pothole-laden road, she always did this. She didn't want to talk about it. She didn't want to make a big deal out of it. Because she didn't think she deserved...

She didn't even know what.

"You're not just tired. Something's bothering you."

"And you just became a father. Your life is...hell, Bennett, I don't even know what your life is right now. My stuff doesn't matter. It really doesn't."

"Kaylee, if you don't tell me, then I can't know. This is why I don't know all your stuff. And then it isn't fair that you're angry at me."

"Bennett..."

"I hope your date goes well."

Dammit. Now she felt like she had been stuck through the chest with an ice pick. That didn't help. It didn't help at all.

"Thanks," she said.

"If you want to talk about your parents..."

"If I did I would have by now. I just wanted to give you a context for the way that I was talking to Dallas. That's all. We're fine. The way that we are. We don't need to change anything."

She turned and stomped to her car, ignoring the fact that he was still standing there watching her. They were fine the way they were. Except that they weren't. Except that as she had realized earlier, nothing was going to change. Touching him was always going to light her on fire. Unless... She didn't even know what.

All the deciding in the world that she wanted to be his friend wouldn't take it away. Not forever. And when she was consumed with him it was...so awful. So hard.

She swallowed, miserable, her throat aching.

The date with Michael had to go well. He had to last long enough that Bennett would have to learn his name. She had to do something to get a hold of herself. She really did.

CHAPTER EIGHT

WHEN CLEANUP DAY rolled around, all hands were on deck. Though, some looked a little bit more enthusiastic than others.

Dallas, specifically, did not look overly enthusiastic. He was wearing a T-shirt, jeans and a pair of borrowed boots that actually fit him, even though he was a few inches shorter than Bennett. He would probably be just as tall in the end, if not taller.

He was like a puppy that hadn't grown into his feet.

And didn't own work boots, apparently. Bennett would have to fix that. He probably needed to get the kid all new clothes.

Over the past few days they had managed to sort out the school situation. Dallas really wasn't behind, and if he was willing to do some testing, he could start at the beginning of the year along with the other kids.

Dallas was quick to agree to that, since summer school hadn't been something he was especially dying to put on his to-do list.

Although, as Dallas pointed out after they left Gold Valley High School, he didn't exactly have a social life to cripple. And until he started school, he wouldn't.

Dallas having a social life would be a whole other thing. Other worries.

Teenagers wanting to be in his house. In potentially large groups.

He wasn't going to think about that now. How had his dad done this? How had he handled four kids by himself?

One was making Bennett insane and Dallas hadn't even done anything wrong.

He was feeling more grateful than he could have imagined for a day of hard labor. He needed something to punish his body badly enough that he wouldn't be able to think of anything but his own physical pain.

On some days, Bennett found Wyatt's overbearing manner to be a pain in his ass, but now, with his older brother handing out orders and giving direction at lightning speed, he found himself grateful for it. Wyatt would have no trouble keeping everyone on track.

He had decided that digging post holes and stringing barbed wire on a new fence was the perfect activity for his nephew, and had sent Bennett and Grant right along with him.

Kaylee had been assigned landscape work with Jamie, and he had heard Jamie muttering the whole way about asshat older brothers.

Dallas, Grant and Bennett drove out to the north end of the property, across a few partially fenced fields to the new area for the cows. Wyatt wanted to have livestock on the ranch. Part of the appeal of Get Out of Dodge as a dude ranch was that it be a functioning ranch.

But he also knew that guests didn't necessarily want animals grazing near their sleeping quarters. He was aiming for a controlled rustic experience.

So that meant designated pasture farther afield.

The land had been clear-cut in the center years ago, creating grazing space, and now the property was hemmed in by what looked like a wall of pine. Tree-covered mountains rose up behind the trees, barricading the property from the rest of the world.

After giving brief instructions on how to dig holes for the fence posts and string the wire between the posts, Grant and Bennett got Dallas set to work. They were each wearing heavy work gloves, wielding the barbed wire as carefully as possible.

"I bet this violates child labor laws," Dallas pointed out.

"Then it's a good thing Wyatt will probably pay you under the table," Grant said, a ghost of a smile touching his brother's lips.

"That's criminal."

"Didn't you know?" Grant's smile turned to a full-blown grin. "The Dodges are outlaws."

"It's true," Bennett agreed.

"Seriously?" They were treated to a skeptical eyebrow from Dallas.

"Hell, yeah," Bennett said. "Stagecoach robbers. Going way back. They terrorized the pony express and all of that."

"Didn't end well for some of them," Grant said. "Obviously some of them survived or the line would have ended. But yeah, basically, they raised Cain all down the Oregon Trail. And camped out on the edges of all the little gold rush towns, taking what they could."

"This ranch was probably bought with a sizable amount of stolen gold way back in the day," Bennett said.

"No way," Dallas said. "That's actually cool."

"We don't rob stagecoaches now," Bennett said. "To be clear."

"I've never known anything about…my family or whatever," Dallas said. "Not bad to find out they were Wild West outlaws."

"We're respectable now," Bennett said.

"Mostly." Grant paused. "Because there is Wyatt."

"True," Bennett agreed.

"Why isn't he respectable?" Dallas asked.

"He's a bull rider," Grant said. "And bull riders are idiots."

"Yes. And Wyatt is chief among them."

"Bull riders and outlaws. And veterinarians. And..." He looked over at Grant.

"I'm a rancher now," Grant said. "I used to work at the power company."

"Oh," Dallas said, frowning. "Interesting."

"It's not. I got married young." The corner of Grant's mouth lifted up on one side. "Had to get a good job. Health benefits and 401(k)s and stuff like that."

"Where's your wife now?"

"She's dead," Grant said, the words flat and bald.

The late spring air kicked up, pushing out the warmth of the sun, and Bennett thought it matched the mood perfectly. He was about to open his mouth to try to smooth things over when Dallas spoke up.

"I'm sorry." And he really looked it.

"Don't be," Grant said. "It was an honest question. And I'm not used to meeting people who don't know the ins and outs of all my business. Hazards of a small town."

"I guess it would be."

"You'll learn quickly enough. You won't be able to do anything without the good people of Gold Valley reporting back to your dad."

Dallas and Bennett exchanged an uncomfortable look.

"But yeah," Grant continued, "now that I'm not married I can take some chances. Now, I'm investing in this place."

They spent the better part of the next hour explaining to Dallas exactly what the plans were for Get Out of Dodge. How they were going to run guest services there, the partnerships with the winery, tours, everything.

"So…Jamie is going to give trail rides?" Dallas asked, clearly trying not to sound as interested as he was.

"Yes. And for some guests she might even do endurance rides. Over fifty miles. Up in the mountains. It's good stuff."

"I've never ridden a horse before," Dallas said.

Bennett frowned. "That's going to change. I mean, if you want it to."

"Hell," Grant said, "Dodges learn how to ride before they learn how to walk. I'm not even exaggerating. I think my dad put me up on the back of a horse for the first time when I was, like, eight months old. With my mom, of course, not by myself."

"We'll teach you how to ride," Bennett said. "Actually, Jamie will love that. We all love to ride, but it's in Jamie's blood. She's a hell of a horsewoman."

"And Wyatt just rides bulls?" Dallas asked.

"No. He rides horses too."

"He probably stays on the back of the bulls longer," Grant said drily.

Bennett chuckled, and Grant actually looked amused with himself, but they were interrupted by the sound of a clearing throat. They turned to see Wyatt standing there looking unamused. "Are you besmirching my horsemanship?"

"Your horsemanship besmirches itself," Grant returned.

It was nice to see Grant smiling. Nice to see him participating in the back-and-forth. But then, they were coming out of winter. Grant didn't do so well in winter. When the sun started to shine again, he always seemed a little bit more himself. At least, the way that Bennett could remember him being back before Lindsay's death. Maybe back before he had started to love Lindsay. Because loving her had never been simple. Loving her, for Grant, had always meant contending with losing her.

"Don't listen to those sons of bitches," Wyatt said. "They're jealous because I'm a badass."

"Yeah, we're really jealous," Bennett said, keeping his face as serious as possible.

"How goes the fencing?" Wyatt asked.

"It's going good," Dallas said.

"Very good," Bennett confirmed. "He's a quick study." He felt a small, unexpected surge of pride go through him as he said that. It was true. Dallas had done a great job keeping up with them, and he wasn't used to this kind of physical labor. Still, he was doing well at it. And he wasn't complaining.

"Great. Lunch is going to be in about an hour or so. That's when Lindy and Beatrix are coming."

"Great," Bennett said.

"Sure," Wyatt said. "Great, as long as it doesn't turn into a brawl."

"You and Lindy are going to have to keep it in your pants," Grant said.

"That won't be a problem. It will be her keeping her fist out of my face that's the problem."

Grant shrugged, but didn't say anything else.

Wyatt left after that, and they continued to work until the lunch hour got closer. "I'm going to go wash up. See you down at the mess hall," Grant said, leaving Dallas and himself alone at the fence.

"How are you liking the work so far?" Bennett asked.

"It's work," Dallas said.

"This is what we do. I know I'm a veterinarian, but this is the family business."

"After robbing stagecoaches."

"Yeah, but robbing stagecoaches wasn't exactly a viable business long-term. In the end, even the Dodges were smart enough to realize that. Eventually."

"So…am I here for the summer? I mean, how long is this going to last?"

"I told you," Bennett said. "This is real. You're staying with me."

"Why haven't you gotten a paternity test done yet?" Dallas asked, the anger in his words sending Bennett back on his heels.

"I'm going to get one." Bennett crossed his arms over his chest. "We have to go do the family court thing and proving my paternity makes everything easiest. But from my point of view, I don't really need one."

"Right. Because if you don't get one then you can still back out." Dallas crossed his arms in an unconscious mimic of Bennett's stance, his expression looking mutinous. "Correct me if I'm wrong, but it's just that you have plausible deniability now."

"I don't *want* plausible deniability," Bennett said, not sure how in the hell he had managed to walk into two conversations in the space of a couple of days that had landed his ass in such hot water.

Kaylee had been bristly with him ever since their confrontation at the clinic the other night about Michael, whose name he remembered now since she had yelled at him about it. And now, somehow, something that had started out as a good conversation had ended up something else entirely with Dallas.

"You're wrong," he said. "I'm not looking for an out. Hell, I'll set one up tomorrow. If that's what you need, then I'll do it."

"Tomorrow is Sunday."

"And it's a small damned town. I can probably arrange to have somebody come in on Sunday if I need to."

"Don't do that," Dallas said, suddenly looking uncertain.

And then, Bennett had to wonder if Dallas was worried that Bennett might not be his father after all. He was never quite sure whether or not Dallas wanted to be with him. Never sure if he hated the small town he had landed himself in a week ago or not. But then Bennett kept coming back to the fact that Dallas had chosen to come to him. He had chosen to tell the social worker who his father might be. And he chose to stay now. Sure, his alternatives weren't great, but nobody had tied him up and forced him to stay.

It was easy to forget that underneath all that bluster, all that teenage bravado, was the heart of a little boy who had been wounded and abandoned more times than Bennett cared to think about.

"I know you don't have any reason to trust me. I know that nobody in your life has stuck by you. You've been exposed to some shady people. I'm not a saint, far from it. But believe me when I say I'm not doing you some great favor by keeping you with me. Sixteen years ago when your mother told me she was pregnant I was ready. I wasn't ready, but I was, if that makes sense. I was ready to upend my life to take care of you. To quit school, to work at the mill. At the power company like

Grant, because that's what you do when you love somebody. You want to take care of them."

"My mother?"

"No. *You.* I loved you before you were born. Right away. I was scared as hell, but I knew that I was willing to do anything for my kid. For the promise of that relationship. And the way I see it now, this isn't any different. We don't know each other. But all the possibilities are there. I don't need to know you to know what I'm prepared to do. *Anything.* To give you the life that you deserve. It's my responsibility because I'm your father. I'm sorry that nobody took responsibility for you when they should have at other times in your life. But it doesn't mean that I won't."

Dallas looked past Bennett, his frown deepening, the scowl line between his brows mirroring the line Bennett had seen growing deeper on his own face over the past few days.

And Bennett realized right then that he had overlooked one crucial thing in that bit of rationalization he just gone through. Yes, he had loved Dallas before he had known him. Before he was born, before he had known if he was a son or a daughter. But Dallas hadn't been wounded then. He hadn't had fifteen years of being let down, time and time again. And now he did. It could never go back and be that exact thing it was all those years ago.

Because Dallas could never be that same kid he would have been. Couldn't go back and be not scarred by the life that he had led.

Dammit. It was such a mess.

"Kaylee told me..." Bennett cleared his throat. "She told me that your mom left you alone? For days at a time?"

"You know what? I don't want to talk about this. It doesn't matter."

"It *does* matter. And if everybody could stop getting mad at me about things that they claim don't matter, that would be great. If you're mad, they obviously matter."

"What?"

"Never mind. But if you're going to be angry, don't tell me it doesn't matter. I told you that I was going to be honest with you, and I am. But I want you to do the same, Dallas. I want you to be honest with me. About what makes you angry. About all the things you think I did wrong. About all the things I'm doing wrong now. Be angry, that's fine, but don't bullshit me. Don't just try to protect yourself. We can do better than that, we can have better than that. I believe it. But we've got to get through this first."

"We've got to get through this? This," he said, waving his hand, "is my life. All the stuff you want me to get through, it's all the things I know. Every last thing. You want me to just…not be who I am?"

"That's not what I meant."

"Maybe I don't want to get over it," Dallas continued. "Maybe I learned some things that I need to remember from it. You don't get to just decide that I should feel different or be different. That's not up to you. Yeah, maybe you loved me before I was born, when you thought I was going to be a precious baby. But that's not what I am now. And I'm not going to be. I'm not going to be that kid that you imagined. Ever. It's too late for that. So get the fuck over it."

And then Dallas stormed away from him, heading off toward God knows where. And Bennett was left feeling like he had failed at everything that mattered.

CHAPTER NINE

KAYLEE WAS STARVING. She and Jamie had spent the morning sweating and planting flowers, which was frankly not in either of their wheelhouses, and then they had ridden out to the far side of the property to take a look at some manzanitas that Wyatt thought could maybe be transplanted to give the place a kind of rustic, natural feel.

Unnaturally. But he hadn't been overly amused when Kaylee had pointed that out.

Jamie had complained the entire way about how she was going to poison her brother at dinner.

There'd been a lot of muttering about bull riders who were far too full of themselves to be of any use to anyone.

There were burgers being served in the mess hall, grilled by the arrogant bull rider himself, so Jamie had to retract some of her earlier venom as she shoved a burger into her mouth and thanked her brother for cooking.

"And thank you for planting flowers, Jamie," Wyatt said, smiling. Then he looked up and his smile faded. It turned into something much different. Not a frown, but something sharp and extremely aware.

Kaylee followed his gaze to the front door of the simple room and saw Lindy Parker and Beatrix Leighton walking in holding boxes of wine. It was Lindy. That was why Wyatt looked the way that he did.

Interesting. When it came to the two of them hating each other, Kaylee wondered if they protested a little bit too much.

Though, maybe not on Lindy's end. Considering the nasty divorce she had gone through only a couple of years ago, and with a friend of Wyatt's no less. But Wyatt… No, it did not look like his feelings for Lindy were entirely negative.

"Where should I put the samples?" Lindy asked.

Beatrix was straining to hold the weight of the boxes, and Kaylee smiled to herself, since the last time she had seen Beatrix holding a box, it had contained a raccoon.

"How is the baby raccoon, Bea?" Kaylee asked, moving across the room to take the box from the more petite woman's arms.

"Oh, he's doing great," she said brightly.

Lindy looked pained. "There's a raccoon living in my winery."

"He's in my cabin, Lindy," Beatrix pointed out.

Lindy made a long-suffering sound.

The door opened again and Dallas came in looking grumpy. He didn't say anything; instead, he walked over to where the burgers were to make himself a plate. Then he looked over at Lindy and Beatrix, and she saw his focus stop hard on Bea.

There was a definite flash of interest in his eyes as he looked at her. Beatrix remained oblivious, but then, that didn't surprise Kaylee since Bea was in her twenties and wouldn't be looking at a fifteen-year-old boy.

Dallas was so focused on Bea that when he picked his hamburger up he lost a whole tomato and didn't seem to notice.

Kaylee groaned inwardly. There was that whole element to teenage boys. How fun for Bennett to manage. Not.

She waited for Bennett to show up, but he didn't. The group of them mixed together, talking about the various plans that Wyatt and Lindy had for cross-promoting events. Including the big grand opening barbecue they would have on the Fourth of July.

"It would be nice if we could get some microbrews to come," she said. "I'll call Ace Thompson down in Copper Ridge and see if he's interested in having something set up. I know they have a big event happening down there on the same day, but maybe he can send out an employee."

"Sounds like a great idea to me," Wyatt said, clearly taking the nonverbal cue that he and Lindy were having some kind of a cease-fire so they could work on business plans.

Kaylee couldn't do things like that. She couldn't draw lines. There had never been such a thing as business and personal to her. Everything just became personal so easily. But then, her body didn't seem to understand the lines between friendship and romance either.

She was a woman who seemed to know very few boundaries. It was *all in* or *not at all*.

Which put her in the mind of thinking about her date tonight. She needed to be all in with Michael. She really did.

She had been wretched and distant from Bennett for the past few days because she was still licking her wounds over that comment he had made about her dating life. She wouldn't be if it weren't true. She wouldn't be, if it had proven so perfectly his lack of jealousy.

All of it was about her feelings, and nothing was

about anything terrible he had actually done. Which made her petulant and awful. But she kind of didn't care.

Except, now Bennett wasn't here, and she was a little bit concerned because everyone else was.

She moved over to where Grant was standing. "Have you seen Bennett?"

"Last I saw him he and Dallas were still working on the fence."

"Thanks," she said, frowning.

She pulled her phone out of her pocket and shot off a quick text. Reception wasn't the best in every part of the ranch, but if he was near the dining hall then he should be able to get it.

She didn't get a response.

Everyone was engaged in conversation, and Dallas was standing on the periphery, clearly looking for an excuse to say something to Beatrix, who had yet to notice him at all. Kaylee took that opportunity to slip away, deciding she was going to try to find Bennett.

She walked across the wooden floor and exited quietly, looking around, listening to see if she could hear any footsteps. Nothing. Nothing but the gentle breeze and the sound of a horse nickering in the field close by. The pine trees swayed gently, the needles whispering as they brushed together. Coursing beneath the sound of the trees was the river, which rushed continually out beyond the clearing.

Kaylee knew there was some seating down by the river. An outdoor dining area for future guests.

She decided to head down that way, since it seemed like as good of a direction as any.

If Bennett had been looking for isolation, that was probably a good place to go to brood.

And if he was looking for isolation then maybe she shouldn't bother him.

But she was going to bother him.

True friendship and everything.

She walked down the freshly barked path, the smell of wood chips rising up with each step, vague notes of smoky hickory combining with the woodsy smell around her. The sound of the river got louder, as did the damp, icy scent of the fast-moving water that had run down from the mountains and still held that biting hint of melted snow.

That was when she saw him, sitting on one of the picnic benches, beneath the rustic covering that was built over the top of the tables, shielding them from the elements.

"What are you doing out here?" she asked.

"Just reflecting on all the ways in which I'm a disaster," he said, sighing heavily.

She frowned. "What happened?"

"I had a fight with Dallas, which is ridiculous. Do you have any idea how stupid you feel standing there arguing with a teenager? I should be…the adult."

"Bennett," she said slowly. "You're thirty-two years old. You're a lot younger than most people dealing with a kid his age. And other parents have the benefit of having raised a kid his entire life. You kind of got dropped into the deep end."

"Stop it," he said. "Stop trying to make me feel better when I'm in the wrong. I hurt you when I brought up your dating history and you brushed it off. Excused me and then wouldn't talk to me. It doesn't help me fix anything."

She frowned. "I was genuinely being ridiculous, and I recognized it. I didn't want to turn it into a thing."

"Well, it's a thing. I handled Dallas badly, and I handled you badly too."

"You didn't." She shoved aside yesterday's pain.

"I did. And something about me must have that effect. Because you know, instead of dealing with me, my ex-girlfriend lied to me about losing the baby and ran off. And then all of this… It all stems, somehow, from me."

"It does not. I think it's pretty clear based on the trajectory of her life versus yours who the mess was in that situation."

"Thanks," he said, "but I'm not interested in total absolution. Not if I don't deserve it. What I said about Michael wasn't called for."

She gave him the evil eye. "You *do* remember his name."

"Yes," he said, "now I'm not going to forget it."

She laughed softly, stepping onto the wooden platform that was built over the top of the soft ground by the river. The hollow-sounding deck echoed beneath her footsteps. "Now it has to work out with him, I guess. That puts a lot of pressure on my dinner tonight."

As if there could possibly be any more pressure on that dinner.

"How did my life turn into this? I had everything planned just a few months ago. Right before Christmas, I was dating a woman I was going to ask to marry me eventually. I was already thinking about that future. And now it's… Nothing looks the same."

He stood and made a very masculine sound as he lifted his arms, stretching. She watched the strong column of his throat rise up and down as he swallowed. She was so keyed in to him. To his every movement. His everything.

It was too much. Too big inside of her. She couldn't breathe around it.

"Yeah." She looked away. "Well."

"You do, though," he said. "*You're* the same." He released a slow breath. "I'm thankful for that."

Kaylee was not. Those words were the absolute worst thing he could've possibly said. Which wasn't fair, because it was obviously the one thing he needed. But it was like bamboo shoots being shoved underneath her fingernails.

"Bennett…"

"Thank you," he said.

She flinched when he spoke the words, almost like they were a physical blow. "You didn't love Olivia," she said, needing to say it, because something inside of her needed the satisfaction of hearing it right then. "But you were actually going to marry her?"

"I…I was putting it off."

"Right. So you're acting now like it was the certain plan that you had, but did you really?" She really didn't think he would have. With absolute clarity right then, she didn't.

He dragged a hand over his face, like he was trying to wipe the tension from his expression. "I told you that Cole Logan knew about the baby. I was scared, and I was upset and I went to talk to him. He let me confide in him. His friendship with my dad was always there. They knew each other all of my life. He's really like an uncle to me. He helped me figure out what I should. Helped me figure out what kind of man I wanted to be.

"He said that the choices I made mattered, even then. Because taking control, doing what was right, that was the thing that would shape me all of my life. It was because of him that I was resolute in asking Marnie to marry me. He made me feel like even though I was sixteen I could step up and be a man. Because he said if I thought I was man enough to be having sex, I had to be man enough to deal with all the potential consequences of it. And that made sense to me. Then Marnie said she lost the baby and I never had to tell anyone what happened."

Kaylee didn't say anything. She just waited.

"Then you know, later… He had a heart attack."

"I remember that," Kaylee said, subdued.

"He asked me to make sure she was taken care of. Olivia. And I said that I would. His health has been fine ever since…"

"So you felt like you had to marry her? Only then you didn't because Cole was fine."

"More than that it…gave me a purpose. A mission, I guess. And I was holding on to that. The reason I hesitated about proposing was because…I didn't love her. Not really and in the end that didn't seem fair. At first I was sure she was on the same page as I was, then it seemed like she…cared more than I did. But I'm not heartbroken. The reason it stings is that I had a plan and now it's…" He let out a slow breath. "I was so sure if I could just reason out a life for myself I could make it perfect. Happy. And still…I don't know. To not have to go through all that messy falling in love stuff. I thought I could game the system and I can't. Now I've got a kid and that's going to be messy and there's nothing I can do about."

She felt fuzzy-headed, a strange kind of out-of-body sensation. It was a lot of new information to process.

Then she looked at Bennett. Really looked at him. Not just a casual glance, assuming that she knew exactly how he looked because she had known him for

years. No, she looked at him now. At the way the lines
that bracketed either side of his mouth had deepened,
at the crease in his forehead that seemed entirely new,
worry added since Dallas had shown up. And all of her
anger, all of her own hurt, fell away.

She moved closer to him, leaning in, and then she
wrapped her arms around him, hugging him. She
pressed her breasts against his chest. His hard, muscular chest. Her heart was pounding erratically, and she
was pressed against him tightly enough that she could
feel his too. Firm and steady.

He curved his arm around her waist, then his other
up higher, one large hand resting low on her back, the
other between her shoulder blades. Big and warm and
right. Like she belonged here against him, even though
she was sure friendship had absolutely no place in this.

But maybe she did. In his arms.

Just for a minute she wanted it to be true.

He was so strong, so big. Not very many men could
make her feel petite, but Bennett did. She closed her
eyes and breathed him in. His soap. His skin. Bennett,
so familiar, but not from this close. Not so completely
wrapped around her.

It wasn't that they'd never hugged before. They had.
They'd gotten drunk together, and she'd seen him cry
the night of their high school graduation after he'd had
three beers and started talking about his mom. But
they'd never held each other.

Right now, she was going to hold on to him. Offer
him strength. Offer him whatever she had. Everything.
She'd give him everything.

He shifted, and she lifted her head, their faces close
together. Her throat was tight, her heart stuck right at
the base of it, pounding hard and heavy.

All she could see was him. His face. The beginnings of a shadow over his jaw, his brown eyes glittering with intense emotion. His lips. She was looking at his mouth again.

It seemed like the most natural thing in the world to close that distance. To brush his lips with hers.

So she did.

It was like lightning. A moment that cracked the sky wide-open and lit up…everything. Just for a moment, a blinding, brilliant moment, everything was clear. Nothing was hidden. This need, this desire, wasn't buried in the cover of darkness anymore.

It was over quickly. Too quickly. She didn't even close her eyes.

Like nothing more than dragging the edge of a feather over the corner of her mouth. That was how light it was. How quick.

But the aftereffect burned through her like a wildfire, along with a heavy slam of her heart against her breastbone.

What the hell had she just done? She didn't kiss Bennett. *Ever.*

She was frozen, her lips right next to his, but not touching anymore.

Then she drew back. "Sorry," she said, her face so hot she felt like she had stuck it up against the side of a wood stove. "I don't know… It was just… You look sad."

Bennett's face was granite, his dark eyes flat and unreadable. She really had done something so horrifying, so outside the code of their friendship that he didn't know how to react. And it hadn't been a hallucination on her end, or he wouldn't be looking at her like that.

"Don't think about it. Don't worry about it." She waved her hand out in front of her, continually moving away from him. "Just… You're doing a good job, Bennett. Don't bring all the past stuff to this party. Don't make our fight somehow part of everything going on with Dallas. That was me. And I'm over it. I'm totally over it." She scrambled backward, stumbling as she did, her heart pounding so hard she could scarcely see straight. She couldn't breathe, each contraction of her chest chasing air that it couldn't seem to capture.

And she was trying to look fine. Just fine. So he wouldn't think it was at all strange that she had hugged him. And then kissed him on the mouth as if that was just something they did.

Oh, *damn*. This was the worst, most embarrassing thing.

Like lightning. She'd thought that when their lips had touched. That it had lit everything up. He would know. He had to know. That she wanted him.

It was obvious now. It wasn't like she'd ever lost it and kissed any of her other friends randomly. Wasn't like Bennett had ever locked lips with Luke because he felt bad for the guy.

She felt hot and cold. Her core molten, her skin clammy and tight with the horror of what she'd just done.

"I'm going to…go. I have a date," she said, almost choking on the words.

"Okay," he said, still rooted to the same spot he'd been in.

"I'll see you later." She turned away from him and wrapped her arms around herself as she headed toward her truck.

She wasn't going to say goodbye to anyone. She needed to be alone for a while. Needed to get her head on straight. She'd go out with Michael and she would forget this had happened. And hopefully by tomorrow

Bennett would forget it too. Hopefully it would get swept up in Hurricane Dallas.

Everything would go back to normal then. Bennett would want it to anyway. That was what he'd said. She hadn't changed. He didn't want her to.

In the end, that would probably be what saved this.

That Bennett wouldn't want to know if it had meant something. Because he didn't want it to.

CHAPTER TEN

THE PHYSICAL LABOR hadn't helped a damned thing.

It was hours since he had returned home from the cleanup day, hours since his fight with Dallas. Dallas, who was now in bed. Presumably. Unless the kid had finally decided to bust out a window and run for freedom.

After that fight at Get Out of Dodge, Bennett wasn't really sure which it would be.

Except the kid wasn't going to run off. He knew that with a strange kind of certainty. Maybe it was a misguided certainty.

Because who hadn't listened to a proud parent talk about their kid in glowing and delusional terms? He had stood around and listened to countless people talk about how their kids were the best, kindest, most well-behaved angels on the planet. All the while Bennett knew that they had been caught drinking or screwing in the back of a car.

Yeah.

There was some kind of heavy denial that took over when you were a parent. He had seen it from the outside. But whether or not this was that, he felt confident in the fact that Dallas wanted to be here.

Now, he also might be angry that he was here, but he had a feeling that Dallas suffered from being angry wherever he was.

Then there was that kiss.

He was putting off thinking about that. Really, the fight with his son was less uncomfortable to go over.

He hadn't known what the hell was happening.

He'd been out there by himself, trying to figure out what the hell the way forward was, and Kaylee had appeared.

He had looked up from where he was sitting on the bench to see her coming down the path, her red hair fluttering in the breeze, her T-shirt molded over her slight curves, and he had wondered if her bra always showed like that through those soft-looking T-shirts, and if he had just never noticed before because...

Because he was an idiot?

He didn't know.

Then she'd hugged him. All those curves had been pressed up against him.

He had the thought earlier today that he might be able to blot out the eternal stream of unsettled stuff running through his brain if he just punished his body with enough labor. But in that moment he wondered if it was something else that he needed. Something he hadn't indulged in for a long damn time.

The reason Bennett had gotten so angry at Olivia when he had first found out she had slept with Luke right after their breakup was that he had been celibate for more than a year. For his part, he had respected what Olivia had asked of him.

She had wanted to wait. Wait till they were engaged.

Hell, she'd been a *virgin*. And then, she'd gone and given it to Luke Hollister. A man who wasn't going to offer a commitment to her at all.

Except that he had.

But it had still left Bennett in the middle of the world's most profound dry spell.

Which was catching up with him, apparently. Because his best friend's curves had felt like a branding iron against his body, and had left his stomach hollowed out. Worst of all, he'd had to fight against his hardening body as she had shifted those slender hips and fitted them against his.

He did *not* get hard-ons over Kaylee. He didn't. He never had. He wouldn't.

Then she had looked up at him, and something in her expression had suddenly seemed so raw. So unguarded, that it had made him feel like an ax had split him in two. Revealing all kinds of stuff at the center he hadn't known was there.

Before he could react to that, her lips had pressed against his.

It had been platonic. He would have called it sisterly if he hadn't felt so decidedly unbrotherly at every point at which their bodies were touching.

The kiss had been nothing. A simple meeting of lips. Barely a breath. A blink.

Except she had jumped back like a scalded cat a moment later. Except that she had run away. Which all spoke to it being *something*. No matter how much of a nothing it should have been.

Was it something he had done? A reaction that he had that had made Kaylee run the opposite direction?

Probably the hard-on in your jeans, asshole.

It hadn't been a full-on erection. He was thirty-two years old, he had a little bit more control than that. However, if the physical contact had gone on any longer...

Well, there was self-control and then there was being able to perform miracles. And he couldn't do the miracle thing.

He had lied to Kaylee when he'd told her that she was

the one unchanged part of his life. From that brief fantasy he'd had of her in the shower, down to this, there was something changing there too. And he hated it. He felt out of control, and he hated that more than anything.

It made him feel like that little kid he'd been on the day he found out his mother had died after giving birth to his little sister.

It hadn't been expected. Not at all. And then, it had just been. She was dead. There was no arguing with that. No coming back from it. No fixing it.

His father had been broken, left with a squalling infant who hadn't been able to be comforted. His oldest brother had gone into a kind of hard, serious mode. Being the man of the house. Grant, for his part, had tried to emulate that. But they were both older.

Bennett had been a little boy. But not the baby.

He hadn't been quite old enough to feel like he could be one of the men, but he hadn't been young enough that he could excuse crying and crawling up into his father's arms. Anyway, Jamie had needed all of that.

He hadn't wanted to cause more trouble. He had just wanted to fix it. What he really wanted was a time machine. To go back and stop it all somehow, but that wasn't possible.

He wished he could have one now too. So that he could go back to before today. Maybe so he could go back months ago, when everything was simpler.

But there was no going back. And all these years of supposed control had only ever been a facade.

He thought he'd made that one mistake in high school and—as sad as it had been—he'd gotten a reprieve. Gotten an opportunity to take all that control back.

But no.

He had never been in control of anything.

And he wasn't doing any better grabbing hold of it now.

He couldn't predict Dallas. Couldn't anticipate where he would put a foot right or wrong. Like climbing a mountain made of loose gravel. Couldn't tell what would hold and what would send him plunging to his doom.

And then there was this whole thing with Kaylee. He couldn't pretend that she hadn't felt whatever weird-ass thing had happened then. Couldn't pretend that she hadn't felt it the last few times.

He had to get a grip. She had a dinner date tonight. With Michael. And he should hope it was going well.

He had stuff to work out anyway.

All right, so he couldn't control Dallas. Dallas was a variable, because he was a person who was going to do what he wanted. Who was going to do what he could to feel in control.

That snapped something into place for Bennett. Dallas was his son. Dallas had done his very best to feel in control of an out-of-control life from the time he was a kid. Right. So he could just assume that his son's actions came from that. That they both wanted to feel like they were in charge, that they both hated feeling helpless. That might put them at odds with each other sometimes, but at least it was something he could understand.

That made him feel better.

As for Kaylee...

This wasn't about Kaylee. It was about his celibacy. It was about the fact that it had been more than a year since he'd had sex, and that was unreasonable.

So there was only one thing to do. He had to get laid.

MICHAEL WAS SO NICE. And he was even trying to be interesting. Maybe he *was* interesting. Maybe there was just something broken, deep down inside of Kaylee.

It was the Bennett cycle. That point of undeniability. When a featherlight kiss shared between her and her best friend was more exciting than the possibility of going to bed with Michael.

They made it through the entire dinner this time, at least. And when Michael had paid he asked if she wanted to take a walk down Main Street.

She agreed.

They exited the restaurant and he took her hand. It felt warm. Pleasant. Nothing else.

It didn't feel like being lit on fire inside, a fire that was probably going to burn out of control and bring on her untimely doom, but nonetheless, an exciting one. No, it didn't feel like that.

It was just fingers entwined with hers. Just skin. It wasn't that extra layer of magic that came from touching Bennett.

But then, there never had been. Not with anyone else.

It was pitiful.

"Kaylee," Michael said. "I get the feeling that you're not with me tonight either."

She stopped, the streetlight overhead casting a golden glow around them. It practically gave the man a halo. She couldn't look at him. Not now. She picked a focal point behind him, the redbrick building they were standing in front of. She focused on the shop window. It was an antiques place with furniture stationed about in casual disarray. Old kitchen appliances she couldn't name. And a taxidermic squirrel looking frozen but feral on a top shelf.

Then she gathered what meager courage she had and looked back at her date. "I'm sorry."

"You're not that into me," he said, treating her to a lopsided smile.

He was cute, dammit. Why couldn't she want to strip

his clothes off him? Why couldn't she want to kiss him, even a little bit?

"I am," she protested, extremely unconvincing.

"I get the feeling that you *want* to be. And when somebody wants something to exist where it doesn't quite as much as you seem to… I have to assume there's another man involved."

That made her feel like crap. It made her feel like a jerk. But there wasn't any way she could deny it. He knew. He saw through her.

"I don't want…" She blinked, her throat getting tight. Tighter. It hadn't stopped aching since earlier today. It was a constant, searing pressure at the base of her neck.

"Is it the other veterinarian you work with? I know I haven't spent a lot of time with you yet, but it seems to me like he's on your mind a lot."

Oh, good grief. Was it so bad that a relative stranger could guess? Or maybe that was why he could. He was coming in from the outside with no assumptions.

"He's my friend," she said. "Like, from junior high. My best friend."

"And you're not in love with him?"

She closed her eyes, wishing she could block everything out. Wishing this wasn't happening. But that damn streetlight glowed even through her eyelids, and she could hear cars, and people leaving the bar across the street and restaurants all around them. It was definitely happening.

"I don't know," she said. "I would like to not be in love with him. Because he's not in love with me."

"I had a nice time tonight," Michael said. "But I'm looking for something serious. And I don't share."

"That's fair," she responded, nodding.

Every man who had ever had her had been sharing

her with Bennett. There was no denying that. Whether she was in love or not.

She liked to think of it as *feelings*. Generic feelings. Because that sounded a whole lot less serious. Less emotionally terminal. Love sounded like…

Well, it sounded like something permanent and final and much harder to deal with.

She felt like someone was pressing on her windpipe.

"I didn't do this on purpose," she said. "I promise. I tried… I tried. Because it's been a lot of years of being hung up on a guy who isn't into me. And I'm not going to just sit around. I have to try to…"

"You're looking for someone to make it go away."

"Yes," she said, relieved that he understood, even if he wasn't entirely happy about it.

"Sitting around and pining after him doesn't work. And we own a practice together. And I care about him. In a way that means not having him in my life is unthinkable. But I just need to find somebody…"

"But if you don't want somebody else, then there's not much you can do with that."

"That can't be," she said. "There can't be just one person for you. Because what the hell are you supposed to do when you're not the one for him?"

"I don't have the answer to that. But I do know that I don't want to be with you in this scenario."

Ouch. That made her feel awful. How many guys had she consigned to that position? Men who had liked her, had cared for her and wanted her, but had never really had her. Because she had been obsessing about someone else. Because someone else held half of her heart.

Hell, more than half.

"Yeah. Okay." She let go of his hand. "I hope I can

still see Clarence. Well, I hope Clarence doesn't get sick, and I don't have to see him. But he's a good dog."

"He is."

"And you're a good man. Maybe too good for me."

"No," he said. "You're just not available. It happens. You're a good vet, and I will definitely bring Clarence back to see you."

"Thank you."

"Just maybe no dinner date."

"Right."

He took a step back and sighed heavily. "If you ever get that guy out of your system, and then it doesn't work out... Maybe then. Good luck to you, Kaylee."

Michael turned and walked away, leaving Kaylee standing there under the light. She felt like she was in one of those old movies where they turn the lamp on and interrogated you. Except she was the one asking the questions.

And she was the one who presumably had some answers somewhere inside of her. No one could answer them for her. She couldn't cut Bennett out.

Getting him out of her system...that sounded like the world's most horrible gamble. Because she could put herself out there and get rejected. Because it could only intensify her feelings. Because he might reject her. Might be the one to walk away when he found out that she wanted him.

Unless he wanted her too.

All she had to do was risk her whole world.

But this was the alternative. This loneliness. Having skin-to-skin contact with a man and having it only be skin.

She didn't know if she could do that anymore either.

She didn't know what she was supposed to do at all.

It was a turning point. But she didn't know for sure which way she was going to turn.

She needed to change something. Change herself. She'd been an idiot thinking she could use another person to fix a problem that was in her. If she didn't sort it out, no other person was ever going to be able to. Her conflicting Bennett issues were on her.

She felt stale. Tired of herself and all of the sameness inside of her she couldn't seem to sort out.

She needed to go ride her horse. Go for a real ride that tested her endurance and got her out of her rut. She needed...needed new clothes and new furniture. Something to change this...feeling in her. To air out her soul.

Maybe then she could find some clarity.

But right now the only thing she knew was that she was going to bed alone tonight. And would be until she sorted all of this out.

CHAPTER ELEVEN

OVER THE NEXT week they fell into a neat, if a bit stilted routine. He and Kaylee hadn't talked about the kiss at all, and he and Dallas hadn't talked about their fight. But they were functioning.

They'd also submitted DNA for a paternity test and were expecting the results any day now.

Not that Bennett was constantly refreshing the on-line portal for the lab.

Every morning, Bennett drove Dallas out to Get Out of Dodge for his day of work, and then he went out and took care of his clients. He hadn't made any steps toward the whole getting laid thing, but he was still figuring all that out. It was the weekend though, and that meant Dallas wasn't going to the ranch. Which also meant that Bennett wasn't working. They spent all of Saturday on the same property but not really near each other. Bennett took care of his animals, riding the horses, and Dallas hung out inside playing the Xbox that Bennett had finally purchased as promised.

Sunday morning, the results posted.

Bennett got them while he was still out in the field, dealing with a pig who had an infected testicle, of all the damn things.

There was a 99.999% chance he was the father.

The only thing that was missing from this moment was Maury Povich and a stiff drink.

He was…relieved. He was damn relieved. He'd known down to his bones that Dallas was his, but the confirmation was…

He didn't have words for it. And he still had a pig to fix.

He managed to make it through the day, managed to make it all the way to the end of Dallas's shift at Get Out of Dodge.

Finally, at dinner, Bennett addressed his son.

"The test results came today," he said when Dallas was taking a bite of steak.

"Uh-huh." He didn't look up.

"I'm your father."

Dallas flicked him a glance. "Wow. Really?"

"Yes."

"No. I meant, you had this chance to make an A+ *Star Wars* reference and you whiffed it. You should start again. Luke, I am your father. Some deep breathing at least. Something. Maybe cut off my hand?"

"Dallas…the test was positive. I'm your dad. Do you have thoughts on that?"

"Not really. I knew you were."

That was the end of that, for Dallas at least. He spent the rest of the evening ignoring Bennett. Which gave Bennett time to think about a few other things that were bothering him.

Kaylee.

And the fact that he had been thinking he wanted to hook up with someone.

The paternity test…that actually just made the stuff with Dallas feel better. He'd believed that Dallas was his son from the beginning. Now they had the legal stuff settled. So he could go to court and get custody.

So it was just the women, or lack of women, in his life that were still unsettled.

He needed to talk to Kaylee.

He went into the living room, where Dallas was sitting on the floor playing Xbox. Pepper was lying on his feet, and Cheddar was sitting next to him, leaning up against him and shedding all over him.

Dallas didn't seem to mind much.

"If I...if I went out tonight would you be all right?"

Dallas laughed and didn't look away from the TV. "I'm fifteen. Also, I've been left alone a lot."

"I know. But I haven't wanted to leave you the last couple of weeks, because this is a new situation."

"You're afraid I'm going to trash your house."

"I'm not."

"A little bit."

"Fine," Bennett said. "The thought crossed my mind at first."

"There is that honesty that you promised me. It warms my heart."

"And," Bennett pressed on, "I was afraid you would run away."

Dallas frowned. "Why would you care if I ran away? Then I wouldn't be your problem."

"Because I want you here. I'm not just keeping you here under sufferance, Dallas. I *want* you here. And if you don't want me to leave because of the test..."

"I'll be fine," Dallas said, pushing that conversation aside. "I don't need you to stay with me. I have the Xbox."

"That's all you did today. At some point, you're going to have to learn to ride."

"Yeah, Jamie said next week she's going to teach me."

Dallas actually sounded like he was looking forward to it.

"Good," Bennett said. "Good."

"Good."

"Great," Bennett added.

"Go. Go out."

"I'm going to," Bennett said.

He paused in the kitchen. He really didn't feel good about leaving Dallas to his own devices. Not completely. Yes, the kid was independent. And yes, Bennett had stayed home alone when he was that age. But it just… he didn't have the parenting thing down even a little bit.

Two weeks with a teenager in his house and it was far from natural to him.

He decided to call his brother. Wyatt picked up on the first ring. "Everything okay?"

He supposed calling his brother after eight was pretty weird. "Yeah. I… I'm headed out for a bit, but I wanted to see if you could swing by and check on Dallas in about an hour. And just be available if he needs someone."

"Going out, huh?"

"Yes. It's been a while." Longer than Wyatt knew.

"Fine with me. But I do have to be up early. Might end up crashing on your couch."

"That's fine. I won't be all night. But I'd…ideally like to be late."

Wyatt made an understanding sound. "Right. Well, I'll be there in an hour or so, so he doesn't feel smothered. But he can text me in the meantime."

"I'll tell him."

Wyatt chuckled. "All right. Good luck tonight, by the way."

"Thanks," Bennett said.

He hung up, then told Dallas about his plans to have

Wyatt stop by. Dallas didn't seem enthused at the idea of being smothered by all the newfound adults in his life, but mostly he was just engrossed in his game. Or at least pretending to be.

"I'll be late," he called out, his hand on the doorknob.

He wasn't used to having to tell anyone where he was going, or when he'd be back.

"Good," Dallas shouted.

"Don't drink my beer."

"You have, like, two beers in the fridge. I couldn't even get a buzz off that. It's boring. And if they're gone it will be because Wyatt drank them. You know he isn't going to let me have them."

"True. I'll see you tomorrow."

His dogs, shaggy little traitors, didn't follow him out. They stayed rooted to Dallas, who they seemed to love already.

That made him smile.

Bennett walked out to the front porch and looked down at the phone in his hand. He wanted to text Kaylee. Hell, he just wanted to see her. Go out with her like they always did. He wanted to talk to her about the paternity test. He wanted to…hug her.

He grabbed his phone and held it in his hand. Busy? She didn't respond.

He stood on the front porch and waited a while. Then he decided there wasn't any harm in swinging by her place before he went to the Saloon. If she wasn't around, or she had a tie on the door or something, he'd leave.

He had never found out how her date went. So maybe she'd be busy. Busy, busy.

And for some reason that made his stomach tighten.

He ignored it, and got into his truck, pulling out of

the driveway and taking the short trip over to Kaylee's place.

She lived in a nice, manicured little house on one acre, with a small paddock for her horse, Flicka, and her fat cat, Albus, who spent his days either on a cat tree in her place, or on a cat tree in the clinic.

She had geraniums in pots on her porch, which he always thought was funny. It surprised him when Kaylee added soft little touches to her home. There seemed to be more and more every time he came over.

He paused and knocked.

The door opened, and he looked up, his heart speeding up for a moment when Kaylee came into view wearing something that was very, very not Kaylee. Well, it was close to her normal clothes in theme, but it showed a hell of a lot more skin.

She was wearing a short denim skirt and a plaid button-up top with a couple of the top buttons undone. Her long red hair was curled slightly at the ends, and she was wearing a little bit of makeup.

"Did I interrupt something?" he asked in a very unsubtle way of trying to get information on how that date had gone.

"No," she said. No other information was forthcoming. "What are you doing here?"

She sounded slightly breathless, and looked a little bit sweaty.

"I texted you. I was headed out to the Saloon and wanted to…see…"

"Oh. Right. Sorry. My phone is across the house and I'm trying to move a hutch."

"A hutch?"

"I went downtown today. I saw a hutch. I bought it. And it's here. And I finally got the damn doors on it but now I can't move it where I want it." She stepped to the side and waved a hand at the massive piece of red furniture standing in the middle of her living room.

"You should have called me," he said.

"I can handle it."

"You're going to throw your back out, Kay," he said, making his way over to the hutch. "Where do you want it?"

"Just right…" She waved her hand toward the back wall. "There in the empty space."

Bennett wrapped his arms around the hutch and started to walk it back toward the wall.

Kaylee let out a frustrated growl. "You make it look so easy!"

"Is that a bad thing?" he asked, getting it backed up against the wall and taking a step back.

"Yes. I don't like asking for help when I can struggle through it. But having struggled for more than an hour, you moving it just like that is obnoxious."

"You help me out all the time," he said, turning to face her, crossing his arms. "Why is it such a bad thing that I came to help you?"

"I just…don't want to be a burden."

"Kaylee," he said, his tone stern. "You're my best friend in the world. You're not a burden to me."

"Well. Whatever."

"Let me take care of you sometimes, Kay. Let me be there for you." That feeling he'd had the other day was back. That urge to comfort her. Touch her.

He would have always been hurt to hear her talk like this, even before he'd known about her parents. But now that he knew that she'd been neglected…

His chest burned looking at her. At that vulnerable expression on her face.

That she felt like a burden because he'd moved some furniture for her.

"Did you get the test results?" she asked suddenly.

"What? How did you…"

"You said you would get them in the next few days. I wondered if you did."

"Yeah," he said.

"And?"

"I'm his dad. But I knew I was."

"But that's a big deal. How do you feel?"

He saw how she was turning the conversation back to him. And well, he knew that part of that was on him. She was his support, and he appreciated that. She also seemed a lot more comfortable with that role than she did with taking anything from him.

"I'm…happy." He was. Strange as that might be. "But I feel like you're changing the subject."

She crossed her arms and looked at him. Defiant. "Of?"

"Of why you didn't call me to help you. Why you're acting weird that I did."

"I just… I told you. My parents didn't pay attention to me. I had to do stuff for myself. Blah blah boring baggage. Who cares? I'm a successful veterinarian and they suck and I've transcended. Why go over it?"

"Because it hurts you."

"So what?"

He reached out and grabbed hold of her arm before he realized what he was doing. And the touch went through him like a shot of bourbon. He let go of her. "You're important to me," he said, his voice rough. "Do you know that?"

"Sure," she said, blinking, moving away from him,

looking down at her carpet, at the dents left behind where the hutch had been before he'd moved it.

"Kay..."

"We don't need to do this, Bennett. I'm fine. Thank you for moving the hutch."

"I'm sorry about how weird things have been," he said, his voice rough. "Do you want to go get a drink?"

"I... Sure." She looked around. "I guess I'm dressed for it."

"Yeah...why are you dressed up?"

"I bought a new skirt. I was trying it on." She looked flustered.

"To assemble a hutch?"

"I mean, that wasn't the plan," she said. "I was going to...and then...whatever. Let's go out."

"Do you want to meet me there in case we leave at separate times?" This was where the whole wanting to meet a woman thing interfered with his desire to hang out with Kaylee.

"Um. Sure," she said, giving him a strange look. "Let me get my stuff and leave some food for Albus."

"I'll meet you over there," he said.

"Okay."

He got in his truck and drove to the Gold Valley Saloon, having an easy time finding parking right in front of the bar. Not typical of a Sunday night, the last gasp of fun before the weekend faded into Monday, but he would take it.

Kaylee wasn't there yet, so he took a seat at a table and surveyed the room. He wasn't worried about anybody thinking Kaylee's presence meant that he was off-limits. Everybody knew that him and Kaylee were only friends.

Kaylee appeared a few minutes later, not looking

much less flustered than she had at her place. She sat across from him, and put her purse on the table.

"You do look nice," he said. "It's a nice skirt."

She squinted at him. "Thank you."

"Is it…for another date with Michael?" She'd dodged his first attempt at figuring out where she was at with Michael.

"Oh. Right," she said, her tone overly casual. "No. I'm not seeing him again."

Well. That was interesting. She'd bought a new skirt. And a new hutch. And her date hadn't gone well.

He could also tell she was irritated by having to make the admission.

"What was wrong with him?" he pressed.

She laughed and shook her head. "What makes you think there was something wrong with him? Maybe it's me."

Without thinking, he reached out and pressed his hand over the top of hers. "There's nothing wrong with you."

She jerked her hand back, her expression unreadable. "I wouldn't be too sure about that."

"Is that why you got a new skirt?" he asked. "To get another date."

She blew out a hard breath. "Bennett. I'm a woman. I don't need an excuse to buy a cute clearance skirt. And yes, I will wear it. I'm wearing it now. So."

"Are you okay?"

"I'm fine." She was clearly not fine. She stood up, grabbing hold of her purse. "What do you want to drink?"

"I'm going to go easy, just get me a beer."

If he was going to find a woman for a potential hookup, he wanted to be sober. Plus, he didn't want to have to strand his truck in town. He was going to have to get back home. So whoever he found, he wasn't going to be able to spend the night with.

Hell, one-night stands weren't really his thing. So, maybe he would find somebody that he could go out with, and have a good time with for a while. That was more his speed. But seeing as it had been so damned long since he'd been with anyone, he was open to just about anything. Kaylee went over to the bar, and he couldn't help but watch her walk all the way over. Watch the way the skirt rode up her legs as she went up on her toes and leaned over while she talked to Laz the bartender for a few moments, before acquiring two bottles of beer and returning to the table.

"So," she said, obviously deciding to let go of the discomfort she had felt with the previous topic. "Did you want to see me about anything in particular? Or talk more about the paternity test?"

"I just wanted to go out," he said.

"Oh."

"I figured we could go out together."

She looked at him sideways and lifted the bottle of beer to her lips. "Okay."

"You know how I told you a little bit about my relationship with Olivia," he said. "That I didn't sleep with her."

Kaylee brought the beer bottle down on the table, her hands rested flat, bracketing it on either side. "Yes."

"It's been over a year. Almost two. And I'm stressed the hell out. I need to get laid."

Kaylee frowned, and then blinked rapidly. "O…kaay."

"I figured you could be my wingman."

All the color drained from her face. "You thought

that I could be your…wingman. Your wingman. Because…I'm basically a dude?"

"No," he said. "I just thought that we could go out and…"

"I thought you wanted to see *me*, Bennett."

He had. He had wanted to see her. Texting her had been the most natural, easy thing. And actually, seeing her in that moment had felt more important than all the sex stuff he'd been thinking about. He missed her. He missed feeling like they were close, and this certainly wasn't helping.

"Of course I want to see you," he said.

"No. You wanted me to hang around and watch you pick up another woman. Because you want to talk to me and bang someone else. I…don't even know what to do with that."

"That wasn't how I was thinking of it."

"Of course it wasn't," she said. "Of course it wasn't how you were thinking of it. But it's how it is."

"What the hell am I supposed to want? You're my best friend. Of course I want to see you. And if you were a man, then I would have called you in this exact circumstance."

"But I'm *not* a man," she said, the words frayed. "*I'm not*. And you know I'm not. You had to move my hutch for me because I have tiny lady arms!"

"You didn't want me to—"

She interrupted him, stamping her foot. "I am wearing a damned denim miniskirt!"

She stared at him hard, her blue eyes glittering. Hell, of course he knew she wasn't a man. Touching her had been screwing with his brain for weeks. The kiss the other day had made it even worse. Yeah, he knew that she wasn't a man.

"I'm trying to get this friendship back on track," he said, the words grinding out of his throat.

This was too much. And it was going too far.

He knew Kaylee wasn't a man. He was so damned aware of it right now it was driving him insane. Or maybe his life was making him insane, and she was a side effect.

She deserved better than that. Better than him losing his grip on reality and morality and doing something that would destroy this relationship they had. The one his life and livelihood was wrapped in so tight.

But Kaylee didn't seem to be interested in backing down. In preserving anything. If it weren't for the overt challenge in her eyes, he would have thought she had no idea what she was tempting. No idea what his body felt like she was suggesting.

"What's on track?" she asked. "The two of us looking at each other until it feels so weird one of us has to look away? Me...kissing you because you look sad and I want to fix it?"

"No. None of that is on track and you know it."

Kaylee leaned back in her chair and tossed her hair back, the level of faux bravado she was trying to project evidenced in the pronounced set of her jaw, at odds with the vulnerable glitter in her eyes.

"I don't want you to leave with another woman," she said, her words coming out far too raw for his liking. "I want you to leave with me."

CHAPTER TWELVE

WHAT HAD SHE DONE? She was screwing this up. She had agreed to come out tonight with the full intention of repairing the crack in their relationship. And instead, she had decided to bust it wide-open.

Or she was a lying liar who was lying to herself.

She'd had kind of a mini-breakdown starting with that disastrous Michael date and continuing into today. She could admit that.

She'd gotten up early and taken Flicka up into the hills and ridden until she'd been ready to collapse from hunger, and hadn't had a single revelation. But at least she'd gone out. Carved out the time to be in nature and to do something she loved.

She'd been starving and restless and had decided to go out to get food.

She'd seen the red hutch at a furniture place in town and had decided she needed it, because her house felt wrong. Or really, her life felt wrong. But she'd made herself believe a red hutch could fix it.

Then she'd bought the miniskirt. Which looked borderline obscene on her, because her legs were endless—her one overtly sexy feature—and it had made her feel good about herself. So she'd gotten it.

Then she'd gotten home and put it on, and had started doing herself up a little. She had put on damned lipgloss. She was wearing a push-up bra, for all the good it did with her teacup boobs.

Then the hutch had arrived and they'd put it in her living room without doors and she'd just gone straight into trying to fix it, only she hadn't been able to.

Then Bennett had shown up. A white knight without his steed.

It had all become shockingly clear in the moment. She was avoiding the fact that things with him were at critical mass. That it wasn't her house that was wrong, it was her heart. And the missing space wasn't red hutch-shaped.

It was Bennett-shaped.

And the miniskirt was not so another random man would notice her.

She'd wanted to see if she could look sexy enough *for him.*

What Michael had said to her kept resonating inside of her. That comment about her getting Bennett out of her system.

It had sparked the desire to get serious about a change that had to start with her—not another man. And she'd been feeling…good. Spontaneous and different and good. But Bennett had shown up. He always would. He would always be there and this feeling wasn't something she could displace anymore.

Everything in her brain was currently scrambled. But she knew two things. That she could not watch Bennett walk out the door with another woman. That she couldn't go on the way things had been. And that those two things scared her far more than whatever other consequences awaited her.

Because she had done this for years. She had watched

him find someone else. She had tried to find somebody herself so that she wouldn't be alone.

She had followed him around when he had gone to pick Olivia up from work. Had been the third wheel when they'd gone out to bars. Had watched the two of them play darts. She had even been there when they had broken up. The emotional support in every way for this man all while wanting him with everything inside of her.

She had been convinced, all that time that Olivia had been getting the one thing that Kaylee wanted most. But she hadn't.

And now, Bennett felt like that dry spell was catching up with him. Well, she felt far too invested in that dry spell. Because when she had assumed he'd been sleeping with Olivia, she had been tortured. And her own bed had been very, very empty.

She'd decided years ago that burying her feelings would be best. But if the past few months had taught her anything it was that her life *wasn't best* right now. It wasn't going to correct itself, and it wasn't going to be fixed with dates, avoidance or red hutches.

"I'm in about the same dry spell," she said. "It's been more than a couple of years for me."

She tried to brazen it out. Tried not to betray the fact that this was something she had thought about for years. Something she had wanted for years.

It was easier if he just thought this was some kind of matter-of-fact offer to help a friend out with something.

Like, she was asking him to loan her a cup of flour. Except she wanted him to lend her his penis.

That was how she wanted to present it. Anything else was…

You're in love with him, aren't you?

She gritted her teeth and blotted out the echo of Michael's words.

She didn't want to be in love with Bennett. Because he wasn't in love with her. But on the other side of this would be something new she could work with. And that was the best hope she'd had for a while.

"What the hell, Kaylee?"

"You're not opposed to it," she said, hoping that she wasn't deluding herself. "If you hadn't ever thought about it then the whole kiss thing... It wouldn't have made things weird. It made things weird, because it made us both think about it."

"Kaylee..."

"Leave with me," she repeated, the words firm. Undeniable. There was no pretending she'd meant something else. No pretending he'd misunderstood. They both knew what she'd said.

They both knew what she wanted.

Her heart thundered erratically, her throat scraped raw. And she just waited. Waited for him to respond. Waited for that hard expression of his to shift. For him to turn away. Lean closer. Something.

It seemed like forever.

And then, just like that, it was all lightning again. A flash of something in his eyes. *Want*. Just for a moment she could see it. Just for a moment it was clear.

"Let's get out of here," he said, flinging a couple dollar bills on the table and grabbing hold of her arm, dragging her toward the exit of the saloon.

"I didn't say I was ready to go," she said, panic suddenly rising up to strangle her.

"We need to talk," he bit out.

He propelled her forward until they were outside,

on the street in front of the saloon. "Get in my truck," he said.

That bossy, alpha tone should have made her mad, but instead, it set off some chain reaction through her body. Made her squeeze her thighs together.

"Why can't we talk in there?"

"Because I cannot have a conversation about possibly having sex with my best friend in a room full of people."

"I don't want to have a conversation. I thought I made that perfectly clear."

"Get in the truck."

"I drove myself," she protested feebly.

"I'm driving you home," he said.

There was something about the way that he held his jaw, granite and uncompromising, that made her stop arguing.

They got in the truck, and Bennett turned the engine over. Her heart was pounding hard, her stomach queasy. She had made it completely clear what she wanted. He wanted it too. She saw it in his eyes. He might be angry. He might want to talk them both out of it. But she had seen the truth.

They started to drive out of town, leaving the main street, and all the buildings behind them. Headed into the darkness, where there were no streetlights. Where there was nothing but trees to stand witness.

It all flooded up inside her then. Fear. Need. Desire. She was about to climb out of her skin, or out of her clothes and onto him. It was crazy. But she'd said the words and there was no going back. She didn't even want to try.

"Pull over," she said.

"What?"

"I don't want to talk."

"We *need* to talk," he said.

"No," she said. "We don't. We've spent the last seventeen years talking, Bennett. I don't want to talk anymore. That's not what tonight is about." She took a deep breath and curled her hands into fists, her nails digging into her palms. "You said you wanted to take care of me. Well…this is how you can take care of me."

He kept driving for a moment, and then they came to one of the many dirt roads that wound around up into the mountains. He turned suddenly sharply. And said nothing as he drove on, the gravel crunching beneath the truck tires. He pulled off at the first turn out, well off the main road. Isolated.

He turned the key. She sat for a moment, staring straight out the windshield, listening to the residual pop and sizzle of the engine as the truck began to cool down.

Then she turned toward him, pressed her fingertips against his cheek. She didn't move closer. Didn't undo her seat belt. She just…touched him.

She was startled when his iron grip captured her wrist, pulled her closer, the shoulder strap on her seat belt biting into her collarbone.

"Are you just going to tease me?" There was something tortured in his voice. Something deep and intense she had never heard before. At least, never directed at her.

"N-no."

"That seems like a tease, Kaylee. Seems like barely more than talking."

She wished that she could see his face. But it was too dark. The trees rose up tall, blocking the light from the moon. She could make out the stars, but just barely. Nothing more than gold dust in the sky.

"If you're going to start it," he said. "We might as well finish it."

He was right. It was acknowledged. That this electric, thick air that had been growing between them recently was attraction. That she wanted him. The damage was done at that point. More than done.

It was the thing she'd always been afraid of. Making a change that couldn't be taken back.

But she was shaking. She didn't know if she could do it. Didn't know if she could take this step.

She had tried. She had tried to be good for so long. Had tried to keep this relationship in its own category. Friendship. Hell, he was almost family. At least, that was what she had told herself. And the attraction stuff... Understandable. Because he was a handsome man and she was just a woman, after all. Because she liked him so much, and all that liking was a hairbreadth away from being sexual anyway with men and women. At least, as long as there was any seed of attraction there.

She had told herself he didn't feel it. But now she knew he did. Even if it was recent on his end, the fact that he did feel it now changed everything.

The fact that they were here changed everything already.

Still, she was scared. She couldn't move. Couldn't bring herself to close the distance between them when she had done it already in the past few days. When she had been the one to commit all the unpardonable sins. The one who had kissed him. The one who'd said he could break his celibacy with her.

It had all been her. She couldn't bring herself to be the instigator again.

But then, she didn't have to be. Because he was

the one who closed that distance. He was the one who pressed his mouth to hers.

The sound he made when their lips touched wasn't one of pleasure. It was one of pain.

Like he was a man enduring the worst kind of torture, rather than a man kissing a woman in a darkened truck.

For a moment it was like the kiss they had shared at the ranch. Closemouthed. Simple.

Still.

But then, it was like something broke between them. Whether it was him or her, she didn't know. But suddenly she found herself flush up against him, her breasts pressed against his chest, his hand on the back of her head, holding her hard against him. She, for her part, was clinging to his shoulders, and they both angled in, parting their lips. When his tongue touched hers it was more than a lightning strike. It was one that touched down to earth and lit the ground on fire. Left it scorched. Left everything singed in its wake.

She was finally tasting him. Really tasting him. She moved her hands around from his shoulders, down to the front of his chest. To those muscles that she had admired for so long, but never touched like this. She was greedy, desperate suddenly. Because this was the chance. Her opportunity to experience all of these fantasies. And she felt like it was too much. Like there were too many things to want, and not enough time to have them. Maybe not enough time in the whole of her life.

Yes, she had wanted to kiss him for years. But also, she had wanted to touch him. She needed him. She needed him so badly. Under her palms, against her skin. Every inch of his body.

He had been forbidden for so long. *This* had been

forbidden for so long. But it was happening now. She couldn't get enough of it.

She'd had hints of it over the years. The familiarity of his scent, brushes of his fingertips against hers. Friendly hugs.

But not this feast. This all-consuming sense of being surrounded by him. The smell of his skin all encompassing, filling her lungs. She slipped her hands up from his chest, loath to stop touching those incredible muscles, but she needed his skin.

She dragged her fingertips over his face, feeling that glorious stubble beneath her palms as she cupped him. It was so masculine. So innately sexual because it was so very different from her.

Except none of the other men she had kissed had impacted her this way. She had never once thought of stubble as being intimate, borderline filthy. But with him it felt like it. Because she had never been allowed to touch him like this, and now she was. So it made the smallest of things, things that would have been innocuous with any other man, seem so deep and raw and wrong. So wonderful and intense.

Between her thighs, a pulse beat steady and hard, that ache stretching from deep inside her core. She was ready for him now. If he unfastened his jeans, and pushed her skirt up he could be inside of her in seconds. Just that very thought had her on the edge. Had her ready to explode.

She had *never* felt like this when kissing a man. She had felt less during sex.

His hands were stationary, holding her still as he tasted her, as he swept his tongue along her lower lip, sending a sharp shock through her body, an electrical jolt that made her internal muscles pulse.

She was ready to come. Just from this. From a kiss. He hadn't even touched her anywhere but her head, and she was ready.

"I need..." She moved her hands from his face, down to the hem of his T-shirt, plucking at it desperately. "More."

He swore and drew away from her. "I have blankets in the back."

It took her a while to register what that might mean, but then he moved away from her, and she protested, feeling muddled and hypersensitized.

"Bennett, don't stop." She couldn't disguise the needy thread in her voice. She didn't even want to.

"Can't," he bit out.

He reached behind the bench seat and grabbed hold of a folded-up flannel blanket, then got out of truck.

She just sat there for a moment, unsure of what she was supposed to do. Her brain wasn't working right. Her thoughts were thick and strange, and she couldn't figure out what he was doing. Then, the passenger-side door opened, and he was there, one hand braced on the open door, the other pressed against the frame. Filling the space.

She unbuckled, then turned toward him, her knees hanging outside the truck. And he wrapped his arms around her again, pulling her up against him. This time, he settled between her legs, the kiss deep and intense. And she could feel him. Hard and insistent between her legs. Pressed up against that place where she was so needy for him.

She saw stars.

She tilted her pelvis forward, letting her head fall back as he kissed her neck, as he rocked his hips up against her. Unconsciously, she wrapped her legs around his waist. Her skirt slid up her thighs, baring her legs entirely. She shifted, capturing his mouth again. He rolled his hips forward, the seam on his jeans biting through the flimsy fabric on her panties.

Suddenly, she saw the merit of skirts. It would be so easy. So easy for him to be inside of her.

Bennett. Inside of her.

She shivered. A full-body response to this madness that was threatening to consume her completely.

Then, he wrapped his arms around her and lifted her up out of the truck. The open door left the light on, casting a very faint glow into the bed of the truck. And she could see what he had been talking about. Blankets. There had apparently been some in the bed already, and they were spread out now, the one from the inside of the truck over the top of them.

He didn't want to stop.

He lifted her up over the tailgate, depositing her on the makeshift bed. He lifted her like she was nothing. He made her feel small, feminine. Almost laughable for a woman who was nearly six feet tall and made entirely of lean muscle with very little in the way of hourglass curves.

But he made her feel beautiful. Cherished.

And that ache in her throat was back. She needed it to go away. An ache between her legs was one thing, because she knew how he could fix that.

It was all the rest. The other feelings that he gave her…that she didn't know what to do with.

But she didn't have to think about it. She couldn't think about it. Because then Bennett joined her in the back of the truck, on his knees down by her feet. He grabbed hold of the hem of his T-shirt and ripped it up over his head.

She couldn't see him well, but what she could see...

The light from the cab of the truck threw his muscles into relief. The shadows showing the dips and hollows on that sculpted body.

She'd seen Bennett without his shirt before. And it was always a whole thing.

Always fuel for her fantasies late at night when she couldn't sleep. When she was lonely and desperate for some kind of release, and could picture only one man.

It was always followed by shame. Shame and feeling weird about him the next day when she saw him.

Because she had always felt like it was a violation of some kind. That his body wasn't there for her.

But now it was. Right now, it was.

She scrambled up onto her knees, moving closer to him. Then she pressed her palm flat against his bare chest.

"Bennett," she whispered, the word like a prayer.

Finally, she was touching him. Bennett. His body. Naked under hands.

She rocked her hips forward, squeezing her thighs together slightly, trying to do something to ease the intensity of the need between them.

Then she swallowed hard, her throat like the inside of a pincushion. She let her fingertips drip down across his nipple, and he sucked in a sharp breath. Then down farther to his abs, to the waistband of his jeans.

He was beautiful. Built tough and strong, the results of years of hard work. The evidence that he was rancher stock down to his bones. One of the few men in the world tough enough to stand up to her.

To make her feel delicate.

Like she could be the girl in that lace bedroom she'd

wanted as a kid. Like she could wear sky-high heels and still be feminine.

Not helpless or powerless. Not a bad feeling at all. It was…it was intensely heady and sexual. To feel like he could overpower her easily. To be so conscious of another person's strength. To have it underneath her fingertips like this, barely leashed and there for her pleasure.

She didn't think she had it in her to say those words. To share like that. But she could show him. With her body. Show him what he made her feel.

"Your turn, Kay," he said, his words tortured, falling back on her nickname from high school. Which just made it seem all the more real.

He was the only person who called her that ever. Which made her all the more aware that this could only be him.

But then, the intensity of the arousal thrumming through her body made certain that she was aware of that too. The fact that she was sitting on a knife's edge, so close to release it was almost embarrassing.

She had never come with a man before. She just could never get herself all the way into it. Could never stop feeling self-conscious. About where to put her hands, about whether or not he was enjoying it. About whether or not she was enjoying it enough. But she had always told herself it was nice to be close to someone. And that she would never be able to have a real relationship if they didn't have physical intimacy.

But now she knew what utter bullcrap that was.

She had tried so hard to make it happen with the small number of other men she'd gone to bed with. And with Bennett…she didn't have to try at all.

She was still up on her knees, frozen, her palm

pressed flat to his stomach. And then his warm, rough hands were brushing against the tender skin on her stomach as he began to lift her shirt up over her head. She lifted her arms, allowed him to remove her top.

He swore, slowly dragging the edge of his thumb across that place where her bra met her skin. And she moaned. She couldn't hold it back. Didn't even want to.

"Let me see," he said, the word tortured.

With shaking fingers, she reached behind her and unhooked that push-up bra, the push-up bra she was regretting now, because she felt like it was promising him things that she couldn't deliver.

She would have said something, warned him, but her tongue wasn't working. She pulled it off and threw it down into the bed of the truck. The cold night air and her arousal making her nipples impossibly tight.

"Kaylee," he said, her name reverent on his lips as he pressed his palms against her breasts, teasing her nipples.

She had to brace herself, holding on to the side of the truck bed, to keep herself from falling back as pleasure coursed through her, with each pass of his calloused thumbs over her sensitized body.

He moved his hands down to her waist, his large hands nearly spanning her slim midsection, then he moved them down farther tracing a line beneath her belly button, that point of contact so strangely intimate somehow. Because he was her friend. Because he had never, ever touched her like this before.

It was weird to think she had known him for seventeen years, had even fantasized about him, but that she didn't really know him. Not really.

Because there was this. All this, that she had never really witnessed before.

The expression in his eyes when he was turned on, the way that he held himself in check, even though she could sense that he wanted to push her down onto the blankets and devour her completely.

She was ready for that. But she also didn't want it to end. Wanted it to go on forever. She was caught and held firmly between those two desires. And so, she just let him continue the slow exploration. Let him undo the snap on her skirt, draw down the zipper and slowly push the denim down her thighs, leaving her in nothing but a pair of lace panties.

"Well, hell," he breathed.

"What?"

"I did not take you for a lace panties kind of girl, Kaylee Capshaw."

Pleasure bloomed over her skin. She didn't know why, but it made her smile. Maybe it was just the idea that Bennett had an opinion on what kind of panties she might wear.

"What kind of panties did you think I wore, Bennett?"

His fingers edged down slightly lower, flirting with the waistband on their current topic of conversation.

"Cotton." The word sounded like it had scraped all along his throat on the way out.

"Sometimes I wear cotton."

"But tonight you wore lace." He looked up at her, his eyes meeting hers. "Did you wear them for me?"

She had. All of this was for him. She could pretend that it hadn't been. That she hadn't been imagining this moment. That she hadn't been committed to trying this.

But she would be lying.

The moment she'd picked that miniskirt up in the store today, she had a feeling she'd been thinking of this.

"Of course it's for you," she whispered, barely able to force the words out.

He growled, the sound so unfamiliar coming from this man she had known all of her life that it made her heart stutter.

He was dangerous, her Bennett. So much more intense, more masculine, than she had even allowed herself to see.

But then, this was the essence of what made him a man. And of what made her a woman. This need. This desire between them.

The way that his body was hard and only got harder, that hers was soft in so many ways, and prepared itself to yield to all that strength.

They were business partners. They were friends. Equals in their daily life.

Having that shift, rip, so profoundly was heady and intense and terrifying all at once. She wanted more of it, as much as she wanted to hide from it.

But she couldn't hide from it.

He pushed his hand down farther, his fingertip grazing her center. It was like the strike of a match. She couldn't hold back the sound of pleasure that built in her throat and escaped on a whimper.

He breathed a curse as he delved deeper and found her slick and hot for him.

"Yes," she whispered, arching her hips against him, meeting each of his movements with one of her own.

"Kiss me," she whimpered. He wrapped his arm around her, drew her bare breasts up against his chest, holding her tight and forcing her lips apart, thrusting his tongue in deep, mirroring the rhythm of his finger. Then he pressed it between her slick folds, rubbing her slowly, methodically. Before pushing inside of her completely.

She broke. And he swallowed her cry of pleasure as her internal muscles pulsed around his fingers, as she gave in to the deepest, most intense orgasm she had ever had in her entire life. The only one she had ever had in front of another person.

And it was Bennett. Bennett was the one who had seen it. Bennett was the one who had caused it.

It was Bennett who had been the first one to taste that pleasure on her lips, to feel her lose her control.

Of course it was Bennett. It was always going to be Bennett.

She could try to care about other people. She could try to want them.

But it had always only ever been him.

She drew in a shaky breath, blinking back an onslaught of tears, trying her best to hold it together when she had already fallen apart. Then, he slipped her panties down her legs, and on autopilot she let him pull them off completely as she shifted so she was sitting on her bottom.

She scooted forward, her legs parted, Bennett kneeling up between them. Then, she placed her hands on his belt, slowly working it through the loops of his jeans, undoing the button and drawing his zipper down slowly. His breath hissed through his teeth as her knuckles brushed up against his hardness.

She was going to see Bennett's naked penis.

She was about to hold it in her hands.

She could barely handle that. But then, he had just had his fingers inside of her when she'd come. So, this seemed fair enough.

She wanted it. So desperately. But she was afraid of it too.

With shaking fingers, she pushed his jeans down,

and he helped her get them off him. And then she scooted closer, pressed a kiss to his taut stomach, just above the waistband of his underwear.

"Kaylee," he said, grabbing hold of her chin and tilted her face up. "You don't have to…"

And that right there confirmed exactly what she was going to do next. She moved her hand to the front of his underwear, black and tight and sexy as hell. Then she tested the length of him, the thickness, through that fabric.

He was definitely a lot more man than she'd ever had before. It felt like her reward. Her just deserts for waiting so long for him. That he would be the most impressive. That he would be the sexiest damned man she had ever touched.

In her opinion, saying size didn't matter was a lot like saying one scoop of ice cream was just as good as two. You might only need one, but you always wanted two.

Bennett was two scoops and then some.

Slowly, she pulled his underwear down, leaving them in the middle of his thighs as she turned her focus to his body. She pressed her palms against his legs and leaned in, pausing for a moment to take in the musky, masculine scent of him. She shivered, all the way to her core. She would have said there was no way she could have another orgasm, not yet. But oh, she was about to. Just from looking at him. Just from being this close.

The light from the truck was weak, and it didn't allow her to see him as much she wanted. She wrapped her fingers around that hard, hot length and she groaned.

"Wow," she said, testing his length, his strength, imagining that thick, glorious arousal surging inside of her. But first. First there was something she needed to do.

She leaned in, flicking her tongue across the swollen head of him, parting her lips and taking him in slowly, inch by inch.

Bennett swore, reaching up to grip her hair, holding himself steady, using her as his anchor. She didn't mind. She wanted to be his anchor.

His everything.

He bucked his hips, pushing himself deeper into her mouth, groaning as he did. She was afraid that he would be tentative, that because he had said she didn't have to, he would feel uncomfortable with it. But clearly, whatever reservations he'd had were long gone now.

And she was glad. She didn't want him to hold back. This was her moment. The culmination of years of fantasies. She didn't want restraint. She didn't want him to be careful. If they were going to burn everything down, if they were going to blow it all up, then it needed to be completely destroyed. There was no point going halfway. At the point when they had acknowledged that they both wanted this, that they wanted each other, it had already been too late.

Hell was hell. Whether you were standing at the door or deep in the pit of it.

When it came to this, there was only all the way.

Maybe it was the way through. Or maybe not. But right now it didn't matter.

She worked his glorious body in and out of her mouth, and he moved his hips along with her. The taste of him, the strength, all of it, it made it a bigger turn-on for her than it might even be for him. Because she was sure that Bennett Dodge had not ever fantasized about her giving him a blow job. But she had certainly fantasized about giving him one.

Bennett. Her Bennett. Finally. Under her hands, in her mouth. It was all she had wanted. All she needed.

"Kaylee," he gasped. "I can't… I can't last."

She could only make a muffled sound.

And then he pulled himself away from her.

"Bennett," she breathed, "it's okay."

"It's not," he rasped, reaching for his jeans and grabbing his wallet. He had a condom, which didn't really surprise her, considering which particular conversation had led them here. She'd had one too, but hers was still in the cab of the truck, so she was happy to let him take the wheel on this. "It's really not okay."

He discarded his underwear, and slowly tore open the packet, taking out the latex and rolling it over his length.

Suddenly, it all became very real. And suddenly, it became very scary.

Because it was all fine and good to think of touching as being the same as wanting. But actually contending with having him inside of her. With being with him like this…it was different. It was more.

She wanted it. But it terrified her. She was not a casual sex kind of girl and she hadn't been with very many people. Always after careful consideration. After they had spent a long time dating.

But actually, if this were casual sex, it would've been less scary. It wasn't casual sex. It was sex with Bennett. And that was the opposite of casual. That was something a hell of a lot more terrifying.

But then on a groan, he kissed her again. So deep and dirty and all-consuming that it made her forget her moment of trepidation. She pushed her panties down her legs, desperate to be completely bare up against him. And then she was. That hot erection burning against her stomach, his chest hair rough against her breasts.

His thighs pressed against hers, one large hand moving down to cup her butt. He squeezed her tight, then pushed his fingers between her legs from behind, stroking her slick channel.

Then he pushed her down, flat on her back, settling between her legs. She didn't want to stop, not anymore. She angled her hips up, offering herself to him as he positioned the blunt head of his arousal up against her. He wrapped his hand around himself, pushing his length through her folds once, twice, again, sending sparks raining down on her before he brought himself against her entrance again.

He pushed forward a fraction of an inch, and she bit her lip to keep from crying out. To keep from crying. As Bennett, her best friend, filled her completely.

She pressed her forehead against his shoulder, trying to hold back the onslaught of emotion that was threatening to crash over her. She didn't want that. She just wanted this. She just wanted to feel. Feel all that hardness stretching her, feel him pulsing inside of her. That was what she wanted. To feel the weight of his body pressed down on hers, his heart beating against her chest.

His breath was hot on her neck, his hands roaming down her back, moving down beneath her ass as he lifted her up and thrust hard into her. He let out a short, fractured sound that hollowed out her stomach, made her feel like she was on the edge again.

She knew his voice. But not like this. She knew his touch, but not like this. She knew him. He had been part of her life for so many years. They had gone to school together. They worked together. They drank together. He had been in her home, in her world, for all of this time, but he had never been inside of her.

It was almost too much. Too real. And she was thankful for the pleasure that began to blot out reality. That made the stars overhead blur and made everything feel just a little bit fuzzy.

He shifted, gripping her hips, jerking her down against him as he thrust forward, the sound of skin meeting skin the only sound in the silence of the forest. Except when he said her name. Short, sharp, pained. But he knew that it was her. He wasn't pretending it wasn't.

She wrapped her legs around his narrow hips, pressing one hand against his chest, the other gripping his shoulder as she rocked against him, desperate for more. Desperate for everything.

This wasn't like any sex she had ever had. It wasn't clumsy or tentative. It wasn't two people stumbling through, trying to figure out what the other wanted.

It was selfish. Harsh and hard. In that way it was perfect. Because they were both taking exactly what they wanted. She was taking pleasure in his body, and he was taking it in hers. And that...that brought all the satisfaction she could ask for.

She wasn't worried about whether or not he wanted it. Whether or not he enjoyed it. She knew he did. It was in the frantic way he moved, in the way he said her name, the way he groaned against her neck, his breath hot on her skin.

She was unraveling again. Bit by bit, beneath his touch. With him all around her, filling her, destroying her. Making her new.

She didn't know what would be left of them when it was over. She didn't know if they would be able to come back from this. To piece themselves together, piece their friendship together. But right now there was this.

It was everything.

A moment in time that so many of her feelings, so many of her desires, so many of her long-held dreams had been leading to. That no matter what happened in the end she couldn't regret it. Because for her this wasn't a spur-of-the-moment thing. For her this had nothing to do with a dry spell or simply being lonely. For her, this was about Bennett.

Whatever it was about to him, she knew what it was to her.

And it mattered enough that it could be everything. For her. For now.

He gripped her thighs, drawing her knees up farther, positioning her so that he went deeper. Impossibly. Beautifully. She gasped, her orgasm breaking over her suddenly, like a sneaker wave on the beach. She had spent her whole life working so hard to find release, she hadn't known it could be so easy. But then, with him it had always been just beneath the surface. With him, of course it was easy. Because it had almost been harder to hold it back.

He followed her closely, his harsh groan loud in her ear as he froze against her, pulsing deep inside of her.

And then it was over. He pressed his forehead against hers, sharing the same breath. He kissed her. And then he pulled away.

CHAPTER THIRTEEN

BENNETT COULDN'T BREATHE. His chest was burning like he had just driven a herd of cattle across a field on foot and Kaylee was lying there in the back of his truck, completely naked, her small, perfect breasts rising and falling with her own labored breathing. He couldn't make out much detail on her bare body, just the vague impression of pale skin, long slender limbs and slight curves in the mixture of white moonlight and the yellow glow coming from the truck.

But even if it wasn't sharp and clear, the fact remained that he was looking at his best friend's naked body. His best friend, who he had just had sex with.

Dammit.

Except, as he knelt there in the truck, he felt...not a whole lot of regret, even if he should. He felt good. He felt better than he had in a long time. Yes, he was a man, so he was pretty basic, but he hadn't realized he was quite that basic. That even with his life flung into turmoil, even with this adding a strange new dimension to his most important nonfamilial relationship, he felt good.

Because he'd just had an orgasm.

One that was so strong, so powerful it was still ringing in his head like he'd gone shooting without ear protection.

"You're going to get cold," he said, his voice rough.

He didn't know why that was the first thing that came to mind. Except she was so slim, so vulnerable-looking. He had a feeling the night air would have her shivering in just a few minutes. Of all the things to be concerned about, that was a strange one.

"I'm not cold," she mumbled, but she mobilized, beginning to collect her clothing, which was strewed around the bed of the truck.

He imagined that he should do the same. He was trying to get his brain functioning again. His jeans and underwear hadn't gone far. He found them and pulled them on. His T-shirt was another matter. He hunted around for that for a while, and finally discovered it buried in the blankets.

He shrugged it over his head and by the time he was finished, Kaylee was completely dressed, wiggling herself out of the truck and back onto the ground. He followed suit, but by the time his boots hit the gravel Kaylee was already in the truck, the door closed firmly behind her.

He took a deep breath, looking around at the darkened forest behind the truck. He had a brief thought that life might be simpler if he just walked into it and kept on walking.

But he couldn't do that. He had a business with ranchers and animals that depended on him. There was a teenager waiting for him at home. His teenager. His son.

And probably, Kaylee wouldn't appreciate him disappearing into the darkness either.

If he felt strange, she must feel even stranger. Hell, strange was an understatement. He felt like he was about to crawl out of his skin.

Kaylee was pretty. He'd known that for a long time.

He wasn't blind. And yes, recently, there had been a sexual edge to that acknowledgment. But this was different than a sexual edge. This had been an explosion. It had blown what he had thought about their relationship sky-high. It had to be the same for her too.

They had never thought of each other that way. Not really. There was a difference between acknowledging the other was an attractive person that maybe somebody else would enjoy having sex with, and actually having sex with each other.

He took a deep breath, gave one last longing look to the inviting, dark forest and got into the driver's side of the truck. His keys were still in the ignition.

He didn't know what to say, so he didn't say anything as he started up the engine and began to drive back down the mountain.

"You can just take me back to my truck," Kaylee said.

"Are you sure? I don't mind driving you home." It seemed wrong to have sex with a woman in the back of his truck and not even drive her home.

He felt weird about leaving her at all, but he had to. He couldn't go back to her place. And he couldn't have her spend the night at his. His stomach twisted, sharp and hard at the thought. Kaylee spending the night. All night in bed together.

That made him hard again in an instant and he shifted, feeling like a jerk. Because he hadn't thought of one useful thing to say and he was sitting next to her getting aroused all over again.

No. He wasn't going to spend all night in bed with her. Even if circumstances permitted…

This was a one-off kind of thing. Like Kaylee had said, they had both been celibate for a long time. Not really by choice, just by circumstance. And they had both needed to scratch the itch. They had scratched it good, but the damn thing about itches was that scratching just made them itch more. Which was about where he was at the moment.

And it was a pretty good indicator that he was going to have to stop.

Let it be a thing that happened once under the cover of darkness with no witnesses except maybe one perverted owl in a tree.

That was the beauty of the compromised lighting situation. He had seen Kaylee naked. But he hadn't *really* seen her naked. It had been an impressionistic nude. Rather than how it might have been if the lights were on, harsh and bright. If he had gotten a good look at all that skin, at the exact shape of her breasts, the color of her nipples, the recovery would be a lot more difficult. The comedown would be a lot harder.

If he knew exactly what color that thatch of curls between her legs was, if he knew how pink she was there…yeah. He couldn't be thinking that every time he went into work in the morning. Couldn't be obsessing about it whenever they had a beer.

He *needed* her. All of her. Not just her body.

She had always been there for him. She had been there for him tonight in a more profound way than usual, but it was kind of an extension of their friendship in many ways. Giving each other what they needed.

Well, that's bullshit and even you know it.

Whatever. He was sticking with bullshit for now. It was that or open up the door and jump out of the moving vehicle. Tuck and roll and hope for the best.

"I'm sure," she said. He sneaked a glance over at her and saw that she was looking out the window, gripping on to the shoulder strap of her seat belt like it was a lifeline. Like maybe it was the only thing keeping *her* from jumping out of the truck.

It didn't surprise him at all that they were on the same page. That was how they worked.

He hesitated. "Thank you," he said finally.

"Thank you?" Her voice sounded hollow.

"Yes. I really… It's been a hell of a couple weeks. It's been a hell of a few months. And I…I needed that."

"You needed that," she echoed.

"Yeah."

"Me too." But there was something strange in her voice, an edge that he couldn't quite place. He didn't know what he had done wrong, but he had a feeling he'd done something wrong.

Hell if he knew *what*.

Maybe the sex?

But no. She'd wanted it. And she'd been into it. Way into it. She'd gotten off, same as him. So it couldn't be that.

"Kaylee…"

"It's fine," she said. "Just weird."

Thank God she'd said it. "*Really* fucking weird," he acknowledged.

"Yeah," she said, forcing a laugh out.

They pulled back into town. The saloon was still open, packed with people, even more than when they had left an hour or two earlier. Just a couple of hours to shift the foundation of his life. That was the theme recently.

His girlfriend breaking up with him during a Christmas celebration on a crowded street, effectively blowing up the future he'd had planned. A son he didn't know he had showing up on his front porch, absolutely destroying any last remaining illusions he'd had that he could control the world or his life.

Getting naked with his best friend.

Yeah. The last few months were just one life-changing moment after another.

This didn't *have* to be one, though. Maybe.

It was just him and Kaylee. And they were stronger than anything. Solid. Close enough to weather this, that was for damn sure.

"I'm over here," she said softly, pointing a block up.

"I'll see you later," he said.

"Yeah," she agreed.

She bailed out of the truck quickly, stumbling a little bit when her feet hit the sidewalk. "Bye," she said.

Then she turned away from him and walked back toward her own truck. He watched her until she got in, until she started the vehicle and drove away.

And then he just sat there for a moment, a hard knot building in his chest, growing, expanding.

No. This was going to be okay. It had to be.

He headed back out toward his house and was relieved to see that his brother's truck was still in the driveway.

He sighed heavily and got out of his own truck, crossing the gravel drive and making his way up the steps. Wyatt opened the door before Bennett's hand touched the doorknob.

"Hey," Wyatt said.

"How is Dallas?"

"He went to his room about a half an hour ago. Probably not sleeping. Back in the Dark Ages we would have had porn under the mattress. I hear tell you can look at porn on smartphones nowadays and I imagine he has one…"

Bennett snorted. "You hear tell? Like you don't know where to get porn."

Wyatt lifted a shoulder. "It does give incentive to adapt to new technology, that's for sure."

"Was he…"

He didn't even really know what to ask. Wyatt jerked his head toward the inside of the house, and Bennett followed him in. Then Wyatt opened up the fridge and pulled a couple of beers out.

"He was fine," Wyatt said. "I mean, I don't have any experience with kids, so honestly, thank God your surprise one is past puberty. Makes them a hell of a lot easier in many ways. If you had randomly ended up with a toddler, I would have been off the babysitting list."

"He was fine, though?"

"He played on the Nintendo thing." Wyatt popped the top off his beer and took a swig. "And we didn't talk much. Mostly about some of the work we had coming up on the ranch that I was going to give him. But you know, he seems fine."

Bennett blew out a long, slow breath. At least there was one relationship maybe he wasn't screwing up.

"You're not home that late," Wyatt pointed out, looking a little disappointed on Bennett's behalf.

"Late enough, apparently," Bennett said meaningfully.

Wyatt arched a brow. "Now, you're implying that you got laid, but you look like somebody just dropped an anvil on your head. That doesn't make any sense to me."

Bennett popped open the beer bottle and took a long drink, then he rested his elbows on the table and scrubbed his hands over his face. "I had sex with Kaylee."

He waited for his brother's shocked response. Waited for any response at all. It didn't come. Bennett looked up slowly and was met by Wyatt's completely blank expression.

"Did you hear what I just said?" he asked, exasperation coursing through him.

He was standing there staring at the smoking rubble of his life, and his brother didn't even have the decency to look surprised.

"Yes," Wyatt said slowly. "You slept with Kaylee."

"Doesn't that shock you?"

"No. Don't you guys…" Wyatt frowned. "Are you telling me you'd never had sex with her before tonight?"

"Wyatt," Bennett said, "she's my best friend."

"Yes. Your best friend who happens to have female anatomy. I figured you guys slept together when you weren't seeing other people. I thought that was your arrangement all this time."

Bennett felt…scandalized. And given the recent events of tonight he had no right to feel that way. But Wyatt thought…did everyone think that?

"Hell, no," Bennett said.

"I figured you had a damn good thing going there, Bennett."

"*I do*. Friendship. Only friendship. Until tonight."

"Now that I find shocking."

"Why?"

"I've never been friends with a woman and *not* slept with her. Really, I've never been friends with a woman."

"Isn't Kaylee your friend?"

"Like a family friend," Wyatt said. "That's different. It's not like I hang out with her alone, constantly all the time. You and Kaylee do." Wyatt shook his head and lifted the beer bottle to his lips. "You must have balls of titanium."

"I just never saw her like that before," Bennett said through gritted teeth.

That wasn't entirely true. He'd been noticing her more and more lately. But in the grand scheme of things, it was almost never.

"You never saw a gorgeous, leggy redhead as a sex object before? I take it back, you don't have balls of titanium. You have broken balls."

"They feel pretty busted at the moment," Bennett said.

"I just mean that's a whole level of denial that I can't even get into, bro," Wyatt said. "If you didn't see her as sexy before, you were *trying* not to."

"She's my best friend. There are always going to be women to sleep with, but man, woman, there's no one like her. No one that's been in my life all this time. I work with her. I go out and have a beer with her."

"And now you have sex with her. It's perfect, in my opinion."

"I don't and I'm never going to be able to see it like you do."

"Sex isn't that complicated, Bennett. You want some, you have some. People don't have to get hurt. That's all mental stuff that doesn't have to be there. It's about expectations."

Bennett shook his head. "I don't agree with that. I think it means something." Yet he'd been about to go out and get some meaningless sex tonight, but in general, he didn't really believe sex could be meaningless. Which was one reason this was bugging him. "It just isn't that casual for me."

"Well, why the hell not?"

"Sex isn't a handshake, Wyatt."

"No," Wyatt said, "it isn't. Because when I shake

someone's hand I'm usually making an agreement of some kind. When it comes to sex, I'm not agreeing to anything beyond a little bit of fun."

"Someday," Bennett said, "some woman is going to screw with your head. And I'm going to look forward to watching that."

"Not me," Wyatt said, kicking his feet up onto the table and leaning back. "I'm immune." He punctuated the sentence with another drink of beer.

"You're cocky."

"It's served me well so far. You don't ride bulls for fifteen years without being a hell of a lot of cocky. And anyway, with that came a lot of women, Bennett. Trust me. I know my limits. I don't have many."

"That doesn't help me."

"It should. You're going through a hell of a time right now, and obviously, you needed some stress release. It stands to reason you would end up looking for it with a woman that you know. That you like. Since this conversation leads me to believe that casual sex really isn't for you. Also, she's pretty. She's really pretty."

"She is," Bennett said, remembering the way that her skin had felt beneath his fingertips. Remembering how it had felt to kiss her.

The slick friction of her tongue against his, the greedy glide of her hands down his back.

She was beautiful, and she had definitely been into it.

"Right," Bennett said. "I guess that's true."

"Bottom line, even though you're friends, you're a man and she's a woman. And you're only human."

"I didn't just have sex with her because she's a woman," Bennett said. "And it wasn't just because she was there. I could have found someone else."

But the way she had looked at him when she'd said

she didn't want him leaving with anyone else... Well, in that moment there couldn't have been anyone else. It had nothing to do with proximity or availability. He couldn't reduce it to that. Because there had been something magic in it being her.

He gritted his teeth, fought against that thought.

Because he didn't want to think about all that magic the next time he saw her. He didn't need that between them. But she knew him. She knew everything he was going through and then some.

Maybe that was why he needed it to be her. Just maybe.

"Sex doesn't have to build or destroy anything," Wyatt said, standing up and clapping Bennett on the back. "Sometimes it just feels good. Don't overthink it."

Bennett nodded slowly.

"I'll see you at some point tomorrow, when you drop the kid off."

"Sure," Bennett said.

"He's a good kid," Wyatt said, his tone suddenly taking on a more serious note. "A hard worker. He's a natural at it. Ranch stuff. I'm glad to have him on my team, and not just because he's my secret nephew I never knew about."

"He is a good kid," Bennett said, believing it all the way to his core, not really understanding why.

"See you later."

And then Wyatt left, his advice still ringing in Bennett's ears. His brother telling him that sex didn't have to build or destroy anything was about the most ironic thing on the planet given that Bennett's secret son was currently sleeping down the hall.

But maybe with Kaylee it didn't need to affect anything. Maybe Wyatt was right. He had needed something, and they had been there for each other. And it didn't have to be life altering or world rocking.

Too bad his world felt so damned rocked.

CHAPTER FOURTEEN

THE NEXT MORNING, Bennett woke up without a single idea of what had happened the night before. But he did wake up with the idea that Dallas needed to start helping with chores around their place.

Because it was their place. And if they were going to share it then they were going to have to work it together. Dallas was going to have to learn to take responsibility for the land he called home.

The kid was less shocked at getting yanked out of bed at six o'clock than he had been at the beginning of all of this. Early mornings were becoming the norm, and Bennett found himself vaguely amused when Dallas stumbled into the kitchen without complaint and poured himself a cup of coffee from the coffee maker.

Bennett had taken to stocking the house with various pastries, since that seemed to add an extra incentive for Dallas to get out of bed, and they were not going to the coffeehouse every morning.

The rumor was sweeping slowly through town that Bennett Dodge had a son. The details were definitely fuzzy in said rumor, seeing as Bennett hadn't gone out of his way to provide any.

And he hadn't called his dad yet. There was that.

But he just didn't know how to broach the subject with Quinn Dodge. Not that he wasn't a good, understanding man—he was. But…it was just a conversation he wasn't looking forward to having, especially not over the phone.

"A little bit early for a wake-up call," Dallas mumbled, taking his first sip of coffee and grabbing a doughnut out of a box at the center of the table.

"Yeah, well, we have some extra work to do this morning. Or, you do."

"I do?"

"Yes. I'm going to teach you how to take care of the animals here. I know you got a basic ranching primer from my brother, but I figure it's time you took some responsibility for this place."

"That sounds like unpaid labor," Dallas said, unimpressed.

"It is," Bennett said. "But it isn't. You live here. That means that this is yours too. That means that the payment is getting to live in a place that you enjoy. But here, we've got lots of land and we got animals that live on that land. They need to be taken care of."

As if understanding they were part and parcel to the topic being discussed, Pepper and Cheddar scooted closer to the table. Though, it probably had less to do with the topic of discussion and more to do with the fact that a sprinkle had just fallen off the top of Dallas's doughnut and landed on the floor. Pepper snaffled it up, and Cheddar looked at Dallas, clearly irritated that her counterpart had gotten a piece of sugar and she hadn't.

Bennett watched, amused as Dallas flicked a couple more sprinkles off the doughnut and onto the floor. He looked over at Dallas, his expression sheepish. "It wasn't fair," he pointed out.

"No," Bennett agreed in mock seriousness. "And they keep score."

"I get that feeling about them."

"You like the dogs," Bennett said.

"Well, you can't not like dogs. I mean, you can, I guess. But when you live in a house with them it's kind of hard."

"Hey, I won't tell anyone you *like* something. But I just mean, you got used to the dogs, maybe you'll like the rest of the animals."

After they finished their caffeine, they headed outside, Dallas wearing a hoodie that he had pulled up almost over his face, his hand stuffed in his pockets.

He guarded any expressions of enjoyment closely, definitely did his best to keep most of his feelings to himself. It made Bennett wonder what had happened to make him see happiness as something that was too expensive to get out.

He had vague ideas, and all of them made his stomach turn.

He took Dallas into the barn, where the horses were still in their stalls. "Okay, so this girl here," he said, indicating the first stall, "gets two flakes of hay in the morning." He walked over to one of the bales of hay. "Has Wyatt explained this to you yet?"

Dallas shook his head. "I haven't fed any of the horses on my own."

Bennett walked over to one of the hay bales that was already untwined and gripped the edge of a wedge of it, separating it easily from the rest. "This is a flake. They'll come off pretty easily. It's the way the bales are put together. So, Lucy here is on a diet. Two flakes of hay in the morning and two at night for her. No grain. She gets a vitamin supplement instead."

He moved on to the next stall. "Shadrach gets two and a scoop of grain. The scoop is in that trash barrel over there, and it's pretty self-explanatory in terms of measurement."

"And Meshach gets two flakes and two scoops of grain. It's a lot, but he's pretty skinny, having trouble keeping meat on his bones."

"They're all old?"

"Yeah," Bennett said. "For the most part I've ended up with my animals because they were at the end of their usefulness for someone else."

"That seems…nice of you."

"I always wanted to fix things," Bennett said. "You know, my mom died when I was seven years old. There was nothing I could do about it. After that…I hated to see anything suffer. It just…got to me. One time I rescued a bird that had flown into the window of our house. It was injured. Really badly. But I picked it up and put it in a shoebox with a blanket, took care of it as best I could."

"And you saved it?"

"No. The fucking thing died anyway. But it would have died sooner if it weren't for me. I did something to change how it went. And…I knew that's what I wanted to do. I didn't want to be a doctor. I didn't want to handle people dying. That's something I didn't want any part of. But the animals… Some of them I save. Some of them I don't. But my intervention matters. And for a kid who felt like he couldn't do anything when his own mother died…"

"I get it," Dallas said. "I wish my mom were dead."

Bennett straightened, like a shot going through his body. "You do?"

"If she were dead then she wouldn't have left me by choice. She just left. At least your mom didn't want to go."

The teenager's words made a strange kind of sense to him. He nodded slowly. "It's true. My mom never would have chosen to leave us. You know, she had just had Jamie. Jamie was a surprise baby. I was supposed to be the youngest. But…she was so excited. I remember that. I remember her putting her hand on her stomach and smiling. And my dad did the same thing. It was a terrible thing to lose her."

"Yeah," Dallas said, turning his focus back to the hay. "So, two flakes?"

"Yes," Bennett said. "Two flakes."

And then, a thought occurred to him that hadn't before. "Dallas, do you want to learn to ride today?"

"I guess," Dallas said, holding back any vague hint of excitement. But Bennett could sense it. Could see the longing in the kid's eyes.

He didn't have any pressing appointments this morning, and he could put off checking in at the clinic. While he had Dallas's attention, he wanted to keep it.

"Then I'll text Wyatt and let him know you'll be late today. I'm going to teach you."

BENNETT DIDN'T SHOW up at the clinic all morning. It was nearly eleven o'clock, and he still wasn't there. That wasn't unheard of, but it was definitely unusual. And combined with the events of last night…

Kaylee's stomach flipped over as she tried to concentrate while scrolling through her schedule on the computer. She had a big block of time available and she could always take a long lunch. But then, she would just sit around stuffing her face and worrying about the fact that Bennett was clearly avoiding her.

Of course he was avoiding her. He was probably

steeped in regret over what happened between them last night.

He had *thanked* her.

Thanked her, like she had done him a favor. Thanked her like she hadn't come apart in his arms like some needy sex kitten that she had never been before in her entire life.

Thanked her.

That thought burned all the way through.

She was going to take lunch. She was going to go get a big greasy burger down at Mustard Seed and try to let go of all the things that were bugging her.

Laura was at reception, gathering her things to take a break and Kaylee stopped her. "Do you want to get a burger? I don't mind closing down for an hour."

Laura looked regretful. "I have plans already. Meeting my mom at Bellissima. But you're welcome to join in if you want."

"Thanks, but I'm married to the burger idea."

"See you after," Laura said.

Kaylee nodded, and flipped a sign saying the clinic was closed for lunch before heading out to the parking lot.

She drove down into town, but she drove past Mustard Seed. Which she wasn't going to do. Because she wasn't supposed to do that. She was supposed to go and get a hamburger. But she seemed to be driving toward Bennett's place.

Her hands were sweaty on the wheel of the pickup, and she readjusted them, not sure if she was trying to talk herself out of this insanity, or mentally trying to bolster herself to sally forth with the crazy.

Bennett was supposed to be her friend. That was the bottom line. He was supposed to be her best friend in the world, and after sharing something completely intimate with her he was avoiding her. She'd wanted this, wanted to be with him for half her life. And she'd been terrified of it, of the potential fallout, for just as long.

Here she was living it. And he hadn't even sent a text.

But maybe he hadn't liked it. And this morning he was appalled and disgusted by it. By her. Maybe she hadn't scratched the itch the way he'd needed it scratched or…or…

And maybe there were *rules*. Rules about how you were supposed to act when a man didn't call the night after you slept with him. Maybe you were supposed to be aloof or cool, acting like a cat, twitching your tail and making it seem like you didn't care whether or not he scratched you behind the ears.

But she had known Bennett too long to play games. It wasn't about pride. Not with him. He knew her. And that meant he knew her well enough to know that he should have damn well gotten in touch with her today.

And so, she felt both resolute and justified in her rage as she turned down the driveway.

She parked in front of the house, turning off the engine and shaking her hands out like it would do something to calm the nerves that were rioting through her system.

She let out a harsh breath.

"Don't be a coward, Capshaw," she said out loud.

Because she had told Bennett that he could have sex with her last night. She had kissed him the other day. She was not a coward.

She was a woman who went for what she wanted.

Maybe she hadn't always been, but she was now. She was resolute, and she was determined. She was shaking, but she was going to ignore that.

Or at least hope that Bennett didn't notice that.

She all but flung herself out of the truck, stumbling on the gravel when her boots hit the driveway. Then she cleared her throat and straightened, running her hands through her hair and giving it a small shake.

His truck was here, but when she knocked on the door to the house he didn't answer. She frowned.

She started having weird wild fantasies, and what began as a pit of disquiet in her stomach sprouted into a tree of paranoia. Perhaps his ex had come looking for Dallas and there had been some kind of ax murder inside of his house and he hadn't gotten in touch with her because he was lying dead on his living room floor.

She scampered over to the living-room window and looked inside, able to see just a small sliver of the room through the closed curtains.

There didn't appear to be any bodies. Which was a relief. But it still left her with unanswered questions.

She took a deep breath and started walking out toward the barn. There was a good chance he was out there. Still possibly ax murder, though. Because now that the idea was in her head she couldn't get rid of it.

Then she heard voices, and she stopped, looking to her left at the wide-open field.

Bennett was standing there, leaning up against the fence, his shirtsleeves pushed up to his elbows, bare, muscular forearms resting on the top rail of the fence. His black cowboy hat was pushed up slightly and he was grinning. It didn't take long to see what he was smiling at.

Dallas was out in the field. And he was riding a horse.

Her heart turned over in her chest, and then crumpled up tight. So tight she could barely breathe.

She had been prepared to be angry. And then, she had been prepared for tragedy—though, only in that detached, paranoid sense—but she hadn't been prepared to fall in love with that man all over again in a moment.

In *love*.

Dammit. She was in love with him.

Always had been.

She hadn't wanted to be. It was the revelation that scared her more than any other. More than wanting him, being in love with him was so, so scary.

There was something about love. It made you hope. And hope was the most insidious, terrible thing. Her entire childhood she'd hoped. Hoped her parents would see her. Hoped she would somehow matter to them.

That she'd be enough.

She hadn't.

She'd loved them. It hadn't mattered.

She didn't want to be in love with Bennett. But she couldn't deny that she was. Any more than she could turn away from what was happening in front of her.

He turned then. As if he could sense her staring at him. And she hoped he couldn't feel the intensity of the emotion that was pouring off her.

"Kaylee. What are you doing here?"

"I was a little bit worried about you," she said, heading toward the fence.

"Sorry," he said, frowning as he lifted his wrist and looked down at his watch. "Damn. I didn't realize how late it was."

She couldn't even stay angry. She hadn't been angry anyway. Not really. She'd been scared.

"How long have you two been out here?"

"Since about six this morning. I gave him a quick primer on the care and keeping of the horses, and then we ended up starting a riding lesson. He's been enjoying himself too much to stop."

"I don't think he's the only one," Kaylee said softly.

The pride on Bennett's face was… There was something about all of this that only cemented her feelings.

No one had ever looked at her like that.

That was a small, petty thought that didn't belong here. That was not about her. Dallas deserved to have someone look at him like that. And even if she was equal parts happy for and envious of the kid, she was going to focus on the happy part.

She was good at that. At taking the pieces and not the whole. It made it all manageable.

She had experienced what Dallas had to a degree. But there had been no wonderful secret father waiting for her on the other side of it.

Though, there had been Bennett. And there had been his family. She was lucky enough. She had no call to get morose.

About that. She was still feeling a little morose about the whole sex situation.

"I guess not," Bennett said. "Good thing I didn't have any appointments today. Just kind of on call. But I didn't mean to *not* check in at the clinic."

She nodded. "Good."

His lips pulled down tight, his brows lifting in an obvious question.

Dumbass man. She was going to have to walk him through it.

"I thought maybe you were avoiding me," she clarified.

The corners of his mouth went down farther, then relaxed suddenly as realization seemed to dawn over him like beams from the sun rising slow up over the mountains. That frown turning into an expression of absolute sheepishness.

"I'm sorry," he said, sounding so incredibly sincere she wanted to punch him.

She would have rather had a smooth line than an apology like that. Than a look of pure bewilderment that let her know he truly hadn't been thinking of what had happened between them last night.

She felt so raw. She couldn't move without thinking about what they did last night, and he didn't seem to be conscious of it at all.

"Will you be all right if I head to the barn for a minute?" Bennett called out to Dallas.

"I'm fine," Dallas said, guiding the horse to turn to the left and taking a broad circle around part of the field.

"Come on," he said, not touching her, which seemed deliberate at this point. But still, she followed him over to the barn and walked inside with him. She turned to face him, crossing her arms and treating him to a hard stare.

"I didn't mean to make it seem like I was standing you up," he said.

"No," she said, feeling beyond wretched now. "Why would I think that? It's just that something completely weird happened between us last night. Something that I haven't been able to stop thinking about. But I can see where you just hadn't paid it any thought. Because it seemed...mundane to you?"

"It did not seem mundane to me. But maybe I pushed it to the back of my mind."

"How nice to be able to do that."

"I'm sorry," he reiterated.

"Well, the apology pairs nicely with the *thank-you* that I received last night."

"What was wrong with the thank-you?"

"Oh, nothing. What girl doesn't like to be thanked for sex, as if she's done a man a favor?"

He frowned. "Kaylee, I'm a little bit lost here. How is it that I've managed to say about five words to you since all that happened but they were all the wrong words?"

"The fact that you can count the words is part of the problem."

She was maybe being a little bit difficult right now, but she felt difficult. She felt offended. She had taken a chance on the one thing she had wanted for so long, the one thing that she had held herself back from. And along the way had come to the realization that she couldn't hang out in denial of what all of these feelings meant.

So if she was a little bit messed up, she was just going to have to apologize for it later. The problem was he didn't seem like any of this bothered him at all. It was all simple *thank yous* and *I'm sorrys*. All going about his daily life in a way that didn't include her.

And nothing had been on her mind from the time she had finally fallen asleep last night, to the time she had woken up this morning, that wasn't about Bennett.

Was it so wrong to have hoped that a corner of his brain was reserved for her?

"I didn't need you to thank me like I did you a favor," she said.

"But I…was grateful."

"Oh my gosh, Bennett!" She was about a second away from banging her head against the side of the barn wall. "You expect any woman to not be mad at you for being grateful that she gave you sex?"

Poor Bennett looked stricken. No. Not *poor Bennett*. She refused to feel sorry for him. "Apparently that is the wrong feeling. But I guarantee you a great many men have that feeling."

"Well, how about this?" She stretched up to her full height, which still put her nose just beneath his. "*Thank you*. Thank you for the orgasm. It was awesome. I'm putting it in my diary. Because you are the first man to ever give me one."

Well, crap.

She hadn't meant to confess that. And right about now you would be able to hear the tiniest piece of straw fall onto the concrete barn floor. Because Bennett had fallen utterly silent, his mouth dropped open in an expression of shock.

"What?" he asked.

Her lips tightened up of their own free will. Like they were trying to save her from her own stupidity. "I've never had an orgasm with a man before. With a partner. *Obviously* I've had them. But by myself."

He blinked. "Oh."

"So, thank you. Thank you for the use of your sensationally magical dick. It was very much appreciated." She waved her hand around. "A fun time to be had by all."

He blinked, his jaw getting hard as stone. "You're right," he said. "I don't much like that."

"See?" she asked, insistent. "It makes you feel weird."

"Not the part about the orgasm."

She frowned. "Well."

His brows snapped together, a look of intense curiosity on his handsome face. "Really? Are you being serious or was that for demonstrative purposes?"

"I'm being serious." She nearly stamped her foot.

It was too late to back out now. She had started on this trail, and she had to keep on it now.

"*No man. None* of them. None of those douchebags I watched you date."

She crossed her arms and shook her head, defiant. "Nope."

"Well, that's just… I'm torn between wanting to beat them up and wanting to take a damned victory lap."

"This is not really more charming than any of the other crap you pulled earlier."

"I'm the first one to give you an orgasm?" he asked as if he hadn't heard her previous statement.

"*Yes,*" she said, "don't let it go to your head."

"It's not my head it's going to."

"*Bennett!*"

And it was almost hilarious. This exchange was almost like something that would have happened between them before the sex. And it was as endearing as it was exasperating for that reason. Of course, it wouldn't have been about her orgasms, but still.

"It's just hard for me to believe."

"That there's something wrong with my body?"

He shook his head emphatically. "It's not you, Kaylee. Hell, no. It was them."

"That's just your favorite scenario because it means they were all defective and you're a stud."

"Well, sure. But I think we all win in that scenario."

"Look, Bennett. I'm feeling a little bit messed up about all of it." She closed her eyes, realizing suddenly that the orgasm confession was actually perfect. Because it gave her a hell of an excuse for being an emotional basket case. One that wasn't: *oh, yeah, I'm deeply in love with you. Fatally. Forever.*

No way. She couldn't handle that right now. One thing at a time.

"I had no idea," he said.

"But you did know that I don't sleep around. And you did know that this would be weird."

"Sure," he said. "But you have to give me some slack then too. For it being weird on my end."

Well, that was reasonable. And it made her mad. Because it wasn't fair. He wasn't supposed to be reasonable about things. She wanted her rage. She wanted it to be all about her. Wanted it to be about her indignity and her feelings. She didn't want to have to worry about his.

How was that for unfair?

"So, your method was just to not deal with it?"

"I'm a guy."

"Sure. But you're the guy that I usually talk to about everything. And something pretty big happened between us, and if we can't talk about it then... I don't have anyone else, Bennett. Which is why this was probably a really bad idea." It was why confessing that she was in love with him was *unthinkable*. "We need to be able to deal with this. We need to be able to come to some kind of resolution. I can't have it be an unspoken thing between us. I can't have it be something that comes between us at all. Bennett, you're my best friend. You were the first person who made me feel like there was some value in me. I'm not being dramatic. We moved all the time until we came here. Until I met you. And my parents cared more about the last drop of whiskey and a bottle than me. They still do. If it wasn't for you, if it wasn't for your family, I would probably be somewhere drowning in a pool of liquor and futile existence. All by myself just like them, because I would never have known that there was another life possible. Your family showed me that there could be something else. You showed me that. And you've been my closest friend ever since. I will be damned if sex messes that up."

"Kaylee, nothing could mess us up," he said, those dark eyes so serious and honest it made her breath catch. "We're bigger than one night. We're long summer nights out at the ball field watching cheesy minor league games and eating stale pretzels. We're cold winter nights around a Christmas tree, and cool spring morning trail rides up a mountain. One night of sex in a truck could never erase all those nights. Ever. It's a new night, the kind we've never had before, I know that. But it doesn't undo all that history."

"But it feels like it could," she said, feeling small and fragile. She closed her eyes, emotion welling up in her chest. "I just can't stand the idea that…that I was thinking about this. All night, all day and…if it didn't matter to you I couldn't stand it. Being that wrong about it. It reminds me…" Her face got hot and scratchy. "It reminds me of when we moved here."

He looked at her, his face turning to stone. Like he was bracing himself for a blow.

"It's not that bad," she said quickly. "It was me being stupid. It's just…where we lived before, I had this friend who had…my dream bedroom. It was all frills and lace and a canopy bed. I loved it. But I could never say that. I always…pretended I hated that stuff."

She swallowed hard, her throat dry. Bennett reached out and grasped her hand, and it made her want to cry. She wished he wouldn't touch her. But she didn't have the strength to pull away either.

"When my parents said we were moving and getting a new house, and I was getting a new room…I somehow thought… I just thought maybe somehow… it would be that room. That there would be a new bed in it, and the wallpaper would have flowers. That I'd have a canopy. Really, I thought…I could move and be different." She blinked heavily. "I'll never forget opening the door, and the room was empty. And then they brought up my same mattress. The same ugly blanket. It wasn't new. And neither was I."

"Kay," Bennett said, his voice rough. He pulled her into his arms, up against his chest. "I had no idea."

"It wasn't the missing lace and canopy. It wasn't that the walls were oatmeal and not flowers." Though that was some of it. "It was feeling so stupid over hoping like that, and being so wrong. I couldn't stand it if this ruined us and I was so lost in the feeling good that I missed it." She closed her eyes. "I couldn't stand being so wrong about us."

"No, honey," he said, kissing the top of her head. "I couldn't think about what happened last night because I had to get through this morning in front of my kid without an X-rated film playing in my head. But it…it matters to me. You matter to me."

"What if this gets all messed up? What if we mess this up?"

"Then we'll make a plan. We'll make a plan and be damn sure we don't mess it up."

That was her Bennett. He wanted plans of action. He wanted to control the situation by laying out the details of what would happen next. And what wouldn't.

And she was just…willing to let him. Because she had no idea what she wanted to do with this. She knew what she felt. But she didn't know what was possible. For her. For them. And the unknown of it all terrified her.

If she could just let go and let Bennett be confident for the both of them then that might actually work for her.

She wouldn't have to take the risks. She wouldn't have to make the choices.

A pushy move, maybe. But she was feeling a bit wimpy. So, there it was.

"What do you suggest?"

"I enjoyed last night," he said, his dark eyes serious on hers. "I mean that. But I would never take what happened for granted. I would never assume that it was going to happen again. You don't owe me a damn thing, Kaylee. And you don't ever have to feel like we need to do that to keep my friendship."

She frowned. "Why would I think that about you?"

"I just want to make sure that's clear."

"It's clear," she said, "because I know you. If you had wanted to use me for sex you would have done it a long time ago."

"That was before. I just want to make sure you know that I would never hold anything over your head."

"Bennett," she said, "if I thought you would do that, then you threatening to take away your friendship wouldn't be so much of a threat. Because I wouldn't want to be your friend. I know that you aren't going to expect anything from me. You don't need to go over-the-top knight in shining armor here."

"Okay. Then I want to do it again."

The words hit her like a punch to the gut.

"You do?" That whole time he had been justifying and protesting so much she had assumed that he wouldn't want to go there again.

"Yes," he said. "I should have gone after you last night. But I let Dallas being at the house serve as an excuse for putting this off. Because I knew once wouldn't be enough, and I wasn't ready to figure out what that meant. Then this morning I had to put it out of my mind for a little while. I had to deal with Dallas and when I think about us…" He closed his eyes and tilted his head back, his throat working up and down. "It's all I can think about. The way that it felt. Kaylee…" He opened his eyes, the uncertainty in them clashing with the desire in her.

"I didn't get to see you," he continued. "Not really. And I want to." He closed some of the distance between them, reaching out and cupping her cheek. "You've been my friend for a long damn time. And I'd be lying if I said I never thought of you as a woman."

"You…you would be?"

"I know you're a woman. And lately… I don't know if it's just because of everything that's been happening in my life, or if it's just inevitable."

She wasn't sure she liked either excuse. That his desire for her was the result of the chaos in his world. But she realized it didn't really matter what reason he gave her. It only mattered what reason he gave himself that he could handle right now.

"I want to see you," he said, his voice like gravel. "Your body."

"What parts of it?" She almost cringed when she spoke the words, but instead, she managed to school her face into some kind of bland expression. Just bland enough that she could stand by those words. Maybe they were sexy, maybe they weren't. She wasn't sure she knew how to be sexy. She knew how to be tough. She knew how to act like things didn't matter. But this moment mattered. She wanted to be…something other than what he was used to her being. Something other than his capable sidekick, his trusty business partner. A woman who could fix the fence and throw a punch and beat some of the guys down at Gold Valley Saloon at arm wrestling. A woman who couldn't wear high heels with most of the men in town because she would tower over them.

She wanted more of what he had made her feel last night.

And so she waited. Waited until the expression in his dark eyes turned sharp. Until she could see that he was tugging at the edge of his control.

His face, that gorgeous face that had been so familiar to her for so many years, suddenly looked foreign to her. Like a stranger. There was a ferocity there, an edge that had certainly never been directed at her. And it made her shiver all the way down deep in her belly and between her legs. Made her want in ways she'd never thought possible.

"I want to see if your nipples match your lips, Kaylee," he said, his voice going deeper, resonating inside of her. "I want to see those pretty red curls between your legs. And then I want to see all of you. I want to spread you wide and see how pink you are. That's what I want. I want to taste you and take my time. And I want to watch your face when I make you come. Knowing full well that I'm the only man who's ever done it. That's what I want. Do you think you can handle that?"

She had no damned idea if she could handle that. She thought she might melt to the floor. Hearing Bennett say things like that to her. Explicit things, dark things that called to gloriously erotic places inside of her she hadn't known she possessed.

Dark erotic thoughts that she hadn't been aware *Bennett* had possessed.

That was the most shocking thing. Standing there, having him look at her like she was something delicious he wanted to eat. Having him say those explicit things.

Bennett. Her Bennett, who was everything good and restrained and steady in her world, knocking it off its axis with a few filthy words.

She had known that he was sexy. She had known that she wanted him. But she hadn't known that he would be…like this.

And she really hadn't known that she would respond to it. That was the funny thing. She had fantasized about Bennett. A lot. And being with him last night had been incredible. But this…this was something else entirely.

Having her friend stand there in front of her and look at her like a lover. A stranger and a friend all at the same time. The man she knew but *more*.

Something about it was almost more erotic than what had come before.

"I want to have you in my bed," he said, his voice rough. "All night. That would be something."

Something a lot like panic fluttered in her breast. "Well, you can't. Because of Dallas."

"I know. I just wanted to make sure you knew that I would. That I wanted it."

She wanted it too. To be between the sheets with him. On a mattress. Another thing that seemed so intimate. Another thing that—in spite of their close friendship— they had never shared. Obviously. A bed.

She had been in his bedroom just to hang out. Ever since they were teenagers, she had been in his room. She had sat on the edge of his bed. She had never been in bed with him.

She ached for that. For that casual intimacy that would come from something like that. Casual and heavy all at the same time.

But it was also relationship stuff. And…

Given everything—her feelings, his situation—it was a dangerous idea.

Bennett was her very best friend. And now, he was her very best sex. She just needed to keep everything in its own neat little box.

To put the sex in one place, and the friendship in another. To keep everything from becoming too big. Too unmanageable.

Hoping for anything more was hoping for that bedroom all over again.

She didn't think she could put herself through that again.

And so she would have this. Another Bennett compartment in her life. Friend Bennett, and sexual Bennett. That seemed…good. Whatever it was, it was more of him. And that could never be a bad thing.

"So…"

"We'll work it out," he cut her off. "As soon as possible. I've got to be inside you again." Her cheeks went bonfire hot, and Bennett's lips curved up into a smile. "Did I make you blush, Kaylee?"

"Yes," she said. "You're being dirty."

"Why do I get the feeling that you like me dirty."

"I do," she said, the words coming out a whisper, even though she hadn't meant for them to.

"More fun for me," he said.

"Suddenly…I'm very curious."

"Are you?"

"Yes."

"What about?"

"It's the weirdest thing. I've known you since we were thirteen. But I don't know about this part of you."

He wrapped his arm around her, pinning one arm behind her back, grabbing hold of her wrist with his other hand, and then he pressed her palm to the front of his jeans. He was hard. For her.

"This part of me?"

"Yes," she said, rubbing him through the denim. "But not just that."

There was no guidebook for having a conversation with your best friend while you had your hand on his dick.

Maybe she would have to write it when all this was said and done.

"What else?"

"We talk about a lot of things. But not really about sex. I told you about the guy I lost it to when I was seventeen."

"Oh, the minuteman?"

She laughed, which seemed absurd when she was touching him so intimately. Or maybe with Bennett it was just right. "Yes. The minuteman. You made me feel better about how horrendous it was."

"It wasn't your fault."

"But we don't talk about our sex lives much at this point and I… I've certainly never seen you…being sexual before all this. It's… I have a lot of questions."

"Go ahead and ask."

"What do you like? How many women have you been with?"

He grimaced. "You don't go easy."

"I never have." Truthfully, she'd had these questions before, but they had been kind of an amorphous blob of sexual wonderment. Now it was… A lot more concrete. Because of those words he had just spoken to her. Words that indicated the depth and need in him that she hadn't fully appreciated before.

Really, she was just so fully confronted with the fact that he was a man. And everything that meant.

Also, she was confronted with how limited her own sexual experiences had been. All the sex she had ever had had been—in many ways—about Bennett Dodge. Trying to forget him. Trying to want someone else. They hadn't taken the time to really explore each other. Hadn't spent a lot of time discussing what she liked. And she hadn't really cared what they liked.

Not really.

She wanted to know everything about Bennett. Every vaguely dirty thought he'd ever had. What it might mean. What she could do to be the fulfillment of it.

"Right now it's safe to say I like you," he said.

"Right now," she said, ignoring the pain in her chest and trying to smile.

"The evidence is in your hand."

"So it is."

"And how many... I don't readily know. Not that many, but enough that I kind of stopped counting."

"Well," she felt perturbed, "that's a fuzzy number."

"How many men have you been with, Kay?" His tone was gentle, but there was an underlying note of steel that made her feel electrified. She couldn't quite explain it.

"Four," she said easily. "That's including you."

"That's it?"

She shrugged. "I told you. Sex hasn't been all that mind-blowing for me in the past."

"You've dated a hell of a lot more men than that."

She shrugged. "Yeah. But I'm choosy."

"I suppose if I asked what you liked..."

"You. *Right now.*"

He smiled. "Touché."

"Bennett, you've always had a plan. And I've always gone along with that plan. It's never steered me wrong. It's why I graduated high school. Went to college. It's why I have a career. What's the plan here? I need to know."

Bennett tightened his hold on her. "We get each other through. Until a new plan comes along."

She could do that. Even if it made her heart feel like it was cracking in her chest. This was more of him than she'd ever thought she'd have.

The sound of a horse whinnying outside broke the moment. Bennett released his hold on her and took a step back. As if he just remembered that there was someone else on the property. It was a good thing he remembered, because she hadn't been thinking clearly at all.

"I should... I guess I have to get to work," he said.

"Me too. I closed the clinic."

"To come down here and yell at me?"

"In fairness, I closed it so that I could go get a burger. At least, that was my intention. Then I started thinking about you, and I got mad at you."

"And I owe you a hamburger, don't I?"

"A hamburger and an orgasm." She grinned at him, gratified when his jaw went tense, his eyes looking deeply interested. "Tonight then?"

He winced. "I just remembered that I promised Wyatt that Dallas and I would have dinner over there tonight. But I bet if I call ahead I can arrange for it to be burgers. Do you want to come over to the ranch for dinner?"

She should have known that she wasn't getting a dinner date out of Bennett. Not with the way things were for him right now. And actually, she didn't really care. She loved Get Out of Dodge. She loved Bennett's family. There was no downside to spending the evening with them.

"All right," she said.

"All right," he agreed. "I'll share dinnertime with you. But after dinner is all mine."

Her heart fluttered at the very intentional promise in his voice. "Okay." Lordy. She sounded like a silly high school girl fluttering over her first date.

In fairness, she felt like one.

Bennett looked over his shoulder and quickly dropped a hard, firm kiss on her lips, leaving her standing there in the barn reeling.

Bennett Dodge was making sensual promises to her. Bennett Dodge seemed to want her.

Bennett Dodge was coming after her.

Kaylee was starting to be afraid that she had woken up in a parallel universe and everything was going to go back to normal a lot sooner than she wanted it to.

But until then… She would have this. Yes. Until then.

Bennett was right. They'd had seventeen years' worth of nights between them. Seventeen years of friendship.

This wouldn't destroy them.

It couldn't.

CHAPTER FIFTEEN

IT WAS TYPICAL of his family to be having noisy, boisterous discussion over food. And tonight was no different. Though, what wasn't quite so typical was that Dallas was joining in the discussion. He was laughing and joking, and talking about Lucy, the horse that he had ridden earlier in the day. Jamie was of course thrilled to have another enthusiast in her midst.

And then, Bennett couldn't decide if he wanted to hug his brother Wyatt or smack him on the back of the head when he started to talk about his experience riding bulls in the Pro Rodeo circuit.

"It's like riding on top of a freight train. Except the freight train wants to kill you," Wyatt announced, in typical Wyatt fashion.

"Wow," Dallas responded.

"Wyatt is an idiot," Bennett said. "And he probably has brain damage."

Wyatt shot him a glare, and Kaylee laughed and stood up from her position at the table, migrating over to the counter to grab a handful of chips.

"You know," Grant said, "a lot of bull riders wear helmets now for a reason."

"Yeah. And do you think those guys get as much action? Helmets don't have the same effect on women as cowboy hats, bro."

The interaction with all of them had been easy tonight, and he was grateful for that. Wyatt knew about the change in his and Kaylee's relationship, but apparently, as far as Wyatt was concerned the fact that it was new was the revelation, so he wasn't acting any differently. No one else knew unless Wyatt had told them, but Bennett doubted it.

Wyatt was tough. He was brash, and he was overconfident at the best of times. He also got under Bennett's skin like a damned weevil.

Bennett was cautious of his older brother's recklessness as well. Wyatt ran his mouth not caring what anyone thought, all the while doing whatever the hell he wanted.

Bennett tended to keep his mouth shut. All the while doing whatever the hell he wanted.

But he didn't like making things a discussion. Wyatt seemed to consider a healthy debate a part of a good day. But Wyatt was also loyal. The amount of blood he'd soaked into the ranch in the last couple years, all the sweat and tears that were here... Wyatt was a cocky bastard, and he ran his mouth about things that didn't matter much.

But he was loyal to family.

"You just rode a horse for the first time today," Wyatt said. "Leave the bulls for later."

"Leave the bulls for never," Kaylee said, breaking into the conversation. "You've got too symmetrical of a face to tempt a wild animal like that."

"Excuse me," Wyatt said. "He's *too symmetrical*. What about me? Am I lopsided?"

"A little bit," Kaylee said. "I mean, in that hot roguish kind of way. But..."

"Yeah," Bennett said. "He was born that way. You can't blame it on the bulls."

Wyatt snorted. "Hasn't impacted my life negatively at all."

"Is this the part where you make great pains to let us know what a stud you are?" Jamie asked. "Because I'm gonna pass on that."

"We'll keep it PG," Wyatt said. "We have a minor in our midst. Anyway, that kind of talk only gets really heated up when the other rodeo guys are here."

Jamie made a gagging noise. "I could do without them."

"Which is half of why having them around sometimes is interesting. It drives you nuts. And that's endless entertainment as far as I'm concerned."

Bennett heard the front door open and he looked around the room quickly, trying to take stock of who was here, and who would walk in without knocking. Well, Luke would. Luke spent more time at his own ranch now than he did on Get Out of Dodge, but he had lived on the property starting at the age of sixteen until he was in his twenties, so he felt pretty at home. But other than him? No one.

He was the only one who had noticed. Jamie was trying to razz a smile out of Grant and Wyatt had just turned his interest in joining in. Kaylee was downing chips and Dallas was watching the whole thing.

Bennett stood and turned toward the kitchen entryway that faced the living room and the entry hall between.

And then his heart dropped to his feet.

"This is just how I left y'all. Sitting around eating."

Well, hell. It was his dad.

CHAPTER SIXTEEN

QUINN DODGE WAS standing in the doorway, his cowboy hat fixed firmly on his head, covering his now silver hair, his petite wife clinging to his side. Freda was only about eight years younger than Quinn, but her hair had only just begun to show small flashes of silver against the inky black. Her dark eyes assessed the situation. And quickly.

"Who is this?" she asked.

"What are you doing back here?" Bennett asked, his heart sinking down low.

"We thought we would come visit," Quinn said. "Got a wild hair. We ended up taking the drive pretty damn quickly."

"Much more quickly than I would have liked," Freda pointed out.

"We camped on the side of the road a couple of nights, but here we are."

He could feel all of his siblings doing their very best not to look right at Dallas. But that concerted effort only drew attention to him. And anyway, he was the unfamiliar face. There was no chance he wouldn't be immediately noticed by his sharp old man. And there was no way Quinn wouldn't see the family resemblance.

"Dad," Bennett said meaningfully, "this is Dallas. And I think you and I need to have a talk."

Bennett began to move slowly, making his way toward his father. He gritted his teeth and gestured toward the living room. Dallas, for his part, stayed put in the kitchen. Which really was for the best. Bennett knew that his father wasn't going to get angry. Well, except maybe about being kept in the dark for the past couple of weeks. But he also knew that it was going to be a tricky discussion that shouldn't have an audience.

"He's not mine, is he?" Quinn asked.

His dad looked genuinely concerned.

Bennett chuckled. He couldn't help it. "That was the first thing Jamie asked."

"I didn't sow a whole lot of wild oats, but I had my moments after your mother died. I wasn't a monk." Quinn's mannerisms were so like Wyatt's in that moment it was almost funny. Except Bennett felt like his windpipe was being crushed so not much was funny.

"He's mine," Bennett said. "No, I didn't know." He took a deep breath. And then, he began to explain the entire story from beginning to end. When it was over, his father was just staring at him with those steady brown eyes.

"Why didn't you tell me at the time?" Quinn asked.

"There was so much in your life already. I would have told you eventually if Marnie had never told me she'd miscarried."

"I would have been there for you, Bennett. Hell, an adult man shouldn't go through that alone. A teenage boy... You needed everybody to rally around you."

Bennett shook his head. "I couldn't have asked that of you. You had your hands full ever since Mom passed."

"Literally in some cases," Quinn agreed. "She died and I was there holding your sister. The other boys... They were older. It was so hard... But...I wonder sometimes, Bennett, if I treated you too much like one of them. Rather than like the little one you were."

"There wasn't a choice," Bennett said. "Jamie was a baby."

"And you tried to become a man much too quickly. But it would never have been a burden to take on your worries, son. Ever."

"I just wanted to be responsible for my own life. I didn't want to add to your problems. Especially when there was no good news to give. The baby was gone. There didn't seem to be a point in bringing it all up. Plus, nobody wants to..."

"Talk about sex with their dad?"

"Yeah," Bennett said. "Particularly not back then. I didn't want to admit to you that I'd been that irresponsible."

"After the hell your brother put me through, that would have been nothing."

"Which brother?" Wyatt was the wild one, but Grant up and marrying at eighteen couldn't have been a picnic for their father either.

His father hesitated a moment. "Both of them, quite honestly."

"But that's the thing. I wanted to have it all under control so that..."

"There's no shame in needing help."

"Well, I might need some now. I've never raised a teenage boy before, and you raised three. Plus Jamie."

Quinn shook his head. "The very fact that you would ask for my help..." He swallowed hard. "Hell, boy. You got me choked up. Makes me think I did something right."

Bennett let out a slow breath. "You did a lot of things right, Dad."

"When did you find out about him?"

"It's been a couple of weeks. But I didn't know how to make that phone call."

Quinn nodded slowly. "I would've rather you told me then. I would rather you told me sixteen years ago."

"I should have. But I'm telling you now."

"Because I showed up unannounced."

Bennett shrugged. "Yeah, that's true. But we're talking."

"I think I need to go meet my grandson. I didn't figure my first grandson would be a teenager when I met him." There was a touch of wistfulness in Quinn's tone.

"I didn't figure my firstborn would be a teenager when I met him."

Quinn paused and clapped his hand over the back of Bennett's back. "I don't figure you did. This must be a tough time for you."

"Tough's not really the right word."

Complicated. A whole lot of things. He could mourn what he'd lost, and sometimes he did. With a kind of hideous breathlessness that would overtake him for a moment in time and make him think he was going to suffocate. But then it would pass. And he would get hold of the moment again.

He hadn't known about Dallas. So really, any time he had with him was something. A chance to build this relationship when it had been lost to them for so many years. He could focus on one end of that equation or the other. The missing years, or the fact that he was going to have years now. It was better to focus on this end. Because it was the one he could do something about.

Then there was Kaylee.

Sweet, prickly, amazing Kaylee. Who had been

through so much more than he'd realized. Who was so much stronger than he'd known.

And so much sexier.

When they walked back into the room, Freda was sitting next to Dallas, forcing affection on him. She had her copper-colored hands wrapped around his, holding him tightly as she said something intently to him. Dallas looked up, clearly at sea being the center of attention.

"These are your grandparents," he said, gesturing between Freda and his dad.

"I figured," Dallas said.

"Good to meet you," Quinn said, crossing the room and sticking his hand out. Dallas stuck his hand out too, and Quinn shook it, firm like he always did.

"You can have a firmer grip than that," Quinn said, smiling at Dallas. "Nothing wrong with a good firm handshake."

And he knew that a lot of people would have found that a distant greeting for a long-lost grandson, but as far as Quinn Dodge was concerned that was the real deal. Teaching a man the value of a handshake was something his father believed in.

Well, not just a man. Jamie's handshake was strong enough to make a bull rider cry. And she'd tried to make more than one cry more than once.

Watching his father interact with Dallas, Bennett had to ask himself what he had *thought* his father would do when he found out. It wasn't like he had ever believed that Quinn wouldn't accept his grandson. Wasn't like he had truly thought he would disown them. But he hadn't told him.

He had avoided it actively. Not just when he had been a teenager when that kind of behavior was some-what excusable, but now, when he was thirty-two years old. A man who should have known better than to do something like that.

But he was used to taking care of things on his own. He didn't like having to lean against people. He wanted to fix things, he didn't want to break them.

The one person he'd really let close had been Kaylee. Not that they shared perfectly with each other. It wasn't either of their strong points. But the first time he'd seen that lonely, lost-looking thirteen-year-old girl at school he'd wanted to make her look less lonely. And she'd made him feel less lonely too.

He had come to understand loss at far too early of an age to ever want to let people be pillars in his life.

That was what he had learned at the age of seven. That when you lost one of those pillars it was so easy for you to crumble.

Of course, he hadn't thought of it in those terms then. He had been a child. And all he had known was the bright, intense pain, the inability to understand what death really meant.

That it was really an end. That it meant they were gone forever. And forever meant no bedtime stories. No being tucked in. Never hearing their voice. Never smelling that perfume. It had taken his brain so long to wrap itself around that concept. Even as an adult he wasn't entirely sure he understood it.

What he knew was that if he had to ask for help, then it meant something had gone wrong. It meant that he had miscalculated, that he was not in control of his life, and for reasons he imagined stemmed back to being that little boy who felt like his world had been turned over on its side, the very idea was unthinkable to him.

But here he was, surrounded by family, with his father and stepmother, and he was… Well, he was leaning on them a little bit. And some of that was for Dallas's benefit.

Quite honestly, Bennett felt like finding out that he was all the kid got was a pretty piss-poor prize. But adding his family to that equation...the uncles, the grandparents. That made it all a little bit more. That made it feel like he was really giving his son something. With all that considered, building a wall around himself was selfish. Because this safety net benefited Dallas, and while Bennett had systematically made sure he didn't need those safety nets, while he had gone to great lengths to make sure he never used them, he could see how foolish it was when he looked at his son.

Could imagine how he would feel if Dallas came to him with news that he had gotten a girl pregnant.

He would be concerned. Maybe even upset. But he'd want to do whatever he could to help. He'd want to be there. Be involved.

This new perspective on the other side of the parent-child relationship was really something. What was actually a burden, and what wasn't.

Basically *nothing* was. Hard, maybe. But he wanted desperately to carry his son's burdens, and they weren't burdens to him. They were blessings. Because it was what he felt like his shoulders had been made for. To carry that. To carry him.

He hadn't understood that before now. Hadn't understood that he wasn't sparing his father by holding all of that back. He was denying him a chance to be a father in the way he would want.

But it required sharing on Bennett's part. And that he found hard. That, he didn't find so appealing.

When dinner wrapped up, Bennett got ready to go.

But after Dallas and Kaylee walked out of the house, Quinn pulled him aside.

"We'll be around for a few weeks. We might even extend the stay. So we can get to know him."

"That's what I'm still trying to do," Bennett responded.

"You've always been strong," Quinn said. "But don't forget to let him in."

That was too close to all the raw, terrible things Bennett had been thinking about. To all the stuff he didn't want to acknowledge.

"All right," Quinn said, clearly reaching an end to how much he could talk about feelings. "We'll see him around tomorrow, I guess. I hear he's working on the place."

"Yeah," Bennett said. "Doing a pretty good job too. And learning to ride."

"Definitely a Dodge," Quinn said.

"Bye, Dad," Bennett said, turning and walking out of the house.

Yes, Dallas was definitely a Dodge. Which meant he wasn't going to make any of that emotional stuff easy. And it wasn't easy for Bennett either. At this point, he just wanted to take a break for a while. Even though he knew it wasn't possible.

But there was Kaylee. She was his port in the storm, always had been. And tonight…

He walked out onto the porch and saw her standing by the truck. She had ridden over with him and Dallas because she had known that he was going to want to spend some time with her after he got Dallas settled at the house.

She was beautiful, with the sunlight shrinking and

fading behind the mountains, threading golden strands through her hair, casting her face in a glow.

He had always been proud of her. Proud to walk around with someone like her by his side. Resilient, beautiful, strong. Smart as hell. But it all felt different in that moment. She was standing with Dallas, making easy conversation with him. Dallas actually seemed a little bit more at ease around her. At least, more than he did around Bennett.

Their relationship was still a standoff half the time, like Dallas was trying to push him away. But he didn't seem to have that problem with Kaylee. Didn't seem to have that need to set her at a distance.

And Kaylee, for her part, understood the kid well. She helped Bennett understand him, which was another point in the column of not trying to do things alone.

But then, he had never tried to do it without Kaylee. She had been the first person he called, and for good reason.

They all loaded up in the truck and Bennett drove them back to his place.

"You can have a reprieve from chores," he said to his son.

And yeah, he had ulterior motives. Ulterior motives that didn't put him in the running for World's Best Dad. But he supposed not knowing about his son for fifteen years had killed those chances already.

"Thanks," Dallas said. "Feeling guilty about all the child labor?"

"Not at all," Bennett said, "but I thought you might be tired."

"Not especially, but I'm willing to go inside and play Xbox instead of clean out stalls."

"Well, whatever works."

Dallas went into the house, leaving Bennett and Kaylee alone outside.

"Why don't we go check on the horses?" Bennett asked.

Kaylee nodded, her expression halting. She clearly knew he had ulterior motives too. But she followed him to the barn, which must mean she didn't mind them. She was silent while Bennett tended to the horses, twisting her hands in front of her as though she were feeling a bit nervous.

He wondered if she was.

For his part, there were no nerves. There was just a growing, expanding need in his gut. One that was starting to blot out all the complicated thoughts from earlier. And that was what he wanted to pursue. That was what he wanted to chase. Because all that other stuff was complicated and confronting. Needing people. Talking to his father. Dealing with all this past garbage that he simply didn't want to deal with.

He didn't know why he felt so desperate, why he felt scraped raw all the way down to his bones. Everything had gone well. There was nothing to fight against. Nothing to insulate himself against. There was just...acceptance. Of his father's love. Of the way his siblings had accepted Dallas as their nephew so quickly.

And then there was Kaylee. Who was always everything he needed, and had been that and more lately.

He needed her now. Needed her to simplify everything. Her touch, her kiss. It would. He knew it. Because weirdly, it was the only thing that made sense from the past few weeks.

Maybe because it didn't have reasoning involved. Because there was no plan in it. Because there was nothing except want, and his wants had been nowhere near any of the recent events in his life.

He hadn't wanted to break up with Olivia. He hadn't wanted a son. He hadn't wanted to open up all the mistakes he made in the past in front of his family and confess them. Hadn't wanted to admit there was a time when he'd lost control.

And yet he had to.

And none of that was for him. Not really. But this was. She was. And he suddenly needed her more than air.

The horses were fed, and everything else could wait.

"Staring at you all night and not being able to touch you has been torture," he said, his voice rough.

Her head snapped around, shock visible in her green eyes. "Me?"

"Yes, you. You're a damned problem, Kaylee Capshaw."

"I'm a problem?" She looked delighted by that information, and not at all abashed.

"A pretty one."

And then, without talking, he pressed her back up against the door of the barn, his chest pressed against her small, perfectly formed breasts as he consumed her mouth like he was a starving man. He was. For more than just sex. For this release, this escape. For a kind of satisfaction that would blot out all the things that had come before.

Maybe that made him a jerk. Using his best friend like this. But maybe that was also the only reason he could do this. Because she was Kaylee. Because she had always been something different. Something special. This small bit of connection he allowed himself to have.

And right now... She was more than escape. She tasted like salvation. All soft and slick and hot.

And he could see her now. The lights were on in the barn, and when he pulled away from her mouth to trail kisses down her neck, he could see the way that pale skin flushed. How aroused she was, evidenced by the way that skin bloomed with red, the way her pupils dilated. The way her breath made her breasts rise and fall in small, choppy motions.

He was going to see her naked. He had to.

"Should we talk about this?" she asked breathlessly as he trailed kisses to the edge of the collar of her shirt.

"I don't want to talk. We've talked enough, don't you think?" he asked, echoing what she had said to him last night.

They'd had years of talking. Years and years of it. And years of not doing this. Suddenly, this was all he wanted.

And that didn't feel like reducing her, or their connection. It felt like growing it. Maybe that was his dick talking, it was entirely possible. But whatever, it made sense.

"I want to see you," he said. "Like I said earlier. I have to know."

"You're obsessed with colors," she said softly, fingertips fluttering down to his chest, tracing a line all the way down to the waistband of his jeans.

Desire kicked in him like a horse, his body getting hard.

"All the colors of Kaylee," he agreed. "Your hair, your skin. Do you know what I like?"

"No," she said, the word hushed.

"I like the way you're flushed all red right now. I like how I can see that you're turned on. I've never seen you turned on before, Kay. Not really. Do you know how hot it is to know what that looks like?"

"Probably about as hot as I find it to see you turned

on," she said, looking down at the bulge in the front of his pants meaningfully.

"Good thing it works for both of us. Can't imagine what it would be like if this only went one way."

She looked down, biting her lip, and he gripped her chin, tilting her face back up so he could look at her.

"Yeah," she said softly. "Good thing."

He pressed his fingertips to the hem of her top, pushing them beneath, dragging the calloused tips over her soft skin. He was rough and work scarred, hazards of the job. But Kaylee did the same work, and somehow managed to be silk over muscle. Soft over strong. He had always focused on that strength in her, because it was something he prized in her as a friend. He hadn't let himself marvel at her femininity. At just how perfect all that skin was. He was doing it now.

He pushed her top all the way up over her head, and threw it down onto the floor, then he leaned in, kissing her jaw as he reached around to unhook her bra.

Lust hit him like a slug in the gut as he took in the sight of those perfect bare breasts. With the lovely, tight pink tips. They were just the right size to hold in his hands, to suck into his mouth. He had done it before, but not when he could see her. Not when he could see this. He was drunk on it. On her.

And suddenly...

He didn't want her to be his port in the storm.

He wanted to be hers.

Everything she'd said to him earlier flooded back. Washed over him. The way she'd looked when he'd come over and helped her move that ridiculous hutch, and how she'd been reluctant to take anything from him.

The first night they'd been together, she'd gone down on him.

Not now.

Now, he was going to give to her. And he was going to make damn sure she liked it.

He gripped her hips, kissing a line down to her collarbone, to that sweet, vulnerable curve just above her nipple, and then he sucked her in deep, gratified when she gasped and grabbed hold of his hair.

"That's right," he murmured against her skin, "you like that, don't you?"

"Yes," she said.

"To think. All this time I didn't know my best friend had such sensitive nipples."

"Doesn't come up in polite conversation," she gasped.

"Then we need to have less polite conversations."

He reached down then, undoing her belt buckle, unbuttoning her jeans and drawing the zipper down slowly. Then he got on his knees in front of her, gripping the fabric of her jeans and her panties and pulling both down her legs, shoving them to the side and leaving himself eye level with those curls he had made declarations about earlier in the day.

She was beautiful. More beautiful than he had imagined she might be. He wanted… He wanted *her*. With such ferocity it jarred him. Wanted to taste her deeper than he thought possible, wanted to sink inside of her and lose himself completely. Wanted to forget that there was anything outside of this barn, outside of the two of them.

Life would be simpler if it could just be this.

Or at least, it would feel better. A hell of a lot better.

He tightened his hold on her hips, moving his hands around slightly to cup her ass. She was lean, and she was toned, his Kaylee, but there was more to grab on to of her backside. It was softer than the rest of her. And he liked that. He liked it a lot.

He leaned forward, inhaling deeply before sliding his tongue through her folds, moving his hand up to part those lips so that he could examine her the way that he wanted to. She was everything. Everything he had wanted her to be. Everything he had needed her to be. And then some.

He didn't think he could match that. He hoped he could do even half of that for her now. Even if it was only sex. Only pleasure.

While he tasted her he was never not fully aware that it was Kaylee. His Kaylee. Naked and wet beneath his mouth, making small noises of pleasure as he flicked his tongue over her clit. As he pushed his fingers inside of her and dragged another release from her beautiful core. As her pleasure coated his mouth, his finger.

He had never gotten quite so much pleasure from lavishing attention on a woman. Because no woman had ever mattered quite this much. He cared about Kaylee. And each sound she made wasn't just one of pleasure. It was Kaylee feeling good. Kaylee feeling beautiful. Feeling wanted.

All the things he'd always wanted for her, but now he was the one giving them to her. He had given her that feeling of being wanted as best he could as a friend. But this was more. She let him be more. Do more.

And selfish or not, she was beautiful, and he had his face buried between her legs. And that was pleasure all on its own. It had him hard as iron, ready to explode.

After her climax he kept on at it, teasing her with his tongue, his fingers, until she begged him to stop. But he didn't stop.

"Bennett," she gasped, "I can't... I can't."

"You sure as hell can," he growled, gripping her hips and pinning her firmly against the wall so that she couldn't move. "Because I'm not done. And don't you worry about whether or not you can come, I've got all the time in the world. And I'm just enjoying sucking on your pretty clit."

And just like that, she came apart around his fingers again. Gasping and sobbing, twisting, as if she was trying to get away from him. But he held her steady against his mouth, stroking his tongue over her a few more times before rising to his feet.

She was panting, sweat beaded between her pretty breasts, her hair hanging lank and disheveled around her.

He was struck dumb. Seeing her like this. His friend, wilted with desire against the wall because of him.

"You take off your clothes next," she said, seeming to find some strength, pushing herself away from the wall by an inch or so. "I didn't get to see you either."

"I think I can handle that."

He pulled his T-shirt over his head, gratified by the expression of open hunger in her eyes as she regarded him. Then he began to work his belt buckle and she eyed him with pure avarice, her gaze never leaving him as he undid his zipper and consigned his clothes to the barn floor along with hers.

He collected a condom from his wallet and tore it open, rolling it on slowly as she watched. He felt her gaze on his body like a physical touch. He took pains to protect them both, his body aching with need for her.

Then he closed the distance between them, working his fingers through her hair, cupping the back of her head and kissing her fiercely as he brought her back up against the wall. She flexed her hips against him and he gripped her thigh with one hand, lifting her leg and draping it over his hip as he positioned himself at her slick entrance and thrust in deep.

She gasped, her eyes fluttering closed, her head falling back, and those delicate, familiar lips parted gently.

He withdrew slowly, before thrusting back in, watching as that lovely, familiar face responded to him being inside of her.

Kaylee.

There was no denying this was happening. No convenient cover of darkness to blunt it all. Last night, it had felt strange and muted, hot as hell, for sure. But there had been some protection in it. None now. It sliced into him deep. Now, it was all her turning him on. Not *sex*, not *a female touch*. But Kaylee. Only and always Kaylee.

He lost himself in the rhythm they established together, in the breathy sighs she made as her arousal began to amp up again. In the way her tight, wet body tightened itself around him.

If he died in this moment, he would die a damned happy man, that was for sure. With Kaylee's fingernails digging into his shoulders, her legs wrapped around his waist as he pounded them both into oblivion.

Wyatt was right. Not seeing her like this before… It had been an effort on his part. And now that he had dropped his guard, now that he had given up on seeing her as anything other than this…his friend who was beautiful. His friend who he wanted, he couldn't imagine ever not wanting her.

That was need. And need terrified the hell out of him. Need was something he had tried so very hard not to feel. But it was sweet right now. Sweet as hell. In a very literal sense. All fire and brimstone and torture, but also something he couldn't stop. Something he couldn't quit. An addiction, one so good he never wanted to be clean.

He wanted to be dirty. With her.

Pleasure gathered at the base of his spine, electric and undeniable. It was like fire building inside of him. One that was going to rage out of control at any moment. One that might consume him completely. That need again. That thing he had known would be a raging, destructive thing. And it was. It was. But he was ready to jump feetfirst into it.

He lost his hold on his control, letting go completely, igniting and bringing Kaylee along with him.

If they were going to burn, at least they were burning together.

They clung to each other, his orgasm taking them over completely, a feral growl on his lips as he let it all go completely.

He kissed her one last time, pulling them away from the wall and walking her over to a cabinet on the far end of the barn. He opened up the cabinet and with one arm pulled out a couple of blankets, clutching them and Kaylee to his chest and heading into one of the empty stalls. He tossed the blankets down onto the ground.

"Gotta put you down for a second, sweetheart," he said.

He did, and she stood there, looking at him, one arm beneath her breasts, her hand gripping her other arm just above the elbow. She looked…lost and a little bit vulnerable, and he wasn't used to Kaylee looking that way. It had been like that after the first time they were together, and he had completely messed it up. He wasn't going to do that this time.

He didn't want to disappoint her. He never wanted

to be responsible for the kind of pain he'd seen on her face earlier today. For the pain he'd heard in her voice when she'd told him that story about her past.

He wanted more. More than just a quick turn up against the wall.

He spread a blanket out over the clean shavings on the floor of the stall that would provide them with some cushion, then he picked her back up, laying her down on the flannel.

"Cozy," she said as he unfolded the other blanket and unfurled it over the top of her, letting it catch air as it drifted down over her curves.

"It'll do," he said, getting beneath the blanket with her and pulling her up against him.

They could hear the horses in their stalls, making small noises and shuffling around. Suddenly, Kaylee snickered against his shoulder.

"What?"

"I was just thinking… This is pretty fitting for us. Considering our lives are bonded over the fact that we take care of animals. But the only thing that's missing is Beatrix Leighton coming in with a box of raccoons."

"It was only *one* raccoon," he said. "And if she came in now, she wouldn't get any help from me."

Kaylee looked mock horrified. "But what about your oath to protect and serve?"

"I didn't take an oath for raccoons."

"You're unfeeling, Bennett Dodge."

"I feel plenty," he said, slipping his hand between her legs and stroking her until she tried to wiggle away, then gave in, going pliant under his touch.

"That's not what I meant," she protested.

"I have more condoms in my wallet," he said.

"Well, that is handy. It's almost as if you were planning this."

"I was," he said unrepentantly.

"Good. I was hoping you would say that."

He kissed her again, drawing her curves up against his body. It felt right. She felt right.

And the plan right now was to do this until it stopped feeling right.

As plans went, it wasn't the best one. But if it meant having Kaylee in his arms, then it was the plan he was going to go with.

CHAPTER SEVENTEEN

WHEN KAYLEE WOKE UP, the sun was just starting to bleed into her consciousness. Rose gold and gentle. It was filtering through the slats on the stall, from the small opens in the barn door.

The barn door. She was in the barn.

She sat upright, and the man next to her mumbled something and rolled over, his elbow beneath his head, acting as a pillow.

Bennett.

She smiled, looking down at him while he slept. She couldn't help herself. She touched him. Ran her fingertips down his bare biceps and sighed a little bit as she touched all that hot, naked skin.

His expression was relaxed while he slept, much less tense than it was when he was awake.

She wanted to keep sitting here like this, looking at him.

But she really had to pee.

She scurried out of the stall, moving cautiously, naked, across the barn, the early morning air chilling her vulnerable bits. She dressed quickly, still mourning the loss of Bennett's warmth and weight as she slipped out of the barn and across the gravel toward the house. She just needed to use the bathroom, and then she would come back to the barn and figure out a way for Bennett to sneak her back home.

She had a feeling he hadn't intended to stay out there all night with her. Hell, she certainly hadn't intended to stay out all night. But after the second or third time things had gotten a little bit blurry, and she had been very, very sleepy.

It had seemed like the most natural thing to do to curl up against his chest and enjoy his warmth. To luxuriate in their connection for just a little while longer.

Plus, she had been so *sleepy*.

And cold.

Damn Bennett Dodge and his seductive coziness.

Well, and the seductive rest of him.

She was reflecting on that as she tiptoed into the house and down the hall to the bathroom. She made quick use of the facilities, casting a critical eye over herself in the mirror. She had hay in her hair. And not a small amount of it. She also looked puffy. The tiny bit of mascara she'd put on for dinner the night before was now imprinted on her cheek. To say nothing of the blanket seam that had carved out a divot on her forehead.

She was not looking her best.

But then, she supposed that was part and parcel to waking up with someone. They got to see the morning after. Which was a mixed bag.

Bennett had looked so gorgeous. So perfect. Not a blanket seam in sight.

That hardly seemed fair.

She sighed heavily and crept back out of the bathroom, heading past the kitchen and leaping like a frightened rabbit when she heard the sound of a clearing throat.

She paused, looking into the other room.

And there was Dallas. Sitting at the kitchen table with his hands folded, his expression amused.

"Good morning," he said.

"Good morning," she said. "You're up early."

"Yeah, well, my... Bennett broke me. I keep waking up at six o'clock like that's something normal people do."

"Damn ranchers," she said, laughing nervously and edging to the side.

He looked at her far too astutely for her liking. "You seem to be wearing what you had on yesterday."

"That's very observant of you. Most guys don't even notice when a woman gets a haircut. You should hang on to that. Your girlfriend will appreciate it someday."

"Did you spend the night?"

She picked at her fingernail behind her back and tried to look innocent. "I did not spend the night at the house, no."

"On the property?"

How the hell was she being interrogated by a teenager and not the other way around? Why did it make her feel *guilty*?

"Well..."

"If I looked in Bennett's bedroom... He's not in there, is he?"

"Maybe not," she said.

The kid smiled. Little snot. "Congrats," he said.

She narrowed her eyes. "On?"

"Making it out of the friend zone."

"That is... This is a bad example. And I apologize."

"Why is it a bad example?"

"Because. Responsible...behaviors and you're far too young to be exposed to adult sorts of situations."

"For one, this is an adult situation I've been exposed to multiple times of my own free will. Yeah. You grow up fast when you don't have parents around. Also, I pre-

fer being exposed to you and Bennett and, you know…
regular meals than I do to neglect and starvation. So,
don't worry. My impressionable youth was scarred a hell
of a lot more deeply by the abandonment of my mother
than by this implied sex scene."

She huffed out a breath. "Your dad is going to be so
mad that you know."

"No, he won't."

"Yes, he will."

"He's never mad at you."

Kaylee sighed and moved into the room, sitting down
in the chair across from Dallas. "He does get mad at me.
And I get mad at him. But we care about each other.
So…we work it out. That's what being friends means."

"And also you spending the night?"

"That's new. But we'll work that out too. Because
you don't quit on someone you love just because it's
hard. And whatever Bennett and I are or aren't…we
love each other."

"That's good," Dallas said, clearly trying to play it all
off like he didn't care. But she suspected he cared. "I'd
hate for you two to have a bitter custody battle over me."

"Well, I've been friends with him for seventeen
years. So, I kind of doubt that would ever happen."

Dallas frowned. "I guess you have to stay in one
place for a while to make friends like that."

"I didn't move here until I was about thirteen. Before
I met Bennett…I didn't have friends like that. There's
a lot of time for you to make friends."

"Assuming I stay," Dallas pointed out.

Her heart felt tender. Bruised. Even after a couple
of weeks, Dallas was living with one foot out the door.
No matter how smooth things seemed to be going, of
course he didn't feel secure yet. Why would he?

She understood that better than she'd like to.

She wished she could reach out and touch him. Offer comfort. But she had a feeling he wouldn't like it.

"That feeling that you have," she said slowly, "that uncertainty…just because you feel it, doesn't mean it's trying to warn you. If you're not sure if you're going to stay here, that's because *you're* not sure if you're going to leave or not. Bennett is never going to ask you to go."

Dallas looked down. "He might."

"He won't. Remember, I've known him for seventeen years. Also, there's his whole family. Can you imagine what Wyatt would do to him? Your grandfather? You have a whole lot of people here who care about you."

Dallas nodded slowly, like he was considering that. "Though," he pointed out, "it's Grant who would beat him up."

"Do you think so?" Grant was much more serious than Wyatt. And it was interesting having known him before he lost his wife and knowing him now. She knew that he had that in him, but she was surprised that Dallas did.

"Yeah. It's always the quiet ones."

"Fair enough."

"You should go back to wherever you were. So that he doesn't wake up and think you ran out on him."

"He wouldn't think that."

"Right. Because you're friends."

"Yes. Not that weird things don't happen, misunderstandings and all of that. But mostly… We know each other. We trust each other. That takes time, and there's nothing but time that can manufacture that. People doing more good things to you than crappy ones." She swallowed hard, finding the next words difficult. But she wanted Dallas to know this. She wanted him to talk about it. She hadn't been able to at his age, and maybe that was part of why it had controlled her life for so long. She didn't want that for them. "My parents never wanted me," she said. "They wanted a baby to try to make them happier, to try to fix their situation."

Dallas frowned. "Why would a kid make anyone happier when your life is shit?"

"They can't fix it," she said. "They just add stress. And I could never be that easy, magic fix for them. So they lost interest in me. Completely. And honestly, if it wasn't for my own stubbornness, and my desire to not let them decide whether or not I went to school looking like a mess, or whether or not I went at all, and the support that I found with the Dodge family, I don't know where I would be. But it's been a lot of years of those people, good people, showing me that someone can be good. And more importantly, someone can be good to me."

Dallas wasn't looking at her anymore. His eyes were fixed on a blank space on the wall. She hoped he'd taken that on board. Hoped he could.

She stood up slowly. "Do you know how to make coffee?"

"Yeah. With these crazy hours it's a matter of survival. I think that's actually the real reason he has me here. To make coffee."

She shook her head. "I'll get Bennett. We'll be in in a minute."

"Do you want me to act cool like I don't know?" he asked, deadpan.

"No." She looked at him and smiled. "Mostly because you wouldn't. You wouldn't be able to pass up the opportunity to say something smart-ass."

Dallas grinned. "Yeah, that does sound like me."

"Just wait. I'll bring Bennett back."

She walked out of the kitchen and out the front door, taking the steps on the porch by twos and back over to the barn. Bennett was still sleeping. "Wake up, sunshine," she said.

Bennett startled, and then sat up, the blankets falling down around his waist, giving her an excellent showing of his muscles. That dark, enticing chest hair that covered his pecs and ran in a slim trail down his abs. It had been perfect last night. Seeing him naked. Really. With the lights on and everything. She hoped to do it again soon.

"I slept in the barn?"

"Yes, *we* slept in the barn."

"You're dressed." The statement was faintly accusing in tone.

"Yes," she confirmed. "I am dressed. I had to go in the house. And the jig is up."

"What jig?"

"*The* jig. Us keeping this a secret from Dallas. He caught me."

"Were you holding a sign that said we had sex?"

"No. But I'm not a good liar, and I was wearing the same clothes as I had on the night before. It wasn't exactly rocket science."

"Great."

"It's fine," she said.

"It just feels complicated," Bennett said. "Like everything."

"I hear you," she responded. "But he doesn't seem especially emotionally scarred or anything."

"You're right," he said, rolling up into a standing position, letting the blanket fall down completely. How were they supposed to have a conversation with him standing there naked like that? His body was a testament to his hard labor. That chiseled line that sat low on his hip, tracing a path down to the most masculine part of him. His perfectly carved thighs and what was quite frankly a glorious behind.

"I'm objectifying you," she said as he began to fold the blankets up. "Just so you know."

He turned his head, a slow smile curving his lips. "Okay."

"You should probably be appalled."

"Should I be?"

"I'm leering."

"Well, I'm not appalled." In fact, he abandoned his blanket folding to cross the room and pulled her against his naked form, giving her a good, thorough kiss. She let her hands flutter down to his chest, moving her finger slowly over his chest hair.

"What's going to happen with us?" The question seemed to burst into the crisp air and add a heaviness to it that she hadn't wanted to inject into the atmosphere. But she had to ask. It was like jerking that bedroom door open as quickly as possible. So she wouldn't have time to build up hope there might be something wonderful on the other side, when it was just more of the same.

Things between them felt so light sometimes, but it was interspersed with this crazy sexual tension. And it had always been there for her. When Bennett had said it would be terrible if this was one-sided, she had nearly choked. Because it had been for her. For years. This horrible one-person torch that she carried, being reasonably certain Bennett would never carry a similar one for her.

And now he wanted her. But in spite of all the confidence she had given to Dallas earlier, she didn't really feel quite so certain. Not because she didn't trust Bennett, or their friendship, it was just... How could she ever go back to only being allowed to see him with clothes on? How could she ever pretend that they hadn't done this?

"It's going to be fine," he said.

"Because you planned it?"

"Yeah," he said, as if that made perfect sense.

"Sorry, Bennett, but given the way that your life has been running lately I don't have the utmost confidence in the universe going along with your plans."

"It's going to be fine," he reiterated.

She didn't know how. But she didn't press the issue as he continued to fold up the blankets and put them back in the cabinet. He collected his clothes, effectively covering her peep show.

"We can all have coffee together now," she said.

Bennett grimaced, and they walked toward the house together. His knuckles brushed against hers, and she was tempted to grab on to his hand. But she didn't know if that was okay. They were...sleeping with each other. But that didn't mean they were also being physically affectionate in a casual sense. Maybe they were leaving behind the whole lover thing along with the blankets, folded up and put away in the barn cabinet until it was time to get them out again.

She shoved the impulse aside, took a deep breath and walked side by side with Bennett up the porch, their footsteps loud on the hollow wood. Bennett opened the door for her and she smiled slightly as they walked inside.

Dallas was still sitting at the table, looking far too amused for Kaylee's comfort. And he had not made any coffee yet.

"If you want coffee, behave yourself," Bennett said.

"Aww," Dallas said, affecting a petulant-sounding tone. "Dad, that's not fair."

Then, he looked slightly stricken, as though he had just realized what he had called Bennett, even as a joke. She looked over at Bennett, whose face looked like it could have been carved from granite.

"How about that coffee?" he asked.

And they didn't talk about anything serious for the rest of the morning.

CHAPTER EIGHTEEN

IN THE WEEKS that passed, they settled into a routine. Bennett would take Dallas to work at Get Out of Dodge, and then Bennett would check in at the clinic, just to see Kaylee, even if he didn't need to go over there. Then they'd do their work, Bennett would pick up Dallas, and they would have dinner.

Then Bennett would go to Kaylee's house for a few hours. They'd drink a beer, talk and inevitably end up in bed together. And then Bennett would go back home and resume his life as father to a teenage boy.

It wasn't all routine. He'd taken Dallas to Tolowa and gotten him all new clothes. Work boots, gloves, Sunday clothes and casual clothes. He'd gotten registered at Gold Valley High School for the following year, and had only made three jokes about whether or not there was a cow-milking class he could take.

"No," Bennett had told him, "but there is a drill team. Jamie coaches them."

"A what?" he'd asked.

"Drill team. Like synchronized swimming, but on horses. With flags and glitter. Boys don't normally do it but I'm sure you could make a case for discrimination."

"Pass."

They spent weekends riding up in the hills behind the house. Dallas was getting to be a much more confident rider. More interesting to Bennett was the bond he was forming with the horse Lucy.

It was hard for Dallas to be sincere, difficult for him to be much of anything other than a wall of teenage cynicism. But not with the horse. His guards dropped for her. Animals were safer than people in a lot of ways, Bennett understood that well.

When he'd been hurting after his mother's death he'd found solace in them. And he'd figured out what he wanted to do with his life from that.

He also knew that you could tell a lot about what a person kept hidden by how they treated animals. Someone who seemed kind and gentle but had neglected cattle, horses with saddle sores and underfed dogs was rotten in their heart, as far as he was concerned. And no matter how tough and hard a man seemed, if he cared for his animals...that showed kindness. No matter how deep he tried to keep it buried.

Dallas's connection to Lucy let him see things that Dallas would rather die than show Bennett. And it gave him hope. It made him feel connected to his son in a way he might not if it weren't for the horse.

They also got a court date to make it all official. It had taken time to get everything transferred over to Logan County from Multnomah County, but Bennett was ready to sign papers for full custody of Dallas.

In reality, this was all a formality. Marnie wasn't likely to show up and demand custody, and even if she did, there was ample evidence she wasn't a fit parent. But this was important to Bennett because it made it legal. Final in a way he had a feeling his word couldn't be.

He wanted to prove to Dallas this would last.

They closed the clinic the day of the court appointment because he wanted Kaylee to be with them. It seemed important somehow to have her there. Quinn and Freda were coming to the courthouse too, adamant that they wanted to be part of it.

Considering it was symbolic in large part, he appreciated it. They were all in this together, even if he could tell it made Dallas uncomfortable—Bennett also thought that could be his tie and button-up shirt that could have been causing the majority of his discomfort. God knew it was causing a lot of Bennett's. But it had seemed like something a man had to put on Sunday clothes for.

Kaylee for her part looked absolutely beautiful. She was wearing that same floral dress she had been wearing the night of her date with that other guy that Bennett had purposefully forgotten the name of already. It was different, though, because this time, she wasn't wearing the dress for someone else. So, as pretty as she had been then, she was even prettier now.

He felt a sense of pride as they all walked into the redbrick courthouse.

The proceedings didn't take long. All that needed to happen was for the papers to be signed and the court to grant the request.

Dallas's caseworker Grace was also in attendance, wearing what Bennett thought might be the same black jacket and skirt she had on the first time they'd met. The actual granting of custody went quickly, and they were back in the antechamber of the courtroom shockingly fast.

Grace smiled at Dallas and reached out, squeezing his arm. "I'm happy for you," she said. "See that you stay out of trouble. And I hope that if I ever see you again it's at a reunion and not because of something bad."

"Well, if I don't behave myself it's not really your problem," Dallas said, shrugging, obviously reluctant to get too sentimental with the woman who had handled his case for the past couple of years.

"If he doesn't stay out of trouble I'll be surprised," Bennett said. "He's working too hard to get up to anything more than Xbox at night."

Dallas grimaced. "Child labor."

"The papers are signed, son," Bennett said. "It's too late. You should have brought that up before the judge."

Dallas lifted a shoulder. "Well, it's not killing me or anything."

"Good to know."

Freda, who knew absolutely no restraint at all, pulled Dallas in for a hug, and the teenager let her, his chin touching the top of Bennett's stepmother's dark hair. She was a small woman, but she was a force of nature. Bennett wasn't at all mystified as to why his father had fallen for her.

And as far as he could tell, Dallas was falling for her too. Because if anyone else had grabbed him and attempted to hug him he had a feeling that Dallas would put up a fight. But Bennett did reach out and pat his son on the shoulder, an overwhelming tide of love and pride washing through him.

It didn't matter anymore that they'd spent fifteen years apart. Dallas was his son. And they were a family. Yeah, he wished they could have had all that time together, but there was no point wasting the years they did have on bad feelings. Not that they would never pop up, that was inevitable. But for his part, he was going to make an effort to focus on the good.

"Congratulations," Quinn said, patting Bennett on the back. "It's good to see you happy."

He was happy. And his life certainly didn't look like the picture-perfect ideal he had wanted so badly for it to be. Hell, he had been determined to make it look traditional even when Marnie had gotten pregnant at sixteen and it had been clear that traditional was not exactly a happening thing.

So, he didn't have that. But he had happy.

He looked over at Kaylee, who was smiling softly, her hands clasped in front of her. She was obviously a little bit uncomfortable to be witnessing all of this. But she didn't feel out of place to him, even if she probably felt a little bit out of place to herself.

"You hungry?" he asked Dallas.

"Yeah," Dallas said.

They walked out of the courthouse, the warm afternoon sun shining down on them. It was almost dinnertime, and apparently, going to family court made you hungry.

"We'll probably head on home," Quinn said. "But we'll see you tomorrow, Dallas."

"Okay," Dallas said.

Freda pulled him in for another hug, and he didn't resist her at all.

"I'll see you guys," Kaylee said.

"Come to dinner with us, Kaylee." Bennett didn't want her to leave. It felt right having her here for this, and he didn't want to let her go.

"Oh, I don't have to…" She shifted uncomfortably. "I bet you guys need some time alone."

"We don't," Dallas said.

Bennett shot his son a look. "We're fine. Join us for dinner. We'll just walk someplace from here."

"Okay. Let me get a sweater out of my car."

She disappeared for a moment and Dallas looked at Bennett. "You know," Dallas said. "You could ask her to spend the night sometimes."

"What?" That was the last thing he'd expected his son to stay.

"I know what you guys are doing when you go over to her house in the evening. Can't you just have her come spend the night? It's not like I think you guys are playing checkers at her place."

"Because it's not... That's like..."

That would be like they were a family. Having Kaylee spend the night, having her have breakfast with them in the morning. It just... It didn't seem like something they should do.

"We'll probably just keep things the same," Bennett said.

Dallas looked a little bit bemused. "Suit yourself. But I'm just saying, it's not like you're protecting me from the facts of life or anything."

"Noted."

Kaylee returned a second later with her sweater. "Where do you guys want dinner?"

"Where can you get a really good burger here?" Dallas asked.

"We always have burgers," Bennett said. "It's like the only thing your uncle Wyatt knows how to make."

"Yeah, but I want a restaurant burger. With French fries. Not potato chips. And a milkshake."

"That sounds good," Kaylee said. "I say we go to Mustard Seed."

Mustard Seed was within walking distance of the courthouse. Just down the street past Sugar Cup, hang a left on the main drag, then another left at the end. They walked down the sidewalk, and it really was hard not to feel like they were a family.

Well, they were family. So why wouldn't they feel like it? Dallas was his son. Kaylee was someone he couldn't imagine life without. He'd eaten here with her countless times through high school and beyond. She was woven into the fabric of his life. Every step of sidewalk in this town, he'd walked with her over the years. He could hardly remember a time without her. Didn't want to. That was family.

Mustard Seed wasn't too packed yet, the diner a popular spot for just about everyone. At breakfast time it was filled with senior citizens, at lunch groups of friends and adult parents and children, and at dinner... basically everyone.

The little place was eclectic, with small creatures made out of silverware adorning most of the available surfaces—an alligator made from bent spoons, a peacock made with forks and knives—a counter with red stools that had buckets of dry erase markers on it so that people could color on the metal countertops.

The windows were always decorated with washable paint, indicative of each season, and right now, the names of the graduating seniors had been scrawled across the windows by the kids themselves.

It was a tradition at the diner for the kids who were leaving town to sign their names at their favorite local spot. Bennett had done it himself, so had Kaylee before they had gone off to school. But they had come back. Not everybody did.

Still, it filled him with a sense of nostalgia when he walked in, seeing all those names, remembering when he and Kaylee had written theirs.

And now he was bringing his son here. In three years when Dallas graduated, his name would be up there.

Something in his chest felt tight.

They took a seat at one of the tables and Lucinda, the owner of Mustard Seed, greeted them immediately. "Hi, Bennett," she said. "Kaylee. And who is this?"

"This is my son," Bennett said. "Dallas Dodge."

Lucinda's dark eyebrows shot upward. "Your son?" She blinked. "I know I haven't seen you in here in a while, Bennett. But not this long."

"I'm a surprise," Dallas said.

"I'd say," Lucinda agreed. "So, what will you have to eat, surprise child?"

"A bacon cheeseburger. French fries. And a strawberry milkshake."

"Sounds good." Lucinda didn't write the order down. She didn't have to. She remembered everything. She looked at Bennett next. "Surprised dad?"

"I'll have what he's having."

"Same," Kaylee said, "but sweet potato fries. And make my shake a chocolate one."

Both Bennett and Dallas shot her strange looks.

"Sweet potato fries?" Dallas asked, curling his lip.

"She's a monster," Bennett said.

Dallas shook his head. "Why, when you could have good, regular French fries, that are not too sweet?"

"Like God intended."

"Excuse me," she said. "I don't need the Dodge men to gang up on me."

"You need better taste in fried foods," Bennett said.

"I will stand on my principles," Kaylee responded. "I will not give in to peer pressure."

By the time their food arrived the restaurant had begun to fill up with rowdy teenagers, some young families and a few couples. Dallas was watching the chaos around them thoughtfully, and Bennett wished he knew what his son was thinking.

Next year, Dallas would be going to school—not with these kids, since they were graduating—but with the teenagers that came into Gold Valley from surrounding areas and from town.

It wasn't a particularly large school, but he would make friends there. He would start to be a part of this. If he chose to. But then, that was what today had been about, really. Bennett had chosen to make it permanent in a legal way. Dallas had been there. Dallas had watched the court papers being signed. Had stood by while the judge ruled that Bennett had full custody.

Dallas had chosen it too.

And eventually, even if it took a while, he wouldn't just be part of Bennett's life, part of the Dodge family, he would be part of Gold Valley.

Bennett wanted that for him. Wanted it so badly it made him ache. To give his son not just himself, not just his love, but this life that he had chosen to live. This life that had been full of pain, yes, but so full of happiness too.

He understood now. That kind of deep nostalgia people talked about with parenting. That desire to pass certain things on to your children.

He more than understood it. He felt like his chest was being pried open, a thousand and one feelings he'd never had before all stuffed inside of him.

Feelings he'd never let himself have.

Feelings he'd been avoiding since he was a child.

They finished eating and brought their ticket up to the register, paying Lucinda before heading outside.

It wasn't dark yet, the sky just beginning to deepen

in color. High school kids were out on the sidewalk, getting rowdy. Driving their trucks down the two-lane street and revving their engines.

Bennett looked over at Kaylee. "Remember when we used to do things like that?"

"Yes. I had a bigger truck than most of the boys," she said, smiling impishly. "The results of a summer spent bagging groceries."

"You were pretty badass." He bumped her shoulder with his, then reached out and took hold of her hand, lacing his fingers through hers.

She looked up at him, her eyes wide. But she didn't let go.

Dallas, for his part, didn't say anything. But he was watching them closely.

They took the walk back toward the courthouse, toward where they'd parked, slowly. Bennett wasn't in a hurry to break this moment. Where everything just seemed good and clear. Right.

"Why don't you come over for a beer?" Bennett asked Kaylee.

She blinked, her eyebrows lifting. "Oh, you're not coming over to my place?"

"I just thought we should hang out at the house tonight."

"Okay," she said, clearly confused.

Bennett wasn't exactly sure what the endgame was. But he didn't feel like leaving Dallas tonight, not after signing those papers. And what Dallas had said outside the courtroom kept on ringing in his ears.

She could spend the night, you know.

Yes. She could.

And his resistance was…

He just didn't want to think about it right now. He didn't need to.

Kaylee released her hold on his hand and walked over to her truck, and Bennett and Dallas got in theirs, heading back toward Bennett's place. It wasn't dark yet, the sky a pale blue with flat, watercolor clouds resting over the top of it. But soon enough the sun would start sinking behind the mountains, turning the fields into mottled spots of gold and deep blue.

"I'm going to go feed the horses," Dallas said as soon as they pulled in, getting out of the truck and heading over to the barn.

"Was he trying to give us time alone? Or is he really that excited about doing chores?" Kaylee asked, moving over to where Bennett was standing. She didn't touch him, which he thought was funny. But then, he realized they didn't do a lot of casual touching. He would kiss her, and once he had done that, once he was holding her in his arms, she would often put her hand on his chest or somewhere else. But when they were talking, when they were walking together, there was no casual, relationship-type touching.

He supposed it was for the same reasons that he had never had her spend the night at his house. It felt like a relationship then. But…was it *not* one?

He had convinced himself that they could do this just to get through. But there was no getting through right now. He was through. He had signed the paperwork with Dallas, and Dallas no longer felt like something that had upended his life. He could scarcely remember a time when he had wanted to marry Olivia Logan. All of that upheaval… It was done with. He felt settled now.

But he didn't feel like taking his relationship with Kaylee back to friendship only. Not even a little bit.

In fact, he couldn't imagine it. There was no plan that felt like it would fix that. And no controlling a damn thing.

That made a strange, sharp pain hit him in the chest.

"Dad!"

Bennett whipped his head around and looked toward the barn, responding to the word *dad*, even though aside from being sarcastic, Dallas had never called him that before.

Bennett didn't even think. He took off running. Heading toward the sound of his son's voice. He heard footsteps behind him that let him know that Kaylee was running right along with him.

When he entered the barn he didn't see Dallas. "Dad, it's Lucy."

Bennett moved to Lucy's stall and looked in. The horse was lying on the ground, rocking back and forth, seemingly unable to stand.

Hell.

Bennett went into action, and so did Kaylee. Bennett had a strong suspicion he knew exactly what was happening, given the horse's past history and her current health issues. Acute laminitis. She hadn't been showing signs or symptoms before this. And that meant there was still time to try to reverse some damage. Before the bone in her leg became a problem that couldn't be solved, only managed. And that was a pretty grim future for a horse.

If she didn't end up requiring euthanasia.

He had a bad feeling Lucy had been into the grain and was on an overload. He had done his best to limit her, but it was entirely possible she'd managed to sneak some if she was able to get into Shadrach's or Meshach's stall.

"What's wrong with her?" Dallas asked.

Bennett explained the situation as best as he could to Dallas, and then started giving him orders. Bennett set up a mobile X-ray, getting ready to examine her hooves.

He took images of all four, and when he confirmed that the front two were affected, Kaylee wrapped the horse's hooves in the hot packs. Then Bennett gave her a dose of mineral oil to counteract some of the grain and set up an IV to administer fluids.

"It looks like the rotation isn't as severe as it could be," he said, eyeing the images from the X-ray. "Basically, we have a couple of days to tackle this really aggressively," Bennett said, keeping his eyes level with Dallas's. "Otherwise she's never fully going to get rid of this problem. And it's going to spring up all the time. And for a horse…it's not a good situation. Their legs have to carry a lot of weight."

"How did you not know she was sick?" Dallas asked, getting angry now. "Why didn't you know that something was wrong?"

Bennett shook his head, at a loss. "It happens. I was trying to control her diet, but she is an animal and she only knows what she wants. Not what's good for her."

"What the fuck good are you if you can't even tell when an animal is getting sick? That's your *job*."

"Yes," Bennett agreed. "It is. But these situations can turn quickly, and I didn't see any signs. I swear to you, if I had I would have done something."

"Right. Or maybe you just don't care very much about her, because she's old and I'm the only one who rides her anyway."

"Every animal on my ranch is here because I rescued them from a bad situation. I *care*."

Dallas's lip curled. "Right. I forgot. You like to take in strays."

Bennett took a deep breath, trying to keep from getting angry.

But it was Kaylee who spoke, softly and over the top of his anger. "He doesn't *take in strays*," she said. "He takes in what he cares about. What should have been with him all along. And gives them the care that they always deserved. He does it the best that he can, but if he can't see the pain, how is he supposed to treat it?"

Dallas didn't say anything to that. Kaylee reached out and put her hand on Dallas's shoulder, squeezing it hard. "Lucy is going to have to let Bennett take care of her. She's going to have to let him give her what she needs. But see, he couldn't, because he didn't know this was happening. He can't take care of you, or me or Lucy if he doesn't know there's a problem, Dallas. We have to let him. You have to let him."

She turned to Bennett. "Should I wait for you inside?"

He could tell she was offering him a moment alone with Dallas, and he was grateful.

He nodded. "Yeah. I'll see you in a bit."

She turned and left them, looking back a couple of times before she slipped out of the barn.

"Is she going to die?" Dallas asked, vulnerability showing through, the anger fading away a bit.

Bennett felt like he'd been punched. He let out a long, slow breath.

"I can't tell you for sure that she won't," Bennett said. "But I wouldn't think so. Most likely the question will be how comfortable she can be after this. And then... That's when sometimes you have to make unpleasant decisions."

"No," Dallas protested. "You're not going to put her to sleep."

"I don't want to. It's all going to depend on how she does over the next few days. And then a few weeks after. But we don't want her walking around suffering."

"Why not?" Dallas asked. "The rest of us are. And we just have to live through it."

"Unfortunately," Bennett said slowly, "physical suffering and emotional suffering are two different things. Especially when it comes to animals."

Bennett sat down in the bottom of the stall, next to the horse, who had now calmed a little bit. Dallas joined him, and they both leaned back against the wall.

It was silent except for the sound of Lucy's breathing. Bennett watched her chest rise and fall. And then he looked back over at his son.

"Dallas," Bennett said. "I love you."

He hadn't intended to say that. He hadn't even been thinking it. And he realized he hadn't said those words to anyone since...

Since he was seven years old.

Since he saw his mother one last time being loaded up into an ambulance, just days after she'd given birth to Jamie.

He had told her that he loved her, and then...she had never woken up.

And he never even thought those words anymore. Never said them to his family. Had never said them to Olivia. He had made it all about keeping control as far as Olivia was concerned. Not wanting to be reckless, not wanting to make a mistake again like he had done with Marnie. But it was so much deeper than that. It went back so much further.

It wasn't like he had told Marnie he loved her either.

He had been crazy about her, true. But he was sixteen in the throes of his first physical relationship and he'd been completely out of his mind. But love? Really opening himself up to people... He didn't do that. He built walls. Strong, sturdy walls, and operated within a fortress of his own making, entirely run by himself. But he couldn't do that with Dallas. He couldn't. Dallas was never going to love him, never going to trust him, if Bennett didn't do the giving first. If Bennett didn't let him in. You couldn't ask for things you didn't give. And Kaylee was right. If they didn't know each other's pain, if they didn't know each other, there was no way to fix it all.

Dallas looked over at him, lines etched between his brows as he pulled them together, the expression in his dark eyes like a frightened, wounded animal. "What?"

"I love you," Bennett said, his throat getting tight. "I love you. Because...you're my son. And I'm so proud of you."

"Because... I'm your *son*. Because we're blood related? And a paternity test proved it?"

"No," Bennett said, his voice rough. "I cared the minute that I met you. And I knew you were mine from that moment. I cared, or I wouldn't have had you stay here. I wouldn't have changed my life around to make room for you. But as I've gotten to know you, and as I see who you are... It's changed. And I get all the things that people say about kids. About babies. That when that newborn baby opens his eyes and looks at them right in the face, that their whole world changes. Dallas, I didn't get to see that with you. You didn't get to change my world fifteen years ago like you should have. It's not fair that we didn't get that. It's not. But I can't sit around feeling angry about it. Not all the time. Because we've lost too many years already. But it's not a burden to have you. It's not a chore to be your dad. This... Now... It's what I want. More than anything. For us to be a family. And maybe what I want isn't a fair thing to ask of you. Maybe asking for you to call me Dad, for you to someday tell me that you love me too... Maybe that's too much. Too much after all the time we spent apart. But I just want you to know it's not too much for me. And I'm okay with whatever you can give. But I'm going to give you everything I've got."

It was silent for a beat. Dallas's face smoothed slowly, his eyes getting blank, unreadable. Then he finally spoke. "Okay."

Bennett's chest winched. He had said all those words, and he had meant them. But of course he had hoped that Dallas would say *I love you, Dad* and give Bennett a hug. He really wanted that. He *craved* it. But he also knew that it really wasn't something he could just ask Dallas to feel.

It was complicated. And it was going to take time.

He had to give Dallas that time while giving 100 percent in return. He couldn't hold back just waiting. He was the parent. That meant flinging himself in front of a moving train to save his son if necessary. Even if his son was driving that train, and it was just a metaphor for something that would leave him emotionally devastated.

"I'm going to do my best with her," he said, putting his hand on Lucy.

"Okay."

On this, Bennett was going to push him.

"Do you trust me?" he pressed.

"I..."

He turned toward Dallas, putting both hands on his shoulders. "Dallas, I promise you I am going to do everything I can to give Lucy the longest life possible. To make sure to the best of my ability that she's not in pain. I'm going to try to do both of those things. I'm going to give it everything I have. *Do you trust me?*"

Dallas looked away, but nodded slowly. "Yes."

Bennett would take that. He would take it as a damned victory.

"Let's go in the house," Bennett said. "She's as comfortable as we can make her."

"I'm going to stay out here for a little while," Dallas said.

Bennett hesitated. "Okay. Do you want me to stay with you?"

"No," Dallas said. "I would rather stay alone."

"Okay," Bennett said, standing up and brushing his pants off. So much for his Sunday clothes. "If anything changes, let me know."

Dallas nodded wordlessly and put his hand on Lucy's neck, stroking her slowly. Bennett turned and left them there.

His heart felt heavy and light all at the same time. He couldn't quite figure it out. As he walked back toward the house, the front door opened and Kaylee came out onto the porch.

She walked over to the handrail and gripped it, looking out at the mountains that surrounded the ranch. The breeze kicked up and ruffled her red hair, rose gold sunlight bathing her face.

What a thing it was. To walk up toward the house and have her come out. To have her be there in his home.

"Is he okay?" she asked when Bennett's boot hit the bottom step.

"I think he will be. I think *we* will be."

"Good."

"Thank you," Bennett said. "For what you said back there. It was exactly what he needed to hear. And it's what I needed to hear too."

"You?"

"Yes. I promised that kid honesty. And I don't think I can give anyone honesty the way that I like to live. I want to protect myself. I want…to not be hurt. But I don't think you can love a kid the way they need to be loved if you're not willing to get hurt doing it. So that means letting go of all my stuff. Letting him know where I'm hurt."

She nodded slowly, but she still didn't move to touch him. So he did it. He was the one that pulled her close, took her in his arms.

"I wish… I just hope that it's not too late," Bennett said. "For him to love me. You know, like a father instead of a stranger who took him in."

Kaylee bit her lip, looking over toward the mountains. "Remember when I told him to be nice to your family because they needed him?"

"Yes."

"It's hard, when you've been through the kind of thing he has. The kind of thing I've been through…it's hard to let yourself need people. To let them care for you. It's much easier to pour yourself into them."

"Hard to ask them to come help you move a hutch?" he asked.

Her cheeks turned pink. "Where is Dallas?" she asked, looking around.

"Still with Lucy. He said he's going to stay in there for a while."

His heart felt raw, bruised. Opening himself up like this meant exposing himself to pain, because when you didn't have brick walls up around every feeling inside, you tended to feel it all a little bit more keenly. But he still wouldn't go back. Not now that he knew. Not now that he understood how much richer and fuller the past few weeks had been than the years before.

Really, it all came down to that moment in the diner. That wrenching feeling of sadness and wistfulness. All the time that he and Dallas had lost. The time they had before them. How much Bennett both looked forward to seeing his son's name written on that diner window, like his had been those years before, and how much he wanted to slow the years down so that they had more time.

Somehow, that moment of pain that came through love held more beauty, more brilliance and more happiness than any time in his life that had simply been content.

It was deep. And it was real. He wouldn't trade it. Not for the world.

And then there was Kaylee. This feeling that he had for her, that had always been there but had grown now, expanded. Like a creek that had overflowed in a heavy rain and become a torrential river. The same feelings that had always been there, made bigger, faster moving, by the injection of new feelings.

And like a river, it was scary. Like a river, it might pull him under, drown him.

But he wasn't sure he wanted it any other way.

In fact, he was mostly sure he didn't.

It was just a matter of figuring out what he was going to do with it. If he was going to try to raft it to the end. Or if he was going to jump in and swim, take his chances. Submerge in it. Go all the way.

He cupped her face, sliding his thumbs across her cheekbones. And then he kissed her. That soft, sweet mouth that had smiled at him more times than he could count. Had frowned at him. Had cussed at him.

His friend's lips.

His woman's lips.

Because she was both, wasn't she? All of it. Not divided into compartments, his lover Kaylee, his friend Kaylee. Kaylee was all of it. The keeper of all these feelings. All these needs. It had to be her.

It really did have to be.

"Why don't you come inside?"

Kaylee balked, chewing on her lower lip as she took a step away from him. "Are you sure you want to… Here?"

"I'm sure."

If he was sure about anything, it was wanting Kaylee with him tonight. All night.

If he could just have that, the morning would be fine.

CHAPTER NINETEEN

"Bennett..."

"Thank you. For today. For coming with me. For having dinner with us. For the last few weeks. And no, I'm not thanking you for sex, like I did the first time. I learned from my dumbass mistakes. But I am thanking you for being there like this. Without you none of it would have gone right."

Kaylee shook her head. "That's not true. You're his dad, Bennett. He needs you. He doesn't need me."

"That's not true. You're the one who connected with him quickly. It took me longer. He understood you. You understood him. That means something. It matters. Honey, it matters a hell of a lot."

He had meant it to come out light, but it didn't. All he could think about was tasting her again. Holding her again. He didn't understand how this day, this person, could be so many different things. The intense triumph and abject terror of taking the step to legally becoming Dallas's guardian. The intense desire to have Kaylee there as a friend. The sadness he'd felt seeing not just Lucy in pain, but Dallas in pain as a result. And also in a strange, twisted way, the pride that the depth of his son's caring made him feel.

And now this.

This desire. Deep and unending, and somehow all part of the same few hours.

Part of the same woman he had wanted at the courthouse, had needed to come to dinner. Needed to help find the right words to ease his son's distress.

The same woman he wanted in his bed. Naked and screaming out his name.

He was used to simple. His life, on his terms. But now it was so much more than that. Life was just happening, all around him. And the people that he cared about were changing the decisions he was making. Changing what he wanted.

Before, he had made a plan and he had set about making it happen. He had seen certain holes in his life, and wanted the puzzle pieces to fit in them. Wanted a friend puzzle piece. A wife puzzle piece. Kids, house. All of it to complement the career puzzle piece.

But now, he had all these pieces, and he wasn't sure where yet to put them. And he didn't even mind. Because it was better. So much better than what he had thought he needed.

He wanted to call Luke Hollister and get down on his knees and thank the man for seducing Olivia. Because if he had gone ahead with things as they had been... It wouldn't be like this now, that was for sure.

More than that...

He wanted to be what Kaylee needed.

He needed her, no question. In so many different ways. But he wanted her to be able to need him. To be able to count on him.

To call him when she needed furniture moved. Or needed to be held.

He wanted to give to her as much as he'd ever taken.

She'd used it to shelter her, he understood that now. She'd let herself be the giver, so she would never be disappointed. He didn't want that. Not anymore.

He took Kaylee's hand, weaving his fingers through hers, and he led her through the front door, down the hall and to his bedroom.

He brought her inside and closed the door behind them. She looked around, shivering lightly.

"What?"

"I'm in your bedroom."

"You've been in my bedroom hundreds of times."

She looked uncertain. "Not for this."

Her voice was so small, so feeble. He wanted to make her feel better. Wanted to put her at ease.

"I think we've had sex about a hundred times now too." He tried to lighten the tone but the exasperated look on her face told him it was the wrong move. That was the problem with being friends first. He knew what to do when he was a friend. He knew less what to do now.

"We have not." She scowled at him. "It's only been a few weeks. We can't have had sex over a hundred times."

He shrugged. "I think it's possible. I think we might have broken some records."

She shook her head. "I'm *serious*. Anyway… I've never been in your room for this. It feels…significant."

There was a heavy note to her voice and he wanted to translate it. Wanted to find a way to figure out exactly what she meant. Exactly what was hidden beneath the surface of each and every word she spoke.

Right in that moment, he wanted to know everything about her. He remembered that day in the barn, the day after the first time they'd made love, when she had suddenly felt the need to question him. About how many partners he'd had, what kind of sex life. He understood it. Understood that feeling beyond a moment of passing curiosity. That need to see it all. The desire to be able to read her mind.

He wanted to know it all. Every last bit.

The details of what it had been like growing up in her family. All the things that she had hidden from him, kept from him. And the things she was hiding from him now. Like why it mattered that they were in his bedroom. Why it made her feel insecure or vulnerable, or whatever had brought on the shiver.

"What made you decide to become a veterinarian?" he asked, taking a step back from her and taking his shirt off.

Kaylee frowned, her eyes darting from his stomach, to his face, his chest, his face. "What kind of question is that? Especially when you're stripping."

"An important question, Kay. Because I don't think I've ever asked you. Because we were…together when we decided, so in a lot of ways I felt like I kind of knew why, but we never really talked about it. We went to school together for veterinary medicine. We planned and plotted this practice together. And I don't think I ever asked you *why* you wanted to do it."

She shrunk slightly, her shoulders folding inward. "I…I like animals."

He didn't believe that was the whole truth. Not at all. But like he'd figured with Dallas earlier, he couldn't take without giving.

"When my mom died I felt like I didn't have any power. I couldn't fix it. I didn't know what to do. Along the way I figured out that I wanted to do something to stop some of the suffering in this world. I wanted to find out some way to be the person who could control the outcome some of the time. And even if it is for animals, and not for people, it's something I feel like I can do. It's in impact I can make in my community. In the lives of the ranchers, and in the animals. It matters to me on a deeper level than just liking animals. It's the way I found to help when I feel helpless. A way I found to feel in control in a world that I really can't ever hope to control." He reached down and started to undo his belt.

"This is an odd conversation to have while you're getting undressed."

"No, it's not. It's the perfect conversation to have while I'm getting undressed. Because it's me. It's who I am. I want to know why." He stripped off the rest of his clothes. Left them on the ground. "Why did you do it, Kaylee?"

She said nothing, so he moved over to her and pushed his fingers against the hem of her dress, tugging it up over her head. She stood there wearing nothing but her bra and panties, goose bumps rising over that pale skin.

He slid his thumb across her cheek, down to the edge of her lips and back again. "Come on, Kay. Tell me."

She looked away from him, and when she spoke, her words were small and halting. "Because you wanted to do it."

He took a step back, shock hitting him like a battle-ax. *"Me?"*

"You wanted to do it, and I wanted to follow you. I…"

She looked like she was about to cry. Like she wanted to crawl underneath the bed and hide from him. Hide from this confession.

For his part, he could hardly believe it. That she had gone to school for something, started a whole career in something, in part because of him. To…be with him.

"My parents had me to fill a void in their life, Bennett. I was supposed to fix things. And you… You had the fullest life of anyone I knew. A father who loved you, brothers, a sister. That beautiful ranch. All the animals. And you *still* wanted me. You had friends already. I didn't. You had all of these things, and you still wanted me. It meant more to me than you can possibly know. And of course you know I love being a veterinarian. It's my passion. When you're a lonely neglected kid you can't help other people. All you can do is hope that someone will help you. Well, you did. You came into my life and you made me believe in myself. You were the one who exposed me to ranch life, to animals. You made me the kind of person who could think about helping others. The kind of person who could be more than small and selfish and mean, needing every good thing in life to come to them, instead of being able to give any of it back. You made me into the kind of person who wanted to help, who loved helping. So yes. What I am now, who I am now, is because of you. So much more than just because you encouraged me to go to school."

He moved closer to her, rested his hands on her slender waist, moved them down to her hips. Then he slid one of them up her back, along the line of her spine and rested his hand between her shoulder blades. He drew her forward slowly, torturing them both with the slow press of her breasts against his chest.

What he wanted to do was crush her up against him, hold her there, not let her go. But instead, he kept it a leisurely pace. Slow. Deliberate. He took his time as he moved his hand from her hip to her chin, as he tilted her face upward. As he spent three heartbeats bringing his lips down to hers.

He pressed his lips to hers slowly, achingly so. Taking his time as those empty spaces between them filled in with each breath. Their mouths together, the ends of their noses brushing, tongues. Teeth. Chest to chest, her stomach against his hardening arousal. Even her legs pressed against his, so that not even the air in the room could come between them. And he just kissed her.

Like he had all the time in the world. Like there was nothing else that came next. Like kissing was the beginning and end of everything.

Not just of sex, but of his entire reason for being.

He cupped her face, worked his fingers back through her hair, silken strands sliding through his fingers. Then he brought his hands down her back, traced a line down to that dip in her spine just above her ass. He slid his hands down farther, beneath the waistband of her underwear, luxuriating in the feel of her soft-as-silk skin.

He pushed those panties down her hips, taking his time to feel every inch of her legs as he went down, taking the kiss down with him, down the center of her breasts, her belly, her center. Then he moved back up, unhooking her bra and freeing those beautiful, perfect breasts.

She looked up at him, and he could sense that there were a thousand different things swirling through her mind. That there was so much she wanted to say, but wasn't. And he would have been content to let that lie all these past seventeen years. But for some reason now he wasn't content to let her have her secrets. Because he didn't much care about keeping his own. She knew him. Every stupid thing he'd ever done now. Knew the ways in which he felt he had failed Marnie. Knew about the pregnancy. About Dallas. Knew about why he had become a vet, about how his mother's death was responsible for it. And it was all fine. Fine to have given her all of that. It felt better.

More real.

He felt more real.

What he really wanted to know was why she had kissed him that day at Get Out of Dodge. The need to know hit him suddenly. It was what had started all of this. Or maybe that was an oversimplification. But still. It was the broken barrier. That first press of her mouth against his. It had been her move. And she had said it was because she felt sorry for him. But when they had kissed after that, and every time since, it wasn't pity that he tasted on her tongue.

Hell, no.

"Why did you kiss me?"

"I kiss you all the time," she said, her cheeks turning a delicate shade of pink when she spoke those words.

"No. Not why are you kissing me now. That day at the ranch, when I was hiding back by the river. Why did you kiss me?"

"Because I felt bad. I wanted to comfort you." But she looked away when she said that. And he knew that if he could see her eyes he would see that it was a lie.

"No," he said. "Don't lie to me, Kay. We're naked here together. Be naked with me."

Tears shone in her eyes, and regret kicked him in the stomach. For whatever reason this was a hard ask. But then, the regret faded away. Because all of this was hard. The past weeks of transitions and changes had been hard. But it was better on the other side.

"I wanted you," she said. "And I didn't know how *not* to kiss you anymore."

The breath left his body in a rush. "You wanted me?"

"Do you think I offered to handle your dry spell out of the blue? Do you think I was acting on some kind of crazy sex whim? I…I've been attracted to you for… forever. And suddenly we were so close, and you looked so sad, and I just forgot that it wasn't what we did. I forgot that it wasn't natural. Because it felt natural to me. It felt easy. It felt like something we were supposed to do."

He remembered then, remember saying to her in that rough voice how good it was they wanted each other at the same time, because it would be hell to be in it alone.

Kaylee had been in it alone.

"But you… You've dated other men."

"I'm not pathetic," she said. "I mean, maybe I am. But I wanted to protect our friendship. And I did. I did until the moment I couldn't anymore. I was… The day you came over and I was frantically building furniture I was really trying to figure some things out. Trying to make some choices. My date with Michael was a disaster and I didn't care. I had hoped he would…fix me. My feelings for you. Feelings I had decided I wouldn't act on. I put myself in a box and then resented it, and it…hit me that I was the only one who could fix it. So I thought maybe if I just…spent some time thinking. If I changed my clothes and my house a little, maybe I'd feel differently."

She laughed. "It was silly," she continued, "and as soon as you showed up I realized that. And when you said you were going to try to hook up… I… Bennett, I knew I couldn't sit there and watch it again and I had to make a choice about *you*."

Suddenly, he saw the foolishness of his own behavior through her eyes and he wanted to punch himself in the face.

"Kay, I'm sorry."

"Don't apologize. That makes it worse. Don't apologize for not seeing me as attractive until I offered you sex."

"That's not it. I told you, I noticed you that way before. Little bits here and there. I thought I was losing my mind. Because you're supposed to be my friend. And you keep talking about how important I was to you, but Kaylee, you mean the world to me. I…"

He closed his eyes and swallowed hard, then continued. "I think if it weren't for you I would have closed everyone out. I think I did for a long time. And then we met. Your first day of school. You were white-faced and nervous, I remember that. Like it was yesterday. But I wanted to…"

"You wanted to fix me. Because that's who you are. It's what you do." She looked at him, her expression a challenge.

"No." He denied it.

"It's okay," she said, her eyes shining, making it perfectly clear it wasn't okay at all. "I understand that. But don't pretend that I wasn't just another wounded bird to you."

Kaylee knew all about that bird. The one he'd tried to save. The one that he credited with changing the course of his life. And in that way, Kaylee and the bird had something in common. But only to a point.

Still, he couldn't deny that at first his feelings had been all about fixing her. Helping her. It was who he was on a fundamental level.

But that wasn't all.

"You know what? Maybe it started that way. But unlike the bird, you didn't need me to save you. You changed *my* life. You became more than a rescue mission. So, maybe at first that's what I wanted. To hold you close and bandage your wing, metaphorically. But in the end… That's not how I see you. And it isn't how I saw you for long. But you know how I am. You know I like to control my life. Everything in its place. That way I know how to fix it when it all goes wrong. I have to understand all the gears, all the mechanics of it."

"Well, that's romantic. I have gears now?"

"So that when something is wrong I can figure out what to do." She looked away, and he grabbed hold of her chin. Turned her focus back to him. "I went out of my way to not look at you as a beautiful woman. Until I couldn't anymore. Until it started sneaking through anyway." He shook his head. "Wyatt said I had to be delusional not to notice that you're sexy."

She lifted a brow. "Wyatt said that?"

"Wyatt knows we're sleeping together," he said by way of explanation.

She let out an exasperated breath. "Of course he does."

"He figured we already had been."

She snorted. "Well, it would have been handy. Easy stress relief."

Except there was something false about those words. He had a feeling she didn't see their situation as stress-free at all. He sure as hell didn't.

He didn't see any of this as easy. Not Dallas and all the feelings his son stirred up inside of him, not Kaylee and his newfound need for her, as a friend, as a woman. As a lover.

Not easy, no. But...worth it.

Still, he wasn't quite sure why Kaylee didn't want to admit that.

But hell, they were in his bedroom, and he didn't know why he was insisting that they talk.

"I can't make up for what an ass I've been all this time."

"You haven't been an ass. It's not like I told you I wanted you and you were cruel to me. I was pining because I was scared. Until I was finally more scared of wanting you forever and never having you than I was of messing up the friendship."

"I hope I don't scare you now."

"Of course you scare me," she said. "Wanting is scary."

He didn't have anything to say to that. Because she was right. Wanting, needing, were scary as hell. So he said nothing. Instead, he captured her lips with his, wrapping his hand around the back of her head and drawing her close, sliding his fingers through that silken hair, luxuriating in the feel of it. The feel of her.

It was Kaylee. *His* Kaylee.

There was nothing off-limits between them. Not anymore. There were no walls. There were no barriers. No dividing lines between friendship and love.

Love.

It wasn't a word he'd thought about before. Wasn't one he'd seen coming. But there it was.

Of course he loved Kaylee. He always had. It was just that there had been boundaries to it. Ways that he could express it, and ways that he couldn't. Because he had loved her *as a friend.* That had a certain set of rules to it. Clear borders. But they'd left those behind weeks ago in the bed of his truck, out on a deserted mountain road.

Without them…

Now he just…loved her.

As everything. There was no boundary, no wall.

Just love. Pure and raw and blinding, burning its way through him like a sword right from the forge.

He'd have fought it, just a few weeks ago. He'd have pushed it all down.

Not now.

He wrapped his arm around her waist, crushed her

bare body against his as he kissed her with everything he had.

There was no being careful. There was no setting up careful fence lines that he couldn't cross.

These feelings were free-range, dammit.

Desire without borders. Feelings without parameters.

And a few weeks ago he would have found that unthinkable. Terrifying. The exact opposite of how he wanted his life to be.

He would have trapped both himself and Olivia in a marriage that didn't have passion. Didn't have feeling. Sure, he had been attracted to her, but in that way that he was attracted to pretty women. Not in a special way. Not in a deep way. Not in this all-consuming brushfire way that he wanted Kaylee.

This was like nothing else. Because she was like no one else.

She was stiff in his arms for a moment, until he traced her lower lip with the tip of his tongue. Then she went pliant, soft curves melting against him. How had he been friends with her this long and not known that she was the one who would fit perfectly in his arms? Fit perfectly against him? How had he missed this?

On purpose. Just like Wyatt had said.

There was only one way a man could be that blind. And that was if he covered his own eyes. Tied his own blindfold. And he sure as hell had.

Because Kaylee could never fit neatly into a compartment. She could never be that puzzle piece. Could never be the best friend piece if he let himself see just how lovely she truly was. Could never be that wife piece the way that he had imagined a wife. Someone who would be at home waiting for him when he got through with work. Someone who would have his children, raise them. Someone who would make a home for him. Basically, somebody to be that image he'd had of what his mother had probably done for his father. But it was a hazy and vague image, because he had been so young when his mother had died.

Love… Well, it looked a lot more like the relationship between his father and Freda. Unexpected. And probably not what his father would have chosen if he had a choice in the matter. Freda was bold, and she certainly didn't spend the days doing his laundry or cooking him dinner—unless she felt like it. Freda, who he cared about enough to leave the ranch, which Bennett would have said his father had never wanted to do.

His father had left the ranch because he wanted to give Freda whatever she needed. Because he wanted to follow Freda to the place that made her the happiest. They compromised. They split their time between Gold Valley and New Mexico, because it made them both happy.

Maybe that was it. Love was the one thing strong enough to entice you to do the things you'd said you'd never do. But also wouldn't ask it of you.

Love was what Olivia Logan and Luke Hollister had found together. And he knew for a fact that Olivia had been spitting mad that Luke was the man for her. She had wanted safe, just like Bennett had. She had wanted to be in charge of that decision, had wanted to create a perfect life. Based around ideals rather than around an actual person.

That wasn't love. It wasn't how it worked.

These feelings that were riding through his chest were messy. They were jagged. And he didn't know how they fit neatly and with anything. He didn't know what he wanted. He had a teenage son that he had to figure out. He had a future that looked like... Well, he had no idea what in the hell his future looked like.

But he had two people in his life that he loved fiercely. And he wanted to figure out how to do the best he possibly could with those feelings.

Whatever it cost.

He kissed her, guiding her over to the bed, laying her down gently on top of the comforter. He propped himself up on his knees, looking down at her body. At all that beautiful, pale skin. At her slight, enticing curves.

She had a freckle just beneath her left breast, another one right next to her belly button. He pressed his thumb against the one beneath her breast, traced it down toward the other. Then he followed the same path with his tongue.

"What are you doing?" she gasped.

"I thought I would spend some time connecting your freckles."

"Don't." She protested. "I don't like my freckles."

She didn't like him looking at her this close. Didn't like sex being all about her. That was why it needed to happen.

"I do." And he spent the next little while finding all of them. No matter how pale. No matter how faint. And he kissed every last one. Until he just started kissing wherever he felt like it. Until he had her shivering and shaking beneath him. Until he forgot exactly what he was supposed to be doing other than tasting her. He forgot if there was any other thing on earth he was supposed to do ever. He wanted to get lost in this. In her.

In that concept of loving Kaylee without walls and fences.

But now that he'd realized that, it was like discovering just how vast the Oregon countryside was beyond the confines of Get Out of Dodge.

That the mountains were endless, the terrain too rough to ride in a day, or two or twenty. That a man could probably spend a lifetime searching for the end and not find it. That he could spend years exploring and still miss some of the wonders.

That brought with it a kind of desperation. To find more time. To find a way to keep her with him so that he could at least come close to reaching the limits.

Or maybe, that was the beauty. That it was limitless.

Like trying to find an exact number in a sky full of stars. Or in the freckles on her body. Infinite. Impossible.

This was life without walls inside of him. Life without protection. Life without borders. Submitting to the fact that there were things he couldn't plan, things he couldn't control.

But as long as he could hold on to Kaylee it would be all right.

Whatever happened, if he had her, it wouldn't be impossible.

The corner of his mouth tilted up into a smile, and he wondered if she could feel it against her skin, against her hip bone as he pressed his fingers between her legs and traced all that slick beauty. As he teased her, teased them both.

He smiled because he realized that as long as he had Kaylee, anything was possible. That was the truth of his life all the way back seventeen years. What he had always known, even if he had been hiding the truth from himself all this time.

He kissed that hip bone, then her stomach, that freckle beneath her breast again and the tender skin right next to her nipple. Her collarbone. Then he captured her mouth again. She grabbed hold of his shoulders, and he slid his hand around her lower back, sliding them both down the bed so they didn't end up smacking against the headboard. Then, he collected one wrist in his hand, followed by the other, squeezing her arms together before he drew them up over her head, held her down, tilted her hips upward with his other hand.

He grabbed hold of some protection and settled himself between her legs.

She looked up at him, those green eyes searching his. For what, he didn't know. He tried to give it to her. He would give her whatever she wanted. He didn't have words. He didn't know how to emote with his facial expressions, or whatever the hell.

"Tell me you need this," he said, pressing against her, denying them both what they wanted.

She arched against him, her body language a silent plea. But he wasn't letting her get away with silence.

"Kay," he said, gripping her chin, tilting her face so she had to look at him. "Tell me what you need."

"I..."

"Tell me, sweetheart."

Her lip trembled. "You. I need you."

Hellfire. He couldn't wait anymore. Not after that.

He surged into her, groaning as he did. He could show her how much he wanted her. How much this meant. He pressed himself inside of her, slowly. Gritting his teeth as need rolled over him like the wind down a mountain, swift and fierce, cutting straight down to the bone.

It wrapped around them like a tornado, carrying them both along, wrapping them up in a storm that was beyond their control.

Destructive. Beautiful in its power.

Kaylee let her head fall back, tossing it back and forth, her wild red hair spread out on his pillow. Kaylee. In his bed. On his pillow, his comforter.

His.

Color crept into her cheeks, and he could feel her drawing close to her release. Once he felt her unravel beneath his touch, he let himself go too. Letting himself get caught up in the torrent.

When it was done, he lifted up the covers and encouraged her to get beneath them. Then he went to the bathroom and took care of the practicalities, before returning and sliding beneath the sheets with her.

He had slept with her in the stall, but it hadn't been on purpose. They had fallen asleep, and woken up together quite by accident. But not tonight. She was staying with him. In his house. In his bed. In his room.

She was right. This was significant. This was different.

This was a step forward to a future.

And he might not know exactly what that looked like, but right now, he didn't mind.

For the first time in his life, he didn't need to see it all planned out.

He only needed to see her.

CHAPTER TWENTY

BENNETT COULDN'T REMEMBER the last time he'd slept in until the sun was high in the sky. But when he woke up, golden beams were already filtering through the window, falling across Kaylee's peaceful face. Strands of spun gold ignited in her red hair, and he just wanted… he wanted to stay there and look at her forever.

Well, maybe not just look. He'd like to do a little touching too.

He couldn't regret how late he had slept. Not when she was so warm and soft against his body. Not when waking up in bed with her was about the sweetest thing he could have ever imagined.

But he knew that he was going to have to get up and feed the animals. More than that, he was going to have to check on Dallas. Dallas and Lucy.

He pressed a kiss to Kaylee's forehead and got out of bed slowly. He dressed even slower, keeping his eyes on Kaylee, watching as she scrunched up slightly, burying her face in his pillow. He bet his bedsheets smelled like her skin. He hoped they did.

He wanted them to always smell like Kaylee. He wanted her to always be in them.

He went out into the kitchen and was surprised to see that the coffee maker was cold, nothing in it. He didn't even smell a faint lingering of coffee, and since Dallas had recently learned to make his own, that was very unusual. He wondered if his son had slept in as well.

He walked down the hall and knocked on the bedroom door. After a few seconds of not getting an answer, he pushed it open.

Dallas wasn't there.

Bennett's heart squeezed, panic moving through his body, a shot of adrenaline working its way through his veins. There were a thousand different reasons why Dallas might not be in bed. Different places he could be. Namely, anywhere on the property. But of course, his first most terrified instinct was to wonder if Dallas had run away.

Without bothering to put shoes on, Bennett tore out of the house and jogged across the gravel, ignoring the way it cut into his feet as he made his way toward the barn.

If Dallas was still on the property, Bennett was willing to bet money he was there.

The cold air hit his lungs like fire, but he ignored that too, pushing the barn door open and making his way inside, ignoring the chill from the concrete that sank through his feet.

He walked down to the stall that Lucy was in and stopped.

There he was.

Dallas was asleep, still wearing his blue shirt from the day before. His tie was undone, draped over his shoulders. And he was holding Lucy's head in his lap. The horse was as sound asleep as her master, her stomach rising and falling evenly.

Bennett would have said that after yesterday he wasn't holding back anymore. That he had reached max capacity for feeling over the past couple of days, and there was nothing deeper, nothing heavier to wring out of him.

He would have been wrong.

Looking at Dallas right now, everything inside of him crumbled.

Love *hurt*. *Damn*, it hurt. It was years lost with a son that meant more to him than he could ever put into words. Years lost with a mother he could never bring back.

It was a kid who had been through enough already spending the night in the cold, on the ground, holding his horse because he was afraid he might lose her.

But it was also the other side of that hurt. That deep, real stuff that made any of it matter.

Without love, there wasn't pain.

But without love, nothing really mattered.

It was like hiding from the sun for years because he was afraid it would hurt his eyes. It did. But anything else was living in darkness.

He didn't want that. He wanted the sun. In his eyes. On his skin. Shining in Kaylee's hair through his window as she lay on his bed.

He wasn't hiding from it anymore.

He walked into the stall and knelt down beside his son, putting his hand on Dallas's shoulder.

"Wake up," he whispered. "Dallas. Wake up."

Dallas startled, then woke, looking down at Lucy, then back up at Bennett.

"She's okay?" he asked, his voice sleepy.

"She's breathing," Bennett said.

"That's good, isn't it?"

"It's always a good sign. We're not out of the woods." Didn't that seem like a metaphor for every important relationship in his life right now?

"What do we do?" Dallas asked, looking up, his expression helpless. Trusting. Dallas was asking Bennett what they were going to do. He was looking to Bennett for answers. And Bennett wished that he had 100 percent reassurance to give his son. But while he might not have that, he did have expertise.

"I want to take another X-ray now that she's been on anti-inflammatories for a while. I need to gauge how much damage we're dealing with here. If it's as promising as it looked last night we're going to try to get her standing."

Dallas nodded.

"Can you move?" Bennett asked.

"Yeah," Dallas said, wiggling himself out from underneath the horse, and pushing himself up to standing. Then, he made a short, shocked sound as his knee crumbled. "Well, except I don't have any feeling in my legs."

Bennett did his best not to laugh. It wasn't a laughing moment. Except that was pretty damn funny. "That would be from sleeping with a giant horse head in your lap."

"I wanted to make sure that she knew she wasn't by herself."

Those words, quiet and serious, stopped Bennett's heart. In them was a wealth of pain, a wealth of meaning. Dallas had been alone. When he was sick, no one had held him. When he'd been scared, there had been no one to chase away monsters.

Bennett understood that unspoken truth. Dallas had gone through it all, all manner of things without anyone. And Dallas hadn't been about to let Lucy go through something without a person by her side.

Bennett got his X-ray equipment and started to get set up to take another image of her foot.

"I wish I could have been there," Bennett said, the words rough. But he couldn't hold them back. Maybe it wasn't the best time. Maybe they needed to put all their focus on to Lucy, but he had to say the words. He had to.

"If I would have known, you never would have been by yourself."

"I've barely been by myself since I got here," Dallas said. "That's one thing that I don't have any trouble believing."

His voice sounded hard, that usual flippant tone that he was given to, but Bennett understood. He did believe Bennett. He did believe that Bennett would have been there for him if he could have been.

"I spent a lot of years trying to control my whole life," Bennett said. "The worst thing I could imagine was another big surprise that changed everything."

"You mean your girlfriend getting pregnant?"

"My mom dying. No one expected it. She had a relatively healthy pregnancy with Jamie. But... She had a blood clot after. And that was it. I lived my whole life trying to avoid that kind of pain. That kind of suffering. Like if I could just control everything around me I could limit what could happen to me. But I had no idea. There were things at work in this world that I could never have guessed at. And not being able to protect you for the first part of your life is about the worst thing I can think of. Whenever I imagine you by yourself... I'm not a violent man, Dallas. But dammit, I want to hurt everyone who hurt you."

"That's not..."

"I know. It's probably not a good thing to say. Especially not to you. But it's true. I don't want to be the bigger man. Not when it comes to you. Not when it comes to making it right with you. I can't do anything big enough to show you how much I love you. How much I wish I could fix all these things that are broken. But I can't. And anger has never fixed a damn thing in my life. But love has. Just these past few weeks, it's fixed a hell of a lot in me. So that's what I've got. It's what I can give. I can't fix what happened in the past. I can only build new things going forward."

Dallas looked down, like he didn't know how to hear it. And like he definitely didn't know what to say.

"It wasn't always bad," Dallas said finally. "When she was sober she was good."

Bennett nodded. "I know. I cared a lot about her when we were together. Though, maybe not as much as she deserved."

"No," Dallas said. "She was always selfish. Even when it was all right. But when I was little her selfishness kind of suited me. It meant we bought all kinds of candy and went to the carnival and things. Because she liked it. But then, she decided she liked drugs more than anything. I don't really wish she was dead," Dallas said. "I just wish she loved me, mostly."

Tears reflected in Dallas's eyes, and Bennett knew what that cost him. Knew just how difficult it was for him to show emotion like that in front of Bennett.

"I love you," Bennett said. "I can't speak for her. What she wishes she would have done different, what she feels. Where she's at or why. We were sixteen when we knew each other. Hell, I didn't know myself back then, much less her. But I can speak for me. I love you, Dallas. And you are the best thing that's ever happened to me."

Dallas nodded. And Bennett knew that meant something. It meant he believed him. Maybe it even meant that Dallas loved him too. Whatever it meant, for now it was enough.

Bennett studied the X-ray he'd taken. The inflammation was down and he could see the bone wasn't rotated too far. It made him hopeful. But only time would tell how Lucy was going to do in the long run.

Either way, he knew she'd have the best person caring for her. Not him. Dallas.

"Okay," he said. "Let's see if we can get Lucy on her feet."

It took a while, but they managed to get Lucy up, and then they were able to get her out into the pasture. Bennett applied wraps to her legs and gave her a few vitamin shots, doing everything he could to make sure that the horse was bolstered.

"Do you think she's going to be all right?"

"You're not going to be able to ride her for a while," Bennett said. "She may not be able to be ridden again. It's tough to say at this point, but I think we can make her pretty comfortable, even if it takes a lot of monitoring and babying."

"I don't care if I can ride her," Dallas said. "I'll still visit her all the time."

"I know. She's going to have a happy life no matter what. Because she has you. She's lucky that way."

"I'm not sure she's the one who's lucky," Dallas mumbled, looking down for a moment, before turning his focus back to the horse in the field.

"Well," Bennett said, "in the meantime, we might have to see about getting you your own horse to ride."

Dallas looked over at him. "Really?"

"You love it. And it's not enough to just have you going over to ride with Jamie. I want to be able to ride with you."

Dallas leaned over the fence, his arms folded over the top rail as they watched Lucy. "I'm staying here, aren't I?"

"Yes," Bennett said.

"I mean, I know you said. And I know that we signed papers. But I have lived in a lot of different places. And a lot of them said that it was going to be permanent. And I did dumb stuff to make sure it wasn't. To prove that they were going to give up. They all did."

Bennett's heart contracted. "You didn't do any of that with me."

Dallas was silent for a minute or so, and Bennett just let it be. "Because if you gave up on me, I really wouldn't have anything. I was too scared to push you that hard. I wanted… I want this. This is where I want to be. With you."

Bennett blinked, his eyes stinging. He turned toward the wind. Let it make his eyes water. Gave him something other than emotion to blame for the moisture there.

"Good," he said, swallowing hard. "But I have to make one thing very clear. You won't lose me. Even if you do your worst. That's not an invitation to test things. But I want you to know…love doesn't have a limit, when you do it right, Dallas. And you're not going to find the limit of mine. It's always."

Dallas looked at him, but he didn't say anything. He just nodded.

Bennett had to take that as good enough.

He clapped his hand on Dallas's shoulder, then tugged his son up against him and the two of them stood and watched Lucy grazing in the field. Last night had been hard. Watching Dallas struggle with the fear and pain over the horse being unwell had been difficult. But it had brought them here.

And that, he supposed, was the important thing to remember.

Pain brought you to more beautiful places. You couldn't hike up a mountain without it. You couldn't get the view without the hike.

His hike had been leading him here all along. To being the kind of father that Dallas needed.

The kind of man who could be with Kaylee. The kind of man she could let herself need.

That was what he wanted. To be with Kaylee.

Really be with her.

He loved her. And all that was left to do was tell her.

CHAPTER TWENTY-ONE

WHEN KAYLEE WOKE UP, Bennett wasn't in bed. Her eyes popped open, and she realized the sun was already up. Of course Bennett wasn't in bed. He got up hours before this every day. Hell, so did she.

Thank God she didn't have any appointments on the schedule, but she should have been at the clinic an hour ago. Hopefully, there were no emergencies.

She scrambled out of bed and looked around for her purse, grabbing at her phone frantically. She had a missed call from her assistant, who was obviously wondering why she wasn't at the clinic.

Kaylee hopped around the room, collecting her clothing while she returned the phone call to Laura. "Have I missed any patients?"

"No.

"I just slept in. If anybody comes, tell them I'm on my way. I just need to talk to Bennett."

"Talk to... Oh."

She could tell by that very meaningful tone that Laura had just realized where Kaylee had probably spent the night.

"Is everything okay?"

"Fine. Fine. It's not...not a big deal," Kaylee said. "It's not that interesting. I'll fill in the details when I get there."

Except it *was* that interesting. And she would only be giving bare-bones details, because embarrassing.

She finished getting dressed and stumbled out of the house, stopping when she saw Bennett and Dallas leaning up against the fence rail. They looked so much alike. It was the most surreal thing. They were so clearly father and son. So clearly family.

Lucy was out in the field, walking tenderly, slowly.

Kaylee smiled, because she had been so afraid of Dallas having to go through a loss when he was just starting to bond with the people and animals here.

Eventually, that was something he was going to have to contend with. But not so soon. He deserved a break from that. Some safety.

She started to take a step toward them, and then stopped.

Like a barrier had prevented her from moving forward. They were family. She wasn't a part of that family. She had loved the Dodge family more than her own because they had given her more than her parents ever had, but that didn't make them family. She was important, but not the same. Not part of it. Not really.

Just like with her parents. They'd had a child in the hopes of fixing some of the things that felt wrong in their life. They'd had her, and she had never really been part of them. Not really.

She wasn't part of this either. Bennett and Dallas becoming a family.

And the fact that it was hurting like this made her feel…stupid. Small. She should be happy for Bennett. Focusing on what a wonderful thing it was he was having this moment with his son. And instead, she was worrying about feeling on the outs. Instead, she was feeling insecure and scared.

Jealous of a kid, really, because he had the kind of belonging that she had never had.

The connection she had found with Bennett was just never...

It never felt like enough.

She still wasn't enough.

Last night, the way he'd looked at her...the things he'd said. She believed all they had was real now, but she couldn't believe it would last. Not for her.

She needed to take her whiny-ass thinking elsewhere. She turned away from the scene in front of her and walked to her truck, grateful that she had driven herself yesterday. Because she needed to get to work. And she really didn't want to interrupt the moment Bennett was having with Dallas. She could shoot him a text later and let him know everything was fine.

She drove over to the clinic, and by the time she arrived Beatrix was there. Sitting in the waiting room under Laura's watchful eye, with a similar box to the one she'd had a few weeks ago when she'd shown up with her bedraggled raccoon orphan.

"What is it now?" Kaylee asked as she approached.

"I just wanted to bring Evan in for a follow-up."

"You named the raccoon Evan?"

"Yes. I wanted to make sure that there weren't any more vaccinations he needs. Lindy keeps saying he's a hazard. But he isn't. And I can pay for them."

"You don't have to pay for them, Beatrix," Kaylee said. "Come on back."

She led Beatrix back to the exam room, giving Laura a cursory wave. Her assistant shot her an evil glare. As if Beatrix's appearance was contrived by Kaylee to keep from having to give details.

It wasn't, but it was welcome.

The raccoon had grown quite a bit. And it was fat. Fat and obviously exceedingly well cared for by Beatrix.

"I hear Lindy is a bit underwhelmed by the raccoon," Kaylee said as she tried to wrangle the little thing into a good position to give it a shot in the scruff of its neck.

"She doesn't mind him. She just acts like she does. Because you know, the winery is fancy. And a raccoon is not fancy, so she says. I'm not really bothered by it either way."

"And she is."

Beatrix shrugged. "Well, I think Lindy feels like she has to try. You know, to make up for her upbringing or something? I already know that if growing up with money automatically made you sophisticated I would have turned out a lot differently. My parents have never known what to do with me."

"Yeah, well, join the club," Kaylee said.

"It's easier having Lindy in charge of the winery. I enjoy working there much better now."

"Are you working there right now?"

"Yes," Beatrix confirmed. "Though, she doesn't really have me do a lot of interaction with customers. Because I'm feral. She says. Though…with affection. I think."

"Bea," Kaylee said, "why don't you work somewhere like…here? Why don't you go to veterinary school? Or work at a shelter."

Beatrix frowned. "I don't know. I guess because I wanted to be free to pick the animals up when I find them and have the time to care for them. Anyway, the winery is ours. And we all have a stake in it. I mean, except for our brother. And my parents. Because of the divorce. But none of us could side with him."

"Yeah. I kind of heard about some of that."

"Lindy is more of a sister to me than Damien ever was a brother. And Dane, you know, Lindy's brother…"

"He's like a brother to you too?"

Beatrix's face went red up to the roots of her hair. "Not quite."

Well, that was interesting. Though, poor Beatrix. Kaylee couldn't think of a worse type of man for a sweetheart like her to have a crush on.

Bull riders on their own were a pretty bad bet, at least that was what Kaylee had gathered from knowing Wyatt as long as she had. He was a womanizer, and every guy she had ever known him to hang out with was the same.

She had met Dane Parker before, though she didn't know him well. He was far too good-looking for anyone's peace of mind, and most definitely not the right kind of guy for Beatrix.

Of course, there was probably nothing really to worry about there. Beatrix was cute. But…she was *cute*. And men like Wyatt Dodge and Dane Parker didn't pay much attention to cute.

"I'd like to hire you, Beatrix. I could really use someone here in the office who's this good with all the animals."

Beatrix shrugged, her curls bouncing slightly with the motion. "I'm fine. I live in a cabin on the winery property. I have… I have money. And I can pay you for the vaccines," she reiterated.

"The care and keeping of Evan is on me," Kaylee said. "Like you said, it's my sacred oath and all of that. But think about the job, okay? I think it's something you'd be good at, and you could enjoy. You could do some certifications to be a veterinary assistant. You would be really great at it."

Bea looked thoughtful and surprised almost. As if it

hadn't occurred to her that she might be good at something. That made Kaylee's heart hurt, because oh, how she understood that kind of insecurity.

"I have your number," Bea said. "I'll...I'll call you about this."

"Please do."

She and Beatrix walked out of the exam room, and Kaylee stopped cold when she saw Bennett standing there. All tight black T-shirt, muscles and cowboy hat. All sexy in ways she could hardly deal with.

"You didn't say goodbye."

"I'm with a patient," she said, waving her hand toward Beatrix and the cardboard box.

"You're with a raccoon."

"The raccoon is a patient."

"Let's talk," he said, grabbing hold of her arm and drawing her toward the break room.

"I need to say goodbye to Beatrix," she said.

He let go of her. And stood there, waiting.

Katie looked beyond him to Laura, who was sitting at the desk looking far too intrigued.

"Bye, Beatrix," Kaylee said. "Call me about the offer."

"Bye, Kaylee," Beatrix said, clearly oblivious to any tension.

She walked back to the break room and Bennett followed her, closing the door behind her. "Why did you leave?"

"It was late. The clinic was supposed to be open, and there was no vet."

"I know. We both overslept. But you could have come and said goodbye to me first."

"You were with Dallas. I didn't want to interrupt the moment."

Bennett smiled. "I think... I think I'm finally mak-

ing progress with him." Then he laughed, a sort of rue-
ful sound. "Well, I'm making progress with myself.
Which is helping."

"Great. Good to know." She didn't know why she was
being so prickly. It was obnoxious of her, really. Bennett didn't know that she was contending with maudlin
thoughts about how she didn't fit, and she hadn't been
able to come and say goodbye to him because there was
no place for her to do it.

"I'm sorry," she said. "I didn't want to interrupt, and
I was feeling nervous about not being at work. I just…
I'm sorry."

Even after the magic that was last night, she really
had no idea what was going on with her and Bennett,
and she had no idea why spending the night with him
and waking up this morning like she had made her feel
strangely distant. She should feel closer to him. But she
didn't. She just felt like an extra piece. Sitting out on her
own. She didn't know what to do about that. Not at all.

"This isn't… This isn't where I wanted to do this,"
he said, looking around the yellow cinder block room.
She followed his gaze, dread clutching at her throat, at
her heart. He felt it too. This weird sensation that she
didn't fit. And he wanted things to go back to the way
they were. Because now he didn't need her. Now everything with Dallas was going okay, why would he need
his sexual Kaylee healing?

She didn't want to do it here either. This was their
break room. She ate sandwiches in here. It was neutral
territory. She was going to have to try to eat lunch in
here forever after, and he was going to hurt her.

"Don't," she said. "Please. Not right now. I have a
whole day of work to get through, and I feel like we
can talk about it later."

"Do you have a patient?"

"No," she said.

"Neither do I. And later, I'm going to have Dallas. And I want to have a chance to talk with you now. Kaylee…"

"It's fine," she said. "I know. I mean, I looked across the field and I saw you and Dallas there, and I knew. I knew then. You don't really need me hanging around anymore. The two of you are… You're family. And it's such a wonderful thing, Bennett. I'm so happy for you. For him. But I get that you want things to go back to normal."

He was looking at her like she had grown another head.

"That's not what I was going to say."

"It isn't?"

"No. I don't want things to go back to normal. Normal… I wasn't happy. Not really. I was going through motions and making steps, and it's just not what I want now."

"What… Then what do you want?"

"My life is never going to be the way that it was," he said. "I had plans. Lots of plans, and all of them have completely dissolved in the past few months. And I don't want it to go back to the way it was. I like this. I'm a father now. I love my son. I'm happy with this life, even though it's hard. And I like how things have changed between us," he said, his voice getting deeper.

Her heart was pounding in her ears, and for some reason there was a metallic flavor on her tongue.

"I want… Kaylee," he said, grabbing hold of her hands, putting them between both of his. "I want you to marry me."

She felt like she'd been hit in the chest. Or maybe just

been hit by a truck. She couldn't breathe. She couldn't…
She couldn't breathe at all. It was like her throat had
constricted completely.

Bennett… *Her Bennett* was looking at her with ear-
nest, dark eyes and he was asking her to marry him.

"Bennett…"

"I want you to be my wife," he said. "The life we can
have… I want to wake up with you every morning. I
want you to go to bed in my room at night. It would be
perfect. Don't you think so? It all fits."

With those last three words the bright, glaring moment of possibility that she had experienced, just a moment of it, was extinguished. His plans had been messed
up.

He saw a new plan here. A new way to make his
life look like he wanted it to. All he was missing was a
wife. He had his son. She could be the missing piece.

But she had been that. That add-on piece for all of her
life. And she knew what that felt like. She knew what
it did to you. And she knew that once she couldn't be
everything that he saw that role fulfilling, he wouldn't
want her anymore. It was exactly like her parents. She
had seen him this morning with Dallas, and they were
family. They had that extra something holding them
together, that something that she had never had with
anyone.

She loved him. And he was never going to love her
in the same way. Because she needed him in a way that
he would never need her. Not really.

She was a good friend to him. She'd spent seventeen
years in that role. Giving to him. Caring for him. Loving him on his terms, because she'd never ever stated
her own.

But this would be different. And once he had her, all of her…would that last?

She couldn't believe it would.

It made her want to curl in on herself. Or lash out.

"No," she said, taking a step back. "No. I'm not going to be your…your new Olivia. I can't just be your wife because the first one didn't work out."

Bennett frowned, looking at her with anger in his eyes that surpassed anything she had ever seen there before. "That's what you think this is? That's what you think I'm doing to you? I would never ask you to be my wife just because I wanted a wife. You're nothing like the woman I planned on making my wife."

She let out a completely incredulous laugh. "Thanks, Bennett."

"I'm serious. I didn't want someone who was involved in my life, I didn't want someone who made me feel all of this. Someone I could go to work and forget about during the day. Someone who would smile at me nicely when I came home and hand me my dinner, that's what I wanted."

"Well, I would never do that."

"No," he said. "You wouldn't. You would have said that you worked all day too, and you expected me to get my own damn dinner. And I like that about you. But I wouldn't have chosen you to be my wife. Because I can't forget you, I can't put you in a box, Kaylee. You don't fit with what I thought I wanted. Because you're too big for that. Too real. Too messy. That's why I could never see you as beautiful. All that time. Because I knew if I did… I knew if I did, everything that I had worked so hard for was going to be ruined. All my control. All of my planning. All that self-protection that was so damned important to me, that I know I can't have now. I don't even want it. I want you. I love you."

Everything in her recoiled, drew back in abject horror and fear. He was standing there saying the right things. Saying them to her. But there was no way... There was no way. It wouldn't last. For her it never did.

Hope made fools of people. It had made a fool of her. And this was why she didn't do it. Why she'd never told Bennett she had feelings for him. Why she made sure there was no way anything could happen, which meant there was no room to hope and no room to be crushed.

And he was trying to change that.

She couldn't...she couldn't.

"No," she said. "You don't *suddenly* love me."

"You're damn right I don't *suddenly* love you. I *have* loved you. For years. I had this...this moment of clarity when I was naked with you last night."

"Yeah, a lot of men have moments of clarity when women are naked, Bennett, that doesn't make it real."

"No. Listen. You have to listen," he said. "I'm trying to tell you something. I've always loved you, but I put limits on that, because if I didn't I knew that it could... take over my life, and I didn't want anything to take over my life. But you know what, then this kid came into the picture and took over everything. Everything that I thought I was. Everything I thought I knew about myself. It was destroyed. When he showed up it was all ruined. And I couldn't play games with myself anymore and pretend that I can control everything around me, not when there's fifteen years' worth of evidence that I can't. He showed me that I had to give something of myself to get anything. And you... I want you. I want everything we can really have, not this careful friendship that we built up over the years because neither of us wanted something that was too big or messy or complicated."

Her ears were buzzing, her entire face numb.

She had dreamed this. Of him wanting her. Of him making promises to her. But suddenly, she realized it had been easier to watch him prepare to marry another woman than it was to stand here and hear this. This was hard. This was borderline impossible. This was wanting on a level that she just… That she was afraid of.

That hope. That need inside of her. Dammit all. She didn't want it. It was one thing to be his strength, his anchor.

She'd never wanted him to be hers. But he was. He *was*.

And the hope of more, of everything, was so very terrifying. It was so much easier to simply believe something could never happen. He was asking for… He was asking for this to last longer than a moment. Asking for this to be real, to be forever.

And she just…couldn't.

She was standing there facing down a dream. Who would have thought that it could be more terrifying than staring down a nightmare?

She couldn't say yes. She couldn't. Because it was going to happen, it was bound to. Maybe not now, maybe not even in a year, but he would discover that she wasn't…

That she wasn't enough.

That she didn't fit.

Her own parents felt that way. And if Bennett had really felt this way about her he wouldn't have been so close to marrying Olivia.

She wouldn't have been a last resort like this.

No, Bennett was lying to himself. Because he was a planner, and he saw the perfect end to his plan. And he didn't mean to lie to her, she knew that. Because Bennett was a good man. But that was the problem. He was a good man who believed firmly in his plans.

But plans weren't enough. And neither was being a puzzle piece.

Because what she knew was that she didn't fit. Not really. He would try. And she believed that Bennett would try with everything.

He wanted a wife. He was choosing a wounded bird. She didn't want to be a wounded bird to him.

"No," she said again. "I'm not going to marry you."

"No?"

"Yes!" she shouted. "No, I will not marry you, Bennett. I know it's hard for you to believe that anyone would dare go up against you and your plans. But I am. I'm not going to marry you. I'm not going to help make your life easier. I did everything for you," she all but screamed. "I became a veterinarian for you. I admitted what a pathetic idiot I am. I can't… I can't keep being this pathetic."

"Is being in love pathetic?"

"I'm *not* in love with you. I'm like a stupid puppy that started following you around seventeen years ago and never found anyone else to follow around. That's it."

"That's it?" Bennett's face was still, frozen like a mask. White with rage.

"Yes. I'm a mess, Bennett. But at least I know I'm a mess. I know enough not to saddle you with me for the rest of your life."

"Did I say that I felt like I was going to be saddled with you?"

"No," she said. "But maybe I don't want to be saddled with you either. With your guilt, and your duty. With this good guy stuff."

"You're the one calling it that," he said.

"Because I'm honest. I'm realistic. About who you are and who I am."

"Who are you, Kaylee?" he asked. "Because I think I know the answer to that question, but you're standing there saying all these things, and it makes me wonder if you have any idea who the hell you are."

"I'm a Band-Aid that has never healed anything. Ask my parents. I'm the sidekick. The helper."

"Have I ever made you into that? Have I?"

"You don't need me," she said. "You have your dad. You have your brothers and Jamie. You have Dallas. You don't need me." She was just saying things now. Anything. Anything to push him away. To get some distance.

"Don't say that," he said.

"I'll say it because it needs to be said. Because I'm not going to live in a fantasy world where I pretend that I'm somehow important when I'm really just a supporting character."

"*That's* the fantasy," he bit out. "This. This thing that you've built up in your head. I do need you, Kaylee. Not because there's a lack of anything in my life except you. You're right. I have plenty of people. Plenty of people surrounding me, plenty of people who love me, and I still want you. What does that tell you? About how important you are? You. Not a woman. Not a friend. Not a wife. You. You're right. I have friends. I have family. There's not a single thing in this world, a single empty role that I couldn't fill without you. But no one and nothing else is *you*. And you're what I need. That's what

I've come to figure out, Kaylee. That love is the most important thing. And that love is never going to play by the rules. That's why all this time I made it nothing. That's why all this time I didn't let myself tell anyone I love them. But I'm done with it. And I'm done waiting until it's safe. I love you. Even if you can't let me do it right now. Even if you can't love me."

Even if *she* couldn't love *him*? She loved him with everything that she was, and that was the damned problem. All she wanted to do was brush aside her fears and run into his arms, but she couldn't do it. She didn't know how. She didn't know how to be anything but this. She didn't know how to do anything but hide.

All of her life she had let herself have just the safest part of caring for Bennett. Because she didn't deserve the rest of him. She just didn't.

He deserved... He deserved a woman who wasn't quite so broken. He didn't need a fixer-upper. And that was what she was.

"No," she said. "No, Bennett. Not us. Not like that. You can find somebody else. You can—"

Bennett cut her off. "I can't. I need you. I won't find someone else. This isn't about me just having a wife. I don't want one or need one in that sense. I need you."

"For what? Why me?"

He took a step back, looking stricken. He didn't speak for a long while. "Because I love you."

"What does it mean? Why me and not someone else?"

He didn't say anything. "That's what I thought," she said.

"Kaylee," he said, reaching out and wrapping his arms around her. She wanted to let him hold her. She wanted to sink into him. Into his warmth. But she couldn't let herself. Already these past weeks had been like a dream, they had been everything that she had never thought she could have. And it… She couldn't put herself through more. She couldn't risk the eventual fallout of it.

"I have to go," she said.

"Kaylee," he said, tightening his hold on her.

"I'm going to go," she said, making her voice louder. "I don't think you're going to stop me."

She started to head out the door as soon as he released his hold on her, but it was his voice that stopped her this time. Harder, shot through with iron. "I never took you for a coward, Kaylee Capshaw."

She turned around to face him. "I'm not a coward."

"You're scared. You're running scared. Don't think I don't know it. All this time I thought you were the strongest woman I knew. I thought you were one of the strongest people I knew. But you're afraid. Just like everyone else."

"Big talk from a man who was no different only a few weeks ago. So here's what I think, Bennett. Either you've undergone a pretty miraculous transformation in a short amount of time or you're just doing what you do. Coming up with a plan. I don't think you're braver than I am, Bennett Dodge. I just think you've come up with more creative ways to mask your fear."

"You're an expert on that, huh?"

"You know what? Maybe not. But you know what I am an expert on? You. And it hasn't escaped my notice that you want all of this from me the minute you want it. Because whatever you say, you think I'm your sidekick. Even if you can't admit that."

Then she turned and walked away from him completely, heading out the door of the veterinary clinic.

She didn't stop to say anything to Laura. She got into her truck and headed to her house, her fingers numb, her lips numb. And only when she was inside her own house did she let herself cry.

CHAPTER TWENTY-TWO

BY THE TIME Bennett got to Wyatt's house that night his face was permanently set in stone. His entire body felt like stone. Like lead. Heavy. Except, it all still hurt. It hurt like a mother.

He had risked himself with Dallas and it had paid off. And as a result he had gotten cocky. He had thought that he might be able to risk himself with Kaylee too. Instead, he had been rejected spectacularly.

But he didn't believe it. He just didn't. That she didn't want him. That she didn't want to be with him. It was that confidence, though, that made him second-guess his own motives. Made him wonder if he was doing just what she had accused him of. Trying to make his life easier. Trying to fill a space and fit a plan altogether.

Dallas met him at the porch, and when he got a look at Bennett's face, his own expression turned to one of concern.

"Is Lucy okay?"

"Lucy's fine," Bennett said. He had been by the house to check on her before he had come to get Dallas.

"Then why do you look like somebody's dead?"

"Nobody's dead. Just…stuff."

"What kind of stuff?"

"Kaylee stuff," Bennett said honestly. Because he had promised the damn kid honesty, which was just obnoxious now.

Dallas frowned and sat on the porch swing. Bennett joined him. "What did you do?" Dallas asked.

"I didn't do anything," Bennett said, feeling defensive. "I told her I loved her."

"Well, she loves you, so you must have messed it up somehow."

"I swear I didn't. I asked her to marry me."

"Then what's wrong?"

"I don't think she trusts me. I don't think she trusts anyone."

Dallas frowned. "Fair enough. You know, because I don't really either."

"You do now," Bennett said.

"A little."

"Well, then if you can trust me after a few weeks she should trust me after seventeen years."

Dallas shrugged. "If you could choose to not be fucked up, then you would just choose to not be fucked up."

Bennett snorted. Sage words of wisdom from the teenager. "Fair enough."

"I'm going to go say goodbye to Jamie," Dallas said, standing up and walking away from the porch. Then Bennett's father came out from inside the house.

"Good kid," Quinn said, taking a seat next to Bennett on the porch swing, watching Dallas's retreating form.

"All things considered," Bennett said, "he is."

Quinn turned to face Bennett. "Something on your mind, son?"

"Why do you ask that?"

"Because you always come out here to sit when you are looking particularly serious. And you're looking particularly serious now, sitting here. So I wondered."

"I asked Kaylee to marry me. She told me no."

"Really?" Quinn asked, rocking back in the seat. "She told you no, huh? Did you have a ring?"

"Not yet. But I didn't have time to get one."

"Rookie mistake, Bennett. Always have a ring. And get yourself down on one knee." He stared at him hard. "You didn't get down on one knee either, did you? I've asked three different women to marry me, Bennett. And without exception I've given them that."

"Three?" The only women that Bennett knew about were his mother and Freda.

Quinn shrugged. "Ancient history. But that's where you went wrong."

Bennett shook his head. He wished it were that simple. "Somehow, I don't think it was the lack of ring that made Kaylee say no."

"Why did she, then?"

"She doesn't believe that I love her. Seventeen years I've been her friend, and I've never lied to her. She doesn't believe that I love her." Without his father pressing for more, Bennett continued. "She thinks that I'm after convenience. That I'm looking to fill a hole in my life. That because of how things were with Olivia I was just… Well, that I was just looking for a replacement fiancée."

His dad looked at him hard. "And you aren't?"

"I sure as hell am *not*. If I was going to choose myself a convenient wife it would not be Kaylee Capshaw. She's *inconvenient*. She makes me feel things. She's a pain in my ass."

"Has she *seen* that? Have you done anything that was just for her? Because it seems to me that if your relationship with her changed around Dallas coming into your life that a woman as skittish as her is going to think the worst."

"But I told her that I loved her, beyond that… I don't know what I can do."

"She was a friend when you needed it. She's been around helping you with Dallas. She's been your work partner. She's been all that for you. On your schedule. And now you're proposing, and she didn't fall in line right away, and that surprises you?"

Bennett felt like he'd been smacked in the face with a board. "I…I never meant it like that. I just…"

"Of course you didn't. But it doesn't change the fact that she's been there for you endlessly. What have you given her?"

He knew what she'd told him about their friendship. About why it mattered to her. How knowing him had helped her to believe in herself. But that…didn't seem like enough. Not next to that towering list his dad had presented him with of what Kaylee had been for him.

"I'm an idiot," he said. "I…"

She had been everything for him. His friend. His support. His business partner. His lover.

Then suddenly he'd decided he wanted it different and she was right: it hadn't occurred to him that she wouldn't fall in with his plan. Because she always did. Because he expected it.

"You can't control love, Bennett. Or how people react to it. When you don't feel particularly lovable, it doesn't always feel like a gift. Just a burden. Something else for her to do."

That wasn't what he wanted. Not at all. He didn't want to take from her. He wanted to give. He didn't want her because of what she could give him. He wanted… he wanted to hold her. Shelter her. Shield her.

"So what do I do?" he asked. "Until she's ready. What do I do if she never is?"

"Love her anyway. If you really love her, and you're not looking to fill a vacancy, you wait. Showing her is the only thing that's going to show her. Forget about what you need. Be what she needs."

"I've loved her for seventeen years. As my friend. And now I love her as everything. I'm not going to stop just because she told me to go away."

"Then take the time to show that. Live it."

And suddenly, Bennett had an idea. But it was going to take some doing. If Kaylee was afraid that she was just a piece being slotted into his life, then he was going to have to do something just for her. Away from life. Away from their regular roles. From the things she thought of as her filling convenient spaces.

"I might need you to watch Dallas for a few days."

CHAPTER TWENTY-THREE

KAYLEE WAS DEEPLY entrenched in her misery by the time her doorbell rang that night. She was completely shocked that somebody would come see her. She had been too much of a troll to Bennett earlier for him to come. Except…he kind of hoped he had. That he had come after her.

Pitiful. She didn't know what she wanted. She wanted… Well, she wanted to be somebody else.

Somebody who wasn't such a coward. That was the bottom line. Bennett was right about her. She was running scared. Because she just didn't know how to make that decision to trust. To let go of all these things that had hurt her so badly and embrace what she wanted most.

She had spent her whole life on the edge of those dreams. Grabbing hold of them was just… It was too hard.

She scraped herself off the couch and padded across the hardwood floor to the front door. She was wearing her pajamas, but oh well. She looked out the little window at the top of the door, shocked to see Dallas standing there, looking edgy.

She jerked the door open. "Dallas? What are you doing here?"

"I drove my dad's truck. And if he finds out he might ground me for the rest of my life."

She was torn between surprise that he was here, the desire to scold him and a strange warmth when he referred to Bennett as his dad. "You know how to drive?"

"Yeah. I mean, it's not legal for me to do it, but I do know how."

"Why are you here?"

"I'm here to talk to you." Dallas walked past her into her house without waiting for her to invite him in. "Why did you tell him no?"

"Oh. He told you about that?"

"It was obvious since he was looking depressed all over the place today. You love him. I don't understand."

"Yeah," Kaylee shot back. "You love him too. But I bet you haven't told him that you do. And you act like a prickly cat with one foot halfway out the door all the time."

"Yeah," Dallas said. "So?"

"So, why do you expect me to be any different?" This was ridiculous. She could hear herself being ridiculous and she couldn't stop it.

"First of all," Dallas said. "I'm fifteen. I have a right to my immature bullshit. You're old. You don't."

Kaylee sniffed and gripped the front of her bathrobe. "I am not old."

"You're older than me. So that's just number one. Second of all...I'm staying. I am. I'm going to take this. Because I want it. And I don't see why in hell you shouldn't take it."

"He doesn't really want me. I'm just...here."

"Well, the same could be said for me. I'm the son he got. He didn't choose me. There's no reason—genetic or legal—that he's stuck with you."

"Convenience."

"I don't think he's upset over inconvenience right now," Dallas said. "He's really sad."

"Well. It's just that I don't… I don't… I don't deserve it," she finished, her voice flat.

"What? And *I* deserve it? I deserve to have the sainted Bennett Dodge rearrange his whole life for me? I have a criminal record. I got myself thrown out of more foster homes than I can count. He still seems perfectly happy to have me around. If deserving it is part of the equation then I'm screwed."

"It's different," she said. "You're his son."

"Yeah, I'm my mother's son too. But it didn't seem to matter much for most of my life."

"It's just different for you, Dallas. It's different with a parent. A good parent. This is…romance stuff. And there's a reason it's never worked out in my life. Trust me."

He continued on as if she hadn't spoken. "You were the only person here that really understood me, Kaylee. And you were the easiest person for me to start to care about. But you gave me a hell of a lot of advice that you don't seem to want to take yourself. Just let him love you. Just love him back. Life is hard enough without making it harder, right?"

"I don't know," she said. "And I… I'm not fifteen. That's the problem. I've spent my whole life loving him and…knowing that I couldn't have him."

"Why didn't you ever tell him?"

"Because I didn't want him to not love me. I didn't want to give all that and then have it be…"

"You didn't want the door closed forever. I get it." Dallas swallowed hard. "I've always known that Bennett Dodge was my dad. In Gold Valley, Oregon. My mom told me that when I was…maybe seven or eight.

I didn't tell anyone because I didn't want him to send me away. My mom let the state take me from her. Over and over again. Why would he want me? I could have been with him all this time. But not until it was the end of the line did I give them his name. Because I couldn't face being rejected by him too. But he didn't reject me. He took me in. He treated me like a son without question from the beginning. I just had to ask. I had to admit that I needed it. Wanted it."

Her heart went out to the child he'd been, so like herself. Still… "I don't know if I can," she said. "Because this hurts. Do you know I had to watch him almost get engaged to another woman? That hurt. But I couldn't survive it if he decided that he wanted me, if he married me…and then he realized what my parents knew all this time. That I'm not worth it."

"You can't get a guarantee. That much I know. Beyond that…" He swallowed hard, his brown gaze meeting hers. "Kaylee, if I was going to have a mom, I would want her to be you. And so maybe coming here is selfish on my part. Because this life here that I have is better because of you. So I think it seems pretty insane for you to stand there and tell me how you're not good enough, or there is something wrong with you when you've been a big part of what was right for me."

That killed her. Just destroyed her. She felt diminished, every wall inside of her crushed. And she wanted… She wanted to reach out and hug him. She wanted to run to Bennett. She wanted… She wanted to be the person that Dallas was describing, and not the person that she felt like.

"How did you do it?" she asked. "How did you…decide to take the chance?"

"Well, my options were a group home and eventually jail, probably, or Gold Valley and Bennett Dodge. So I guess it's when you realize the alternative is no kind of life."

She nodded, but didn't say anything.

"A lot of people love you, Kaylee," Dallas said. "Eventually, you're going to have to let them."

Dallas turned and started walking back out the door.

"Was it that easy?" she asked.

"For me? No. I'm still working it out. But…like I said, it's better than what else is out there for me. It's better than anything else. Anyway, I'll see you around. I hope."

He turned to go and she stopped him. "Hey, wait a second, juvie. I'm not letting you go out and get arrested, okay? I'll drive you back in your dad's truck."

She held her hand out, waiting for the keys.

"How will you get home?"

"I'm old, like you said. Don't worry about me, I'll figure it out."

They kept mostly silent for the five-minute drive up the road to Bennett's place, and at his guidance she pulled the truck into the barn, where Bennett wouldn't hear the engine or see the headlights.

"Stay out of trouble," she said when they got out of the truck.

"Why don't you come to the house?" he asked.

His tone was hopeful, and it hurt.

"Not tonight, Dallas. I'm sorry. I have to…figure this out."

He nodded, seeming to accept that. "Good night, Kaylee," he said, turning and walking across the gravel drive toward the porchlight that shone in the distance. Kaylee stood there considering her next move.

She could call Jamie to come pick her up, but she didn't actually want company.

She looked up at the clear sky. At all the stars overhead, at the black ridge of mountain and trees that rose up in the distance. She remembered running through a field on a night like this. With Bennett.

She headed out toward the highway and crossed over the fence line into a field that ran along the side of the road that wasn't on the shoulder. She picked up her pace, going faster and faster, until she was running.

Like they had back then.

She wanted to go back in time. When it was simple.

When it was her and Bennett against the world, and not her against Bennett. Her against herself.

She ran until her lungs burned. Until she thought her heart might burst.

She stopped in the middle of the field, tears streaming down her face. She bent over, bracing herself on her thighs.

What was she doing?

What was she running from?

She had wanted Bennett all of her life, and then he had offered himself, and she was too afraid to take it. Why? Because she doubted him?

No. She didn't doubt Bennett. He was the best. Good right down to his bones.

She doubted herself.

More than that, she was afraid. Afraid of what it would mean if she changed her life like this.

Because the truth of it was her feelings for Bennett had always been manageable. She had been able to sit back and be a martyr to them. Allow them to hurt her, but just enough.

She had held herself back from him, so that if he rejected her he wasn't rejecting all of her.

She had accused Bennett of having plans, of being in control. But she was even worse. What she had felt for Bennett… Had it even been love? What she had felt had been all selfish and self-protecting.

A chance for her to marinate in all of her glorious pain and the injustice of the fact that she wanted a man she could never have. Because she didn't ask for what she wanted. Because she didn't give him honesty.

And yes. She had conveniently filled a lot of spots in his life, but she'd done it willingly. She'd never asked for anything different. Had never pushed for more. She'd just pretended. That everything was fine. That she was happy.

He had given her honesty. He had stood there and professed his love for her, had stood there and faced down rejection. He had been naked for her in a way that went beyond clothing.

But she hadn't been. Not really. She was protecting herself, always protecting herself. Because she was every inch the coward he said. And she covered it up in all this self-pity. She had been wounded, convinced she wasn't good enough, that he didn't really want her.

But what if he did? What if he really wanted her with everything that he was? What if they could have everything if she would just stop hiding?

She was going to have to come up with a plan to do just that.

She stood up straight and looked back up at the stars. She couldn't go back in time. She had no choice but to go forward.

And she was going to have to be brave. No more hiding. No more protecting herself.

Because if she really loved Bennett, then she was going to have to show him. If she really loved Bennett, she was going to have to risk something.

Anything else wasn't love at all.

CHAPTER TWENTY-FOUR

WHAT KAYLEE DIDN'T expect was for Jamie Dodge to show up at her front door the next morning, her dark hair tied back in a ponytail, her expression grim and grouchy. "I'm kidnapping you," she said.

"You're...kidnapping me?"

"Yes," Jamie said, shifting her weight from one cowboy boot-clad foot to the next. "You have ten minutes to pack a weekend bag and get in."

"I have...the clinic..."

"It's closed today," Jamie said, sounding maddeningly like her brother when she made definitive statements like that. "All emergencies will be allocated to Copper Ridge's clinic by Laura. It's all been arranged."

"Is Bennett behind this?"

Hope flooded through her, but she didn't want to hope too much. Or maybe she needed to. Maybe she needed to trust in the man that Bennett was, in the truth of his feelings, and let herself hope fully. Because she didn't allow herself that. Ever. And if she was going to follow through with what she intended to do, she had to.

She had a speech prepared. And she was going to give it. She was going to tell him everything. About how she felt. For how long she'd felt it.

Even if she had to do it in front of his whole family.

"I'm not at liberty to say," Jamie returned crisply.

"Just let me... Let me get dressed."

She went back inside, packed a bag with essentials, and slowly selected an outfit, put on a little bit of makeup because unless Jamie was planning on dumping her off the side of a cliff she was going to see Bennett at some point today, wherever this was leading.

Though, given that Jamie Dodge was protective of her family and certainly not squeamish, Kaylee had to accept the fact that the cliff dumping might be a viable possibility.

On unsteady legs she met Jamie outside and got in her red pickup truck.

She stole a glance at the other woman who was determinedly looking at the road and not at Kaylee.

"So," Kaylee said. "How is…everyone? I mean, with the changes. Quinn being in town. Dallas. Luke and Olivia having a baby." Put in a list like that, the Dodges were having quite the time.

"Fine," Jamie said, keeping her answer short and unfriendly.

"And Bennett and Dallas are…?"

"Fine with each other." There was a break in the conversation. And then Jamie pressed on, her tone sharp. "You love him," Jamie said. "I always suspected that you did. So…don't hurt him. Not now. He's been through enough, Kaylee. He's lost enough. And he's the best man, the best brother. He's being the best… the best father to Dallas." Jamie's tone suddenly thickened. "He never acted like he hated me. Not once. And he could have blamed me for her death. He could have. But he was my big brother always. He protected me. I will damn well protect him now if I can."

"I don't want to hurt him," Kaylee said, her head aching. "I'm just trying not to hurt myself."

"Sure. I get that. I know how it feels to be hurt. To

lose someone. But what's the point in protecting yourself if that means losing all of the good things? Isn't it
better to risk the bad than to end up with nothing at all?"

Kaylee wasn't sure what to say to that, but then Jamie
spoke again. "If my dad... If Bennett, and Wyatt and
Grant... If they'd chosen to let losing my mother keep
them from loving me, I wouldn't have anything. I'm
grateful for their bravery. When people make the choice
to be brave for love. It makes all the difference in the
world."

They drove on in silence until they reached the town
of Copper Ridge. They drove through the main street,
and Kaylee did her best to stop from asking questions
as they went by all the little classic, shingle buildings.
They bypassed the town and went out into the coun-
try, turning left off the main highway and down a long
driveway. It was a ranch, that much she could tell. But
they bypassed the fields and what looked like a large
log cabin, going back into the trees until they stopped
at a Victorian-style house, set in the middle of the rustic landscape. It was painted rich cranberry colors, the
little yard full of azaleas.

"What's this?"

She saw that Bennett's truck was already there.

Her heart sped up, and she got out of the truck.

"Don't forget your bags," Jamie said, her expression only marginally friendlier than when she'd first
appeared at Kaylee's door.

She grabbed the bags, and then watched as Jamie
drove away, leaving Kaylee stranded in front of the
house. Well, she wasn't really stranded, seeing as Bennett was there. But that depended on whether or not
Bennett intended to take her off into the woods and
leave her like she was a problem cat.

As if it had heard her thinking about cats, a little gray one hopped up onto the porch and rubbed itself up against one of the planter boxes in front of the door, looking at her plaintively. "I'm not sure what I'm doing here," she said to the cat, getting down and scratching him behind the ears. "I'm hoping that you're a good omen."

She straightened and walked up the porch steps, stopping in front of the door. There was a little sign that said to enter, so she did.

It was a bed-and-breakfast, that much was clear when she walked in and saw the little podium with the guestbook sitting on top of it. There was no one attending the front room. But she looked down at the guestbook and saw a familiar name.

Bennett Dodge. Room two.

She swallowed hard and looked around, then headed toward the staircase, making her way up slowly, going down the hall and pausing in front of the door with the number two on the outside.

She felt frozen. Like she was standing in front of another door, in another house, in another time.

She was hoping now. Hoping she knew what she might find on the other side. Her defenses were destroyed. She couldn't be cynical, she couldn't hold back.

But she was afraid to open the door.

"Kaylee." She heard Bennett's voice through the door. "If that's you standing out there hedging, just come in."

As if it's that simple.

Except…it was. She could stand out here and never know. Never have to face disappointment. And never, ever have a chance at what she really, truly wanted either.

With those options…well, there was no question.

She took a deep breath and pushed the door open. There he was, sprawled out on the bed, his black cowboy hat over his eyes. It was an incongruous image. The room itself was frilly. Lacy bedspread, a canopy over the top of it. Matching curtains. There was floral wallpaper that definitely went with the Victorian theme, but did not go with Bennett. And there he was, in a black T-shirt she loved so much, his regular jeans, his feet bare, his boots on the floor. And that hat over his face.

It was the bedroom. The one from her fantasies, only more. Richer. Better. The kind of princess room fit for a grown woman, and not a little girl.

The big, sexy cowboy on the bed added to that angle, for sure.

It hit her then, standing there, looking at her gorgeous masculine man in this frilly bedroom, that he wasn't asking her to choose. He was offering her everything. The everything that she hadn't thought she could possibly possess.

And here it was. Just all of it. Her business partner, her friend, her lover. On a lace bedspread.

Showing her that she could have it. That she deserved it. That he would be the things she needed. The things she desired.

"I...I don't know what to say," she said, closing the door behind her.

He moved his hat back and looked over at her. "Well, this is for you. And whether or not I stay is your call. But it's paid for either way. So if you want a weekend with me...I'm here for that. If you want one without me, I'll go.

"But this... Kaylee, I love you. But my loving you can't be all a series of demands. It can't be about where you fit in my life. It can't be about just me being ready.

I love you. And I'll…do that however you want. If you
want me to marry you, or if you don't. I'll still be there.
If you want to just be friends… I can try that too. I feel
like I've been awfully selfish with loving you, and that
has to stop." He took a breath. "I want to be what you
need. The fulfillment of your dreams. That's…that's
what I want. Really."

"You aren't selfish," she said, making her way over
to the bed and sitting on the edge of it. She placed her
hand on his chest, could feel that, for all that his posture
was relaxed, his heart was beating overly fast.

"Kaylee…" he began.

"No," she said. "I've got some things to say to you.
And I need to say them first. Bennett…I've been in love
with you for most of my life. And the only way that I
could deal with that was to comfortably assure myself
that it could never turn into anything. I was just hiding.
Loving you and never taking a chance. It was one thing
to sit around and feel morose because you were with
Olivia, because you were going to marry her… But I
accepted it, Bennett. I accepted that you were going to
marry another woman. I…I can't even reach back that
far to figure out what in hell was going through my
mind. I feel like… Like that was another person. That
person who wouldn't fight for us. She couldn't hope."

She looked around the room, her heart swelling in
her chest. "But…it's me. It was me yesterday. When you
said that you loved me and I turned you down, and I said
all that stupid stuff. About not loving you, and about
how you didn't really love me. And it was all just…me
protecting myself. It's what I've always done. I told myself it was somehow benevolent of me not to ask you
for anything more than friendship. But it wasn't. I am
a coward. Just like you said. Because I am so afraid of

wanting and not having. I'm so afraid of confirming that we can't be together. I would rather be the tragic figure in the story than someone who tried and didn't succeed. I'm the one that made myself a sidekick. And it was…" She cleared her throat. "Do you know that your son snuck out last night?"

Bennett frowned. "What? No."

"He did. He came to see me. To tell me that I am an idiot. And that I am less mature than him. He's right about all of that. He came to talk to me because he said of everyone here I understood him. And I have to admit that means he kind of understands me. He said that… that he knew your name. But that he had been protecting himself by not going to you."

Bennett nodded. "We actually had that talk last night."

"I realized that's been me. All this time. I never took the chance because I didn't want to confirm that you couldn't love me. And when you stood there telling me that you did… To think that I can have that is so scary. Because opening myself up to it completely means that I could be hurt. So badly. Worse than I ever have been. Because I love you so much that you have that power that no one else has."

"Kaylee," Bennett said, "why do you think I've spent my life planning things out the way that I have? Why do you think I was so obsessed with having all those pieces I thought were the right pieces? Because it was what I could control. And you can't control love. The love that I have for you, I can't control. I think something in me had to know that. And it's why I kept you as my friend. It's why I held out all this time. Why I insisted that I didn't see you that way. But loving Dallas broke down the first barrier, and being with you broke down all the rest. When I held you in my arms the other night I realized there were no more barriers between kinds of love. I love you. I'm in love with you. When I quit holding back…it was so clear."

"What made you fall in love with me?"

"There just came a point where I couldn't not be in love with you anymore," he said. "It was pointless to resist it."

Her heart swelled up, everything inside of her feeling so full, so swollen with happiness that she thought it might burst inside of her, that she thought it might be too much. But she didn't care. She'd spent her whole life having not quite enough. Too much was better. So much better.

"I got this place," Bennett said. "For the next four days. Hoping that you'd want to spend them with me."

"I do," she said. "I really do. I promise you're not forcing this on me."

"Do you know why I wanted to do this?"

"No," she said, feeling all choked up. "Why?"

"Because I want to take us away from real life. To get away from my family, even Dallas, for a few days. We don't need to fit in my life. We just need to fit together. I wanted us away from all of that. My timing and everything. I believe in this. I believe in *us*. You are the longest, most important relationship I've ever had. I think it was love all along. But this is for you, all these days. Just for you. Whatever you want. Whatever you need from me, I want to be there for you. So for the next few days, it's just you and me. This room, this bed. Nice breakfast. Maybe some walks. Some time on the beach. Whatever you want. I want to take time out of my life to be with you, to show you how much you matter. Enough to change me. Enough to rearrange things."

"Bennett… You didn't have to do this. Dallas…"

"Is fine. He's with his uncles, his aunt and his grand-parents. And he's completely fine. You and I need to be together. Just us. Not forced together by emotional stuff happening back in Gold Valley. Not breaking dry spells. You and me. Because we want to be together."

"I already know that I want to be with you," she said.

"What do you want me to be, Kay? I want to be all that. Whatever you need. Your furniture mover. Your friend. Your lover. Your smile when you're sad. Arms to hold you when you can't stand up. Your hope when you can't find any."

"You are," she said, swallowing hard. "You have always been the one who could be that for me. I was just too afraid to tell you it was what I wanted. But it is. It's you, Bennett. I want you to be my everything."

He kissed her, deep and long until neither of them could breathe. "Do we really need a walk on the beach? Or should we spend the weekend in bed?"

"Hey," she said, pushing at his shoulder. "You promised me walks on the beach. I want walks on the beach."

Bennett laughed and suddenly he mobilized, pushing her onto her back, grabbing hold of his cowboy hat and putting it on his head as he gripped her wrists and push them over her head, holding her down to the mattress, his weight over the top of her. "Are you sure about that?"

"Okay, now you're making a case for this staying in the room business."

"You're my best friend," he said. "The love of my life."

"Mine too," she said.

"We can do this. Just this. Sex and working together. Until you're ready for more. I want marriage, Kaylee,

I won't lie to you. But I'm willing to wait until you're ready for it too."

"I'm ready," she said, the words coming out a whisper.

"Thank God. My dad said I had to get down on one knee, but I think I like this position a lot better."

"I'm not complaining," she said, gasping as he rolled his hips forward, and then teased her with a kiss.

"I bought a ring and stuff too. But..."

She reached up, pressing her fingertips against his cheek. "That can wait."

"Do you think we need to talk more?" he asked.

"I think we've spent the past seventeen years talking," she said. "You say you love me. And I believe it. But why don't you show me."

"I think I'm going to take a lot of joy in showing you for the rest of our lives."

She was never again going to spend a sad date she didn't want to be on hoping she got a phone call from Bennett. Because finally, forever, she had Bennett.

Her friend. Her lover. Her everything.

He kissed her, and she kissed him back. She gloried in every erased boundary, every blurred line.

Kaylee Capshaw had been convinced she needed a new life. But that hadn't been true at all. She'd had what she needed all along. She'd just needed to find the courage to embrace it.

The love she'd had all along.

EPILOGUE

IT WAS THAT time of year again, and the seniors' names were written on the window at Mustard Seed. And this time, Dallas Dodge's name was among them.

Bennett could not possibly have been prouder of his son, or the work he had put in over the past three years to graduate. He had been behind, and it had been a struggle getting here, but he was here, he was doing it.

And so much of Bennett's own work as a father was done. It was strange. The past three years had been the most defining in his life. They had made him a father. And he had become a husband.

As he sat down in the bleachers at the football field while the graduates readied themselves, Kaylee grabbed hold of his arm, her ring shining in the sunlight.

That weekend at the bed-and-breakfast, he'd eventually gotten around to getting down on one knee and giving her the ring properly. Sometime much, much later in that first day. After he made love to her so many times he'd lost count.

Even now, the memory made him smile. Made his heart beat faster.

That weekend had been important. It had established a foundation for who they were as a couple. After so many years of being friends, it had been…necessary. To find that romance. To find out who they were as a couple, away from everything else.

It had been surprisingly easy. Like everything they'd been holding back for years had just been waiting. Waiting for them to wise up and realize what they both needed.

When their son was called up to the stage, Bennett and Kaylee stood, cheering and clapping, the whole Dodge section making a spectacle as Dallas crossed the stage to collect his diploma. When the ceremony was over, they all met on the field for a barbecue, families and students in black robes milling around. Dallas, for his part, ditched his hat almost immediately. But he held on to that diploma.

He surprised Bennett by crossing the lawn quickly, heading away from his friends and his girlfriend and straight for Kaylee and Bennett. He grabbed hold of Kaylee and gave her a hug. And then, he wrapped his arms around Bennett.

"I love you, Dad," he said.

Bennett's chest tightened, emotion almost overwhelming him. "I love you too, son."

"I'm going to go hang out," he said, clapping Bennett on the back as he headed back toward his friends. And Bennett just stood there, staring.

"I guess we did it," he said to Kaylee. "We're empty nesters."

"He doesn't go to school until fall," Kaylee pointed out.

"Still," Bennett said, "it was like we were on some kind of accelerated program."

"We were."

"I guess so," he said, rubbing his chest.

"Bennett," Kaylee said, grabbing his hand and pulling him close. "You don't have to worry about us being empty nesters for very long."

Bennett jerked back. "What?"

"I would say that with Dallas not leaving until October, we're really only going to have an empty house for about five months."

"Kaylee Dodge," he said, grabbing hold of her chin and looking at her square in the eye. "Are you telling me what I think you're telling me?"

"Yes," she said. "I'm pregnant."

Bennett picked up his wife and swung her in a circle, kissing her right on the high school football field he should have kissed her on years ago. Back when he'd been too stupid to know she was the one for him.

Back when he'd been too afraid for her to be.

A baby. More family. More love.

Things in his life definitely hadn't gone according to his plans. And thank God.

Because it had all gone much, much better.

* * * * *

Mail Order
Cowboy

CHAPTER ONE

JACKSON REID KNEW what he liked. He liked riding the perimeter of his family ranch, liked working from sunup to sundown until his muscles ached and his body was worn out. He liked drinking. And he liked women.

Women were the reward for all that work he did.

Work hard, drink hard, fuck hard.

He had no intention of settling down, no intention of changing. If he could die on the back of a horse, or with a tumbler of whiskey in his hand, or in the bed of a beautiful woman? Any of those things would be a fitting end for him. So why in hell would he change his life? He was on the path to any one of those ends, which meant he was on the right path for him.

His stepmother didn't approve, but she'd moved away from Gold Valley six months ago, and his father was dead. So there wasn't anyone around to mourn the fact that he wasn't after marriage or babies.

He'd worked damn hard that day, like he did every day. It was pouring down rain and he'd been soaked to the bone by the time he'd come in. He'd had a hot shower, and now he was about to get down to the drinking. But that was when he heard a knock on his door.

He stood up, ambled over to the door and opened it. For a moment, he thought the sex had been delivered right to him. There was a blonde on his doorstep, bundled up against the cold and the wet.

Then he realized a few things. The first being that he recognized her. The second that she was tearstained and miserable. The third…that she wasn't as bundled as she had initially appeared.

She was holding a blanket. And in the blanket was a baby.

"I can't do it," she said. "I thought I could, but I can't."

"Sasha?" That was her name. He vaguely remembered her from a liquor-soaked night quite a few months ago.

More than nine months ago, as a matter of fact.

Hell.

While that realization was rolling over him, she reached forward and thrust the baby at him, into his arms.

The bundle felt fragile, and at the same time…heavy. He looked down at the tiny thing in his arms and felt… He couldn't explain it. Couldn't reason or rationalize the expanding sensation in his chest, or the ever-increasing sensation of weight. In his arms. On his shoulders.

"I can't," she said again. "I know you can take babies to a hospital or a police station, but she's yours. You can take her there if you want."

"Mine?" he asked.

His. His baby. He'd never even held a baby before, and now it turned out the one he had now was…*his*.

"I have to go. I need to go get… I need to get out of here."

And then Sasha turned and ran. Ran away from the front door and down the steps, through the rain and back to her car.

He should do something. Go after her. Stop her. But

he was frozen in place, staring down at the bundle in his arms. He moved the blanket away from the baby's face and something in him shifted. Changed. As he looked at that tiny, vulnerable bundle in his arms, Jackson Reid felt like he no longer knew a damn thing.

Three months later...

I have a degree in early childhood development. The daycare that I worked at recently had to close, so I'm out of a job right now. I'm also out of an apartment, but that's a long dramatic story.
—S

Lily is four months old. She doesn't sleep through the night and I think I'm about to die of exhaustion. Cows don't delay their care, even if babies don't sleep, it turns out. She doesn't take after me. If I hadn't had a paternity test done I almost wouldn't have believed she was mine. Too sweet, for one thing. And she's the prettiest little thing I've ever seen. I don't know a damn thing about babies.
—J

She sounds perfect.
—S

She would be, if I weren't drowning. I need help. Room and board, plus the pay we discussed previously.
—J

I can get there in a week.
—S

I've got all your flight info. I'll be at the airport to get you.
—J

You can't miss me. I'll be the one with the bright, flowered suitcase. I'm plain and tall.
—S

A week after that...

SAVANNAH STURM STOOD in the tiny airport and looked around. She'd come into gate number three, and it turned out it was... Well, it was gate three out of three. In the only terminal the airport had.

She had been worried that her new employer, Jackson, might need a sign to help her find him. Now she imagined she'd just look for the man with the baby, assuming he *was* a man with a baby and *not* an ax murderer. The possibility was there that all of this was a scam of some kind. She was counting on him ringing alarm bells while they were here in public if she needed to be scared of him.

She adjusted the strap on her carry-on bag and stuffed her hands in her sweatshirt pockets, walking in line with the people who had just gotten off the very small plane and through a revolving door that led to...

What looked like the lone baggage carousel.

She stopped and looked around. The waiting area had a smattering of people in it. Not many, but that wasn't terribly surprising since her plane couldn't have had more than fifty people on it.

She didn't see a man with a baby.

The main doors to the outside slid open. The man who walked in was head and shoulders above everyone else in the room, a black cowboy hat pulled low over his eyes. He was wearing a flannel shirt with the sleeves pushed up, revealing muscular forearms that had lumberjack-caliber definition.

And he was holding a little pink bucket seat with a lacy blanket draped over the top.

Fathers of infants should not look like that. They should not look like every bad boy fantasy she'd never allowed herself to have. Fathers of infants shouldn't look like fantasies at all. They should look softer. Less angular. And he certainly shouldn't make her stomach tighten, and her body remember that it had been a very, very long time since she had been touched by a man.

And even longer since she had particularly wanted to be.

She blinked, grabbing hold of herself and retrieving her consciousness from that strange space it had just been in. She wasn't here to check out a hot man. She was here to do a job. To reclaim the broken pieces of a life that hadn't even been hers anymore after a particularly traumatic divorce.

She had herself firmly back together. Breathing normally.

Until she realized with absolute certainty that this wasn't just any hot dad wandering through the airport terminal.

It was the hot dad she was waiting for.

Jackson Reid.

He was nothing like what she'd expected. She felt silly suddenly that she'd had an expectation at all. But a single dad with a tiny baby made her think of someone soft, and the man she'd corresponded with online had seemed...maybe even sweet.

Checking out her boss in the first ten seconds of meeting him was kind of a bad start. But then, she sup-

posed she could forgive herself that. She'd been with
Darren for five years, and during that time, it had never
even occurred to her to check another man out. Finding herself unattached again was presenting some interesting side effects.

That was all this was. That part of herself naturally
inclined toward seeking attachment reminding her that
she currently didn't have one. And all she had to do was
remind that part that she didn't want one. She squared
her shoulders and crossed the space, standing closer
to the baggage carousel, but also a little bit nearer to
Jackson.

Who was apparently a hard-bodied cowboy.

She waited for him to see her. Waited for him to close
that remaining distance. But he didn't. Instead, he continued to scan the crowd, such as it was, his eyes skip-
ping over her easily. She didn't know how to feel about
that. Particularly since her eyes had gone immediately
to him, and had had a nearly impossible time leaving.

She cleared her throat and looked back at the baggage carousel. Maybe it wasn't him. Maybe she was
still waiting for Jackson Reid. Maybe it was some other
man all by himself with a little baby. Maybe *this* man
was waiting for his wife.

A wife who would no doubt be pretty and petite and
as striking as he was.

A wife who was probably sexually confident and
not frigid and buried under years and years of issues.

She took a deep breath, and the conveyor belt on
the carousel began to turn. People crowded in, collecting their bags. She wasn't expecting hers to show up
anytime soon. It was her own little Murphy's Law that
her bag was always last off the plane. She wasn't quite
sure how.

Not that she had traveled very much. She'd gone on a few little trips before her marriage. A post-graduation excursion to Disney World with some friends, a couple of spring breaks where she had been fully out of her element and had spent most of the time in the hotel room sober and trying to pretend she didn't know her friends were hooking up with strangers a floor above her.

Then she had met Darren and they'd taken that first trip to Colorado to meet his parents, and then had moved to his hometown to be surrounded by his family. A family that had, at first, seemed like a dream to her, given her own parents. She'd settled into a life that had slowly grown more and more confining in ways that Savannah hadn't totally realized until she had been free of it.

Lost in her thoughts, she hadn't realized the baggage carousel had emptied out, and her flowery, purple bag was going by. She grabbed hold of it, happy that the cheerful color and pattern made it easy to spot. Always being the last bag helped, too.

She hefted it off the carousel and turned around, and her eyes collided with his.

Oh, it was definitely him.

"Are you waiting for someone?" he asked.

"I *think* I'm waiting for you," she said, looking down meaningfully at the little pink bundle.

"Savannah Sturm?"

"Yes," she confirmed.

His eyes landed on her suitcase. "I suppose your description of the bag was true enough."

She blinked, looking up at him, and wondered if he had been thrown off because she had characterized herself as tall. Well, at nearly six feet, she was. But then,

Jackson had to be nearing six-five, so it was entirely possible he didn't see tall the same way that she did.

"Sorry. I guess tall is subjective."

His scorching brown gaze moved over her, and for an instant she thought she was going to be singed alive. She waited for him to say something, but he didn't. Instead, he simply turned. She moved to follow him, and he stopped to take the bag from her hand without asking if she wanted him to.

"You're holding the baby," she pointed out.

"Yeah, well, Lily doesn't weigh fifty pounds, and I assume the suitcase does. Either way, I can handle both just fine."

She had no trouble believing that. Still shamefully taking a visual tour of his muscles, she watched the way he maneuvered both baby and bag easily outside to where his truck was parked against the curb. There was an old security guard standing right next to it, looking officious, like he was about to make a proclamation. Jackson zeroed that gaze onto the guard. "I'm leaving."

"It's for loading and unloading only," the guard pointed out, tapping the sign with his forefinger to illustrate the point.

"And I'm loading," Jackson returned, his voice and glare as hard as steel.

Well. He was a whole thing.

Savannah gave an apologetic wave and got into the passenger side of the truck. Jackson hefted her suitcase into the bed, and then opened up his door, gently installing Lily's car seat in the small bench seat behind the driver side. Then he got in and started the engine, pulling them both away from the airport.

"How was the flight?" he asked.

"Quick," she responded. "It's only a couple hours from Colorado."

"It's going to take half that time to Gold Valley," he said. "Near enough."

"So there's no airport in Gold Valley."

"Nothing beyond a tiny municipal airfield. Not for commercial flights."

"I figured as much when you told me to fly into Tolowa."

"Our ranch is a bit out of town. Hope that doesn't bother you."

"Who's... I thought you were... I didn't think Lily's mother was in the picture."

"She isn't," Jackson said. "But I live on a family spread with my brothers and my stepsister. Lily and I live in our own cabin, and you'll stay there with us."

The idea of living in a cabin, which sounded cozy to the point of being tiny, seemed almost impossible now that she had actually laid eyes on the man. He was so large. He would fill up so much...space. It was impossible that he wouldn't.

She didn't say that out loud, though, and hid any discomfort. She'd been looking for a change. Looking for a new job in child care, because that was what she did, and when she had run across the ad from Jackson it had seemed like a godsend. Because wherever she ultimately landed, this job would provide her with the means to get away. And she *desperately* needed to get away.

Living in a small community where her ex-husband was a hometown legend, where his family owned half of everything, was impossible. She'd been choking on the mile-high air in her old life. A clawing desperation to be anywhere else taking over her every thought, as her options in her little town had been eliminated little by little. But moving was expensive, and it required a hell of a lot more credit than she had at this point in her life. Everything being linked to Darren had been fine when she had assumed that it would be forever. But when her marriage collapsed, she'd been left with nothing.

Jackson's ad seeking a live-in nanny had seemed perfect, and their back-and-forth conversation online had been effortless, making the decision to take the job even easier. But she hadn't considered the stark reality of being in such close quarters with a stranger.

"What do you do on the ranch?" she asked. She was desperate to fill the silence. If she didn't, she would be left with her thoughts, and her thoughts were perplexing her at this point.

"Cattle ranch," he said. "We supply USDA-approved beef to a large distributor."

"It keeps you pretty busy?"

He chuckled. "You could say that. In fact, I'd say my life was packed full before I found out I had a kid."

He hadn't given her the full story of why he was a single dad, but his choice of words just now was odd. She didn't know if he was divorced, but it had been pretty clear based on the tone of his messages that there was no one else involved. Maybe his wife had died. But then, he hadn't mentioned that. He hadn't mentioned a woman at all. It was like...

Like he had just found a baby on his doorstep.

"I see," she said, not really seeing all that clearly.

Neither of them said anything else for a while, and Savannah turned her focus to the scenery. It wasn't completely unlike Colorado. Mountainous and full of pine trees. She liked that. She loved the mountains. Compared to the exceedingly tame neighborhood she'd grown up in on the East Coast, she really liked the way that things were out West. She hadn't wanted to leave Colorado, per se. She had just needed to escape a town dominated by her ex, where he was still making choices about her life even when he wasn't directly in it. The way he manipulated things in town…

She'd had to get out.

She had thought that Oregon might be a natural place to get to. It had either been that or Montana, maybe Wyoming. But Oregon was where the opportunity had arisen, and she was also attracted to the idea that she would be able to drive out to the beach. Something she hadn't been able to do living in Colorado.

They drove through the small town of Gold Valley, all redbrick buildings and Wild West aesthetic, which burned a bright spot inside of her soul. Made her feel like—in spite of the initial awkwardness—she had made the right choice.

They continued on out of town, down a winding two-lane highway lined with thick trees, ferns and thickly carpeting the floor of the forest encroaching over the side, nearly to the road.

He was right, the ranch *was* quite a ways outside of the town itself, and if not for the two wooden posts holding up a sign over a narrow driveway that said Box R, she wouldn't have known there was even a ranch there at all.

They turned onto that dirt road. The trees cleared and revealed pastures, several empty, and one with a herd of cattle, before the road narrowed and the pines thickened again. It was just remote enough, just isolated enough that a jolt of adrenaline shot through her. Maybe she'd been stupid to come out here. Maybe there was no cabin and she was just on a dirt highway to murder.

But then they came to the end of the drive and she saw a little cabin. It was rustic and rough, but then it was what she'd expected a cabin to be, she supposed. She sat there while he got out, watched as he tended to his daughter. As strange as it all was, the way that those large, battered hands cradled the tiny infant when he took her out of her car seat made her feel…

A whole jumble of things. Most of them centered down deep in the pit of her stomach.

"I'll just get Lily laid down in her crib, and then I'll show you to your room and get your things," he said.

She nodded and watched as he walked up the steps to the front porch and disappeared inside the cabin.

She climbed out of the car. She supposed she could follow him in, but he hadn't said to, so she just stood there out in the gravel drive, turning a half circle and looking around the isolated place. What in hell had she gotten herself into? She realized it didn't much matter. She didn't have anywhere to go back to. She had no real friends left to speak of, no family that wanted anything to do with her.

For better or for worse, this was the place from which she was starting over.

So she had to make it work.

At least for a while.

CHAPTER TWO

Plain and tall.

Jackson played those words over and over in his head as he prepared his coffee and breakfast the next morning.

After he and Savannah had arrived at the cabin, he'd given her a quick rundown on Lily's schedule and where everything was. He'd shown her to her room—which was across the house from his, and next to its own bathroom—and he'd told her not to worry about taking care of Lily that night, because while he was an ogre sometimes, he wasn't enough of one to make her interrupt her sleep on a night when she'd been traveling all day.

She'd gone to bed early, early enough that he was pretty sure she was avoiding spending time in his company. Not that he minded. But he didn't think she'd eaten at all. Which meant he was making up a double portion of bacon this morning.

He hoped she wasn't a vegetarian, because everything was cooked in the bacon grease, and it was too late for him to do anything about that.

Probably would have been a good idea to ask.

There were some aspects to having a stranger in his house that he hadn't fully considered. He had just been desperate for the help. And since he needed round-the-clock help, offering room and board had seemed like the smartest thing to do. Of course, that meant sharing his space. Which he didn't like to do. But then, he was already sharing it with a woman, a bigger diva than he'd ever encountered before in his life.

Apparently, the tinier the female, the more willing a man was to submit to her whims. He couldn't explain the way that having Lily made him feel. He didn't like babies. He didn't like kids. He'd never wanted any of his own. He wasn't sure he did *now*. But the fact of the matter was he *had* a child, and he would die for her. Hell, he'd kill for her.

He didn't know what exactly the feeling was that had invaded his chest, but it was intense. He wasn't...content or happy, necessarily. No, the kind of feeling that Lily gave him wasn't settled in the least. It was entirely opposite to the way he had always imagined domestic life would go. Which he had imagined as death by monotonous inches.

The appearance of Lily in his life had taken everything he thought he'd known about himself, and about what he wanted, and turned it all on its side. He was sleep deprived, his chest ached when he looked at her, and every damned morning when his feet hit the floor, he had no idea what he was doing.

He'd been a rancher all of his life. When it came to working the land he knew what he was about. Backward and forward. He'd lost his virginity at fifteen to a pretty, older teenage girl who'd shown him exactly what to do, and hadn't been shy about demanding he do it better. Since then, he'd considered himself something of an expert on women. Everything he did in his life, he had a firm handle on.

Until now.

Feeling like a greenhorn was a total mind fuck, and apparently caused him to make decisions he might not have otherwise made. Like inviting this so-called plain, tall nanny to come live with him.

That was a far cry from reality. She was… She was stunning. It was a problem. Leggy and blonde, with sea-green eyes and full, gorgeous lips.

He hadn't been with a woman in quite some time. And that was playing havoc with him. The messed-up thing was he hadn't even thought about it. Not since Lily. He hadn't had the energy to even consider that kind of thing. He'd been so busy coping with the new life he found himself with he hadn't spared a thought to his old life.

But then the nanny had shown up, and he wanted to fuck her, which told him everything he needed to know about what kind of asshole he would be in a more conventional life. Because wasn't it only asshole husbands who wanted the nanny? Yeah, he knew that it was.

He wondered why she thought of herself as plain. Maybe because she wasn't fussy. She didn't have any makeup on when he picked her up at the airport. She had been wearing a T-shirt and a pair of leggings, but that seemed par for the course for travel. Maybe that was how she was all the time.

But if that's what she thought made her plain… Well, he wondered what kind of men she'd had in her life before.

Doesn't matter. You're not a man in her life.

He needed help with Lily. At least until she was old enough to go to a daycare or preschool part-time. He and Savannah had discussed that over email. And if he went and messed with the only help he'd been able to find, and earn himself a shady reputation on top of it, he was going to be more screwed than he already was.

It was getting late, and he shouldn't waste any more

time standing around in his kitchen. He had work to do, but seeing as he didn't have to strap Lily to his chest this morning and go about his work, trading her off between his siblings as they went through different tasks, he was going to hang around the house for a while. He needed to get Savannah established in her new role.

As if on cue her bedroom door cracked open and she appeared. Her blond hair was pulled back into a ponytail, a gray T-shirt molding over her slight, but perfect curves. She was wearing similar black leggings to the ones she'd had on yesterday.

"Good morning," he said. "Bacon?"

"Coffee before anything," she mumbled, stepping into the small kitchen, her gaze avoiding his a little bit too neatly.

As if it was intentional.

"How did you sleep?" he asked.

Her green eyes collided with his and he wondered if he had overstepped. Honest to God, he didn't know how to talk to her. Three months out of the game and he was this bad at communicating with women? Or maybe the problem was he didn't know how to communicate with a woman he was attracted to that he couldn't touch.

He hadn't exactly lived a life of restraint.

"I slept fine," she said. "I feel bad that I didn't help with Lily. Tonight I'll be ready to take the baby monitors."

"I might be a little bit of a tyrant," Jackson said, "but I wanted you to start out with a good night's sleep. No sense in us both being sleep deprived from the get-go, right?"

"Right," she agreed.

He poured her a mug of coffee and set it in front of her. "Cream and sugar?"

"Please," she said.

"All the food in the house is yours," he said. "My stepsister, Chloe, grocery shops once a week, and she does delivery. So if there's anything you like, be sure to get it to me and I will put it on the list."

"I can get my own groceries," she said. "I don't mind taking Lily to the grocery store."

"Food is part of your pay," he said. "It's fine if you want the outing, but you don't have to buy your own."

"I appreciate that. I...I need to figure out getting a car. I have the money. I sold my car in Colorado."

"We can work on that, too."

"Are you a good cook?" she asked.

"I'm terrible," he said. "Which is another thing. Chloe cooks for us sometimes, but often we fend for ourselves, and you may not like that. So, while I did not hire you to be a chef..."

"If I want to enjoy my dinner I might have to cook for both of us?"

"Just a fact," he said.

"Good to know."

"I'm happy to eat frozen pizza. And a lot of garlic bread. Throw a steak in a pan with some butter. I'm not picky."

"That's going to catch up with you someday," she commented, eyeballing his midsection.

"Hasn't yet," he said. "Other things have, obviously, but not my eating habits."

She hesitated for a moment, taking two very pointed sips of coffee. Then she put her mug down and looked at him. "By other things do you mean...Lily?"

He sighed heavily, rubbing the back of his neck. He supposed there was no way around having this conversation.

"Yeah," he said. "I'm the last guy on earth that should be raising a baby by himself. I don't know a damn thing about kids. And I was not exactly in a white picket fence place. But here I am. When I say I don't know anything about babies and fatherhood, I mean it."

"Who is her mother?"

"I know her name, but beyond that, I don't know much," he said, shame sliding over him when he said that.

He'd already had to explain this to his brothers, his stepsister, and to their stepmother. He'd never been bothered by his behavior before. Until this.

Because when people talked about him and his reputation it was all euphemistic. Elbowing, winking and nudging. Nobody came right out and said that he had sex with every woman he talked to in a bar, but the fact of the matter was he did. And Lily was undeniable evidence of that.

The fact that he didn't really know her mother was further evidence of who he was. And put all out in public like that, it shamed him. Knowing that someday he would have to explain to his daughter how he'd acted bothered the hell out of him. Knowing he was the kind of man that he would never, ever want Lily to even speak to was another layer of that altogether. Because he was raising her. And he had to find a way to be better.

"So, she wasn't your wife."

"She wasn't even my girlfriend," he admitted. "I didn't know she was pregnant. I hadn't seen her again, not since we hooked up. And she showed up a couple of months ago with the baby. Told me that she couldn't do it. I had a paternity test, and I have full, legal custody. Permanently. Lily's mother gave up her rights."

"Oh," Savannah said, looking down.

"It's not a great story," he said. "But when I said I was in over my head…"

"You really meant it," she said softly.

"I sure as hell did."

Their eyes met and held, and he felt something stretch between them, something that was definitely mutual, and clearly unwelcome. Both for her and for him. He looked away.

"For a while I could wear her for a lot of the ranch work I do, but it's getting harder."

She was staring at him, a perplexed expression on her lovely face.

"Yeah," he said. "I can't believe those words all just came out of my mouth, either."

"I have to admit, you don't look like someone who would have a lot to say on the topic of baby wearing."

"I never thought I would." He sighed heavily. "Babies are scary. And I say that as someone who is not scared of much. But…I can't tell you how many times a night I have to check and make sure she's still breathing."

"I don't have any children of my own," she said. "But I've heard that before."

"It's a hell of a thing."

"Hopefully I'll make it a little bit easier."

"What exactly are you getting out of it?" He couldn't help but ask. After all, she was living in his house and taking care of his daughter. He had a right to know exactly why. Another thing that was hitting him a day late and quite a few dollars short.

"Room and board? Pay?"

"I imagine you could get a job taking care of kids a whole lot of places."

"I needed to get away," she said.

It occurred to him then that he maybe should have

done a background check on her or something. But he didn't know how to do a background check on someone. He'd never had to. He'd never had to concern himself with anything like that, but he was letting this woman take care of his baby.

"I'm going to have to ask you why you needed a fresh start," he said, lifting his coffee mug to his lips. "I want to keep this as professional as possible. But I do need to know a little bit about you personally. And I realize asking you now, on the first day, is maybe a little bit late, but I'm new to all this. I'm not exactly thinking of everything here."

"I feel the same way," she said. "I mean, I don't know anything about you, either. Except for what you told me. But I wanted to get away. I needed to. I'm not running from the law or anything. I just got divorced. Actually, I got divorced about eight months ago, and I tried to keep on living where we were. I loved our little town. But my husband—ex-husband, that is—has lived there all of his life, and there's no way I can combat that local mentality. His whole family is there and they own half the businesses in town. And they are… They're angry at me for leaving him."

"So the asshole made it impossible for you to live there?"

"Basically. And I was not going to go back home to live with my parents. I lived with them until I could legally leave, and as far as I'm concerned, a phone call home once a month is enough."

"Fair enough. I work right here on the property, and I'll be back to check on you probably more often today than usual. Just a warning."

A smile curved the edge of her lips. "Are you afraid to leave her?"

"It doesn't feel real yet," he said, his voice rough. "I've been afraid to take my eyes off her since the moment her mom handed her to me. Still. And I'm not going to lie, sometimes the responsibility feels so big I almost wish the whole thing was a dream. But then, the minute that thought enters my head…it's followed by total terror. Because sometimes I feel like nothing in my life was anything until her. I'm not sure I can ever go back."

That was the worst part. Wanting something of his old life, and knowing it wouldn't feel the same. He could never see himself or the things he used to do the same way again. Not now. "I better head out."

"I'll be fine. I remember where everything is."

"If you need anything…"

"I have your phone number. I have your stepsister's phone number. I have both your brothers' numbers."

"And I'll be back."

"I know."

For the first time in three months, Jackson Reid stepped outside with empty arms and headed out to work.

CHAPTER THREE

THERE WAS A larger housekeeping element to this job than Savannah had expected, but she didn't mind it, either. In fact, over the next couple of days she found a strange kind of bliss in it. Jackson was gone most of the time, and she usually woke up to coffee he had made and some leftover bacon, which she helped herself to, and then set about to preparing Lily's first bottle, and getting set up to change diapers.

She read to her. Made sure she had the recommended amount of tummy time, and sang to her off-key. But at Lily's age, the bulk of what she did was sleep and wiggle. And that gave Savannah a decent amount of free time. So she cleaned the tiny cabin, she made herself lunch, and then she prepared a dinner for both herself and Jackson.

Jackson had come in late the last couple of nights, and they didn't take dinner together, but Savannah didn't mind eating by herself.

It was a revelation, to be in a new setting like this. She had lived on her own for the last eight months, and had been distant from her husband before that, but still, she could feel his specter looming over her the entire time. Actually living in this new place with this fresh start was awfully blissful. Tonight she was making pot roast, which was even more blissful. She had never made it before. She hadn't done a lot of cooking even when she'd been married, not because she couldn't, but because she'd worked full-time and had usually been too exhausted at the end of the day to put together anything more spectacular than a pot of spaghetti.

She and Darren had often eaten out, or gone to his parents' house for dinner. He didn't really enjoy her cooking. That was the biggest part of it. And so they had settled into a routine where they had what he liked to eat, when he wanted to eat it. And often, his mother facilitated that. Darren had certainly been the one in charge in their house, but if there had been anyone pulling rank above him it'd been his mother.

She frowned. It had all been so slow and insidious, and she hadn't realized that nothing in her life was hers until the end, when Darren finally pulled the plug on that marriage by announcing he had found someone else.

That was the worst part.

She'd been unhappy for a long time, but she had been primly pressing on because there was nothing else to do. Because she'd made vows and she would honor those. And that someday, maybe they would find the kind of happiness they'd had when they were dating.

It wasn't until they'd divorce that she realized she'd walk herself right into the same marriage her parents had had.

She hadn't given it the necessary amount of thought until it was too late, but somewhere, deep down, she'd believed her parents had always been unhappy. That they'd never been giddy about each other, that they'd never felt reckless and young. And so, when she'd met Darren and fallen in love for the first time, experienced attraction and infatuation for the first time, she'd imagine she'd gone and sidestepped her great fear.

But then it had just been…bad. Such a *quiet* bad that it had seeped into every pore, every crack in her life before she'd fully realized. Like the slow settling of a fog over the tops of the mountains, creeping over the peaks and rolling down until she had forgotten how high they were supposed to be. Until she had forgotten what it was like to look out on a clear day.

It was clear now. In this little cabin, with Lily. Right now, it was clear enough.

Obviously, Jackson wouldn't need her forever, but it was a great place to land for now. If only she could get her reaction to him under control.

He came in to check on Lily at varying points during the day, and Savannah wasn't prepared to deal with his random appearances. He was always somehow taller and broader than she remembered, his jaw more square, his face more arrestingly handsome.

It was a problem.

But most especially with the memory of her marriage so bright and clear, she shouldn't allow those feelings to mean a thing. Feelings like this were a lie. She knew it. What was *real* was this cabin. This beautiful part of the world. And the beautiful baby she got to take care of.

She'd always loved children. She'd gotten into child development because she wanted to do what she could to bring happiness to children who might not have the best home lives. Or to be extra support for those who did.

Her own home life hadn't been so great. Void of affection and any meaningful attention, it was her teachers, her coaches and her Girl Scout leaders who had provided the support she needed in her life.

It had inspired her to want to do the same. Lily

needed her. Jackson didn't, and her hormones needed
to get a grip.

That was the one drawback to living with Jackson,
really. She didn't know what to do with what he made
her feel. It was a restless edginess that she would put
down as *attraction* if she didn't know that she just…
wasn't all that sexual. She tried to put that thought out
of her mind and busied herself until the smell of dinner was beginning to kill her. When she couldn't wait
any longer, she opened up the cupboard and took down
a bowl, ready to serve herself some food. Right then,
the front door opened, and in came Jackson, wearing a
cowboy hat, heavy boots and a flannel shirt.

She didn't know why that was particularly sexy to
her. She'd never been into that kind of thing. Darren
had been polished. A small-town businessman, nothing
like the kind of men strolling around Fifth Avenue, but
his neat style had appealed to her at the time.

Jackson was rugged and a little bit dangerous and
there was no earthly reason she should find that interesting. But she did.

She looked over the counter, and their eyes collided.
She felt it hit her square in the stomach. It was…*attraction*. On a level she had never experienced before,
something she would have thought was completely impossible for her to experience until this moment.

She'd been married for nearly five years. Had shared
a bed with a man for most of that time, and for some
time before. She thought she had known all about sex,
and what her limitations were in that arena. But Jackson made her feel more with one look than Darren had
made her feel with dinner, foreplay and the main event.

He made her feel more like a woman than anyone or

anything else had before. More aware of her body, of what it meant to be feminine to his masculine.

It was a problem. A serious problem. They were sharing this tiny house, and she was taking care of his daughter. They needed boundaries.

So many boundaries.

For a moment, she thought she saw the heat that burned her stomach reflected in his gaze. But then he looked away, took his hat off, and hung it up on the peg by the door. "What's for dinner?"

"Pot roast."

She suddenly wished she hadn't cooked something so domestic. It added a strange layer to the whole interaction. Or maybe that was just her. Her and her completely inappropriate thoughts about her boss. Her boss that she lived with.

"I'm starving," he said. "How's Lily?"

"Getting in one more nap before she eats again. Before she sleeps for a while longer."

"Did you stay home today?"

"Yeah," she said. "I took her outside for a little while. She seemed to enjoy the leaves crunching under my feet while I walked."

"You know," he said, walking into the kitchen, his presence so intense, so imposing that she had to take a step back, "it's Friday night, and normally I would be heading down to the Golden Valley saloon to have a drink. Or three. Pick up a woman." His lips quirked up into a half smile. "Instead I'm eating pot roast."

Her chest was tight, and she could barely breathe. "You're welcome to go out if you want."

"Looking to get rid of me?"

"I didn't say that," she said.

She was frozen in the back of the kitchen, holding on

to her bowl, waiting for him to finish dishing his own food. She didn't want to walk past him. She felt like if she got that close, she might spontaneously combust.

She needed to get a grip. This was ridiculous. Profoundly ridiculous.

She took a fortifying breath and walked past him toward the little table set against the wall in the open living area. When she walked past him, she could feel him. His energy. His heat. He looked…so hard. Like he had been carved directly out of rock.

She had never touched a man like that. She had never particularly wanted to before. But…but her hands itched when she looked at him, and her body ached.

She blinked and sat down quickly, pulling her bowl of food close, and turning her focus resolutely onto it. For his part, Jackson stayed in the kitchen, standing against the counter, the bowl placed in front of him.

"Have you gotten a chance to explore the town much?"

He was being polite, which was very nice of him, and she supposed a lot less self-conscious than sitting there in silence, like she was. "A little bit," she responded. "When Lily and I went grocery shopping yesterday I made a few stops. It's cute. It reminds me a little bit of Colville."

"That's where you're from?"

"Yeah. Well. I mean, that's where I've lived since college. Since… Since I got married."

"You mentioned something about that. The divorce, I mean."

"It was…messy."

"What happened?"

"That's kind of personal," she said, looking back down at her pot roast.

"You're living in my house taking care of my kid. You might work for me, but it's a pretty personal situation."

The way he was looking at her made her want to tell him. She hadn't told anyone. In the end, she hadn't had anyone to tell. Darren had made her feel so stupid she hadn't wanted to tell anyway. But suddenly here…with him, in another town, another state, in his house in the woods…she wanted to tell someone.

"Okay," she said slowly. "He cheated on me. And then he ended the marriage. So…it doesn't even really matter that he cheated. I didn't even get the chance to get righteously angry and say I'd never take him back. He didn't want to be with me. He said we were unhappy. And that I wasn't…" She wasn't going to finish that sentence. She wasn't going to tell Jackson that Darren had told her she was disappointing in bed. And that he never should've married a virgin just because he felt guilty for being her first.

All of that was way, way too personal. And it might be fine for him to get the bare minimum details, but that was too deep.

"He sounds like a prince."

"Unfortunately, he was. The Prince of Colville. His uncle is the mayor. His family has been there for generations. His dad owns the hardware store, and his mother owns the flower shop."

"Did that relate to you losing your position at the daycare?"

She sighed. "Yes. The woman he ended up with was a single mom at the place I used to work. She convinced all of her friends to withdraw the kids, because of course she couldn't be around me."

"And the place had to close?"

"The owner was close to retirement anyway. Otherwise, she just would've fired me." She thought of Eliza Elton, who of all people had been kind to her when everything had fallen apart. "Well, maybe she wouldn't have fired me. She was about the only person who took my side. Or, if anyone else did, they certainly didn't tell me."

"I don't get that. How did this guy cheat on you and end up with people on his side?"

"People love to blame the woman," she said drily. Again, that was far too close to the personal for her to want to get into it. "The woman he... His new fiancée... She's very popular. She's lived there most of her life. She's a widow, and her husband was much beloved in the community. And Darren was helping her out, which was why me feeling weird about him going over and hanging up curtains for her at ten at night was immature. It's an example of what a good guy he is, don't you know. And I was only ever an outsider. One of Colville's own needed Darren and he was there." She bit the inside of her cheek. "How could he resist when all he had at home was a frigid wife?"

She'd said it. Frigid. She hated that word. She *hated* it. And Jackson didn't need to know that about her, but...she was just angry. And she hadn't told anyone all the ugly things he'd said to her. Who would she tell, when they were all whispering similarly ugly things behind their hands?

Jackson arched a brow. "That was his story, was it?"

"Yes," she said, her eyes meeting his in defiance of her embarrassment. Her cheeks were hot, and she was sure they were lit up bright pink.

"Well, he sounds like a Grade A dick."

In spite of herself, she laughed. "You're not wrong.

And a mama's boy. I wouldn't be surprised if his mom threw him right in Elizabeth's path. She would have suited my former mother-in-law much better. More involved in the community and all of that." She cleared her throat. "Not just a daycare worker."

"Sounds like you were in a hell of a situation," he said.

"Yeah, it could have been better."

"Doesn't exactly make me sorry that I haven't given the institution of marriage a try. Or commitment of any kind."

"I should have known better," she said. "My parents were unhappy. I thought that I could do better. I thought that by watching them I could figure out exactly what not to do. More fool me."

"Are your parents divorced?"

"No," she said. "They still live in their venom-filled suburban nightmare, trading barbs back and forth over the dinner table I imagine."

"My father was married four times," he said.

"Really?"

"Yep. He was not a good husband. A pretty nice guy, all around, but shitty at commitment. He was more married to this land than he ever could have been to a woman."

"Chloe's mother?"

"She was the one that stuck. And I could never figure out if that was just the two of them being ready to settle for whatever they got or if they actually changed for each other."

"You couldn't...tell?"

He shrugged. "Ella is a great woman. She moved away after my dad died, wanted to be somewhere a little less rural. I don't blame her. But we still see her.

She was the only one that had a kid of her own, and sometimes I wonder if Dad was more attached to being Chloe's father than he was to being Ella's husband. Though, like I said... I don't really know."

"How old was Chloe when they got married?"

"Ten or so. Them getting a divorce certainly would have been the toughest for us. Because of her."

"Is that why you don't do commitment? Your dad?"

"I'm a little bit too much like him, is the thing. I like women, but I love the ranch. I love freedom. I don't want to be accountable to anyone."

It was a good answer, and it seemed direct enough, but something in the way he spoke the words made Savannah doubt the authenticity of them. There was something else. He told that story in such a detached way, it made her wonder what more there was. But he was her boss and it wasn't her business.

She shouldn't want to know him. Shouldn't want to get closer to him. Shouldn't want to press her thumb between his eyebrows and smooth the crease that was there.

She shouldn't want to touch him at all.

This should be polite dinner conversation only. Nothing more.

"How long has it been since your divorce was final?"

"Eight months," she said.

"What have you done in those eight months?"

"I moved here."

"Before that."

"Came to terms with the fact that I was going to be alone."

"Why do you think you're going to be alone?"

"I don't know. Probably for similar reasons to yours."

"I've never spent eight months alone."

"I assume you mean that as a euphemism," she said, picking up her bowl, which was now empty, and heading back toward the kitchen to put it in the sink.

"Yeah."

She cleared her throat, her face feeling hot. "That is… That is definitely not your concern."

"Maybe not. But…" In spite of her best efforts, that long pause he took made her turn her focus to him. "He's not right."

"About what?"

She regretted asking the moment the words left her mouth. When Jackson's eyes connected with hers, she felt like all the air had been sucked out of her body. She wasn't imagining the heat there. She wasn't.

"You know perfectly well *what*."

She regretted that she'd chosen this moment to spill her guts. "That's not… That's not for you to comment on. And anyway, you don't know. Maybe he is right."

"That you're frigid?"

Heat prickled her scalp. "Like I said. You don't know me."

"If that's the way he feels, if that's how things were in your marriage, I'd put the blame squarely on him."

"This really isn't something we should be talking about."

"I'm not an expert on much, Savannah, but women's pleasure happens to be one thing I am. I don't know a damn thing about babies, and here I am, thrown into the deep end on that, and you're helping me out. So, give me a minute to talk about what I know. If things weren't working out for you, that's his fault."

"Maybe it isn't," she said.

"No. I'm sure it was."

Silence stretched between them, thick and meaningful. And she could feel herself being drawn to him. Like a band had been wrapped around the two of them and was slowly contracting, bringing them together. And she couldn't fight it. She took a step toward him, then another.

He lifted his hand, and stretched it out, like he was going to touch her face. His fingertips on her bare skin… She knew that she would go up in flames.

Unless she froze his fingertips.

That was what they were talking about. About the fact that she wasn't able to…

She took a step back. "I'm going to go to my room. I have some email and things to catch up on."

He jolted, his hand dropping back down to his side. "Good idea."

"I'll see you tomorrow around lunchtime, I'm sure."

He took a deep breath, his broad chest expanding. "I'm sure."

And then she ran, like she was running from the devil himself. And for all she knew, she might have been. Because she had never known temptation like she'd experienced just now.

But it wasn't the temptation, or the fact she might give in to it that scared her. It was the idea that it would be another disappointment. Another opportunity for her to fail with a man.

More than anything else, she didn't think she could face that.

CHAPTER FOUR

JACKSON HAD SLEPT for shit that night. He blamed Savannah and the conversation they'd had. *Frigid.* He wanted to find her ex-husband and pull that bastard's testicles out through his mouth.

In his opinion, any man who put that kind of thing on a woman was beneath contempt. Jackson might not be a knight in shining armor, but he knew where his responsibilities lay in the bedroom. There was no damned point to sex if your partner didn't get as much out of it as you did, if not more. A woman's pleasure was part of his own. Any man who not only put that responsibility on the lady, but also made her feel bad about herself when he couldn't perform, was a lowlife in his mind.

That kind of man certainly didn't deserve to get off.

But the problem was, Jackson shouldn't be thinking about *his nanny* and *getting off* in the same sentence. Not at all.

That was the trouble with not having Lily out with him while he worked. He had too much time on his brain to do thinking. And his thoughts were in the damned gutter.

He sighed and lifted the ax he was holding over his head, bringing it down hard on the piece of wood sitting on its end, sending half of it flying across the lot.

He looked up and saw his brother's truck pulling up

toward him, and he swore. The last thing he wanted was to deal with Tanner or Calder right now.

And sadly for him, it was both of his brothers. They stopped the truck and got out, the two older Reids looking at him, and then looking at each other.

"Can I help you?" he asked, feeling testy as fuck and just as mean. He had sexual tension to get rid of, and he aimed to chop a cord of wood, not have a discussion with his brothers.

"Just haven't had a chance to chat in a while," Tanner said.

"You're full of shit," Jackson said. "We work together every day."

"Yeah," Calder agreed, "but Chloe's been around."

"What exactly do you want to talk to me about that you can't say in front of Chloe?"

"I want to know what's really happening with you and the nanny," Tanner said.

"What do you mean *really happening*?"

"You're living with a woman that beautiful in your house, and you want me to believe that you're not doing anything with her?" Calder asked.

Tanner's expression tightened, his whole body going tense. It seemed he didn't find Calder's questions any more amusing than Jackson did. "It *is* possible to live with a beautiful woman and not touch her," Tanner pointed out.

"Sure," Calder said. "It's possible. But Jackson doesn't have any experience with restraint. And we know that with even more certainty than we did a couple months ago."

"Yeah, because you're a snow-white virgin," Jackson said, glaring at his brother.

"I'm no such thing. But I'm not half the manwhore you are."

"Even half the manwhore I am is pretty bad," he responded drily.

Tanner snorted. "That is true. Though, I've been much too busy running this place to get up to even half of what Calder has."

"That's a dirty lie," Jackson said. "You've been a bit busy raising Chloe."

"I am *not* raising Chloe," Tanner said, his tone hard. "She's an adult."

"What is she? Twenty-two? And she's half-feral."

"At least you don't have to worry about her sneaking off with guys," Calder said, humor on his face. "Anyway, if a man gave her trouble, she'd just shoot them herself."

"We are not talking about Chloe," Tanner said, his voice taking on an edge when he said their stepsister's name.

He knew Chloe could be irritating, but she and Tanner had lived together in the main house for ages. It had only been about six months since Chloe's mother had moved away, but Jackson couldn't imagine things had changed that much since Ella had gone.

"We're talking about Jackson. And his transgressions," Calder said.

"If you call Lily a transgression one more time, Calder," Jackson said, his tone warning, "I will personally put my fist through your face."

"That isn't what I meant," Calder said, looking contrite. "I was just giving you a hard time."

"I swear, everything with Savannah is on the up-and-up. I needed someone to help me out. I don't know shit about babies, and you know that."

"Neither do we."

"Neither does Chloe," Tanner said.

"Yeah, it's basically a nineties comedy around here, except that we're not going to magically figure it out, so I needed to do something. And I hired Savannah. End of story. I'm not touching her, and neither are either of you. She's the only way I've gotten any sleep for a week, and if you fuck that up for me I will…"

"Fist through the face," Tanner said. "I think we got it."

"Hey," Calder said, "I'm more worried about you messing it up."

"I can keep my dick under control, thanks," Jackson said.

"*Can* you?" Tanner asked.

He would be offended, but Tanner had a point. If he could keep himself under control, he'd never shown it. He'd never had to.

"I have a *reason* to," he bit out. "The best reason I've ever had. I know that you might not… I never wanted to be a father," he continued. "But the fact of the matter is I *am* one. Everything that I wanted has changed now. I care a hell of a lot more about that little girl growing up happy than I do about when I'm going to get laid next. And hell, I don't know when that's going to be. Maybe not till she graduates from high school."

Well, he hoped that wouldn't be true. But there was a serious chance he wasn't going to be getting any action on a regular basis for quite some time. He couldn't bring a parade of women through her life. That was the kind of thing their father had done, and he wouldn't do that. He wanted her to have more stability than he'd had. Didn't want her to go through a series of attachments and separations over and over again. It was too hard.

Her mother had already left, and God knew he understood that pain. Of knowing your mother couldn't handle you. Couldn't raise you. Already, Lily's childhood was a shade too much like his own. For his father's part, when it came to their mother, at least it hadn't really been his fault. He had married her. Had tried to have a stable life before bringing children into the world.

Jackson had just been indiscriminate. Yes, he'd used protection, but the fact of the matter was, there was always a chance that protection could fail. And any grown man who was sexually active had to take that risk on. It had never come back to bite him in the ass before.

But now it had, and he had to man up.

"I never realized you were so self-sacrificial," Calder said.

"I'm not. But what else am I supposed to do? She's here," he said gruffly.

"We're here for you," Tanner said, clapping him on the back. "Even though I don't think we're any more qualified than you."

"Maybe if we put all of our heads together we can equal one qualified parent," Calder said.

Jackson chuckled. "You might be about right."

But he had Savannah. She was qualified, and she was giving Lily a good start. She knew what to do. She knew things like tummy time, which Jackson hadn't known about. She was going to provide that early stability. Be that mother figure for Lily. And he knew it wouldn't last forever, but if he could just make it the best situation possible, he had a feeling it could last for a while.

And that meant no more thinking about Savannah, or her problem.

And letting go of the idea it was his to solve.

Lord almighty. He wanted to solve it.

Dick. Under. Control.

His brothers took off, and while he went on chopping that wood, all he could think about was that Savannah wasn't staying forever. It was already temporary.

And there was no real way to mess up something that wasn't forever anyway. Was there?

CHAPTER FIVE

SAVANNAH WAS READY to fall asleep on the floor right next to Lily. The baby hadn't slept at all the night before, which meant Savannah hadn't, either, and then for some reason Lily had defied every reasonable expectation and hadn't napped the entire day, either. She really hoped this wasn't indicative of what was to come.

Finally, the little wiggling thing had fallen asleep on her blanket, and Savannah was stretched out beside her, the ceiling spinning above her head as she fought to stay conscious.

Jackson would be back soon. She had already texted him to warn him that she wouldn't be cooking dinner. She simply didn't have the energy. She had managed to eat a few grapes while spoon-feeding Lily some squash, but that was it. She was hungry and exhausted. She wasn't sure how she was going to go on.

And while she lay there, her thoughts turned to Jackson.

That was the biggest problem with being sleep deprived. She had almost no control over her thought process. All damn day she had thought of him. Of the way he talked about how it was a man's fault if a woman didn't find pleasure in bed with him.

It made her wonder.

Wonder a whole lot of things that were half-formed and blurry. Wonder a lot of things that she knew she should have a better handle on, but she didn't. Because her curiosity about sex had basically shut down over the past few years. She felt like a failure at it. A failure as a wife. And instead of trying to figure it out with Darren she had just locked everything away. Pretended that she didn't care. It was better—she had rationalized—than being her parents. Always unhappy and yelling and screaming.

But then she had discovered just how quiet unhappiness could be. How many forms bad marriages could take.

She had tried so hard to be different, and it had ended up the same.

Well, not quite. Her husband had actually cut her loose. Her parents didn't have the common decency to set each other free. They just suffered together in misery. Savannah could honestly say she felt her choice was the better one. Or rather, the choice that Darren had made for the both of them. Though, she refused to be grateful to him.

But there was Jackson.

His lips were beautiful, and they made her want to kiss them. Kissing she had liked. At least at first. It had always sparked in her stomach the promise of something that she could never really have. So, eventually she had stopped liking kissing quite so much.

She wondered if kissing Jackson would be any different.

He was rarely clean-shaven. Somehow, he always seemed to have a perpetual five-o'clock shadow, and it looked like it would be rough to touch. She licked her own lips in response to that thought, closing her eyes and allowing her vision to fill with images of him.

She heard the front door open and close. Her eyes popped open.

"Hello," said Jackson softly, looking down at her position on the floor.

"Don't wake her up," she said. "I'm desperate."

"Yeah, your text seemed a little bit on the desperate side."

"I haven't slept." She sat up, rubbing her face.

"Do you need to take a nap?"

"Yes," she mumbled. "But I need to eat. I haven't eaten today, either."

He frowned. "If it's ever that overwhelming you should call me."

"You hired me to take care of things. I'm not going to call you away from work. This is my job."

"Which you won't be able to do if you're not functioning. I don't expect you to be working twenty-four hours a day. That's not reasonable."

"Well, I'm fine," she said, stretching and then standing. "Just tired. And hungry."

"I did bring food."

He held up a bag and she sniffed the air. "What did you bring?"

"Burgers," he said. "From Mustard Seed. I brought regular fries and sweet potato fries. I didn't know what your philosophical stance was."

"I will put any french fry in my mouth. All of them. So, I hope that you got two orders of each. Because if you didn't…I'm still eating them all."

"Oh, don't worry. I got four orders."

"Perfect," she said, standing up and rubbing her hands together. She really was starving. Beyond reason. And suddenly, all she could think of was how perfect it would be to eat a hamburger.

Which was much less unsettling than pondering the merits of devouring Jackson's mouth.

He set the paper bag down on the table, and she crowded around, digging inside and pulling out one of the containers of fries. The sweet potato. She dug into them immediately while Jackson sorted through the rest.

"Beer?" he asked, heading toward the fridge.

"Coke," she said. "A beer is just going to put me to sleep."

"Nothing wrong with that," he said, but returned with a beer for him and a Coke for her.

"I need to be able to wake back up if Lily needs something."

He frowned. "Let me take a shift tonight."

"No. I already told you. This is my job. And I really don't mind doing it."

"And I told you that I don't expect you to work twenty-four hours a day. I want you sharp enough to take care of her tomorrow. That means you need to sleep tonight."

"Jackson, I will tell you when I need you to be a mother hen. That time is not now."

His lips quirked upward into a smile, and she recalled the fantasies she'd been having about those lips not long before. "A mother hen?" He shook his head. "That's the first time I've ever been accused of that."

"Well. You're being ridiculous. I'm a grown woman, and if I need something I have no problem letting you know."

"Is that right?" His dark eyes burned into hers, and her heart leaped up in her chest. It was not a caring look. It was…loaded. It made her stomach tighten. Made her fingers feel numb.

"Don't look at me like that," she said, stuffing a french fry in her mouth and chewing indelicately.

"Like what?"

"You know. If I… If *I know*, then it's really not very subtle, Jackson."

"I'm not looking at you like anything," he said. "Because things need to stay professional between us. I was pondering that earlier today."

"Were you?"

"I was."

"Why did you…" She hated herself for asking this question, but she was going to anyway. "Why did you come to that conclusion?"

"Because I was having some decidedly unprofessional thoughts," he acknowledged, his voice getting rough, the heat in his eyes intensifying.

She shifted, stuffing another french fry in her mouth.

"That…" She cleared her throat and reached down for the burger that he had put in front of her. "I hope this has onions on it."

He chuckled. "Believe me. Onions are not a deterrent. The fact that you're taking care of Lily? That is."

"Right." She took a bite of the burger and moaned. She hadn't meant to have such an obvious response to eating a burger, but she was starving. When she looked up, Jackson was watching her far too closely.

They ate in silence for a while, a strange awareness settling over her. They had acknowledged it. And he hadn't denied it. Not at all. He was attracted to her.

It was strange. She didn't consider herself the kind of woman men like him would be attracted to. She wasn't stunningly beautiful. She was tall, and some men were into that, but since she had never been big on dating, she hadn't much explored it. And then, she had been married and found out what a disappointment she was as a sex object, so really, this whole thing with Jackson was weird.

He was attracted to her. She was attracted to him. Right from the beginning. From that first moment they had seen each other in the airport.

The problem was, it was all a lie.

Well, the real problem was Lily. But beyond that, even if they were two strangers that just met… Whatever he thought being with her might feel like…he was wrong.

Whatever her own body thought being with Jackson might do to her, it wouldn't.

"I'm not that exciting," she said. "Really. In fact, I think if you're actually finding yourself attracted to me right about now it's mostly because of the forbidden aspect to…to us being together."

"Really?" He raised his brows, and he looked maddeningly unconvinced.

"Yes," she confirmed, hoping he didn't know she hadn't a clue what she was talking about. "You said yourself you…are well-traveled."

"Is that a nice way of saying I'm the town bike?"

"Well. Yes." She cleared her throat. "That leads me to believe that not very many things have been off-limits to you. Until recently. And now you find yourself… chained to your house. So… Not *traveling* as much. So to speak."

As she said it, it made sense. It made a hell of a lot more sense than this man randomly wanting her for… her.

"You're not wrong about that," he agreed.

"And I'm here."

"Yes, you are," he said, his face almost comically serious.

"Look, the thing is…maybe Darren is a jerk, but he's also right. So…even if we…did something…it wouldn't actually be that fun. I would be prudish and disappointing. And you would be disappointing, too, and it wouldn't even be your fault. It would be mine."

Silence fell between them. But it wasn't awkward, and it wasn't harmless. It seemed to crackle. With heat and fire.

He leaned forward, his dark eyes intense. "Let's get one thing straight, honey. I am never disappointing."

Her cheeks felt scorched. "Well, there would be a first time for everything, and it would be with me."

Jackson leaned back, taking hold of a french fry and putting it in his mouth, chewing thoughtfully. "The real problem," he said slowly, "is that I suspect there might just be some firsts between us, Savannah. But they wouldn't be disappointing firsts."

Her heart thundered hard. "Good thing we're not going to find out."

He shook his head. "It's very important to me that Lily have stability in her life."

"It's important to me that I get some stability in mine."

He nodded. "Stability is very important."

Except he was leaning closer to her, and she could smell the aftereffects of his long day of hard labor, mingled with the body wash he used. And none of it was objectionable. Not in the least.

She swallowed hard, feeling dizzier than she had earlier. But right now, lack of sleep had nothing to do with it.

"The thing is," he continued, "I'm a bad bet."

"I'm sure you say that to all the girls," she said.

"I do." He nodded. "I don't want to upset what we have here."

"I don't, either."

"Although," he said, "there's a couple of things I'd add to that. The first being the fact I'm a bad bet might actually make it a better idea. There isn't going to be a romantic entanglement, even if there's a physical entanglement. That's not in me. Fact of the matter is, I didn't think fatherhood was in me, and stretching myself to be that… There's not going to be any more character growth coming for me for quite some time."

"Noted."

"And we've already talked about it. I'm attracted to you. Hell, I can't remember the last time I wanted a woman as badly as I want you."

She hadn't expected him to say that. He didn't need to say things like that.

He didn't need to lie.

"You really shouldn't have said that," she said, looking down at her hands.

"Why the hell not? We've been dancing around it. So, there it is. Now, those are the first two things."

"What's the third thing?"

"I want to send your ex-husband to a fucking early grave for telling you all that about yourself. But since I have a child to think about, and I can't go getting myself arrested for murder, the next best thing I can think to do is try to erase some of that. You came here for a fresh start, Savannah. I can give it to you. You can stay here with Lily for as long as you want and during that time…if the two of us have some fun, then I consider it an added bonus."

"Another perk of the job?" she asked drily.

"Forget the job for a second. I want you. You want something different than what Darren showed you. Right?"

"What if it's me?" she insisted.

"You need to get over that. That fear. You're not going to stay here and be Lily's nanny forever, right? That was never your plan."

She shook her head slowly. "Well. No."

"This is just a stopover while you figure out what to do with the rest of your life. And that's fine. But I assume that in the future you're going to want children of your own. A husband."

"Husbands don't have a lot to recommend them as far as I can see."

"Lovers then. Who wants to be alone? No one." He shrugged. "Even I don't like to be alone at night."

"Just because you like sex," she said.

"Sure. But most people do. Let me prove him wrong. *You* prove him wrong, Savannah. I'll show you it was him. His fault. You can let that go, leave it behind. Burn it to the damned ground. Isn't that better than letting his words live inside you like that? Next time you tell someone your ex-husband said you were frigid you can do it with a laugh."

"But what if… What if…"

He didn't let her finish that sentence. Instead, he reached out, grabbed hold of her arm and dragged her over to his side of the table. Onto his lap. And then, she didn't have to wonder about those lips anymore. Didn't have to wonder about those whiskers. Because Jackson Reid was kissing her, and it wasn't like anything she'd ever experienced before.

It was *better*.

CHAPTER SIX

SHE HAD THOUGHT she liked kissing. Had thought that it was her favorite part about physical intimacy. That it was sweet and undemanding, that it allowed her to feel those warm, fuzzy feelings that always vanished once her clothes came off and expectations began to grow.

But this kiss was something else entirely.

It wasn't sweet. And it was more than demanding.

His lips were hard and hot on hers, his tongue insistent as he devoured her mouth, sliding it against hers. And as for warm, fuzzy feelings...

This was too sharp to be anything like fuzzy. It was something ferocious, something that went deep and hard and on forever. Something that reached parts of her she hadn't been aware of.

His hands were large and rough from all that outdoor labor, just like she'd known they would be. He didn't hold her gently. Not at all. His blunt fingertips bit into that space between her shoulder blades as he held her tightly against his body. And they didn't stay still. No. Not at all. One slid down the center of her spine, tracing a line on the way down to cup her ass, and then he lifted her, easily, quickly, positioning her on his lap, her legs straddling his thighs. She could feel him between them, hard and insistent and already pushing her outside the boundaries of kissing.

She would have said that she didn't like that. That

she didn't like to be rushed through this part, and taken to the portion of events where she failed.

But she couldn't say anything. Because he was still devouring her mouth, and there was something about the way he held her, something about the way he moved his tongue against hers, about the way his hips bucked beneath her, that made her forget there might be something she wasn't doing right.

Her fingers ached, and it took her a moment to realize it was because they were wrapped around the collar of his T-shirt. So tight that in spite of the fact there was fabric between her fingertips and her palms, she could feel her nails digging into her skin. It was a miracle she hadn't worked little claw marks through the material.

Dimly, she wondered if she cared if she did.

He shifted his other hand, the rough pads of his fingers an erotic sensation on the delicate skin of her neck as he moved his palm to cup her head, tangling his fingers in her hair. He broke the kiss, his lips hot against her neck, her cheek, and then against her ear.

"What did he do?" he whispered in her ear, the words rough and harsh.

"What?"

"Your ex. How did it normally go?"

She didn't want to think about him. Not at all. "It doesn't matter."

"It does. I'm not setting you up for failure."

"I...I..."

"How about this?" His voice grew huskier. "Why don't you tell me something he never did?"

Her brain froze. That felt too... To have to admit to him all the things she'd never done. To have to sit there and try to think of sexual things she had no experience of was humiliating. And not only that, it would take too long. And there were probably about a thousand things she wouldn't think of because she was too inexperienced to know them.

How could a woman who had been married all that time be inexperienced? It was... Well, she came back to the word *humiliating.*

So she simply froze above him, her entire body going stiff. He drew his head back and looked at her, those dark eyes boring into hers.

"Never mind," he said, his tone gentling. "I'll handle it."

"You'll..."

He slid his hand forward, tracing the line of her jaw to her chin, and then pressing his thumb against her lower lip. The movement was slow, deliberate, and his eyes never left hers. "You don't have to worry about a thing."

"How... How am I supposed to..."

"Honey," he said firmly, "I don't need you to problem-solve this. You're not *my* nanny. I don't need you to take care of me. I know exactly what I'm doing."

She chose to forget for a moment that it was because he had been with a lot of other women. Because he had been with any number of people he would be able to compare her to. Because really... That just meant that he'd had a lot of sex, and if this sex was disappointing she wouldn't feel that bad. She was not, after all, the be-all and end-all for him, like she had been for Darren.

Somehow, that put less pressure on her. Made her feel more settled.

His large hands were so firm and sure, it made her feel like she could relax into them. That demand that she had felt in his kiss earlier wasn't a demand being placed on her. It was a demand he placed on himself, and all she had to do was surrender to it.

He kissed her again, firm and certain, slow and thorough, taking the time to trace her mouth with his tongue before he delved back in deep. She shivered, warmth pooling low in her midsection as he explored her mouth.

He didn't move his hands. He kept them right where they were, kept his exploration confined to her lips alone.

There was something incredibly erotic about that. It made her whole body feel more alive somehow. Made her feel restless, aching for a touch he wasn't giving. Her breasts felt heavy, achy. As did that soft, slick place between her legs. He wasn't pressed against her now. The only place they made contact was where her legs draped over his thighs, and where he held her fast with his hand, where his mouth met hers. She wanted more.

She couldn't remember how long it had been since she had wanted more. He kissed her like that until she was trembling, until that ache between her legs had become a hollow, intense pain. Until she was ready to beg.

And then, just when she felt like she couldn't stand it any longer, he moved his hand down the side of her neck, to her breast, cupping her gently, his thumb sliding over one tightened nipple.

The sensation was like a jolt of electricity arrowed down to that place where she was wet and needy for him. She bucked her hips forward, the movement involuntary, bringing her into contact with his arousal again. He chuckled, but didn't make any movements of his own. He just continued to stroke her breast, lazily almost, as if he had all the time in the world.

He broke the kiss, those dark eyes knowing as he stared into hers, as he continued to toy with her. Looking at him while he touched her like that was… She shivered, a strange aftershock seeming to echo inside of her core.

"That's my girl," he whispered, pausing to find her nipple again and pinch it lightly between his thumb and forefinger. Her eyes widened, a shocked gasp on her lips. And he swallowed it, claiming her mouth with his own again. Then, he lifted them both up out of the chair, not breaking the kiss as he walked her back into his bedroom.

She was not a petite woman. And no man had ever… picked her up like she was a delicate, fragile thing. But Jackson made her feel like she might be. His strong arms held her easily, his big, hard body a firm and steady resting place.

It was exhilarating. Incredible.

It was the one room of the cabin that she hadn't been in over the course of the past couple of weeks. It was sparse and masculine, and exactly like she had imagined his room would be. Plain, wooden furniture was paired with a red-and-black flannel bedspread, which she soon found herself deposited onto. He didn't join her on the bed. Instead, he took a step backward, his hands going to the hem of his T-shirt.

He dragged it up over his head and her insides hollowed out.

He was the most… The most incredible, *beautiful* man she had ever seen. His muscles were honed from years of hard work, a bit of dark hair covering his chest and trailing down over his well-defined abs. His jeans were low, showing off that band of muscle that formed an arrow, pointing down toward that most masculine part of him that remained hidden from her sight.

Then his hands went to his belt buckle, and her throat went dry. "I figured I ought to get naked first," he said.

"Of course you think that," she said, her voice trembling. "You know there's not a woman alive who could turn you away once you do that."

She hadn't exactly meant to say that out loud, but she had. He chuckled, continuing to work his belt through the loops, and snapping his jeans and drawing the zipper down slowly, shedding the denim and his underwear in one fluid movement, and leaving her staring, open-mouthed.

She shifted restlessly, that hot, hollow ache between her legs suddenly taking on a very clear and obvious purpose. But if she was going to fill it with a man that size she was going to need to be seriously wet. She squeezed her legs together. She *might* already be wet enough. Just from looking. Just from kissing.

Although, calling what had just happened between them just kissing seemed a little bit disingenuous. He looked at her with purpose, closing the distance between them and bending over, kissing her until she couldn't think straight. Kissing her until she couldn't breathe. Then he stretched them both out on the bed, her body draped half over his, still fully clothed. Her hand was planted against his bare chest, and she could feel his heart, raging hard against her palm. He was naked, and she was fully clothed.

It should feel—in some ways—like he was the vulnerable one. But she had no idea how a man like him could ever be vulnerable. He was so large that he made her feel tiny and delicate, which was unheard of at her height. But he was so broad and muscular and tall. Perfect.

Touching his bare skin made her shake. Feeling all

that leashed strength beneath her hands… She had never experienced anything like it.

Those big hands moved down to her hips, pushed up beneath the hem of her top, the heat of his touch burning through the thin lace of her bra as he cupped both breasts and teased her nipples. Then, with very little fanfare, he wrenched her top up overhead, sending it flying across the small bedroom. He grinned as he turned his focus to her leggings, dragging them down her legs and leaving her before him in nothing but her black lace bra and underwear. She gave thanks for the fact that she kept it simple when it came to unmentionables, and it just so happened she had white and she had black, and that meant most of the time they matched.

Though she had a feeling he wouldn't care either way.

He was looking at her like he wanted to eat her whole, and she didn't think—no, she *knew*—that her husband had never looked at her that way. Not even once. And he was supposed to have loved her. Jackson didn't love her. But he seemed captivated by her body. That did something to her. Ramped up the already intense sensitivity in her body.

He made a sound that was halfway between a groan and a growl, moving toward her and kissing the curve of her breast, just above her lacy bra cup. Then he reached behind her back and unclasped it, sending it sailing the same way as her T-shirt.

"Shit," he breathed, the curse like a prayer as he stared at her. He touched her again, like he had done through her shirt, cupping her, teasing her. The effect of those calloused fingers, with nothing to blunt the sensation was… She arched and squirmed beneath him, that restless ache between her thighs growing wider, more insistent.

Then those wicked lips quirked into a grin as he pushed his other hand down beneath the waistband of her panties, sliding his finger through the center of her slick folds, his touch like lightning against her sensitized flesh.

She gasped in shock, trying to squeeze her knees together as he drew lazy circles around her clit, his fingers moving easily because of all the wetness that he'd created there. She was almost embarrassed. For him to realize how much she wanted this. To be revealed in this way. That thought sent a zip of panic through her. She couldn't hide. Not like this. He knew exactly how desperate she was. How needy. Knew that he had created this effect in her body.

As if he could read her mind he removed his hand from her breast and drew it down to his cock, wrapping his fingers around his hardened length and slowly sliding his hand from base to tip and back down again, bringing her focus to his arousal. To how turned on he was. How much he wanted her.

Maybe she was wet and needy for him, but he was hard for her.

She licked her lips, desire drowning out that momentary panic as she watched him take himself in his hand, as she took in the full sight of him, thick and heavy and beautiful.

She could honestly say she had never thought of that part of a man's anatomy as beautiful before. His was. *He* was.

He continued to tease her with his fingers, sliding one finger deep inside of her and continuing to move his thumb over her clit as he worked it in and out of her body.

She let her head fall back, arching her hips against his hand in time with his rhythm. She was lost in it, and only dimly aware when he pulled her panties down her legs, exposing her to him completely.

He leaned in, kissing her hipbone, the touch of his mouth on her skin a shock.

Then he shifted, moving downward, parting her legs, his focus right there on her center.

She squirmed, trying to close her legs like she had done earlier, but he held them open, his gaze never leaving her body. Then, he met her eyes, a question in them.

He wasn't going to ask, though she knew exactly what he was wondering.

If anyone had ever done this for her. What he was about to do.

Part of her wanted to stop him. For the same reasons she had been horrified by her own signs of arousal earlier. Because what he was clearly getting ready to do was so intimate, so raw, that it terrified her. Just the idea of it.

And no, no one had ever done it to her.

But neither of them said anything, and he kissed her inner thigh, the scrape of his beard on that delicate skin sending an erotic shiver through her body.

She could tell him to stop. But as he kissed and licked a path to the most intimate part of her, she could only wait. Wait and anticipate.

She didn't know what kind of magic he had worked on her body, only that it was very real. And that she was under his spell.

He pressed his hand against her intimate flesh, spreading her open and sliding his thumb over that sen-

sitized bundle of nerves there a few more times, bringing her back to her body. Bringing her back to that state
of need that superseded everything else. Then he leaned
forward, replacing his thumb with his tongue, tracing
shapes, drawing the most intense pleasure from her that
she'd ever experienced.

It was so sharp it almost hurt, that slick glide of his
tongue over her clit. She was bucking her hips in time
with his mouth, unable to worry about embarrassment,
unable to care what it said about her. What it betrayed
about her desire for him.

She could only feel. His every lick, his every kiss,
the welcome invasion when he pressed two fingers inside of her and worked them in and out of her body in
time with the rhythm of his tongue.

He lifted his head, just for a moment, his eyes burning into hers. "Good girl," he said, before lowering his
head and sucking her clit into his mouth as he spread
his fingers inside of her wide. She hadn't felt it building. Not really. It had been an ache, something sharp
and fiery. She hadn't realized the explosion was coming.

It was hard and intense, lightning behind her eyes
as her internal muscles clenched tightly around him, a
wave pulsing through her body. It went on and on. She
didn't know if it would ever end, and she didn't know if
she could survive it. The pleasure felt like it might break
her apart from the inside out. Deep inside, where she
had never been touched before. And he didn't stop, his
fingers drawing out deeper, harder responses while she
shivered and cried out, her cheeks wet with tears. Then
he moved away from her, leaning over and opening up a
drawer by the bedside, taking out a small plastic packet
and tearing it open quickly. He rolled the condom over
his length and returned to her.

She was boneless. Spent, her mind reeling with what had just happened. Her body still trembling with the aftereffects. She couldn't handle more. She couldn't. But she couldn't find the voice to say it, and much like right before he had placed his mouth on her, she wanted to push herself. Dare herself.

She didn't want to allow herself to be the one that stopped what was happening.

He had said that she could trust him. So she was going to. He positioned himself between her thighs, that thick, blunt head teasing her entrance.

She was so wet, more than ready for him. She looked up at him, at that beautiful face, so acutely aware of the fact that it was Jackson slipping inside of her now. He felt different. Every inch of him. From that hard, muscular chest pressed to her breasts, to those big, rough workmen's hands. To that thick, glorious cock that made her feel so full it took her breath away.

He flexed his hips forward, hard, and she gasped as his pelvis made contact with her clit again. She had never felt it like this when Darren was inside of her. Had never felt stimulation there before. It was something about the way Jackson moved, or the way he had so thoroughly aroused her before. The way he had already brought her to completion. She was sensitive. So sensitive. She could barely stand any more stimulation.

He kept moving, and each thrust deep inside of her found some glorious place deep in there, sparking need against those nerves.

She felt like she would die of it. Another orgasm built from somewhere deeper inside her this time.

And she recognized it. What that ache was. That need that verged on pain.

She didn't fight it. She chased after it. Suddenly she

was desperate. For more. For everything. She wrapped her legs around his waist, trying to take him deeper as he whispered filthy things in her ear. Working her hips in time with his as he claimed her, over and over again. As he seemed to lose his control, his movements becoming fractured and uneven, harder.

Harder.

She realized she was saying that out loud. Making demands of her own.

And he obliged.

He slammed his mouth against hers, his tongue going deep as he froze above her, his hardness pulsing inside of her as his muscles shook, trembled. It was his own release, and the realization that he was in the grips of an orgasm as powerful as the one she'd had earlier pushed her over the edge again.

Her internal muscles gripped him tight, pulled him deeper, drew out their pleasure longer. Impossibly so. She clung to him. Held on to him until her breathing slowed. Until her heart rate returned to normal.

And she realized she had made a huge mistake.

Sleeping with a man she was living with. A man she couldn't get away from. A man whose baby she was taking care of. A man who paid her wages.

She also didn't care. She couldn't.

"I didn't know," she whispered.

He kissed her forehead, pulling her against his chest. "Now you do."

CHAPTER SEVEN

JACKSON WASN'T SURE what woke him up. He had been sleeping better than he could remember sleeping in months, and suddenly he wasn't. His bed felt empty, and for a moment he couldn't figure out why that was notable. Not when it had been empty since Lily had come into his life. And then he remembered.

Savannah.

He had taken Savannah to bed last night.

Thoroughly.

And while part of him wanted to give himself a pat on the back for rocking her world the way that he had, because damn, she'd been shaking and crying in his arms, she'd come so hard, another part of him knew that he didn't deserve to feel proud of what he'd done.

But then, he didn't feel proud of much. He wasn't sure why suddenly that was a requirement. She hadn't stayed in bed, and that did concern him. It made him wonder if maybe she was feeling...regretful or something.

It wasn't like he hadn't had his share of sexual encounters that had some regrets in the end. Tipsy hookups ended that way a lot. On both sides, frankly. But... he cared. Because hookups that ended in regret weren't something Savannah normally did. And he didn't want her to feel any regret over what they'd done. Mostly because he wanted her to be able to enjoy the fact that it had felt good.

Is that why?

What other reason could there be?

He got out of bed and put his jeans on with nothing underneath, zipping them and walking out into the main part of the house. It was quiet, and then he noticed that there was a small shaft of light coming from under Lily's bedroom door. He walked that way and pushed it open.

Savannah was there, dressed in a simple pair of gray thermal pajamas, cradling Lily to her chest, rocking in the chair and rubbing his daughter's back as she hummed.

Her voice was sweet sounding, soothing.

It reached down inside of him and made him feel like she had grabbed hold of his heart. Like she was cupping it in her palm, and could decide whether or not she was going to squeeze it, twist it or destroy it completely. On her whim.

At the same time, she was holding his daughter in her arms, an extension of that feeling. That she had his heart in her hands. But she was gentle, the look on her face serene.

"Hi," he said, his voice rough.

She looked up, her green eyes wide. "Did she wake you?"

"No," he said. "The fact that you weren't in bed did."

"Lily started crying, and I realized we forgot to bring the monitor in. I could hear her through the walls."

He shook his head. "I didn't hear her at all."

"I wasn't… I wasn't sleeping," she admitted.

"Are you all right?"

Her smile turned dreamy. "I'm fine."

It was hard to breathe all of a sudden. "I was worried that you were upset," he said heavily.

"No," she said. "I was just… It's silly."

He walked farther into the room and stood in front of her, leaning back against Lily's crib. "I'm here for silly."

"Are you?"

"It would be a pretty dick move if I was here for sex and nudity but wasn't here for silly."

Savannah looked down at Lily, her expression concerned. "I…"

"She doesn't understand," Jackson said.

"I don't know," Savannah replied. "This could be an early repressed childhood memory situation."

He chuckled. "I'd make a joke about how she needs something to tell her therapist, but sadly, I have a feeling she's actually going to have a lot of things to tell a therapist."

"I don't know if that's true," Savannah said softly.

"Why weren't you sleeping?"

"I didn't want to sleep because I was afraid that it was a dream. I spent so long feeling like there was something wrong with me. And I just had to let go of the idea that I was a woman who didn't enjoy sex. Sometimes it was okay, and sometimes it wasn't. But most especially when it caused problems in my marriage… I just felt like a failure. This clarified a lot for me. An orgasm, of all things."

"Two," he said.

She laughed softly. "Two. But…what happened to me with Darren was a lot more him than I realized. I think I came into our marriage with more baggage and more fears than I thought. And I think that he exploited that, used the places where I was naive and afraid to create a life where he never had to be the bad guy."

She shifted, adjusting the blanket over Lily. "He managed to have an affair and *still* make it my fault. I accepted it to a degree because of how I felt about myself at that point. And now...I just don't. I'm mad at him. And he deserves it. But I'm also relieved. I don't think there's anything wrong with me, Jackson," she said, meeting his gaze, the words making his chest feel too tight. "And I can honestly say it's been years since I thought that. Since I thought I wasn't broken."

"Definitely not broken," he said roughly.

"Do you know why I was such an easy target for Darren?"

"Why?" he asked.

"This goes back to why I think Lily might not be as messed up as you think."

"Okay," he said cautiously.

"I didn't have parents in my life who built me up. If it weren't for my teachers I wouldn't have had any affirmation. My parents were too busy screaming at each other. Too busy fighting and reveling in their own unhappiness to care much about me. That isn't true with you, Jackson. I know that Lily's mother abandoned her. But you changed your entire life to give her a home. To be her father."

"I don't deserve any kind of medal for that," he said. "It's just what a man should do."

"But my point is men don't. And women don't. People can't get past themselves to give to others. Not my parents. Not my ex-husband. But you are doing it. For her. And tonight you gave me something, too."

He shifted uncomfortably. "I don't like you thinking of it that way."

"Why not?"

"Because I'm not a vibrator and it wasn't a charity

orgasm. I didn't have sex with you just to make you feel good."

She looked down at Lily and kissed the top of her head, and the simple action tilted his world over on its head. Then she slowly put Lily down in the crib. Silently, she walked over to him and took his hand. He grabbed hold of her and pulled her up against him, her other hand splayed over his bare chest. "I really, really liked fucking you," he said, making sure her eyes stayed trained on his. "And I want to do it again as soon as I possibly can."

She shivered in his arms. "I think…now is as good a time as any," she said, looking up at him, her expression hopeful.

For just one moment he had the thought that this was a mistake. In this small, cozy house, where his daughter was sleeping in the other room, it was a mistake. This little place that was built for families, where it would be so tempting to…

To imagine that something was happening here when it absolutely wasn't, and most definitely couldn't.

But then her fingertips trailed over his chest, and she stood up on her tiptoes, bringing her mouth scant inches from his. Whatever caution he'd been about to exhibit evaporated. All that was left was need. So he closed that distance and he kissed her. All the concern and all the thinking better could wait until another day. Right now, he just wanted Savannah. Back in his arms. Back in his bed.

And he wasn't going to let himself wonder why.

CHAPTER EIGHT

"Your sister texted me to ask if we wanted to come over for dinner tonight. To the main house."

"Stepsister," he commented.

"Sorry. Does it matter?"

Jackson frowned. "Not to me."

"But to someone it does?" she pressed.

"I get the feeling it matters to Tanner," Jackson answered, "though, I don't know exactly why." He knew how Chloe felt about Tanner. It was obvious to anyone with eyes. But Tanner would never, ever reciprocate the feelings. But even so, there was a definite difference in the way Tanner treated Chloe versus the way Calder and Jackson did. He was meaner and less patient with her, for a start.

Though that didn't seem to dent Chloe's hero worship. Not at all.

"I don't have to go," she said. "If it makes you uncomfortable."

He frowned. "Why would it make me uncomfortable for you to come?"

Her lips twitched. "Well, I think we both know it doesn't make you uncomfortable when I come."

He couldn't help but smile at that. She'd changed a lot in the weeks since they'd been together, in the weeks since she'd been here. She was more confident, in bed and out. And he liked it more than he should. "True enough. But I meant to dinner."

"Just… Boundaries."

"We're not doing the best job with boundaries," he said. "But I don't really mind."

"I assume that you'd like it if your family didn't realize just how badly we were doing with boundaries?"

He nodded slowly. "Yes."

"Then we won't tell them."

"It doesn't bother you?"

"If you think I'm going to get a dirty secret complex, you're talking to the wrong girl. I already know what it's like to have half a town involved in my relationship. I'm not saying that this *is* a relationship. It's just…I don't have any interest in having a whole ton of people commenting on us and what we're doing. Doesn't appeal to me at all."

He shook his head. "Me neither."

But he couldn't help but feel slightly guilty about it. He never brought women he was sleeping with around his family, so he didn't know quite how to handle the politics of it.

He, Savannah and Lily had set up a little isolated hideaway of sorts, on his corner of the ranch. They did venture out, sometimes taking afternoons to go to some of the local farms with petting zoos. A pumpkin patch to get Lily's first pumpkin, even though he knew she wouldn't remember it.

And then there was what they did at night.

That was just for them.

It was much simpler, and less political, if they simply didn't know. There was no reason for them to know.

But it gave him an even stronger sense that he might be taking advantage of Savannah in some way.

Though she had made it abundantly clear she didn't feel that way. Still. "Do you have any work to do before dinner?"

"Yeah. A bit."

"I'll see you then." She hesitated, and then stretched up on her toes, pressing a soft kiss to his lips. "Since I won't be able to do that later."

That kiss burned. And it kept burning all through the rest of the day until it was time to pick Savannah and Lily up from the cabin and take them to the main house.

When he saw Savannah standing on the porch, her blond hair blowing in the early-evening breeze, wearing a floaty, flowered dress and a pair of leggings, his heart honest-to-God stuttered. She was holding Lily on her hip, his baby girl clinging to Savannah's dress like Savannah herself was a lifeline.

She felt like it just then. To him, too.

In the time since she'd been here, his life had changed. Again. He expected to see her in the house when he got in from work. Warm and waiting, with a kiss. Dinner sometimes, but the kiss was what mattered. He was used to seeing her car, a little Camry he'd helped her choose, in the driveway.

He was used to *her*.

He parked his truck and got out, walked up to the porch. Lily flapped her arms and rocked back and forth, making a series of cooing sounds as she tried to launch her body toward his. Shock, and another feeling, deep and painful, overwhelmed him as he reached out his arms and took hold of his baby girl.

"She knows her daddy," Savannah said, smiling.

"I guess so," he said, damn near flabbergasted by the whole thing. Babies were weird. You could mark the passage of time with them. In the months since Lily had been with him, she had changed so much. And in the months since *Savannah* had been with them, Lily had changed even more. She was making sounds and moving more, kicking her feet, rolling onto her stomach. He had lived a long, steady life of bachelorhood where very little had changed. He lost his father, and that had been devastating. In his experience, change was usually bad. But Lily had brought a series of changes to his life, each one kind of miraculous.

He deposited Lily in her car seat, much to her chagrin, and he and Savannah got into the truck and made their way down the dirt road that led to the main house.

Savannah filled him in on everything Lily had done that day, and he found that he enjoyed hearing about it.

If a few months ago someone had told him he would live for a daily update on the menial activities of a baby...

Well, he would have thought he was having a stroke.

But everything in him was changing. From the way his heart kicked when he looked at Savannah, to the way he worried about the damned future. Because of Lily. For Lily. For himself. He wanted... He wanted to be good. Hell, he wanted to be the best. And he couldn't remember having aspirations like that before. Not ever.

No, he'd just wanted to please himself. Had just wanted to get by. It hit him then, as he pulled up to the front of his brother's house, that he had never in all his life contemplated what living for another person meant. He had lived for himself, and he had done it proudly.

But that wasn't enough. Not anymore. Living for his own temporary satisfaction was the grind. Living for Lily, for her milestones...her smiles. Her first laugh. The first time she rolled over. It was something else.

It turned the passage of time into something brilliant and miraculous.

By the time he and Savannah were standing on his brother's doorstep, he was fully realizing that his life was changed forever. Being a father—it was who he was now.

Savannah felt like part of it. Which was a worry all on its own.

"Come on in," Tanner said when he opened the door.

Calder and Chloe were already sitting around the table, a plate of burger patties in front of them, and a stack of toppings and buns off to the side. "I was about to start without you," Calder said.

"So was I," Chloe responded.

Chloe smiled at him, but he noticed how quickly her gaze slid over to Tanner.

The fact that she wasn't over her crush yet was… well, not ideal. But Tanner was oblivious to it and he would also never do anything. Which was the one consolation, Jackson supposed.

"Well," he said, "I thank you for not devouring the hamburgers before I arrived. I was out working. Apparently the three of you were sitting here lounging."

"I never lounge," Tanner said, walking over to the table and beginning to fill his plate. Jackson retrieved Lily from her car seat and cradled her in his arm, holding her with one hand while he grabbed his burger with the other. Savannah took a seat beside him. He wasn't unaware of the way his siblings watched him, or the way they exchanged glances between them.

There was a strange feeling to all this. Not because he was the one with the baby, but because he felt like a unit with Savannah, who reached down and grabbed a burp cloth and wiped Lily's mouth when she needed it while making casual conversation with Tanner.

The worst part was it felt *natural*. It felt good.

That was like a hammer throw back to reality. Because the bottom line was the reason he had cultivated the life he had was that it meant he didn't have to count on anyone. No one. The life that he led was geared toward the solitary and the familiar. He and his siblings had always stuck together. Through his father's endless marriages and their mother's abandonment. Through their father's death. No one else had ever stuck by them.

No one who wasn't bonded by blood—or in Chloe's case, a bad puppy love problem—had ever stuck around one of the Reid men, save their last stepmother. That was just a fact.

Savannah was temporary, too. Destined to be. There was no use crying over it or lamenting it. It simply was. He could deal the hell with it.

He just had to remember that no matter how much he liked going to sleep with Savannah every night and waking up with her in his arms, no matter how much he liked seeing her hold Lily, seeing her play the part of mother…she wasn't. Lily had been abandoned once and he would not set her up for it again. Not because he was an asshole who couldn't remember what was real and what was magic dick feelings.

Hell, he had a ton of sexual experience, but not with women who had never had an orgasm before. And never with a woman who was caring for his child. It was unrealistic to think that there was actually something appealing to him about being in a committed relationship when before there hadn't been. Not at all.

It was a byproduct of Lily. And when she wasn't a baby, he wouldn't feel this way anymore.

Savannah was a nanny. She wasn't Lily's mother.

She was his lover. She wasn't his wife.

He sat there around the dinner table with his whole family, who were all effortlessly filling in dead spots in conversation and laughing, and Savannah. It all felt so real, and very much not the casual get-together he'd wanted. And he found himself shoving his burger away. "I'm going to go for another beer," he said, standing and making his way into the kitchen.

He heard tentative footsteps behind him and expected it to be Savannah, but when he turned he saw his stepsister, Chloe. Her red hair was in a tangle around her face, her expression curious.

"She's so nice, Jackson," Chloe said finally, taking a step toward him.

"She wouldn't be taking care of Lily if she wasn't," he responded.

Chloe stuffed her hands into the pockets of her dirty jeans. "I didn't mean for Lily. I meant for you."

He stiffened, opening the fridge quickly and grabbing a bottle of beer, curling his fingers tightly around it. "I don't know what the hell you're talking about, Chloe."

"Don't give me that. I know men are dumb assholes, but you're pushing it a bit."

"You know men are dumb assholes? Because of all your experience?" He narrowed his eyes. "Or do you just mean Tanner? Who is your brother. And shouldn't be considered a man."

"Stepbrother," she said through gritted teeth. "And it doesn't have anything to do with this. I have no idea what you're talking about."

But Jackson was feeling mean and cornered. A hell of a lot like a bear whose nose had been stung by a bee.

"The hell you don't, Chloe. The only person it's not obvious to is Tanner. And you're damned lucky that that's the case, or he'd throw you out on your ass and tell you to find another place to live."

"Well, he can't," Chloe said. "Because the ranch is part mine, too. As you well know."

"Honey, he would pick you up and drop you off in the wilderness like a feral cat."

"And I'd find my way home. If Tanner was stupid enough to underestimate me to that degree, he'd also deserve the mauling he would get when I got back. I know you don't like to be seen as soft, Jackson, but the fact of the matter is, you are soft for Lily. And there's nothing wrong with that. If it extended to someone else… would it be the end of the world?"

"You don't know what it's like, Chloe," he said. "To open your heart over and over again and lose people you thought were going to stay. My mother, countless stepmothers, and now my dad is just dead. I'm not going to take lectures from you."

"It's not like everything in my life was great before my mom married your dad, Jackson," she said. "It's not like I haven't been hurt."

"Right. And you handle that by staying here and panting after the one man you can't have."

Chloe firmed up her chin and crossed her arms, staring him down. If he had thought that he was going to make her cry or something, he had clearly been mistaken.

"I stay because it's easier to run. I stay here and care for this ranch, for the land, because that's tough. Starting over a hundred times, that's easy. That's what your dad did all those times. Right? New things. New relationships. He had more fights with my mom than any of the women before her. I know, because I heard him tell her that. And she would just smile and tell him that's what happens when you're with someone past the honeymoon phase. I stay because staying is tough."

"Good for you," he said. "But I know what kind of life I'm going to have. I know it well. I'm not bitching about it, but I'm not spinning fantasies that are never going to come true."

"I believe that it could. Why do you think it can't?"

He didn't have an answer, so he just opened the beer. "Go back to the table and eat," he said.

Chloe shook her head. "Fine. But you know, I never figured you for a coward, Jackson. A woman showed up on your doorstep with a baby, and you embraced Lily with everything. I don't understand why you can't embrace this other good thing that's right in front of you."

"And I don't understand why you're obsessed with the thought that one of my employees could become something more."

Chloe rolled her eyes. "Because it is more. I'm not blind. Even I can tell that you're sleeping with her," she said. "And I don't know anything about that sort of thing."

Jackson gritted his teeth. "It's not what I want. I never wanted to be a father, much less a husband. I don't have a choice on the father part."

"And you love it," Chloe said softly. "You love Lily."

"What else was I going to do? She's a baby. No one else is going to take care of her but me."

"So that's it? That's the only reason. Because she's a baby? Because you have to? That might be how you handle obligation. But it's not how you handle love. And you love her. I think you could love Savannah, too."

Jackson looked behind Chloe's shoulder, and saw Savannah standing half in the doorway looking stricken, her face pale, holding on to Lily. She quickly turned and shrunk back out of sight. Whether trying to act like he hadn't seen her, or trying to avoid a confrontation in front of Chloe, he didn't know.

He shook his head and walked past Chloe, heading back into the dining room. The rest of dinner passed slowly, but incident free. Jackson did his best to ignore everything that Chloe had said to him.

Neither he nor Savannah spoke the entire way home.

Home. As if it was *their* home.

That was the problem. The real problem. It wasn't just that Chloe had irritated him. It was that she had scraped up against that little fantasy he had started to have. That feeling of family he was starting to want. Starting to ache for. Lily was asleep when they got inside, and Savannah took her into the nursery and laid her down. When she reappeared, Jackson was pacing, trying to contend with the reckless energy that was riding through his veins.

Savannah's soft lips parted, and he did the only thing he could think to do. He closed the distance between them and hauled her into his embrace. She squeaked, and his mouth crashed down on hers. He didn't want to feel anything. Not in his heart.

He was happy enough to have it be in his dick, but nowhere else.

It was all a lie, anyway. No one was ever going to stay with him. Savannah could never love him. Nobody that wasn't blood ever had. And sometimes, he had even wondered about his father, who had poured more sweat into the ranch than into the raising of his sons.

This tenderness in his chest was all because of Lily. It had nothing to do with Savannah. It was all getting tangled up because he had made a damned mistake taking her to bed. But at this point, the mistake had already been made.

He had to remind himself why he had these feelings, and where they came from. From tangled limbs and intense orgasms. Physical intimacy and that hot rush of need. From the novelty of having a familiar lover, which he never had before. A woman whose body he knew, and was learning better and better with each passing day.

At this point, Savannah and her orgasms were a science. A dirty, wet, fun science.

He knew just where to stroke, just where to lick, just where to suck.

He was in control of this thing between them. Not her. Not his heart. Just him.

She sighed and leaned into his hold, and he knew that she wouldn't resist him. Knew that she couldn't. That was the other problem. He was the only man who had ever made her feel this way, and the temptation to make sure that was always the case snarled inside of him like the caveman idea it was. The plan had been to set her free with more confidence. Or at least, that had been the excuse. The thing he had told himself to justify sleeping with her in the first place.

But he didn't want anyone else to touch her. Didn't want anyone else to learn the things that he had about what made her tick. Made her whimper. Made her moan.

She was his. *His*, dammit.

For now.

He ignored the roaring of his blood that seemed to echo forever in his veins. He stripped her clothes off and walked her back to his room, taking her down onto the bed quickly. Ferociously.

But she reached up, a gentle hand on his stomach that stilled his movements. She scooted toward the edge of the bed and with delicate fingers, undid his buckle. Soft green eyes stayed on his as she opened up the front of his jeans and curled her fingers around his cock, drawing her hand slowly up and down his length.

"Don't," he bit out. "This isn't about me."

"I hope that's not true," she said softly, her eyes never leaving his, her hand working continually. "It's been going on for a few weeks, Jackson, and I thought at this point it was about us."

Us.

That word made his stomach feel hollowed out, or maybe it was the light pass of her fingertips over his aching flesh. He couldn't work it out. Not with her touching him like that.

He was about to demand she stop when she leaned forward, the tip of her tongue flicking over the head of his arousal, sending a shot of white fire through his body. Her mouth was tentative and sweet, and when she wrapped her lips around him he could hardly think, could hardly breathe, let alone demand she stop anything.

It wasn't so much the slick friction of her tongue, the delicate suction of her lips, though it was good, but it was the way she looked at him. Those blue eyes trained on his the whole time she pleasured him with her mouth, and damn it all, he couldn't look away. All he could do was watch. This beautiful, fair-haired angel brought down low. Being dirty. Just for him. Because this wasn't about her getting off, wasn't about her having an orgasm. This was just about...

Her wanting to do this for him. Her wanting him.

His teeth ached, and he clenched his jaw together.

Damn, how he wanted that to be real. Her wanting him. Her needing him. But everything was way too tangled up, and there was just no way that could be true. No way in hell.

She worked her hand in time with her mouth, and all he could do was buck his hips against her as he started to lose his control. He reached down, grabbing her hair and wrenching her head back. "No," he said. "Not like that."

"Jackson…"

He rolled her onto her back, then reached for the condoms in the drawer. Then he had an idea.

He flipped her over onto her stomach, grabbing hold of a couple pillows off the head of the bed and putting them under her chest. "Let's try this."

"Jackson…" She sounded uncertain.

"Let me take care of everything," he said. "Remember?"

He rolled the condom on and pressed himself to her entrance, that particular angle allowing him to get deep. So deep he thought his head was going to blow off.

He gripped her hips, slammed inside and relished the throaty sound that she made. Now he couldn't see her face. Now he couldn't see those angelic green eyes. Now she could be anyone. Any woman.

Except she wasn't.

She didn't feel like, smell like, sound like another woman. And she didn't make him feel like any other woman ever had. It was different. It wasn't just pleasure centered around his cock. It was need. Need that pierced his soul. And it terrified him.

The dark, empty well that had been torn open inside of him the moment Lily had been thrust into his arms had only grown deeper since Savannah arrived in his life. And deeper still in this moment. He would never find the bottom of it. No one would ever, ever be able to satisfy it. And he had no idea what the hell he was supposed to do with that.

How the hell he was supposed to survive?

Pleasure began to tighten in his gut, and he gripped her so tightly he made dents in that pretty white skin. He went hard and fast, and then reached his hand between her legs, rubbing her clit in a circle as he drove home. She cried out, internal muscles pulsing around him, and that was it. He couldn't take it anymore.

He squeezed his eyes shut tight and came hard, his jaw held so firm he was sure he was going to shatter the bone. But even with his eyes closed, even with her facing away from him, he could still see those green eyes in his mind. The way she had looked up at him. The way that she cared about him.

And all he wanted to do, every part of him, was reach out and take what she was offering.

But he couldn't.

He just damn well couldn't.

CHAPTER NINE

SAVANNAH DIDN'T SLEEP after that particularly raw experience with Jackson. She wasn't sure how she was supposed to. Yes, she was discovering that orgasms were a bit of a sleeping pill. But not after something like that.

It had felt loaded.

When he had turned her over like that.

It had been hot, there was no denying that. But for some reason, he had found the blow job confronting.

In her experience men didn't find *that* confronting, they found it nice. But there had been something in his response that made clear that it had been different for him. He certainly didn't act like her ex-husband. Ultimately, she couldn't even compare the two men. Darren had loved his veneer of respectability and had been prideful about his position in the community. His reputation. Jackson didn't seem to care about his reputation. He didn't care what anyone thought—he only cared what he did. What it meant to him. And now, what it meant for Lily.

She was fascinated by that. By the way he was. By the way that interacted with who she was, and how she had always seen herself. By what she had thought about marriage and what she thought of it now.

Her parents had had a particular sort of marriage. One she had never wanted to emulate. And still, even though she had ended up in an entirely different situation, it had been a bad one. She had started to think it was marriage.

She rolled over onto her side and looked at Jackson's silhouette. She was so different with him. There was no expectation of a future between them, and maybe, because of that, she hadn't held pieces of herself in reserve so that they couldn't be hurt. Couldn't be destroyed.

But she had told him about herself. About all her failures.

She had been married to her husband for five years, and other than him using it to insult her at the very end of everything, they had never discussed the fact that she hadn't orgasmed before in her life. Why hadn't they talked about that? And why had she been able to talk about it with Jackson?

She had a feeling the answer was complicated. A little bit her. A little bit him. A little bit of them together. Just like his reaction to what they'd shared earlier.

Maybe it wasn't marriage that was wrong. Maybe it was sometimes just the person. Because she could imagine forever with Jackson. With Jackson and Lily in this cabin on this beautiful ranch. In this adorable town. Yes, she could imagine that. More than that. She wanted it.

She loved him, she realized.

The thought was terrifying. Enough that she sat bolt upright in bed, clutching the covers to her chest, breathing hard.

She had fallen in love with him.

It had been nothing like her previous experience with love. It had just…happened. And it wasn't as simple as wanting companionship. Wasn't as simple as wanting to live in the same house and build a life that looked a certain way. It was something deep and terrifying. She would live with him with no wedding ring—and it wouldn't matter. Whether he was her lover, boyfriend, fiancé, husband. All that mattered was that it was him.

What she wanted went deep. An ache in her soul she didn't know she'd ever find the cure for. She suddenly felt terrified, panicky, like she would never have enough of him.

She wanted it all. All and everything. This man. This life. This baby she had grown to love with everything inside of herself.

All of her life she had kept walls up around her heart. Her parents had placed her at a distance, and she had wandered around the world doing the same to other people ever since. She had learned to carry everything she needed in her chest, self-contained and protected, and never wounded by the people around her. Because they could never get inside.

Not even Darren.

But in Jackson's house, in his bed, she had found intimacy. The reason that people couldn't get enough of each other's bodies. She had discovered the meaning of sex. And what it meant when two people found pleasure together.

It wasn't just nice to be close.

An orgasm wasn't *nice*. It wrenched down your defenses. Made you scream, contorted your face into expressions that would be humiliating if you weren't sharing it, glorying in it together.

She'd had sex with one man for five years and it hadn't made her love him. But sex with *this* man…

Oh, it had made her love him.

The sex, the closeness. That it made her understand *making love*. The way he was with Lily. The way he was with his family. The ranch. *Her*.

She loved him.

It was novel. New and terrifying. She didn't want it. But she needed it.

She brushed her fingertips over his bicep and he moved slightly.

"You're not a slave, either, are you?" she asked softly.

"No," he said.

If she'd been on the outside looking in she would have thought it was insane. To fall for another man less than a year after her divorce would have been insane. If she'd ever really fallen for her husband in the first place.

The fact of the matter was, she was falling for the first time.

With Jackson. Only with Jackson.

"I…" She cleared her throat. "Jackson."

He turned over, and she couldn't see his face in the dimly lit room. "You sound serious," he said.

"I feel serious."

He shifted. "I'm not sure you really want to have the conversation you think you do."

She flashed back to that moment in the kitchen at his brother's house. To the things that Chloe had said. And the way that he'd denied them.

She knew that he had been avoiding talking to her after that. That his kiss had been to shut her up, to distract her. To reroute her. But that was okay. It didn't scare her. Well. It did. But at this point, it all did.

"Don't tell me what I want," she said. "I spent too many years telling myself what I wanted, instead of just letting myself want it. I'm not going to let anyone else tell me a damn thing."

"Savannah…"

"I love you," she said. "I do. This whole life. Living here with you. With Lily. I love you."

She felt him get stiff beside her. "No," he said firmly.

"You love what you just said. The life. But eventually, honey, that's gonna wear off. And it's not going to be fun for you. When it quits feeling like playing house, you're not going to like it anymore."

"What is it you think of me?" She adjusted so that she could see him better. "Have I ever acted like a person who just gets tired of her responsibilities? Do you think that I'm someone who says that I love someone else? I've told you about my life. About my marriage."

"And I already know that you're willing to walk away from a marriage."

"That's not fair. You know how awful all that was for me. You know that he wasn't a good husband."

"*I* wouldn't be a good husband. It's why I never plan on being one. My father wasn't a very good husband. I can tell you that for a damned fact. If he were, he wouldn't have had to try with so many different women."

"Why did your stepmother stay married to him?"

"She had grit. More grit than desire to be happy every day, I guess."

"You just don't think anyone could possibly be happy with you? Because I'm happy, Jackson."

"Honey," he said, "that's the sex talking."

"That is the most insulting, ridiculous thing you could've said."

"We both know you don't have experience with this kind of thing. Not with anyone else."

"Jackson…"

"I am not crazy enough, I don't hate myself enough, and I sure as hell don't hate my daughter enough to sign her up for the kind of life that I had growing up. I won't do it. The only reason I ever started anything with you, Savannah, is that I knew you were temporary. I already knew you were going to leave. Move on to your real life. I'm not going to promise Lily a mother and then let her lose it."

"That's what you think I would do?"

"It's maybe not what you think now, but nobody starts serious relationships thinking they're going to end. I think you know that."

"No. I know that who you're with matters. How do you not see that?" She rolled over, the sheets and blankets rustling. "Staying married is not the be-all and end-all. You have to compromise, make yourself vulnerable. Expose parts of yourself you wish you didn't have to. That was where I failed in my marriage, Jackson. I never let Darren know who I was. That's not what this is."

"No." Jackson shook his head. "That's where you're wrong, honey. You might not believe it, but you have made me into an ideal. If you hadn't, then you wouldn't be trying to get me to change my mind right now. You don't want me. You want the husband you think you could make me. But I'm not built for it."

"You didn't think you were built for being a father, either. And look at you."

"Yeah. So I could marry you, Savannah. I can make this little arrangement permanent. Pretty damned convenient for me, don't you think? And how would you ever be sure it was real?" He reached over, grabbing her arm, squeezing her tight. "How? I didn't want any of this, and here I am, doing it. Is that why you want a man to marry you? Because he wants a permanent nanny?"

She took a deep breath, sliding out of the bed. "I'm not your nanny, Jackson. I never have been. What I want from you has nothing to do with that."

She started to collect her clothes, her hand shaking.

Then she stopped, turned to look at him. "Tell me you don't love me."

"I don't love you," he returned. Easily. Lightly. As if it cost him nothing to say it.

She nodded, her heart splintering in her chest. She stood out in his living room for a long time after that, debating going in and kissing Lily on the cheek. Lily felt like part of her. A part of her heart. As necessary as air to her existence. What would she do when she couldn't start her day by picking her up from her crib and feeling that precious weight against her chest? Resting her cheek against that soft, downy head.

She couldn't go back in there.

She would fall to her knees and howl over the loss and never get back up.

It occurred to her, when she walked on numb feet back to her bedroom and began to pack the minimal things she had brought with her, that she had never once asked Darren if he loved her.

Because she hadn't cared about the answer. Not in the end.

This was love. This was what it meant to be vulnerable to another person. What it meant to open herself up.

It was terrible.

It hurt.

But she had a feeling that in the end this would be the only way she would ever heal. From the life she had been born into that she ultimately couldn't control. This was her taking control. She wasn't going to let the way other people treated her determine what she could have. Not anymore.

Not even him.

She walked out the front door, tears pouring down her cheeks. The thought that echoed in her mind as she got into her car and drove away from Jackson's house was that the worst part about all of this was that Lily could have been hers. Jackson could have been hers.

And now they wouldn't be.

Now she was alone. Again.

CHAPTER TEN

WHEN HE WOKE UP, she wasn't there. He hadn't slept, not really, but he had stayed in his bedroom and waited for her to come back. Waited for her to cool down. Apparently, she had done neither, because when he woke up early in the morning and went into her bedroom, her things were gone. He went into Lily's room, hoping Savannah was just there, and that for some reason her room was just uncommonly neat.

But she wasn't there.

Lily was sleeping peacefully on her back, her fisted hands up over her head, her expression serene. She wasn't aware that she had lost the woman who had been taking care of her for the past month. Wasn't aware that anything had changed at all. How many times had that happened in his life? Too many.

He whirled around and went back out into the living area, pounding his fist onto the wall. How could he have let this happen?

How could he have put himself or Lily in this position?

He had to remember that he could never care about anyone. Could never trust anyone. There was only himself. That was all there would ever be. Lily would be able to depend on him, he would be sure of that, but he wouldn't expose her to this ever again.

He looked around, still somehow unable to fully take

on board the fact that Savannah had left. She'd said she wouldn't.

And you said you didn't love her.

Pain exploded in his chest, bursting behind his eyelids. Yes. He had said that. He hadn't meant it. He hadn't. But this was the problem. He wasn't supposed to love her.

He knew better than to love anyone.

He remembered his mother leaving. Remembered what it was like that strange, surreal morning when he had walked out of his bedroom and everything had been exactly where it had been the night before, and yet felt utterly and completely different.

Much like now.

And then after that, his father had brought home a new woman, and Jackson, at five, had hoped that she would be his mother. Had hoped that she would be the answer to that hole in his chest. That open, lonely space inside of him. But then she had left, too. And so had the next one. And the next one. By the time his father had married Ella, he had already known there was no point getting attached to the older man's latest bride. No point at all. He'd had his heart ripped out too many times at that point. Had already learned that love meant giving someone a piece of your heart to take with them when they decided to head somewhere better to be.

Love meant losing that piece of yourself, without having that other person leave anything behind.

Except Savannah had left too damned much behind. The house might feel unchanged, but his insides had been turned upside down and rearranged. His life was... He didn't know whose life this was. And he wanted so very desperately to go back to the one he and Savannah had carved out for themselves.

And what an ass he'd been. Asking how she would know it was real.

You're the one that's afraid she's more in love with the idea of being a mother to Lily than she is in love with you.

He gritted his teeth and fought against the sharp, cutting truth of that thought.

He was afraid. That was the bottom line.

Afraid of losing her, and so he had. And no amount of denying his feelings for her made him feel insulated from that. Not even a little bit. But she was gone. And this time, there had been no quiet space beforehand. No lingering questions as to why. Possibly for the very first time, it had been him who had well and truly driven someone away. He had no idea how the hell he was supposed to live with himself now. Had even less of an idea as to how he was supposed to live without her. But it didn't look like he had a choice.

"WHY DID YOU bring Lily out this morning?" Tanner asked, looking at the carrier that was strapped to Jackson's chest.

There was fencing to be repaired and heavy equipment repairs to see to, and if Jackson had to sit at home and think about what an ass he was, he'd lose his mind. So he had gone out and gotten to work.

The appearance of Tanner on the fence line made him regret it.

"Savannah's gone," he said simply, keeping his eyes fixed on the layered mountains that surrounded the ranch. Deep green fading back to pale blue. A sight he normally took solace in.

Not now.

"You gave her the day off?"

"Nope," Jackson responded. "She's gone." He figured if he said it enough, maybe he would be able to feel it. Accept it. Maybe it wouldn't hurt so bad.

But he doubted it.

"She left?"

"Yes," Jackson said.

"What the hell did you do?"

"I fucked up," Jackson said. "Majorly."

"How?"

"She told me she loved me," Jackson said. "I told her I didn't love her."

"I would leave your ass for that, too. You love her, though," Tanner said, his words confident. "I don't know what the hell changed between the time we talked after she got here and you telling me that you were going to keep it professional, and that dinner we had at my place last night, but it's obvious to me that something did change. And that you love her."

Anger spiked through his veins. "Are you and Chloe having slumber parties over there? Braiding each other's hair and giggling and talking about my love life?"

Tanner shrugged. "I didn't talk to Chloe at all."

"Well, she was up in my business, too."

"Maybe because you need an intervention."

"Fuck off, Tanner. It's not like your life is together. When was the last time you were with anyone?"

"It's been a while," he admitted. "But I don't see how that's relevant."

"Isn't it in the Bible or something? Don't worry about the dust in my eye when you have horseshit in your own?"

Tanner snorted. "Pretty sure that's not in the Bible."

"Deal with your own stuff, that's what I'm saying."

"I'm fine being alone," he said. "Which is the big difference between the two of us. You're not fine, Jackson. You're not."

"Don't you think if I went after her it would just be… Isn't it a little bit convenient, Tanner? That suddenly I want to be with a woman who happens to be a great… She'd be a great mother for Lily."

"No. I don't think it's convenient. But I think the fact that it matters shows that you care. Do you think that Dad ever cared if the women he brought home would be good mothers to us?"

"I don't suppose. Seeing as only a couple of them were."

"Don't you think it would've been a better thing for him to consider us with a decision like that?"

"I guess."

"That's not convenience, Jackson. That's being a good dad. Our lives would have been better if our father was that good. And you know it. You weren't looking for a mail-order bride, just a mail-order nanny. You got more. Why let it get away? Why miss this chance?"

"Because we'll just get in deeper," he admitted, his voice rough. "Deeper and deeper until everything in my life, everything in Lily's life is tangled up in her. I mean, even if it's not…convenience for me, what if it is for her? What if it's not…me she wants really?"

"I don't know what to tell you about that. I don't think you can have that guarantee. I just think you have to…take a chance."

"What if she leaves me?"

"She *did* leave you, dumbass. The ship has sailed."

"But at least now Lily won't remember. Not like me. I remembered."

"Are you afraid for Lily or for you?"

He let that blow hit. "I don't… I don't know. But does it matter if she's safe?"

"And she won't have a chance at having the life she could have, having as great of a mother as Savannah. Because you're scared. But more than that, because of course you can't marry someone just to give Lily a mother. More than that, you're destroying your own happiness to keep yourself safe."

"Great lecture from a guy in a codependent relationship with his stepsister."

Tanner stiffened. "She's going to get her own place soon."

"You said that before. You could build another house on the property. But neither of you have made that move."

"I don't know what you're implying. Chloe is family."

"To me. To Calder. To you? I'm not sure about that."

Tanner gritted his teeth. "This isn't about me. You're the one letting the love of your life walk away."

The love of his life. Was that what this was? He'd heard that expression a thousand times and never once applied it to himself. He'd never loved a woman he was romantically involved with. Ever.

But he loved Savannah. He didn't even have to question that now. It just was. The only question was what he was going to do about it. She was gone. He couldn't very well negotiate with someone who wasn't there.

But he could do something he'd never done before.

I could go after her.

"Can you watch Lily?" he asked, his voice suddenly tinged with desperation.

"Hell, yeah," Tanner said.

Jackson was going to find her. Even if it meant breaking some minor laws to do it.

CHAPTER ELEVEN

AT LEAST SHE was close to the ocean now. The air smelled like salt here, and mixed easily with the salt of her tears. She had wandered down the main street of the little town of Copper Ridge for most of the day before going back to the little bed-and-breakfast she had booked herself on a neighboring ranch.

She and Jackson had never taken Lily to the beach before. Oh, she would love it. Love to squish the sand in her fist and kick her feet in it.

She could just see Jackson's face. The way he lit up when he looked at his little girl...

It was the most beautiful thing. The only thing that was better was the feeling she got when he looked at her.

And right now, no matter how charming the B and B was, she felt like she was going to be crushed beneath the weight of her own pain.

The hostess at the B and B was sweet, and she had a little gray cat, and several beautiful children with a hot cowboy who also happened to be the sheriff in town.

She shouldn't have come here. She felt surrounded by cowboys after she had just managed to escape one. Here, there were two, the sheriff and his older brother, their wives and children, and she felt surrounded by both Stetsons and happiness.

She wasn't particularly in the mood for either.

Still, the quiche had been delicious this morning, and

the room was adorably appointed. She couldn't really complain about that.

Well, she could. But it would be churlish.

Everything was terrible. The benefits of flaky crust and a soft mattress could not be minimized in those circumstances.

She heard heavy footsteps in the hall and wondered if someone was staying in the room next to hers. But the footsteps paused, and there was a knock on the door.

"Hello?"

"Savannah," came the familiar voice on the other side of the door. "Thank God."

She jumped back, her hand on her chest. "How did you find me?"

"Think of me as a small-town James Bond. I have a select network of informants."

She scrambled across the room and cracked the door open. "What does that mean?"

"Exactly what it sounds like it means. I follow the gossip chain and it led me here. Asked at Sugar Cup if anybody had seen you leave this morning. Called around to see where the vacancies were in these parts. It all led me to the B and B."

"How did you know which room I was in?"

"You left it in the guest ledger," he said. "That was easy enough."

"They need better security for this place."

"I suspect security's not a real big issue around here."

"Clearly it is!"

"Can I come in?"

"Why?"

"Because I need to start over. I need to try again. Last night... Early this morning... Whenever it was. I messed up. I don't know how to do this. In my experience, loving someone just ends with loss. But in this case it was a self-fulfilling prophecy. Somehow, I justified that to myself because it was protecting Lily. From getting more attached to you. From thinking of you as her mother and losing you."

"Jackson...even if something ever happened between the two of us I would always love Lily."

He nodded. "I know that," he said, his voice choked. "That's the real problem. I really can't stand losing you. For me. For selfish reasons. And I was a dick last night asking you how you would know if it was real. It was me. I was the one that was worried it wasn't real. I want you. I would never have met you if it weren't for Lily, but I would want you even if I didn't have her. It's you, Savannah."

She grabbed him by the front of the shirt and dragged him into the room, slamming the door behind him. And then she kissed him. Kissed him with every ounce of pain and pent-up anger that she had inside her. "Why did you do this to us?" Tears filled her eyes and she looked up at him, at that beautiful, familiar face. "Why did you put us through this?"

"When my father divorced my mother, well, after she left him, there was a big hole in my life. I was five when my mother left. I can remember her. Just enough. And not enough. And when he brought home my first stepmother, I wanted it to be real. I wanted it to be real every time. But it wasn't. Over and over again. How many times can you open up your heart only to let it get kicked around?"

"Jackson," she whispered, her heart tightening in pain for him, for the little boy he'd been, the man he was now. "I'm sorry. I don't know what it's like to be physically abandoned. But I know what it's like to live with people who aren't really there for you. I know what it's like to love people who don't love you back. And to decide you're not going to let yourself get hurt again. But you're worth it. I would love you and take the risk, every day, forever, rather than go back to a world where I don't know what it's like to have you in it."

"Me, too," he said gruffly. "Me, too." He pulled her into his arms and kissed her. Kissed her until her walls broke down again, until the pain vanished. Until there was nothing between them. No defenses, no past hurts. They kissed until they might as well have been the only two people in the world.

They would go back home, to his place, and there would be three of them. A family. The very idea made her heart swell.

But right now, just for now, it was her and Jackson. Nothing and no one else.

When he laid her down on the bed, he looked into her eyes. "I love you," he said.

"I love you, too," she whispered back.

"Do you want to know what made me the maddest when I went to pick you up from the airport?"

"What?"

"You said you were plain. Plain and tall. There's nothing plain about you, woman. You were sunshine in the dark. There's no way to hide from the sun. And I think part of me knew it from the first moment I saw you."

"I'm not the sun. I'm not anything special," she said.

"You're everything special. You told me you were plain. And, honey, the first moment I saw you...I couldn't believe you thought that. You're beautiful, do you know that?"

"You look at me and I...I feel like I might be."

"You are," he said. "Beautiful. Perfect. Everything I needed. Everything I *need*."

There was such deep, real love in his eyes. She felt the furthest thing from plain. She felt singular. Special in a way she never had before. And she was damn glad she didn't have any walls left, because she didn't want anything between them at all.

"You're everything I need, Jackson. Because without you...I would still be buried behind all those rock walls. But now look at us. There's none of that left anymore. Just love."

"Good thing," he said.

Savannah had come to Gold Valley with nothing but one flowered suitcase, hoping to start a new life.

But she'd found so much more. She'd found everything.

She'd found love. A family.

And home, in Jackson's arms.

EPILOGUE

JACKSON REID KNEW what he loved. He loved riding the perimeter of his family ranch with his daughter seated in the saddle in front of him. He loved working from sunup to sundown, with his brand-new baby boy strapped to his chest.

He loved coming home at the end of the day to a warm house that was full of crying babies, a barking puppy and a pissed-off cat that hated him. He had no idea how they'd ended up with a cat. Savannah had come home with her one day after a shopping trip in town, and Lily had already named her on the ride home. He'd been outvoted.

He loved finding sippy cups hidden in strange places, although he loved cleaning them less. He loved his life.

He loved his wife.

He used to think that hedonism was a reward for all the hard work he did. And now he looked around and couldn't find a single thing he'd done to earn this.

There was no other way he wanted to live. In this house, with his family. Waking up every morning with the same woman. His life had changed.

Work hard. Play hard. Love harder.

And they loved him back. Beautifully. Wonderfully. Forever.

* * * * *